COLD
JUSTICE

OTHER BOOKS AND AUDIO BOOKS
BY KATHI ORAM PETERSON:

The Forgotten Warrior

An Angel on Main Street

The Stone Traveler

River Whispers

COLD JUSTICE

A NOVEL

KATHI ORAM
PETERSON

Covenant Communications, Inc.

To my husband,
for supporting me in everything I do.
I love you, sweetheart!

Cover image: *Black Crow Taking Off* © Anton-Marlot, courtesy istockphoto.com.

Cover design copyright © 2012 by Covenant Communications, Inc.

Published by Covenant Communications, Inc.
American Fork, Utah

Printed in the United States of America
First Printing: June 2012

18 17 16 15 14 13 12   10 9 8 7 6 5 4 3 2 1

ISBN-13: 978-1-62108-046-6

ACKNOWLEDGMENTS

A WRITER SPENDS COUNTLESS SOLITARY hours in front of a computer. The magic of creating a fictional story is amazing as characters come to life and plots unfold. But this is only one stage in the process of getting a manuscript in shape for publication. Many wonderful and knowledgeable people have helped me along the way, and I am deeply grateful.

I'd like to thank Marc Otte, chief deputy of the US Marshals Service in Alaska, for answering some of my naive questions about what could and couldn't happen in remote communities of his great state.

I'm very grateful to my brother, Lyle J. Oram (Bud)—a pilot and seasoned sailor—for bringing me up to speed on planes and what could happen to a boat out at sea.

I want to give special recognition to my publisher, Covenant Communications, Inc. They have a fantastic team. There are a few people I'd like to mention by name: my editor, Samantha Van Walraven, who patiently guides me and keeps me on track; Kelly Schumacher, who does an outstanding job promoting my novels; managing editor Kathy Jenkins, who took a chance on me; and designer Jennie Williams, who does a fantastic job on the cover art for my books.

I must thank my writer's group, the Wasatch Mountain Fiction Writers, and especially Dorothy Canada, Maureen Mills, Brenda Bensch, Charleen Raddon, Nikki Trionfo, Ann Chamberlin, Roseann Woodward, and Tina Foster. Week after week they have listened to my story and have given me sage advice on everything from motivation to punctuation. Also, two other members who have gone above and beyond in giving me feedback are Kathleen Dougherty and Kerri Leroy. They read the entire manuscript, and their attention to detail and logic was truly a blessing. I'd also like to thank my mentor, Elizabeth Lane, who gives me faithful encouragement in everything I do.

A big thank you goes to my ever-supportive family and the love of my life—my husband. On days I'm discouraged, my family lifts me. When I think I can't do everything plus write, my husband steps in, clearing the way so I can do what I love—write stories.

And thank you, readers, for joining me on this suspenseful adventure.

AUTHOR'S NOTES

AFTER MY NOVEL *RIVER WHISPERS* was published, I wanted to write a sequel that would not only keep my readers on the edge of their seats but also give more depth to the characters my fans had grown to love. I needed a rugged setting—somewhere that would test my characters' mental capacity and strengthen their faith. Alaska was the perfect place.

Beautiful Alaska was rich with history and a breathtaking environment that I couldn't pass up. I knew Regi, Samuel, and the rest of the characters would find out who they really were in a place God's hand had touched in so many different ways: the beautiful ocean and harbor villages, the northern lights, the snow-covered mountains, the Native Alaskan people, and the myths and legends that keep that area grounded and humble yet mystical.

I wanted to stay true to that authenticity, so in my research of Alaska and the people who live there, I came across three different books that caught my attention: *The Wolf and the Raven: Totem Poles of Southeastern Alaska* by Viola E. Garfield and Linn A. Forrest, *Keepers of the Totem* by the editors of Time-Life Books, and *Spirits of the Snow: Arctic Myth* by Tony Allan, Charles Phillips, Michael Kerrigan, and consultant Dr. Piers Vitebsky. These books contain short stories of the myths and legends of the north and helped me shape the setting, ambiance, and plot for my book. With the help of these books and specific terms in them, I created my own myth for *Cold Justice*. This myth runs in excerpts at the beginning of each chapter and dovetails the storyline of the actual novel.

The Raven Clan referred to in this book is fictional, as is the town of Malamute.

Alaska has a strong Russian and Native Alaskan heritage; therefore, I have used terms indigenous to the region but only as a means of giving flavor to this fictional story.

I hope you enjoy this journey to Alaska.

Bundle up!

CHAPTER ONE

"Come out! Come out!" Raven caws.
A life taken; a heritage lost.
Only one can answer the Call.

HE STOOD AMONG BARREN ASPEN trees, knee-high in winter snow—watching.
Always watching.

The binoculars were cold as he pressed them against his eyes. Freezing weather would neither impede him nor stop him from his mission.

He asked Raven to guide his every step. Raven helped his eyes to see and his ears to hear, but would he help him kill if he must before completing the task?

Justice must be served.

He'd found his enemy in Trailhead, Idaho, a small town in the Rocky Mountains. For days he'd waited for the right moment to strike. His prey had done well since leaving the Clan: purchased rich land and heavy cattle with the stolen heritage from his Alaskan past, built a fancy, white-pillared house, and found a beautiful woman to love.

They were together even now, smiling and laughing on the walkway between the house and the vehicles in the parking lot. The Jeep was hers; the truck, the prey's.

Even from this distance, he knew the woman loved the man because of the way she smiled, tilted her head as she listened, and leaned into him. Little did she know this visit would be her last with the man standing before her.

The day of reckoning was at hand.

"Regi, don't worry; I'll be there." Samuel Tanner grabbed Regina Bernard's parka sleeve and pulled her to him, wrapping his arms around the woman he'd loved all his life. Her long, honey-blonde hair, with strands of lightly aging white woven through it, hung loosely about her shoulders and down the back of her parka. He yearned to place his face in it and breathe in her luscious jasmine scent. But instead, he bent and kissed her lips, sweet as honeydew, and hugged her even tighter against him.

How he loved this woman!

In only twenty-four hours, she would walk down the aisle and finally marry him, like she should have done more than twenty years ago. The Lord worked in mysterious ways, but Samuel was relieved that His ways had at last brought them together.

Samuel pulled back and looked into her love-filled eyes. Though she was thirty-nine, she would always be the young girl of his dreams: creamy complexion with a sprinkling of freckles across her short nose, fire and fight in her gaze, and a long, slender body.

The sun sparkled off the snow around them, burning this moment into his memory. "Look, woman of mine, I promise in"—he checked his Rolex—"two hours and fifteen minutes, I'll be at the church, ready to be baptized. I just have a few chores to take care of, and then I'll shower, pick up Clifford, and meet you there."

"Your *chores* are chopping wood, aren't they? And you've already started." She pushed away and stared up at him.

Samuel didn't answer. In the short months they'd been together again as a couple, she'd learned that when he chopped wood he was mulling over a problem. He'd been chopping behind the barn before she arrived, but he'd stopped as soon as he'd heard her drive into the parking lot. He'd pulled his parka on over his vest and hoped she wouldn't notice that even though it was two below zero on this brisk February day, he'd worked up a sweat.

Her worried eyes pleaded with him. "You're still a little doubtful about being baptized, aren't you?" Her frosty puffs of breath added emphasis to the concern of her words.

Samuel thought about all that had happened over the years—being apart from Regi for so long, the rivalry between Samuel and Regi's late husband, and then the nightmare they had lived through months ago when Samuel had learned that his family had conspired to frame Regi for the murder of Ranger Curtis Romney. They'd attempted to cover it up by trying to kill Regi. Grief washed over Samuel as the horror of watching his delusional aunt Ida force Regi at gunpoint into the Snake River claimed him. Samuel had been stuck on the other side of the water. His first instinct had been to yell at his aunt and swim across to help Regi. But a still, small voice had prompted him to wait. Fortunately, he had and was able to save Regi. Marveling at the woman before him, he said, "As I pulled you out of the water, wet and weak as a newborn calf, I knew I was guided by a divine power."

Regi sighed heavily. "So why were you chopping wood?" She studied his face, her worried brows bunching together.

He tugged off the old, work-stained Stetson he always wore outside, rubbed his forehead with the back of his hand, and pushed the hat back on. Doubts about the Church shadowed him. But he didn't want to try to explain them to Regi. Besides, he truly felt that once he was baptized and committed not only to the gospel but to Regi as well, their love would be enough to truly convert him.

"Okay, Reg. This is going to shock even you." He watched as she steeled herself to hear what he had to say. "Don't tell anyone, but I'm going to burn that wood in the fireplace."

"You jerk!" She slugged him in the arm.

He grabbed hold of her and hugged her tight again. She smiled, and his world was right. Today was a big step toward building their life together. Their wedding tomorrow would seal the deal. He kissed her nose—her short, thin nose.

"You know," Regi feigned anger, "that dry humor of yours is going to get you into a lot of trouble someday. And don't think I'll ever let you forget that you compared me to a cow."

"I said a newborn calf. There's a big difference. Calves are cute, all bright eyed and helpless." He added the last word, even though he knew he was flirting with danger.

Fire lit her gem-green eyes. "A helpless calf? Really? You're sticking with that?"

"Nooooo. You're my wild mustang." He kissed her soundly on the mouth and released her. "I do love wild horses."

"And don't you forget it!" A smile tugged at her lips as they walked toward her Jeep. The crunch of snow beneath their boots echoed their footsteps. The freezing air tingled in his nose. He wanted to take Regi back into the house and have another warm muffin her sister had sent, but he knew better. "Thank Claudia for the muffins. Are both she and Wakanda really coming to my baptism?"

Regi smiled and nodded. "Yes. Claud wanted to tell you herself, but I couldn't pass up an opportunity to see my man, so I delivered the message and muffins for her." She kissed his cheek and started to walk toward her vehicle again. "Claud and Wakanda are getting pretty serious about the Church, but they need to see someone else take the big plunge first—no pun intended."

He followed her down the sidewalk, reluctant to see her leave yet knowing she must. "So . . . I'm testing the waters for them, huh?"

"You're good at diving into water to save people." She chuckled, opened the Jeep's squeaky door, and paused. "Why don't you have Morgan pick up Clifford instead of going yourself? Then you won't have to leave quite so early. Morgan's probably out on patrol and would be more than happy to do it."

"He's taking the day off from his sheriff duties so he can bring Hannah, probably Effie too." Samuel felt bad for his friend. "He's hired Effie to live with them full time."

Regi climbed into her Jeep. "Knowing Effie, she would have moved in to help without being paid. I was at Morgan's the other day, and Hannah could barely talk."

Samuel caught the flicker of anguish over her best friend's illness in Regi's eyes. "Maybe taking her out more will help."

Regi peered at Samuel, shielding the sun's reflection off the snow with her hand. "Would you take care of me if I got Alzheimer's at an early age like Hannah?"

He bent over and kissed her. Staying eye level, he said, "You bet. After tomorrow, I'll never let you go. Count on it." He tweaked her nose, stepped back, and closed the door.

Regi rolled down the window. "Samuel, it's really going to happen, isn't it?"

"Yes." He patted her pink cheek chilled from the frosty air and was amazed that this beautiful woman loved him again. There had been a long spell when she'd hated him.

With a deep sigh, she turned the key in the ignition. The Jeep roared to life. "See you in a few." She shifted into drive and pulled away.

Samuel watched Regi round the snowy curve to the main highway. She would always be the wild mustang in his life that brought a smile to his face and warmed his heart. He looked up to the blue sky and said, "Thank you, God."

Putting his thermal gloves on, he decided to pull his truck behind the barn so he could load the wood he'd chopped. Driving down the path he'd made in the snow during previous trips days before, he realized that in his haste today he'd made his pile on the wrong side of the chopping block. To save time, he'd need to park on the other side. He swung the truck around the tall stack of logs to the wood waiting to be loaded. As he did, he couldn't help but think about how lucky he and Regi had been.

She was one feisty lady. And she was always curious, like she was a moment ago about why he'd been chopping wood. He hated that he hadn't told her about his doubts regarding the Church, but he just couldn't.

He got out of the truck and walked around to open the tailgate. All at once, a feeling of being watched came over him. He turned, expecting to find someone, but he could see only snow-covered land and the familiar dense grove of aspens on the hill overlooking his place. A sudden shiver skittered across his skin. He glanced at his watch. What was he thinking? He didn't have time to load his truck. If he were lucky, he might have time to feed his horse, Rufus.

Samuel opened the back door to the barn, kicked clinging snow from his winter boots, and, before closing the door, scanned the horizon once again.

Nothing.

Odd how the feeling of being watched kept riding him.

It was probably because he was plagued with leftover guilt. His past was riddled with it. He'd failed his late father by running away. At the time, Samuel had felt that if he stayed, his drunken father would beat him to death, or worse, Samuel would kill him. Leaving like he did, Samuel had abandoned not only his father and Regi but also his brother, Jedidiah. The years of being alone with their father had changed Jed, making him calloused and turning him into a monster. Scenes of that horrible night on the river reeled through Samuel's mind again. Sorrow filled him, cutting deep as he remembered how Aunt Ida had killed Jed and then turned on Regi. If Samuel had been more aware of what was going on in his brother's life, he might have been able to stop the unraveling of his family. He would have noticed the signs of his aunt's madness and would have saved them both. But at least Samuel hadn't failed his mentally challenged nephew, Clifford.

Since that fateful night when Cliff had helped save Regi, Samuel had promised God he would always take care of his nephew. He'd sought out the professional help Clifford needed. The doctor recommended that Cliff live at Stony Creek Care Center. Living there would give him a sense of independence, yet people would be near if the need arose.

Samuel quickly gave his horse grain and added fresh hay to the animal's stall. As he pulled the hose to the water trough, he checked the large goldfish in the water. In subzero temperatures, most ranchers used them. Not only did the fish help keep the trough clean, but they were also a good barometer of water temperature. Too hot or too cold and the fish would die. He kept the trough warm with an electric trough heater. The fish swam around as Samuel added more water. Rufus nudged his arm, wanting attention.

"Sorry, old boy. I'm in a hurry." Samuel stroked the roan's neck and rubbed the animal's soft velvet ear before leaving.

Upon entering the kitchen, he pulled off his gloves, shoved them into his coat pockets, and hung his coat on a wall peg near the door. He paused a moment, tugged his Stetson off his head, and hooked it on the back of one of the breakfast nook chairs. He proceeded to wash the dirt from his hands in the kitchen sink but paused when he heard the front door open.

Had Regi returned?

Shutting off the water and grabbing a hand towel, he pushed through the swinging door between the entryway and kitchen, fully expecting to find her walking toward him. But the hallway was empty, the door closed.

"Good grief. Now I'm hearing things."

His imagination had gone wild. Maybe the pressure of getting baptized and married within two days was too much, but he really didn't think so.

Becoming a member of The Church of Jesus Christ of Latter-day Saints was something he wanted to do. Something divine had happened out there on the river the night he'd pulled Regi out of the water. Of that he was certain. To gain more understanding of Regi's church, Samuel had read the Book of Mormon cover to cover and had taken Moroni's challenge of getting down on his knees and praying to know the gospel was true. The confirming knowledge that had befallen Samuel as he'd knelt beside his bed had brought him near tears. So why did he still have these doubts?

He just needed more time on his knees, more praying. He stepped back into the kitchen, hung up the hand towel, and got a glass of water to take upstairs. He planned to read Joseph Smith's account of the First Vision one more time and then plead with the Lord that he would gain understanding.

As Samuel passed the den on his way to the staircase, he couldn't help but stop and think how Regi had told him that this room was broody. She always seemed to characterize inanimate objects with feelings. He smiled as his gaze panned over the cobble-rock fireplace, his darkly stained desk, the walls lined with shelves of leather-bound books, his suede couch, and the Navajo rug on the floor. He noticed that the raven statue Big Jake had given him was missing from its usual place.

"What the . . ." He stepped toward the end table where he kept it. Suddenly he was struck hard from behind. He dropped his water as he fell to the wooden floor. The glass shattered into a hundred pieces. His face landed in the water. He attempted to get up and turned slightly.

For an instant, he saw a dark ski mask.

Tar-black eyes glared at him with hatred.

The intruder struck again, and Samuel slipped into nothingness.

CHAPTER TWO

Circling, swirling overhead,
Raven watches humankind struggle
to find the Great Beyond.

SITTING ON THE CUSHIONED FOLDING chair, Regi nervously stared at the baptismal font filled with water. She heard people whispering behind her. The Relief Society president, Sister Busterudd, was inviting Sheriff Thomas Morgan; his wife, Hannah; and Effie, their nurse and housekeeper, to stay for refreshments after the baptism. They were close friends of Regi and Samuel, but they weren't members of the Church. Sister Busterudd was probably trying to make them feel comfortable. Regi noticed that Stew, the owner of Twiggs Café, was in the back. He too wasn't a member, but he was here for Samuel.

Regi wanted to talk with her friends and ward members who had shown up, but she couldn't face them. Samuel was over a half hour late. From of the corner of her eye, she saw Bishop Caldwell standing near the piano, nervously checking his watch and comparing it to the wall clock. He was a tall, thin man who looked like he never ate a complete meal. Did he have doubts that Samuel would show up?

"He'll be here." Claudia leaned over and put her hand on Regi's arm.

Regi glanced at her older sister, who seemed to always know when Regi needed support. Since fall, Claudia had cut her long, blonde hair to a more manageable shoulder length. It framed her oval face, making her look younger than her forty-one years. Her concerned blue eyes seemed larger with her hair shorter.

Regi patted her sister's hand. Claudia was always worried about others. Regi couldn't help but think of Claudia's late husband, Congressman Morris

Osborne. Out of respect for the dead, Regi had never told her sister what a two-timing skunk she thought he was. And she truly felt bad that he'd killed himself rather than tell his wife he was being blackmailed because of his infidelity. His lies had come to light during the Romney investigation. Claudia bore life scars as deep as Regi's, though hers were different.

"Claud, I know he'll be here." Even though Regi agreed with Claudia, a nagging doubt needled her. Wakanda, Regi's offbeat friend who believed she was a descendent of Chief Joseph of the Nez Percé instead of the white woman she truly was, sat on the other side of Claudia and wore a nice pair of black dress slacks and a dark, red-flowered blouse. Her long gray braids were twisted into a bun at the nape of her neck. Wakanda had come a long way in the last few months. At times, Regi got a glimpse of the woman she once was. Her speech patterns were less stilted. More and more she spoke in clear sentences. This was possibly because she'd quit drinking. In fact, Regi couldn't remember the last time Wakanda had mentioned her "ceremonial potion."

Regi smiled, thinking about the shopping trip Claudia had taken with Wakanda. Her sister was certain she could convince Wakanda to wear a dress for Samuel's baptism if she bought her one. But when they returned from their quest, crimson frustration smeared Claudia's face. Regi didn't ask what happened but believed they had at least made progress because Wakanda had let Claudia buy her something other than her usual jeans and sweatshirt. Wakanda now smiled at Regi and nodded, agreeing that Samuel would come.

But where was he?

Surely, he wouldn't back out now.

Even though he said he believed in the gospel, deep down Regi knew he still had doubts about the Church . . . or were they doubts about marrying her? Something had been bothering him. Maybe after all these years, he didn't think he deserved to be happy. *Or maybe after all these years, he decided he really doesn't want me?*

"Regi." Bishop Caldwell stood in front of her and leaned over to speak. "Did Samuel say anything to you about being late?"

"No." She tried to think. "He was going to pick up Clifford on the way. I'll call the care center and see if he's been there." Regi was grateful for something to do other than sit and stare at the baptismal water.

As she walked down the aisle of folding chairs, she smiled at Morgan. Without his sheriff's hat and sunglasses, his bald head and rugged face weren't nearly as intimidating. Waiflike Hannah sat next to him. Regi saw a flicker of recognition in her friend's eyes, but it quickly faded. Effie had a protective arm poised on the back of Hannah's chair. The older woman nodded to Regi.

Morgan gave Regi a concerned look. She would have stopped, but she didn't want to talk about why Samuel wasn't here yet. Not to Morgan. Not to anyone. No, the only person she wanted to speak with at this second was Samuel Tanner himself.

Regi rushed into the foyer, where the phone sat on a table. First she dialed Samuel's number in case he was still there. The phone rang and rang with no answer. If only he carried a cell phone, but Samuel refused to use them. So did Regi. And for that matter, so did half the community of Trailhead since reception was spotty at best in this remote, mountainous region.

She had to call the care center. She'd written down the number and stuck it in her wallet for safekeeping. Digging through her shoulder-strap purse, she finally grasped the wallet inside. She flipped it open and pulled out little bits of paper she'd written notes on.

"Want some help?" Claudia's voice surprised Regi, making her drop the papers on the floor.

"Blazes! Don't sneak up on a person like that." Regi scooped up the papers and laid them on the table.

"What are you doing?"

"Looking for the number of the care center where Clifford lives." Regi sat on the sofa as she tried to smooth out the crumpled scraps: several gas receipts, an appointment card to the vet for Oscar, a grocery list.

Claudia picked up a gum wrapper. "This has something written on it."

"That's it. Thanks!" Regi took it from her and dialed. On the second ring, the receptionist answered. "Stony Creek. This is Tamara. May I help you?"

"Hi. Can you tell me if Samuel Tanner has picked up his nephew? This is Regi Bernard." In a split second, Regi realized that by tomorrow at this time her last name would change to Tanner. Regina Tanner. The name had a very nice ring to it.

"No, Ms. Bernard. Clifford's been waiting at least an hour. Mr. Tanner always comes when he says he will because he knows how upsetting it is for his nephew to wait."

"I'm sure Samuel will be there any minute. Thanks." Regi slowly placed the phone back on the hook without saying good-bye. More than anything, she didn't want to turn around and tell her sister Samuel was a no-show at the care center.

"I take it Samuel hasn't been there yet?" Claudia asked.

Shaking her head, Regi crammed the paper scraps back into the overburdened wallet and stuffed it all in her purse. "Something's not right. Samuel would never leave Clifford waiting." She started walking down the hallway back to the Relief Society room, where the baptismal font was . . . and where all those people waited. She slowed down, reluctant to tell them she couldn't reach Samuel. Some would remember how he'd left her years ago without saying a word. She couldn't face their pity, not now.

"He could have a flat tire." Claudia put her arm around Regi's waist. "It happens. By the way, have I told you how beautiful you look in a dress?"

Regi glanced down at the teal, cross-dyed TravAllure dress she'd purchased from a catalog. She felt as uncomfortable as a trapped pigeon, but she had to admit she liked how it drew attention to her womanly curves, and she so wanted Samuel to see it. "Thanks. Look, even a flat tire wouldn't take him this long to repair."

"Unless he doesn't have a spare and he's walking."

Regi looked at her sister like she was brilliant. "Right!" She swung around and headed for the exit, grabbing her black trench coat off the wall hook on her way.

"Where are you going?" Claudia started to follow.

"If he's walking, I've got to pick him up."

"But . . ."

"But what, Claud?"

Her sister nodded toward the Relief Society room. "What about them . . . your and Samuel's friends?"

"Would you mind telling them?" Regi felt bad for dumping the responsibility on her sister, but Claudia'd had a lot of practice cleaning up Regi's messes in their youth; plus, having been married to a politician, she was good at reassuring people everything would be all right. Regi shrugged, hoping Claudia would realize the difficult situation Regi was in.

"Don't worry." Claudia shook her head. "I'll take care of it, but you owe me."

Regi chuckled. "The list grows ever longer." As she turned to leave the building, her eyes caught the picture of Jesus walking on water, reaching out to save a drowning Peter. The image remained in her mind as she fled the church house.

She sped down the snow-packed highway, watching for Samuel's shiny red, one-ton Ford. He could have slid off the road or gotten a flat tire. What if he'd crashed? Instantly, in her mind's eye, she could see him stretched out on the pavement, bleeding, with no one there to help him. Her imagination was having a field day with horrible scenes of him bloody and hurt.

This can't be happening.

Not now.

Not when we're so close.

She drove to Samuel's. By the time she came to his turnoff, it was four forty in the afternoon, the sun was beginning to set, and the countryside had already begun to fade into a cold gray. Pulling into the barnyard, she couldn't see Samuel's truck, which had been parked out front earlier. Obviously, he'd left. Could be he was between his place and the care center. Not getting out of her Jeep, she spun the vehicle around and drove toward Stony Creek.

Samuel awakened face down on the floor. His head throbbed like he'd been bucked from a horse and had landed head first on a sharp rock. When he tried to rub his head, he found his wrists were bound behind him. He craned his head back and glimpsed the silver duct tape that held him captive. Adrenaline shot through his body as he recalled the ski mask and tar-black eyes. He immediately rolled onto his side and, with the aid of the coffee table, gained his feet.

A tall, thickset man clad in a bulky parka, jeans, and ski-mask held the raven statue in his hand. Using the statue as a weapon, he lunged at Samuel. Samuel dodged the attack and, turning about, shoulder-slammed him. They both fell hard to the floor.

On top of his assailant, Samuel tried to head butt him, but the guy veered to the side and shoved him off. The attacker quickly regained his feet and kicked Samuel in the gut. Pain ricocheted through him. He curled into it, rolling onto his knees. As Samuel tried once again to stand, the intruder punched him hard in the face.

Blood gushed from Samuel's nose and mouth. Numbing pain pinged in his head. The man hit him again, this time in the right eye. The force knocked him flat on his back.

Samuel heard the rip of tape being pulled from the roll. He raised his head. His vision swirled. He struggled to get his feet under him. The tilting room made it impossible. Again, the man punched him in the face, spinning him backward until he crashed to the floor. Blinking hard to focus, Samuel spat out, "Who are you?"

The intruder said nothing as he cut a strip of duct tape with a bowie knife.

Samuel's eye was already swelling. Blood dribbled from his nose. "What do you want?"

He didn't answer but stood there staring at Samuel.

"Take my wallet. It's in my hip pocket."

The man grabbed Samuel's wallet from the coffee table and held it open. Samuel should have known he would have searched him already. The intruder pulled out what cash was in it and tossed the bills and wallet in the air. A picture of Regi fluttered to the floor.

Samuel stared at his attacker and knew this was something more than a mere robbery. "Coward! Take off the mask, and let me see your face!"

The man grabbed the duct tape he'd cut and stuck it over Samuel's mouth, silencing him. The intruder slowly straightened and peeled off the ski mask.

Long, black hair fell to his shoulders. A menacing glower streamed from his gaze. He was Native American and looked vaguely familiar, and yet, he didn't. Samuel's mind reeled. Where could he have seen him before?

The attacker had a calm bass voice. "The Raven Clan sent me to deliver justice."

Samuel felt icy memories from his Alaskan past wrap around his throat and squeeze.

Had Samuel taken a different route? Regi thought as she sped down the highway. Two roads led to the care center from his place, but surely he'd taken the straight shot. Yet, there was no sign of him as she drove the entire distance to the care center.

After parking, Regi raced into the brick building, hoping Samuel'd already been there and taken the other road to the church, though why he would was beyond her reasoning. The building smelled stuffy and felt too warm. She hurried down the corridor filled with homey pictures and dried floral wreaths.

Tamara, the receptionist, sat at her post, watching Regi rush toward her. Before Regi had even reached the station, the gal shook her head. "He hasn't shown up. Do you want to take Clifford with you? His nurse has him in the dining room working on a jigsaw puzzle to take his mind off waiting for his uncle."

"It would probably save time. If Samuel is running this late, I'm sure he'd want me to take him." As Regi started down the hallway to the dining room, she began to think. *If I take Clifford and something's happened to Samuel, Clifford will only become more upset. Darn you, Samuel Tanner, for not calling me. The least you could have done is find a stinkin' phone and call the church or call here, for that matter.*

But what if he was physically unable to call?

A panicky feeling came over her.

She stopped, swung around, and went back to Tamara. "On second thought, until I know what's going on, I don't think I'd better take Clifford. I'll let Samuel explain where he's been to his nephew."

Tamara smiled. "Oh, he's probably busy ranching. I know how it is. Everything and everyone else comes in second to cattle. I learned that from my first husband. You might rethink getting hitched to that man."

"Too late. Claudia already has a hundred pounds of shrimp and four fifteen-pound prime-rib roasts thawing in the fridge for the wedding tomorrow." Regi said it with a chuckle, but underneath she wondered.

"That man doesn't know how good he has it." Tamara chuckled.

Regi quickly made her way to the front door and walked out into the cold.

The air should have been refreshing after the heat inside. Instead, it reminded her that the man she loved was missing. And she didn't know where to find him.

He could have returned to the ranch for some reason. What if Samuel wasn't feeling well? What if he'd had a heart attack? At this point, she wasn't ruling anything out. Maybe she'd missed something at his house.

Regi knew she had to get back to Samuel's place.

And fast.

CHAPTER THREE

Raven eats the sun, the moon, the stars,
while Seal Hunter and Caribou Girl
hunger for wisdom and knowledge.

BRUISED, BLOODY, AND UNABLE TO use his hands or speak, Samuel remained kneeling as he watched his captor. Why would the Clan send him? Samuel had to learn who this guy was and make him talk.

He shook his head and felt the pull of the duct tape on his lips as he tried to communicate. The intruder ignored his pleading and disappeared into the kitchen but quickly returned with the garbage can and a hand towel. He picked up the broken glass, dropped it in the trash, and mopped up the spilled water, along with Samuel's blood, from the hardwood floor. "People need to think you disappeared—which you will."

Disappeared . . .

Samuel twisted his arms against the bands that held him. The tape stuck to his skin, pulling the hairs on the back of his wrists. It stung like needles. His wrists burned, but the tape still held him captive. Frustrated, Samuel managed to stagger to his feet.

"Look. For the pain you've caused, you deserve much more than what I've done, but I won't hurt you anymore if you do what I say." The man pulled out his bowie knife. "Make no mistake though. I'll use this if I have to."

At that moment, Samuel heard a car door shut. He glanced at the clock on his desk. He was an hour late for his baptism. That had to be Regi.

The man heard the sound as well. He rushed to the window and peeked out. "Your lady friend's come back."

Come back? Samuel was confused.

As if noticing the question on Samuel's face, his captor said, "She pulled in while you were unconscious. Lucky for her, she took off for some reason." He returned to Samuel. "She's not happy."

Panic rifled through Samuel as he madly fought the tape holding his wrists together.

"She's very pretty." Eyeing the knife's blade, the man said, "Do what I say, and I won't lay a hand on her."

Samuel would do anything to spare Regi.

"Got a basement?"

Samuel nodded and started toward the kitchen, where the door downstairs was located.

"Wait a minute." The man stopped and went back, wiped the blood off the raven statue, and returned it to the end table. Next, he grabbed the duct tape, along with Samuel's wallet, and scooped up Regi's picture from the floor. He crumpled her smiling face in his hand and dropped the paper in the garbage. As he picked up the trash can, he quickly scanned the room then shoved Samuel forward. "The basement?"

Quickening his step, Samuel led the way. As the basement door closed behind them, he heard Regi's key in the lock.

"Samuel!" Regi scanned the den and living room on her way to the staircase. No Samuel in sight. And, of course, everything was neat and orderly as always. Maybe he'd fallen in the shower and been knocked unconscious. His prone lifeless image flashed in her mind.

Even though she wore heels, she dashed up the steps two at a time. "Sam, honey!" She knocked on his bedroom door. No voice called for her to come in.

Pushing through, she found his king-sized bed was made, no clothes strewn on the plush carpeting. Again, Regi realized—as she always did when she saw how meticulously clean he was—that she was going to need to tidy up her act to live with this man. Claudia was forever after Regi to pick up her clothes.

Regi noticed Samuel's Chisholm chair, with its high back and tooled leather. On the seat lay an open book with his reading glasses on top. As she rushed by, she saw that it was the Book of Mormon. He *was* seriously studying. She hurried to his bathroom door.

"Samuel!" She knocked. "Honey, are you all right?"

No reply.

The thought of him lying unconscious on the floor guided her hand to the doorknob. She opened the door to find the room empty. Quickly feeling the fluffy burgundy towels hanging on the antler towel rack, she realized they were completely dry. That meant he hadn't showered. She glanced at the copper sink. No droplets of water left in the basin. Maybe he was still outside.

Samuel's truck wasn't parked out front. Maybe he'd pulled it in back where she couldn't see it? She went to his bedroom window and moved the suede curtain to see outside. The only vehicle was her Jeep. *Shoot! This window looks out front.*

Regi dashed out of the room, down the stairs, and through the kitchen to peer out the back door window. No truck.

She gave a deep sigh and turned away. Maybe he'd decided not to pick Clifford up because he was running late. But that didn't make sense. He'd never leave Cliff waiting.

But he could have called the center and told them he wasn't coming after Regi had left. Samuel could have gone straight to the church, so while she'd been coming from the care center, he'd been on his way to his baptism. But why hadn't he showered? *Maybe he hung up fresh towels after he was done. I mean, it's possible. Look at this clean house.*

Fighting her apprehension, she found the phone book on the counter, looked up the number of the church, grabbed the receiver, and dialed. He was probably there now, wondering where in the heck she had gone. That would be so funny. They'd laugh about this day for years—the day Regi missed Samuel's baptism because she was searching for him.

"Third ward, Bishop Caldwell speaking."

"This is Regi. Has Samuel shown up?"

"No. And Sheriff Morgan had to take his wife home, and others need to leave as well."

Regi didn't know what to say. She bit at her bottom lip as tears began to cloud her vision.

Bishop Caldwell cleared his throat. "Regina, I'll wait as long as you need me to. Your sister and Wakanda are still here and several of your friends. We can wait."

Regi thought about Samuel. His absence spoke volumes. "Bishop . . . I guess we'll have to reschedule," she softly said, not wanting to tell him her true fear and trying not to cry.

"Are you sure?" He sounded concerned.

"Yeah." Her voice was but a breath.

He paused. "Um, I hate to ask this, but what about tomorrow . . . and the wedding?" Of course, the bishop needed to know what to do. He was supposed to marry them . . .

At the church . . .

In the chapel . . .

With all their friends witnessing it.

"I don't know." The words slid from her lips. "I guess we'll reschedule that too."

"Regi, I'm a good judge of people. I know Samuel loves you. Something must have happened. If you need me to help you look for him, I will." Bishop Caldwell was trying his best to help her through this nightmare. But she knew the truth. It had been whispering to her for days, and she'd ignored it until now.

"Thanks, but I think it's obvious that he's changed his mind." She hung up.

She remembered that Samuel'd been chopping wood earlier, which was a clear sign of his inner turmoil, yet she'd allowed him to push her worries aside with his usual teasing and kissing. Why had she ignored that nagging doubt riding her shoulder and reminding her of their past? Just because Samuel'd come back after he'd run away when they were young and in love didn't mean he'd never run away again. He'd been beaten by his father, and, in order to survive, he'd taken off, leaving his family and Regi behind. That was many years ago. If she'd stuck to her guns today and listened to what her gut was trying to tell her, she could have found out what was wrong. But instead she'd been dazzled by his charm, and he'd slipped away yet *again*.

Samuel was a master at keeping secrets. After the Romney investigation last fall, Samuel told her that when he'd returned to Trailhead years ago and found out that Regi was married, he still loved her even though he didn't show it. He'd even tried to help her after Earl died by buying her cattle, land, and horse, yet he'd never once told her how he felt about her. Of course, at the time, she wasn't listening either. She'd seen only what she'd wanted to see, like she had when they were teenagers in love. Maybe that's what she was doing now. Maybe Samuel never wanted to be baptized, never wanted to marry . . .

No! She couldn't think this way! She knew him. He wasn't the same person who'd abandoned her in their teens. Samuel had changed.

He'd saved her life.

He'd built this house and had responsibilities here.

He wouldn't walk away. There was a reasonable explanation for his not showing up. She noticed that the coat he'd worn earlier was on the wall peg, and his Stetson hung from a ladder-back chair. Obviously, he wasn't out on the range working like Tamara had suspected. What if Samuel had cleaned up, gotten all ready to go, and left for . . . where? A drive to Bounty Falls to catch a movie? No, he wouldn't do that. She picked up his hat, put it over her face, and smelled his musky scent in the leather. *Where is he?*

Slowly, she put the hat back. The only explanation that made sense was that he couldn't go through with getting baptized. And he knew she wouldn't marry him unless he did, so . . . he'd ditched the whole thing.

Of all the times for him to turn tail and run, why now? Why not four months ago when they were going through that horrible ordeal with Curtis Romney? Why stay through all that mess? Unless . . . he just liked the challenge of winning her over.

And he won me over.

Samuel's craggy, tanned face, weathered from months in the saddle and working outside, came to her mind. She loved his thick ledge of brows, his strong, solid chin, and the way his rich chocolate eyes turned all tender before he kissed her. Tears clouded her gaze as bitter reality crept into her thoughts. *He made me love him.*

"Darn you, Samuel Tanner. Have you run out on me again?" she yelled into his empty house.

Samuel's heart shattered, hearing the hurt in Regi's words. He never thought what had happened in Alaska would come back to haunt him now, not when he finally had his life together. He stepped toward the door, wanting to go to her, hold her in his arms, and take away the doubt and pain. His assailant pressed the knife's blade hard against Samuel's side, cutting through his shirt and into his gut. Gritting his teeth against the pain, Samuel immediately stopped. What would this creep do to Regi if she got in the way?

She had to leave.

Leave now.

Samuel mentally blocked the torture of the knife and listened to Regi pacing back and forth in the kitchen. With each step, he thought he'd go mad.

After what seemed like an eternity, Samuel heard her footfalls walk away. She was finally leaving.

Samuel held his breath, praying she wouldn't check for his truck behind the barn. He wanted her to go. *Please go, Regi. Just go.*

As if in answer to his pleading, he heard the front door slam shut. It seemed to take forever before he heard her Jeep roar to life. Regi was gone, and with her went his heart.

His captor pulled the knife away and opened the basement door. He guided Samuel to the kitchen. Seeing blood on Samuel's shirt, the guy grabbed a chair and made him sit. Glancing around the room, the man's gaze stopped on the paper towel holder. He quickly grabbed a wad and pulled Samuel's shirt away from the wound. As the assailant wiped up the blood, he said, "Didn't mean to stick you this deep. Only meant to stop you." He folded a clean square to make a bandage then tore off another length of duct tape to keep the paper towel over the wound. Once finished he said, "That should do until we can get away from here."

He grabbed the pencil and notepad by the phone, setting them on the table near Samuel, then cut Samuel's hands free. The man pulled out a semiautomatic, 380-caliber Ruger from inside his parka. "I prefer to use a knife, but this is more convincing. Sounds like you ran out on your lady friend once before, so you're going to tell her you're running away again. Don't want anyone looking for you." He pointed the gun at Samuel's forehead. "Get writing!"

The pencil felt odd as Samuel picked it up. He didn't want Regi to think he'd up and left like he had years ago. He had to somehow leave her a clue that she could pass on to Morgan.

His captor pressed the gun barrel to Samuel's head. "This is what I want you to write: *I can't go through with it. I need time away. Please don't look for me.*"

With a trembling hand, Samuel wrote the note, all the while trying to think of a way to clue Regi in that something was wrong. As he signed his name, he realized what would work. Finished, he dropped the pencil.

The man read it. "Good." He retaped Samuel's wrists behind him, stored his gun in his parka, then began to tape Samuel to the back of the chair.

Samuel stared at him as he tried to figure out what this guy's motive was. If he wanted Samuel dead, why dress his wounds? His attacker continued to wrap the tape several times around Samuel and the chair. "It will be dark soon. Need to get my truck before we can go. Don't want to leave, do you?"

Samuel tried not to show emotion.

"People have to do a lot of things they don't want to do—like die."

Did he plan to kill Samuel but just not here?

He continued. "I'm sure Big Jake didn't want to die either. Everyone believed he'd been lost at sea, but a curious thing happened. The pipes froze at your cabin and broke." He stared at Samuel like he should know what he was going to say next.

Samuel knew about the pipes. He'd told Herman, the man he'd paid to take care of the place, to have them fixed. Samuel failed to see what this had to do with Big Jake dying.

"You probably never expected that they'd have to dig quite so much. They had to dig clean away from the cabin."

The man was still looking at him expectantly, so Samuel shrugged as though to say, so what?

"You never expected anyone to find Big Jake's body. You thought you'd gotten away with murder."

Big Jake? Murdered?

That couldn't be. The coast guard had found Jake's seiner fishing boat adrift in the middle of Malamute Sound. No sign of Jake. What sort of cock-n-bull story was this idiot going on about? Something was seriously screwed up.

"The Clan demands justice. And I seek vengeance for Grandfather's death."

Grandfather?

Samuel studied his attacker: long-limbed yet thick in the shoulders, bladelike nose, and hollowed eyes. A cold frisson overcame Samuel. Maybe this man wasn't a full-blooded Native American. Maybe he was a Native Alaskan. And maybe he was part white.

And *maybe* he was Shada's child.

Regi tried calling Samuel again. The phone rang and rang. Glancing at the kitchen clock, she saw it was well past midnight. Where in blazes was he? She hung up.

How could he do this to me again? Had the man never learned how to communicate? A simple phone call. How hard can that be? Pick up receiver; punch in numbers.

Hot anger flashed through her, prickling her skin, and was quickly followed by sorrowful hurt that wrenched her heart. She felt hollow, like a shell of the person she'd been only hours ago. How could she be hollow when she hurt so badly inside?

And then her stomach growled.

She hadn't eaten since noon.

Regi'd driven straight from Samuel's to the Raindancer Bed and Breakfast that she and Claudia owned and lived in and had locked herself in her room. Claudia had knocked on Regi's door several times, asking if she was okay. Regi had told her she was all right and just needed to be alone for a while.

After the bed and breakfast had been quiet for several hours, Regi sneaked downstairs to get a bite to eat. All at once, she remembered her kids, Jack and Lisa. The twins were leaving Richmond College early in the morning—no, *this* morning—so they could be here for the wedding . . . the wedding that would never happen.

She decided to call them around six. They'd be getting up to leave about that time. If she called then, it would be enough time to reach them before they left. Right now, she needed something to eat, even though she felt like a horseshoe was lodged in her stomach. How could she be hungry when her world was collapsing? All her dreams had been displaced by this drama of not knowing what was going on. Was she doomed to always be stuck in this neverworld, always peering through the window of other people's happy lives while she was stuck out in the cold?

Quit feeling sorry for yourself.

Opening the fridge, she saw packages of jumbo shrimp and prime-rib roasts. What were they going to do with all this food? Regi slammed her fist into the wall. Pain crushed her knuckles and streaked up her arm.

"I thought I heard you." Claudia seemed to float into the kitchen, her long satin robe billowing in her wake. "What you need is some herbal tea to help you sleep." She glanced at Regi's hand. "And ice for your knuckles."

Regi plopped down on a dinette chair. "Sheesh!"

Claudia turned on the sink faucet and filled the chrome-plated teapot then set it on the stove and turned on the burner.

Oscar, Regi's arthritic Irish setter, moseyed over to her and placed his snout on her lap, sympathizing as best he could. Regi made sure she gave the dog his arthritis medicine every morning. It eased his pain during the day. He'd bound around the ranch like a young pup once he had it, but at night, his age would catch up with him, as it had now. She stroked his head, taking comfort in his presence, while Claudia wrapped ice cubes folded in a towel around Regi's smarting hand.

"You called him again?" Claudia sat in the chair beside her.

"An hour ago. Still didn't answer."

"Sis, I know Samuel loves you with everything he's got." The conviction in her sister's voice almost made Regi believe her. Almost.

"But, Claud. What's the deal? When I took him your muffins"—tears threatened, but she forced them back—"he was excited, talking about how we'd finally be together, but now . . ." She'd known something was bothering him, but like most men, he didn't want to worry her. As if not showing up for his baptism wouldn't worry her!

"Well, whatever he's going through right now, he has to be as devastated as you are. The man has loved you all these years." The teapot whistled. Claudia rose and pulled it from the burner. She took three cups from the cupboard and set them on the counter.

"There are only two of us." Regi looked at the dog. "Oscar doesn't care for tea."

A quick knock came at the door, and in walked Wakanda, dressed in her deerskin coat. The chill of subzero temperature slipped in behind her.

Claudia gave Regi a knowing glance.

Wakanda hung her coat on the back of a chair. She was dressed in her ragged jeans and tattered sweatshirt. Her long gray braids that now dangled to her waist made her look the part of an old-fashioned Indian chief. "Took your time coming down. Now, what happened?"

Regi's friend was forever a surprise. In the last few months, Wakanda had become part of the family, though she insisted she needed her space and stayed in the bunkhouse. It gave her the distance she needed yet made her feel part of their lives.

Claudia added herbal tea bags to the cups, poured steaming water into each, and carefully carried them to the table.

Regi grabbed the plastic honey bear that was always on the counter and squeezed some into her mug. "I don't know what happened. But I do know there's not going to be a wedding today."

Claudia plopped down beside her, patting Regi's arm.

Regi didn't know how her sister would react to what she would say next, so she decided to get it over with. "All that food in the fridge is going to go to waste unless we eat it, so I say we have a party."

Wakanda took a sip from her cup, peering at Regi and Claudia like she was waiting to see if this was a joke.

Regi gazed at her sister.

Claudia's right eyebrow rose as she gave her sister a concerned look, but she shrugged. "Why not? What else are we going to do with all that food? I'll start cooking first thing in the morning." She glanced up at the clock. "Actually, in a couple of hours." She leaned near Regi. "Maybe Samuel will show up, and you can still get married."

"Maybe," Regi replied, but she was really thinking that notion didn't stand a chance. If he was such a coward that he couldn't manage to tell her what was bothering him, they weren't meant to be together.

Regi forced a smile, but underneath she knew Samuel would be a no-show.

CHAPTER FOUR

Devilfish beckons
Seal Hunter and Caribou Girl
into the mouth of Fire.

"WHAT ARE YOU STARING AT?" Samuel's captor growled, glaring back at him.

Could this really be Trace, Shada's son? Ten years had passed since Samuel'd seen the boy. He was no longer a nine-year-old child.

Unable to answer the question because his mouth was taped, Samuel shrugged.

Trace stored his bowie knife in the scabbard on his belt. He turned and opened the cupboards, taking out cans of soup and stew and placing them on the counter. As Samuel watched Trace work, thoughts of Big Jake came to mind, along with many questions.

Hadn't the man, who'd been more like a father to Samuel than his own, drowned as everyone thought? What if, for some reason, Jake had deliberately faked his own death, making people believe he'd been washed overboard? No! There was no reason. Besides, Big Jake wasn't devious like that. He was outspoken and would tell anyone right to their face what he thought of them. He'd done that to Samuel.

When he'd first met Big Jake, the man's imposing figure had reminded Samuel of a Russian version of Grizzly Adams with a dose of Native Alaskan peeking through. Big Jake had been on the dock next to his fishing boat, the *Isabelle*. At the time, Samuel was a gangly eighteen-year-old, desperate for a job and a place to live.

The first words Samuel heard from Big Jake's mouth had been, "Get off my dock."

Samuel had been near starving since he'd been on the run for months, eating out of garbage cans and even stowing away on a boat until he'd ended up in Malamute. He'd barked back, "Give me a job."

Jake had stopped fussing with the buoys and glared at Samuel. "Not hiring."

"You need me," Samuel had begged, which galled him more than hunger.

Jake had kept checking his boat but threw out over his shoulder, "Where you from, boy?"

Not wanting to be specific, Samuel had said, "South of here."

Jake had stopped and studied Samuel while stroking his gray beard. "Can't use you." He had turned to walk up the gangplank to his boat.

"I'm a fast learner," Samuel had spat out.

Without saying a word, Jake had shoved Samuel off the dock into the water. The shock of mind-numbing coldness had swallowed him in one gulp. Samuel had surged up for air, gasping. Frantically treading water, he'd looked into Jake's penetrating eyes and heard the growly man say, "Climb out on your own, and you've got a job."

Though cold as an iceberg, Samuel had somehow managed to grab hold of the dock a good foot above his head. And with sheer willpower, he'd pulled his soaking and quivering body onto the weathered wood. He shivered even now from the remembrance. No, Jake would not hide away for years, letting people think he was dead. According to Trace, they'd found Jake's body. But what condition was it in? If he'd been killed recently, they could surely tell. And if it had happened recently, they wouldn't suspect Samuel because he hadn't been in Alaska for years.

Trace finished pilfering for food. He filled a paper grocery bag, turned, and said, "Don't get any ideas. I won't be long." He slammed the door behind him as he left.

Samuel feverishly fought against thick layers of tape around his wrists. Because his wrists were behind him and his upper body was taped to the chair, it was difficult for him to see what he was doing.

However, Trace had not bound Samuel's legs. Standing up the best he could, he tried to open the knife drawer, but with his hands in back of him, and the chair in his way, his fingertips barely touched the lip of the handle. He had to think of something else and fast.

Sitting down, Samuel heard the chair's legs creak. These chairs were old. It wouldn't take much to break the legs off and possibly break the chair's back as well, giving him more mobility.

Desperate, Samuel stood and thrust his body down on the chair using his full weight. He felt the legs give a little. *One more time.*

Rising again, he jumped up and flailed backward, crashing to the hardwood floor and hitting his head. Pain shot through his brain and the knife wound in his side. Dazed and forcing his injury from his mind, Samuel looked around. The chair's spindly legs lay in pieces beside him. Yet, the seat and back of the chair were still intact. Rolling back and forth until he had momentum, Samuel managed to get on his side. He pushed and slid across the floor against the wall. Using leverage, he gained his feet, though he was bent like an old man because of the chair. Now with a little more mobility, he tried once again to open the drawer. He still couldn't grasp the handle.

Then the phone rang. Samuel shuffled to it and read the caller ID. Clifford's care center number. His nephew was probably anxious because Samuel had been a no-show to pick him up for the baptism. Staring at the phone, Samuel knew if he knocked it off the base there was no way he could talk with duct tape covering his mouth, but he might be able to moan loud enough for Clifford to hear him.

Samuel nudged the phone with his shoulder. It fell to the floor. The dial tone blared.

He had to somehow call Clifford back. But how could he talk to him? *Get the tape off.* Rubbing the side of his cheek against his shoulder, Samuel frantically tried to peel the edge away from his lips. The corner came loose. Encouraged, he tried to moisten his lips with spit beneath the glue, hoping that would help.

He heard the sound of a car engine and the closing of a door.

Samuel glanced out the kitchen door window. Trace was walking away from an old Dodge truck with a camper. He was heading for the house. Time had run out.

Kneeling down, Samuel leaned to one side, trying to grasp the phone. He craned his neck to see his hands behind him. His fingers brushed against the receiver. He managed to grab the phone. If he remembered correctly the recall button was near the right side. He pressed it with his thumb.

Dialing!

Ringing!

"Hello." Clifford.

"Mmmm!" Samuel tried to move his lips beneath the duct tape. No use.

"H-e-l-looooo." Clifford wouldn't stay on the line much longer.

The kitchen door opened. Trace kicked the phone from Samuel's hand and stomped it to pieces. "Should have known you'd try something." Trace pulled a syringe from his pocket. "Have plenty more where this came from." He stabbed the needle through Samuel's shirt sleeve and into his arm.

Immediately, dizziness swirled Samuel's vision. He collapsed to the floor. Clifford's voice echoed in Samuel's mind: "Hello, hello . . . h-e-l-looooo."

The muffled sounds of people talking awakened Regi. As her vision cleared, she realized sunlight streamed through her bedroom window. She sprang up. What time was it?

She grabbed her alarm clock.

9:00 a.m.!

"Shoot, shoot, shoot, shoot, shoot." Leaping from her bed, she scavenged for her comfortable jeans. "Claud and her dumb sleeping pills." Regi had swallowed a tablet around two o'clock, hoping to find rest from the torment of Samuel ducking out on her yet again. But she didn't think the pill would keep her under this long. She needed to call her kids to stop them from driving home. Finding her pants, she tugged them on. She scooped up a T-shirt and smelled it before slipping her arms and head through. Sprinting barefooted from her room, she flew down the stairs two at a time and burst into the kitchen.

Claudia was at the stove cooking, and Lisa stood next to her, holding a plate. Jack and Wakanda sat at the kitchen table eating breakfast.

"Shoot! I meant to call you guys." Regi went to her daughter and gave her a hug. Lisa reminded Regi of a Precious Moments character, with wide, bright eyes and a creamy complexion.

"I'm sorry about your wedding, Mom." Lisa hugged her tightly. Regi was tempted to boo-hoo on her daughter's shoulder, but she knew she couldn't. For Pete's sake, she was the mom. She couldn't show her kids her emotional pain.

Jack rose and came to her as well. Her son was a Brad Pitt look-alike with a dimpled smile and a twinkle in his eyes. But today that twinkle held concern. Regi knew she looked pathetic if even her carefree son felt sorry for her. She hugged both of her kids.

"I'm all right. Aren't I, Claud?"

Looking over her shoulder, Regi caught her sister's I'll-play-along-but-you-can't-hide-your-feelings-from-me look.

"Yes," Claudia said. "In fact, instead of a wedding, we're having a party this afternoon." She placed a slice of nutmeg-cinnamon French toast on Lisa's plate and handed it to her.

Lisa and Jack took their seats so they could eat.

"A party?" Jack asked as he took a bite of his French toast slathered with peanut butter and maple syrup. He glanced at his mother as he chewed.

"Yep. A party!" Regi snagged a piece of crust from his plate and winked. "Claudia, tell them about it while I take care of something."

Regi could feel Wakanda's eagle-eyed gaze trailing her, but she fled the kitchen anyway and crossed the dining area to the reception desk near the front door. Picking up the phone, she dialed Samuel's number.

She let it ring. Where in the world was he? A dark foreboding shadowed her, as strong and intense as if a ghost hovered above.

"No answer?" Wakanda asked, scaring Regi and making her drop the phone.

Picking it up and placing it back on the hook, Regi shook her head.

Her friend stood with her deerskin coat draped over one arm and Oscar by her side, wagging his tail. Regi stroked the animal's head and looked at Wakanda. Of course, her friend knew exactly who Regi had called. Wakanda's aged eyes were filled with knowing and compassion, which should have made Regi feel better but, instead, only agitated her more. But she wasn't agitated with Wakanda. Heaving a sigh, Regi said, "This is all my fault. If I hadn't fallen for that man, I wouldn't be in all this turmoil. Why didn't you stop me?"

"Couldn't." Wakanda shrugged. "He saved your life."

"You would bring that up." Regi glared at her friend.

Wakanda's eyebrows rose. "He loves you."

"Well, he has a funny way of showing it," Regi said, as she felt the emptiness of not knowing where Samuel was growing bigger and bigger. "Something's not right."

Wakanda nodded. She too must have sensed the ghost circling.

"You feel it, don't you?" Regi asked, relieved that she wasn't the only one. Her shamanlike friend nodded again.

"Want to go for a ride?" Regi shoved her feet into her fur-lined boots by the door and grabbed her mocha-colored parka from the hall tree.

Oscar's ears perked up, and his tail wagged. Regi figured Claudia had given him his arthritis medicine because he was suddenly anxious for any adventure that would take him outside.

"Right behind you." Wakanda tugged on her coat.

The odd trio of Regi, Wakanda, and Oscar sneaked out the front door and sprinted toward Regi's Jeep. She unplugged the engine's heater. With the subzero temperature, she had to keep the car engine warm overnight or it'd never start. Regi blew in her hands, cursing herself because she'd left her gloves behind.

Oscar jumped in the back as Wakanda and Regi climbed into cold seats. Quickly turning on the engine and dialing up the heater, Regi paused, wondering if she should return to the kitchen to tell Claudia and the kids where she was going. But she couldn't. Jack and Lisa would think their mother was nuts. Claudia would give her that pity look she used so well. Nah, by the time they realized Regi was gone, they'd probably assume she was out in the barn with Wakanda. They'd never think she'd drive all the way to Samuel's. Until a moment ago, Regi didn't think she would either. Shifting into drive, she pressed her foot on the gas.

Though the sun shone brightly over the snow, steam rose from the river as they rode over the bridge on the main highway. Just last night she'd driven down this road and looked for Samuel's truck. Little did she know at the time that she wouldn't find him or that she'd be worried out of her mind about him today.

Oscar whined for attention. Wakanda and Regi said nothing. There was really nothing *to* say. Regi felt like she was driving a luge down the mountain. She kept an eye out for any sign of Samuel's truck, hoping he might pass them. Several cars passed, but none were Samuel's.

Finally, she pulled into his barnyard and leaped out of the vehicle. Hustling down the path toward the house, she called to Wakanda over her shoulder. "Please check the barn and see if Rufus has been fed this morning."

Her loyal friend raced to the structure with Oscar tailing her.

Regi fumbled with the key, her fingers stiff and cold. Finally, it fit, and she went in. "Samuel!"

The house was deathly quiet. Slamming the door behind her, she sprinted up the stairs to check his bedroom. Without knocking, she burst in and found his bed still made. The tan suede comforter that covered the mattress was as she'd seen it yesterday.

So he didn't go to bed last night. The Book of Mormon still waited on the chair with his reading glasses on top; the bathroom door was still ajar. Samuel had not been there. "I wonder if he came home at all."

Sometimes he left her a note on the kitchen table. Leaving his bedroom, she made her way downstairs. Keeping hope alive the best she could, Regi pushed through the swinging door, leaving the entryway. She immediately went to the table. No note. However, she noticed one of the kitchen chairs was missing. She remembered it had been here last night. That was odd.

Wakanda tapped on the kitchen door, startling Regi. *Good grief, must I jump at everything?* She opened the door. Grim faced, Wakanda said nothing but motioned for Regi to follow.

"What is it?" Regi hurried to keep up.

Wakanda didn't slow down. "You need to see."

The churning in Regi's gut grew claws. She hadn't seen Wakanda so upset since Curtis Romney's murder. Oscar bounded across drifts of snow, coming toward her. The Irish setter wanted to play. She pushed him away as she fought an all-out panic attack.

Wakanda had left the barn door open. As Regi stepped inside, she saw Samuel's horse, Rufus, in his stall.

"No fresh feed, water low." Wakanda pointed to the animal's nearly dry trough. The goldfish swam in mere inches of water.

Rufus stuck his head over the top of his stall, wanting Regi's attention. She stroked between his eyes and looked at Wakanda. "This isn't good."

"Gets worse." Wakanda went to the back door and motioned again for Regi to follow.

Stepping from the shelter, Regi saw Samuel's one-ton Ford. He hadn't gone anywhere in his truck or on his horse. Fear rifled through Regi. She dashed around the truck, looking for Samuel or unusual tracks or anything out of the ordinary but found nothing.

But something was wrong.

Very wrong.

She stared at Wakanda. "We need help. It's time to call Sheriff Morgan."

CHAPTER FIVE

Devilfish tricks the fools,
but he cannot outsmart
Raven.

SAMUEL WAS RUNNING HARD AMONG barren trees, trying to reach the river. His breath grew ragged. His side ached. Still, he raced on. If he didn't get there in time, Regi would die. He lunged forward. The air caught his arms, and he was soaring high above the clouds.

He wasn't alone. Big Jake was beside him, arms outstretched, beard blowing in the wind beneath his girth. He smiled at Samuel.

Samuel was thrilled to see his old friend, and it took awhile before he thought, *Why am I flying?* "Am I dead?"

"Not yet." Big Jake soared toward him, coming closer and closer, his eyes as penetrating and cold as the first day they'd met. All at once Samuel was immersed in freezing water, trying to climb onto the dock. Jake morphed into Trace and kicked Samuel into black, inky darkness, frigid as a crypt.

Regi needed him! Samuel had to go to her. She was waiting. He saw a small light. It grew brighter and brighter, blinding him. Shielding his eyes with his hand, he tried to peer through the light.

He had to find her. He tried to yell her name, but his mouth wouldn't open.

Regi! Regi!

Samuel awakened with a start. He heard a motor and felt the sensation of movement. To his left were small cabinets; to the right, the bottom of a bench seat and the base of a dining table bolted to the floor. His mouth was still taped shut. Daylight streamed from somewhere. The hard floor he lay on was freezing cold.

What happened? Where was he? As he became more coherent, he realized he wore his parka and was covered with a blanket. But his wrists were taped together behind him. His hands felt numb; the side he lay on ached.

A camper! How had Trace managed to put Samuel's coat on him and get him in here? Maybe Trace wasn't alone.

As Samuel tried to sit up, the wound in his side throbbed with pain. Favoring his side, he leaned against a cabinet. The blanket fell from his shoulders to his legs that were now taped together from his knees down. Ignoring the pain in his side, Samuel gazed about fully expecting to find someone watching him, but he saw only a vacant dinette and no one in the upper bunk. By the light shining in the windows, he knew it was no longer evening. He'd been out all night and half the day. How long had Trace been on the road?

Bracing his elbow on the bench seat, he dragged himself off the floor until he was able to sit on the cushion. His thoughts went to Regi. She was probably out of her mind with worry. He prayed she understood what he'd scrawled on the notepad. If she didn't, surely Morgan would.

Even so, chances were that he was far away from home. Samuel had to get out of here. He looked around for something he could use to break a window. The counter was bare. Bracing himself against the table, he managed to stand and made his way to the closet. Turning so his hand could work the knob from behind him, he pulled but the door caught. Next he tried a drawer and cupboard. They gave a little but then stopped, as though something kept them from opening.

He stared between the cracks. Childproof locks. Of course. Campers don't want their stuff flying around, and with his hands bound behind him, he couldn't open them.

Samuel knew he had to calm down and gain his bearings. Where could Trace be headed? Samuel went back to the bench seat, sat, and peered out of the parted curtains above the dinette table. Flashes of pine trees raced by, but from this scenery, there was no way he could tell where he was. They could be in Idaho, Montana, or even Washington.

Maybe Samuel'd have a better view from the door. Struggling to his feet again, he went to the back. Turning around, he was able to grab the knob. Twisting it, he pushed, but the door didn't budge. He'd been locked in from the outside.

Trace had been thorough. Peering between the curtains, Samuel saw the highway trailing behind them. A vehicle followed in the distance. If he could communicate with whoever was in that car, this might all come to an end.

Trace hadn't been thorough enough.

Regi burst through the kitchen door of Samuel's house and reached for the phone to call Morgan. But the phone was missing from the hook.

She glanced around the room, thinking that maybe after she'd used it last night she'd left it somewhere else. She couldn't see it. Remembering the phone in Samuel's den, she motioned for Wakanda to follow her from the kitchen.

They crossed the entryway into the broody room, and Regi sprinted around the desk to the phone. Grabbing the receiver, she stopped when she saw a note addressed to her. She scanned the words and froze. Her knees became weak. The room tilted.

"What's wrong?" Wakanda had stayed in the entryway but now rushed to see what had captured Regi's attention.

Oscar crawled under the coffee table as if to escape.

Regi's blood ran icy cold as she read the words out loud.

> Regi,
> I can't go through with it. I need time away. Please don't look for me.
> Sam

Her worst nightmare had come to pass. Samuel had left her again. She slumped into the leather chair next to the desk.

Wakanda folded her arms. "Some men can't be tamed."

"But I thought he'd changed. You saw it, didn't you?" Regi looked up at her friend, trusting her to tell the truth.

Wakanda glanced over at the couch in front of the fireplace. "Last fall I watched him sit right there and hold you in his arms." She pointed to the spot. "He loved you."

Regi stared at the couch, remembering how Samuel had held her as she'd recovered from hypothermia. That night, a fire had flickered in the cobble-rock fireplace, and the broodiness of the room had changed to hope, life, and love. Now it was cold, empty, and broody . . . again.

She studied the couch and coffee table. Was the furniture further apart than usual? Eyeing the Navajo rug, she found where imprints of the couch legs had matted down the nap. The couch had been moved a good half foot. That was odd.

Her eyes trailed to the empty end table.

Empty?

"Wakanda, Samuel's raven statue is gone." Pointing at the vacant spot, Regi said, "It was right here yesterday."

Wakanda stood beside her. "Are you sure?"

"Yes!" Regi's mind raced. "That's the second thing missing. There's a kitchen chair gone . . . oh, and the phone from the kitchen."

"Maybe he took them upstairs for some reason." Wakanda shrugged like that was the only conclusion she could fathom.

"I didn't see them when I was just up there." But Regi hadn't looked for them either. Surely if all these missing items had been there, she would have noticed, but they could have been in the other rooms. It was a big house.

Regi looked again at the note. "You know, he never signs his name just *Sam*. Even in little love notes, he writes *Samuel*. And look at how shaky his handwriting is."

"Maybe he'd been drinking."

"No." Regi immediately dismissed that notion. "Not Samuel. He was going to be baptized."

Wakanda cocked her head to the side as though to say drinking might be why he never showed up.

"He gave up liquor long ago. When his father was drunk, he nearly beat Samuel to death."

Wakanda raised a skeptical brow.

"It's true. Samuel doesn't touch the stuff because of that." She stared down at the note again. "So why did he write that way and sign his name just *Sam*, like he was a totally different person?"

Wakanda stood totem-pole straight, arms folded as though she was stumped as well.

"Some of his things are missing, his truck is here, the horse is here but hasn't been fed, and now this note. I have a bad feeling, and it's not that I've been left at the altar. I'm seriously wondering if he's ill or something. Which doesn't account for the missing items, but he could be in serious trouble, lying on the floor somewhere." She glanced around the room like she might see him behind the bookcase or on the other side of the recliner. "We have to check out the house."

Wakanda gave her a sideways glance that asked, are you sure? "What if he's all right, comes home, and finds us snoopin'?"

"I'd like to see him try to get angry with me after what he's pulled." Regi stopped. Actually, between thinking he might be passed out from a stroke or coming home and finding them rummaging through his house, she'd choose the later. She would rather argue with him than sit by his bedside worried about whether he would live or die.

"Come on. We have to look around." Regi and Wakanda hurried up the stairs. Regi stopped outside of Samuel's room. "I really don't think I can go in there again. Would you mind checking while I search the other rooms?"

Wakanda nodded.

Regi went through the two guest rooms, the laundry room, and another bathroom. Weeks ago when Samuel had given her a tour of his place, she'd only glanced in them. But today nothing seemed out of place from what she could remember, and there was no sign of Samuel, the chair, the phone, or the raven statue.

She walked into the spare room next to the master suite and stood in the center, where Samuel had once stood. Memory overcame her like she'd stepped into another dimension.

Samuel had stammered, hemmed, hawed, and finally cleared his throat. "Don't you think this room would make a good, um . . . nursery?"

"Oh yeah." She'd loved how the sun had streamed in through the curtains. White shelves had hung on buttercream-colored walls. She could imagine stuffed toys and books on them, could see a bassinet in the corner and a crib along the wall. "Our grandkids would love this room."

Samuel's brows had knit together as he'd given her a wistful look. "We're not that old yet."

She'd chuckled. "Samuel, the twins are in college. I'm thirty-nine. You're forty. We don't want to start over, do we?"

"Regina, *we* never had a beginning." No chuckle had echoed in his voice.

"You're serious?" Regi hadn't known what to think. She'd gone through the baby thing, messy diapers, early morning feedings, school, trips to the doctor. She'd done it with two at the same time.

He had slowly nodded that he was serious.

How could she say no to this man? She loved him and would give him anything he wanted if he asked . . . but a baby?

He'd drawn her into his arms. "A baby. Yours. And mine." He'd pressed his forehead to hers. "I know we're not spring chickens, but that's better. We've made all the mistakes. With our love secure, this child would have everything. We have no financial problems. Jack and Lisa would love him or her to death. And Claudia and Wakanda would make wonderful aunts. I always wanted to have a child with you. Have since we were young."

Tears puddled in her eyes with remembrance of that day. Samuel had backed off from pressing for an answer. Now, she'd give anything to have the chance to tell him yes.

Wakanda walked in. "No sign of Samuel or the missing stuff. Did you check the other rooms?"

"Yeah. Nothing." Regi turned so Wakanda wouldn't see her blink away tears. They hurried downstairs and continued their search in the sunken living room across from the den.

Stepping down to the plush carpeting, Regi checked around the grand piano while Wakanda looked over the sofas that faced each other and the mantel above the fireplace. Again they found nothing out of the ordinary. Regi rarely saw Samuel go into this room, though she remembered him talking about how next year they'd set up their Christmas tree in the bay window.

A knock came at the front door. Answering it, Regi found Morgan dressed in his sheriff's uniform right down to his spit-polished black boots and Stetson patrol hat. He took off his sunglasses and fur-lined gloves then unzipped his parka, which had the sheriff's star logo on the upper sleeves.

At first he looked surprised to find Regi there, but then he tipped his hat back and asked, "Did Samuel have a reasonable explanation why he was a no-show yesterday? Got worried, and since I was out and about, I swung by to give him a bad time."

"He's not here. And I can't find him." She let Morgan in. He waved to Wakanda. She nodded, acknowledging him.

"Morgan . . ." Regi motioned him toward the den. "I found a message from Samuel."

She pointed to the note on the desktop. Morgan didn't pick it up but quickly read it. When finished, he gazed at Regi. "I'm sorry, Reg." He slung his arm around her shoulders. "Samuel told me awhile ago that he was having doubts about the Church, but I thought he'd overcome them. I really didn't think it would stop him from getting baptized."

"Look at the note again." Regi drew his attention to the evidence. "Handwriting's mighty shaky, don't you think?"

"Yeah, and I've never seen him sign anything with just *Sam*." Morgan looked at the note with renewed interest. "Yesterday, he was probably pretty nervous and wasn't himself when he wrote it."

"Something's not right, and I can't put my finger on what it is. There's a chair and the phone missing from the kitchen and his raven statue." She pointed to the empty space.

Morgan's entire demeanor changed from a consoling friend to an alarmed officer. "The statue is missing?"

"Yeah." Regi had wanted Morgan to see that something could have happened to Samuel, but his deeply concerned expression was more than she'd expected.

"Big Jake left it to him in his will." Morgan took a deep breath.

"I know. Samuel told me. The statue meant a lot to him." Regi glanced at Wakanda to see if she'd caught on to what Morgan was getting at. She stood with her arms still folded, expression unchanged, just listening. She looked back at Regi as though to say, wait for it.

"Inside was a deed to his cabin and property in Alaska." Morgan rubbed his chin. "Said he wanted to give you the cabin as a wedding gift."

"Wait a minute." Regi had never heard about this. "Samuel doesn't have that much money. I mean, it's obvious he has money—look at this house—but a cabin in Alaska? Come on."

Worry lines furrowed Morgan's brow. "You said other things were missing from the kitchen?"

"Yeah." She had wanted him to take her seriously and help her look for Samuel, but the fearful urgency in Morgan's tone was more than just worry about an ill friend. "Let me show you."

In a surreal daze, Regi led the way, doing things mechanically instead of facing the fear that breathed over her. When she was almost to the door, she realized Morgan hadn't followed. He was back in the den, gazing down on the wood floor where it looked like something had spilled but someone had tried to wipe it up. Squatting, he studied it. He took a sticky notepad from his pocket and pulled a paper off, placing it on the floor next to the stain.

"What are you doing?" Wakanda squatted beside him.

"Could be blood stains. I need to mark it." His eyes scanned the carpet.

"Did you say blood?" An alarm went off in Regi's head as she came back into the room.

"Yes. Did you move the couch?" he asked, walking around it.

"No. I thought it looked like it had been moved too." Regi studied Morgan's face, wishing she could read his thoughts.

Wakanda stepped beside her. "We searched the house for the missing things."

"You two have been all over the house?" His expression became grim.

Regi didn't understand but still felt like they'd done something wrong.

"Basement too?" he asked.

Regi quickly looked to Wakanda, who shook her head. "Forgot the basement."

Regi and Wakanda followed Morgan as he left the den and went to the kitchen. The basement door was right next to the swinging door from the hallway. He opened it, flipped on the light, and paused, staring down at spots on the top wooden step. He marked them and stepped around them. "Stay here while I check." He disappeared downstairs but quickly came back up. "He's not down there."

Getting down onto his knees, Morgan dug in his pocket and brought out latex gloves and a small paper bag. From another he pulled out his pocketknife. He flipped open the knife and slipped on the gloves. Carefully, he cut the wood beneath the spots, lifting both the wood and stains from the step. Then he placed it in the evidence bag.

As she watched, Regi heard fear hum in her ears as loud as a dial tone. Nausea swelled in her throat. "Morgan, what do you think happened?"

"I have little evidence. I mean, a missing chair and phone aren't much, but add them to the raven statue and what looks like bloodstains . . . On top of that, he didn't show up at his baptism, and he's not here for his own wedding to the woman he loves. Plus the strange note he left . . ."

He stared at Regi, biting his lips together.

"Do you think he's sick somewhere?" As soon as she said it, Regi realized they'd moved past that idea. It didn't fit the evidence any longer. She knew deep in her heart that Morgan was gathering evidence like a crime had taken place. She was just hoping beyond hope that she was wrong.

Morgan got up off the floor. "This has all the earmarks of a kidnapping."

Regi shuddered. Out of the corner of her eye, she caught sight of Samuel's weather-beaten cowboy hat on the back of a chair. It had been there when she'd visited yesterday. If he had left of his own free will, he would have worn his hat. With trembling hands, she picked it up. "This is where it was when I came last night looking for him." Regi put on the hat. Too big, but she didn't care. Wearing the hat made Samuel feel near.

Her eyes trailed to where his Gore-Tex parka had hung on the wall peg. It wasn't there. "His coat is gone! It was here last night!"

"Let's go in the living room where you can sit down." Morgan guided her out. Wakanda followed, not saying a word but ever watchful.

"Morgan, the coat was here last night. If someone had kidnapped him and that's what kept him from showing up at the baptism, why isn't his coat still here?" Her mind kept skipping like a scratched CD.

Morgan settled her on the couch and stood in front of her. He sighed and swiped his hand over his face, blinking a few times. "Blood on the top step could mean they hid there while you were here."

Regi thought of how she'd stomped through the house. *And a kidnapper could have been here with Samuel, watching me?* She thought she was going to be ill.

Wakanda sat beside her, patting her leg.

This could not be right. Fighting Morgan's scenario, she asked, "Still, why kidnap Samuel?"

"Don't you know how much Samuel is worth?" Morgan glared at her. Regi shrugged.

As if he couldn't believe her ignorance, Morgan said, "*Millions.*"

"*My* Samuel?"

"Your Samuel took the inheritance he received from selling Big Jake's fishing business and invested it *very* wisely." Morgan grew impatient. "As we speak, someone could be forcing him to withdraw much of his fortune from the bank."

"But then they'd release him, right?" Regi bit her chapped bottom lip.

"Chances are, it's someone Samuel knows and could identify. Whoever it is probably kept him here last night, waiting until this morning to take him to the First National."

"And I could have stopped it if I'd looked in the basement?" Regi desperately needed the sheriff to disagree.

Instead he said, "I need more evidence to back me up, but I'm going to radio Sheriff Talbert in Bounty Falls."

As they walked to the entryway, Oscar crawled out from under the coffee table, carrying what looked like the brown knitted scarf Wakanda had given Samuel for Christmas a few months ago. "Come here, boy," Regi coaxed him over. The Irish setter went to her.

As Regi took what he had, she saw it was black not brown. And it wasn't a scarf. It had holes for two eyes, a nose, and a mouth.

A ski mask. And it wasn't Samuel's.

"Here." Morgan motioned for her to put it in another evidence bag. "Could be hair inside the cap or saliva on the mouth hole where we could collect DNA."

Regi dropped the mask in. Clamping a hand over her pursed lips, she stifled a moan. The room swirled.

Morgan guided Regi to the couch in the den and motioned for Wakanda to help. "Keep her here." He took the evidence bags with him as he made a quick exit.

The nightmare Regi had awakened to this morning had morphed into a horror show. Regi stared at the cold fireplace. She had been through some tough times in her life, like losing Earl to cancer and being accused of murder, but *this*—thinking that someone had kidnapped Samuel and may have killed him for his money—was more than she could bear.

Please, God, bring Samuel home!

CHAPTER SIX

Seeking daylight, Seal Hunter and Caribou Girl
call to Him who owns the stars, the moon, and the sun.
No answer.

THE CAR SAMUEL HAD SEEN in the distance was now much closer. Turning, he tried to reach from behind for the curtain covering the window in the door. Because his wrists were taped together, he fumbled until he was able to grab hold of the material and jerk. The rod loosened slightly. He jerked again and again until the hooks sprang free. Dropping the curtain to the floor, Samuel gazed out the window at the automobile.

A black Camry. The front Montana license plate read, "Winkie." *Odd choice for a vanity plate.* At the wheel was a white-haired, stern-faced, elderly man whose eyes reminded Samuel of Mr. Magoo. *Ah, thus the Winkie plate.* To his left sat a sour-faced, blue-haired, elderly woman who looked none too happy.

Samuel had to gain their attention. He moved from side to side and jumped up and down.

The woman was first to notice. She squinted at Samuel. Never taking her eyes off him, she nudged her husband and pointed.

Progress!

The elderly man peered up.

Samuel turned sideways. He held his wrists high so the couple could see he was tied up. He also shook his head so they could see the tape on his mouth.

The Magoo-eyed man jerked back and yelled something at the woman.

Dang, what was he saying to her? Samuel strained to read the man's lips but with no success.

The woman bristled and spat words back at the man, her lips moving too fast for Samuel to catch anything she said.

The man drove to the left like he was checking for oncoming traffic in the other lane, and then the Camry jettisoned out of sight. The last Samuel saw of the couple was the woman folding her arms and glaring at her husband.

Samuel still clung to the hope that the man would motion for Trace to pull over. But the truck never slowed or deviated from its course.

Apparently, Mr. Magoo didn't want to get involved. Or maybe, if luck were on Samuel's side, he'd call the authorities. And *maybe* he'd taken down the truck's license plate number. *That's as likely as Big Foot jumping in the road and stopping the truck.*

Discouraged, Samuel shivered as he gazed at the empty road with miles and miles and no car in sight. He made his way back to the bench seat and sat so he could still peer through the window in the door. Surely another car would come along soon.

Though Samuel wore a parka, his teeth chattered against the cold. His thoughts went to Trace . . . and Shada.

When Samuel had left Malamute over ten years ago, Shada was as mad as a rogue cougar that the courts had ignored the tribe and upheld Big Jake's will. Samuel had felt bad for her, but she and Big Jake hadn't gotten along. The man loved his wayward daughter, but she never showed him respect and spent much of her time at the Thirsty Beaver Bar picking up men. Jake didn't care for the company she kept, especially when she was supposed to be taking care of her child. And he never forgave Shada for getting pregnant out of wedlock and refusing to tell him who the father was, though Samuel felt Jake had had a good idea of who the guy could have been. Shada called her father only when she needed to be bailed out of financial trouble. Because of the boy, Big Jake helped her, but in his will, he'd left Shada nothing and asked Samuel to send her child support until Trace turned eighteen. That had ended a couple of years ago. Shada threatened legal action and even sent Samuel a blistering letter several months ago, but since then, he hadn't heard from her.

Samuel could well imagine the stories she'd told Trace. The poor kid had really received a raw deal from life. Most kids who had crappy childhoods felt alone, unworthy, and rejected. Samuel knew because that's how he'd felt when he was young. Samuel had run away from his abusive father and experienced all those feelings until he met Big Jake. If Samuel could tell Trace how much his grandfather had loved him, it might help.

Samuel peered out the window again.

Still no car.

He couldn't afford to wait. Each second took Samuel further away from his life with the woman he loved. He had to do something to make Trace stop the truck.

An idea struck. Samuel once again made his way to the door. It had been locked on the outside to keep him in, but camper doors were flimsy. If he could kick the door out . . . then what? Jump? Not likely. But if Trace heard Samuel, he'd stop.

Stopping would be good.

Stopping would get Trace out of the truck, and the chances for Samuel to escape would increase.

Samuel glanced down at his taped legs. He couldn't run, and with his arms bound behind him, he couldn't put up much of a fight. However, Samuel could make a scene. And maybe a car would drive by. The odds were horrible, but deep down that's what Samuel felt he had to do.

The question was, should he do it now or wait until a car was close?

Now!

He couldn't wait.

Samuel eased down, sitting on top of the curtains he'd pulled off the door. Lying back, with his bound hands propping up his behind, he drew his legs up and kicked as hard as he could.

The door gave a little.

He did it again and again, putting all his might behind each kick. The bottom half of the door cracked.

The vehicle slowed to a stop. Samuel heard the motor shut off and Trace curse as he slammed the driver's side door.

He was coming.

And so was Samuel's chance to either escape or die trying.

Unable to wait any longer for Morgan to return to the house, Regi stood up, sat down, stood, and sat again. She didn't know what to do. Wakanda was next to her, not saying a word, only watching Regi as if she expected her to combust. In an effort to avoid uncontrollable tears, Regi walked around the coffee table in the den.

All her hopes and dreams for the future were wrapped up in Samuel Tanner. She loved him, plain and simple. The love she'd felt for him when they were kids had been rekindled after all these years. For a second, she thought of the empty room upstairs, the would-be nursery. More than ever she wanted to give Samuel a baby—a baby he would never have if someone killed him.

Tears clouded her vision. She gazed at Wakanda. "When I came here last night . . . if I had known maybe I could have helped Samuel."

"No good comes from talk like that. Getting yourself killed would not help Samuel." Wakanda strode to the desk and reached for the phone. "You need your sister."

Remembering how careful Morgan had been, Regi said, "Wait!" She dug in her jeans pocket and pulled out a clean tissue. "Pick it up on the bottom, and use this."

Wakanda scoffed, took the tissue, and dialed.

Watching where she walked so she wouldn't step on evidence, Regi paced. Her legs were jumpy. She had to do something. And pacing was something; plus it helped her think. Before Morgan had gone to his patrol car to call for help, he'd said that Samuel was worth millions. Maybe something in Samuel's business correspondence would give them a clue as to who would do this.

She joined Wakanda beside the desk and, carefully touching only the very edges so as not to leave fingerprints, glanced through a small stack of papers on top. Only bills for feed and utilities. Nothing out of the ordinary. She'd have to search in the desk drawers.

Regi tried to pull one open but broke a nail when the drawer refused to budge.

Locked.

She tried all of them. They were all locked.

Wakanda finished talking to Claudia and hung up. "On her way. Be warned. She's mad we slipped out."

"Yeah, well . . ." Regi kicked the desk. "This stupid thing is locked."

Wakanda dug in her ragged Levi pocket and pulled out a long-hook pick. At first Regi was surprised, but thinking about how much she didn't know about the friend she loved like a sister, she realized Wakanda had lived a long, hard life. Nothing should surprise Regi. Wakanda set to work on the middle drawer lock.

Morgan returned, stomping snow from his boots. He held what Regi thought was a tissue box.

"Were you able to reach the sheriff's department? Is help coming?" Regi tried to sidetrack him while she thought of a way to explain what they were doing.

He came to stand beside her. "Yes, but . . . use these," he said, placing the box on the desk. It wasn't tissues but a box of disposable latex gloves. "When the sheriff from Bounty Falls eventually gets here, he's going to go ballistic that we've touched everything, but each moment we wait could take away from Samuel's . . . chances, and I need your help." He stared at Regi.

She knew he was going to say *life*—moments away from Samuel's life. Knowing that Morgan believed Samuel's fate was dire increased Regi's own sense of urgency.

Wakanda continued working. As Morgan watched her, he said, "Sheriff Talbert said they have their hands full right now. A little two-year-old girl has been taken, and they have a tri-state Amber Alert out for her; plus, some wandering ice fishermen from Grey's Lake didn't come home when they were supposed to. So Samuel's disappearance is low on their list of priorities until I get the test results back on the blood samples and ski mask. That will take days."

Regi's heart went out to the parents of the little girl and to the families waiting for their men to come home, but her main concern was for *her man.*

"'Bout all Talbert could do is put out an APB. And he did that as a favor to me." Morgan tapped the box of gloves. "Put these on."

Regi took a pair and laid another on the desk where Wakanda could get them once she'd finished. The old woman's arthritic fingers worked the pick with expertise.

They heard a click. Wakanda's broad face smiled as she brushed one of her long gray braids over her shoulder. She picked up the gloves, pulled them on, and opened the drawer.

Morgan stared at her with disbelief and wonder. Was he thinking of other break-ins around Trailhead he couldn't solve and pinning them on Wakanda? Ignoring the fleeting thought, Regi pulled the drawer completely out.

The three of them started shuffling through the contents. Regi set extra staples and a stack of business cards out of the way. With Morgan and Wakanda searching the middle drawer, she tried the side drawer. Within was a file full of the ranch's bank statements. She placed it on the desk and opened it, drawing Wakanda's and Morgan's attention.

The statements showed that Samuel had paid Intermountain Farmers, a vet, and some excavating and construction company. She flipped through the statements, finding nothing out of the ordinary for a working ranch.

Regi closed the file, looking back in the drawer. From the outside, it appeared deeper.

A false bottom perhaps?

Wakanda seemed to notice what Regi was looking at. She eyed the drawer more closely, feeling the bottom and the top. She tapped on the wood. It made a hollow sound. Wakanda felt around the inside seam and found a catch. Pulling the bottom up, she discovered another compartment with yet another file. She stared at Regi as though expecting she would know what was in it.

Shrugging, Regi grabbed the folder. These statements were from a bank in Alaska. Several payments went to a person named Herman Degelder. It appeared that Samuel sent him money every month. There were also payments to utility companies, an attorney, the Alaska State Tax Commission, and other expenses. Only a year's worth of statements were inside.

Regi gazed back in the drawer. Inside were more manila folders with the years written in black marker on each. As Regi set them on the desk, she heard car doors slamming. Claudia and the twins must have arrived. Jack and Lisa had never been to Samuel's place. Regi hated that their first visit was this. *Samuel should be here to welcome them.* A lump rose to her throat. She was suddenly very hot. It could be because she still wore her coat. But Wakanda still wore hers as well.

Morgan motioned for Wakanda and Regi to follow him to the entryway. "I don't want a lot of people walking around in the den." Oscar followed Regi like he was afraid to lose sight of her.

They met Jack as he walked into the house. He stomped snow from his feet, tugged off his gloves, and unzipped his parka. As soon as he saw his mother, he hugged her and said, "What's going on? Wakanda told Aunt Claudia you needed us." Worry furrowed his forehead. Claudia and Lisa were behind him, concern in their eyes. Lisa skirted around Jack, took hold of Regi's arm, and squeezed. The warmth of her family around her gave Regi strength. She looked to Morgan. "Can we go in the living room? Nothing was disturbed in there."

Morgan rubbed the back of his neck. "I should tape off the entire house until I can thoroughly search it, but it's too cold outside, and since you've already been through it anyway, yeah, go ahead."

Everyone took off their coats and hung them on the hall tree. Morgan led the way to the living room. Wakanda, Regi, and Claudia sat on one couch, and Jack and Lisa sat on the other, facing them. Oscar settled at

Regi's feet. Morgan stood in front of the fireplace. Everyone looked to Regi as if expecting her to say something, but she didn't know where to begin. Morgan seemed to understand her need for backup and explained the evidence they had found. He finished by telling them about the blood on the floor.

Lisa gasped. Jack's mouth gaped open. Claudia rubbed Regi's arm. "Sis, are you all right?" Maybe seeing Claudia staring at her with sympathetic eyes or having the kids she loved more than life itself looking shocked and worried for their mother was too much because all at once an emotional tsunami hit Regi. The strength she felt earlier vanished. Her hands shook; her insides tied into square knots.

Gazing at her sister—who had helped Regi during every disaster in her life—Regi was unable to answer. In fact, she was having an awful time focusing. Regi closed her eyes.

Claudia took Regi's hand. "Thomas will do everything humanly possible to find Samuel." She always called Morgan by his first name, a leftover habit from their teen years when they had dated. Claudia continued. "Whatever happens, I'm here for you."

Whatever happens . . . Claudia sounded like she didn't think Samuel was alive.

Wakanda, on the other side of Regi, nudged her in support.

Regi stared at Wakanda then Claudia. A trace of pity smeared their faces. *They think Samuel is dead.* Unable to look at them, Regi glanced over at Jack and Lisa. They seemed shell-shocked. She wanted to go to them and tell them everything would be all right, but she couldn't. She had no clue how this was going to end.

Unable to bear their looks, Regi stood. "Excuse me a minute. Morgan, would it compromise your investigation if I used the bathroom? I'll be careful."

Morgan stared at her for a second and, as though realizing she desperately needed to be alone, he nodded for her to go ahead.

Regi fled up the stairs, Oscar trailing behind. She crossed through Samuel's bedroom to the sanctuary of his bathroom, motioning for Oscar to wait for her and closing the door. She had to be totally alone. As she leaned against the door, she knocked Samuel's hat off her head. Seeing it on the floor made her miss him all the more. She sank to the hardwood floor as tears spilled down her cheeks. She felt so alone and isolated, and she knew she needed to turn to her only comfort—the Lord.

Getting on her knees, she poured her heart out to her Father in Heaven, begging Him for strength, pleading for help to find Samuel, and, if it be His will, to find Samuel alive. Then she rose to her feet and put cold water on her face.

She turned to leave and grabbed Samuel's hat, but the lip of the counter caught the brim, knocking it from her grasp. She picked up the work-worn Stetson again and noticed a piece of paper tucked in the inside rim. She pulled it out. It was a scripture in Samuel's handwriting:

Romans 5:3-5, "And not only so, but we glory in tribulations also; knowing that tribulation worketh patience; And patience, experience; and experience, hope: And hope maketh not ashamed; because the love of God is shed abroad in our hearts by the Holy Ghost which is given unto us."

Samuel had been working so hard to develop a testimony that he must have put the scripture in his hat as a constant reminder. She stared at the last line—*And hope maketh not ashamed; because the love of God is shed abroad in our hearts by the Holy Ghost which is given unto us.* Burning flooded her heart with the sure knowledge that Samuel was still alive.

Tears collected in her eyes. Regi folded the paper and placed it back inside the rim. She looked in the mirror, about to put the hat back on, but stopped. Just yesterday Samuel had worn this hat as he'd walked her to the Jeep. Just yesterday he'd promised that he was finally going to get baptized and that today they'd get married. *And just yesterday* he'd kissed her good-bye.

No, it wasn't good-bye. Deep down in her soul, she knew he was still alive. She had prayed for guidance . . . and the Lord was giving it to her. She *had* to believe Samuel would come home and they would have a life together—the life they were always meant to have. After all they'd been through, she couldn't give up on him now.

No, not now.

Not ever!

She put Samuel's hat on then. The Stetson was too big for her, but she didn't care. She decided that too big or not, she was going to wear it every day until Samuel himself took it off of her. Wrangling her emotions under control and determined to be strong, she left the bathroom and went downstairs.

All eyes were on her and Oscar as they joined the others in the living room. "Samuel is going to be all right, and we are going to find him."

Jack and Lisa sat on the edge of the couch, staring up at their mother. Wakanda smiled. Claudia's eyebrows rose, but she nodded in agreement. She knew better than to get between Regi and her determination.

They heard car doors shutting outside. Regi glanced at Morgan.

"Must be Cameron Elliott," he said. "When Sheriff Talbert was too busy, I gave Elliott a call. Even though most of the rangers are searching for those missing fishermen, I thought there might be some who could help us." Morgan walked toward the door but looked at Jack. "Want to give us a hand searching the ranch?"

"Sure. Where do we start?" Jack and Morgan grabbed their coats and headed for the door.

"Son," Regi called to him. "Please feed Rufus before you head out. I don't know how long the horse has gone without something to eat. He needs water too."

Jack nodded as he and Morgan left.

Claudia went to the window and pulled the curtain aside. Regi knew she was looking for Elliott. "Why don't you go out and talk with him?"

Claudia scoffed. "Just wanted to see who was with him was all." She turned away from the window and gazed at Lisa. Something passed between them. Regi wasn't certain what. Surely Lisa wasn't concerned about her aunt's attraction to the park superintendent.

Last Christmas Lisa seemed to be over the nightmare that had put her at odds with Superintendent Cameron Elliott and his daughter. The super's daughter had married Curtis Romney shortly after he dumped Lisa and spread lies around the town about her. Even though Romney had broken Lisa's heart, Regi knew her daughter mourned his death. Lisa, being the terrific person that she was, had welcomed Elliott and his daughter to their family celebration with open arms and compassion.

And in the last few months, Cameron had become a constant visitor at the Raindancer Bed and Breakfast, and it wasn't to check in as a guest or to see Regi or Wakanda.

Wanting the awkward moment to pass, Regi motioned for Lisa, Claudia, and Wakanda to follow her to the desk. They carefully stepped around the marked evidence on the floor. Oscar crawled under the coffee table to his usual spot. Regi gave Lisa and Claudia gloves then reached for one of the manila envelopes she'd set out earlier and found more bank statements. "We need to look through each of these folders and the statements. Set aside anything that stands out as not being a business expense." Regi stacked papers she'd already looked at in a pile.

Claudia opened one, pulled out the contents, and turned the pages. "An Alaskan bank?"

"I just learned today that Samuel has a cabin and property there," Regi replied, not wanting to explain but knowing that she had to. She glanced at her sister and daughter. Of course, they were puzzled. She went on. "And it seems that he's . . ." Regi didn't know how to tell them her fiancé had money, so she just blurted, "Samuel is loaded."

"Loaded? Do you mean he was drunk when this happened?" Lisa didn't quite grasp the meaning.

Wakanda explained as she kept thumbing through the statements. "No. He's a millionaire or something."

"Why did he keep it a secret?" Claudia stared at Regi instead of Wakanda. Regi knew her sister hated secrets. She'd been burned by them too much in her past. Secrets had a way of catching fire and ruining lives.

"I don't know. But Morgan said Samuel wanted to surprise me and give me the cabin as a wedding present. So I'm guessing he was keeping it a secret so he could tell me then." Regi had no idea why Samuel had never told her. He'd said he had no financial worries, and maybe he assumed she understood what that meant.

Lisa glanced over the den, at the ornate western pictures hanging on the walls, the expensive bookcases filled with leather-bound books, and the high-end furniture in the room. "Makes sense. But money doesn't mean that much to Mom." She smiled at Regi. "She'd love him even if he were broke."

Regi was touched by her daughter's high opinion; she didn't know what she'd done to deserve such good kids, but she was grateful.

An hour ticked by as they flipped through the papers. Regi discovered another file folder tucked way in the back of the drawer. It held correspondence from someone named Herman. Regi remembered the name from the bank statements. This fellow could be the same Herman who Samuel had sent checks to every month. Seemed he was the caretaker of Samuel's property. He was reporting to Samuel on the cabin and land upkeep and mentioned something about turning the water off because a water pipe broke and he needed to hire a plumber and backhoe to fix it. He wanted Samuel's approval because it was going to be costly due to the time of year.

About to close the file, Regi noticed another letter with different handwriting. Someone threatening to talk to a Clan about justice. The person called Samuel some vulgar names and claimed that judgment day was coming. The signature was only a large *S*.

"Look at this." Wakanda broke Regi's concentration, showing her what looked like a printout of an actual check. "This entire folder is filled with these. No one prints checks anymore unless they need to prove something. Who is Shada Baranov?"

As Regi took the check from Wakanda, the front door opened and Morgan, Jack, and Elliott walked in, stomping on the entry mat and unzipping their parkas. Their cheeks were pink from the cold, but they all had grim looks on their faces. Morgan was carrying a large garbage bag.

"What's that?" Claudia asked before Regi could get the words out.

Morgan glanced at Elliott and Jack as though he were checking with them to see whether or not he should say anything. Then realizing he had to, even if he didn't want to, he said, "Looks like pieces of a chair, a broken phone, wads of duct tape, a broken glass, a bloody towel and . . . Regi's crumpled-up picture. But no raven statue."

Regi's throat closed off, leaving her speechless. This had to be solid proof that Samuel had been kidnapped.

"Where did you find it?" Wakanda asked.

"In the borrow pit by the turnoff to Samuel's," Jack said. "I noticed a garbage bin there. It's brim full. Several bags had been placed beside it. The kidnapper probably thought his wouldn't stand out."

"And it didn't," Elliott added. "But Jack was determined to look in each one of them. Tore several apart before coming across this one."

Regi got up and gave her son a hug, still holding the check she'd found. Filled with a whirlpool of emotions, she didn't know what to say. She was grateful they'd found the evidence but also horrified that Morgan had been right. Someone really had kidnapped Samuel.

Regi gazed back at the check in her hand. Five hundred dollars. The date, two years ago. In the description was written one word: *Trace*. She turned it over. The printout was front and back. The endorsement signature was crude, the *B* in the last name much bigger than the other letters. But the *S* in Shada's name was identical to the one on the letter Regi had read. Why would Samuel pay five hundred dollars to this person? And why would he go to the trouble of printing out the processed checks every month? Must have been someone he didn't trust, so he wanted an actual copy.

"What's that?" Morgan asked, pointing to the letter.

Regi sat in Samuel's leather chair, staring at the name. Words from the handwritten letter played back to her: *Clan*, *justice*, and *judgment day*. A large chunk of this mystery had fallen into place. But with it came a mountain of fear.

"What's wrong?" Claudia asked. Both she and Wakanda stared at Regi, but Regi was unable to put her fear into words, unable to tell them anything. Claudia noticed the letter and check printout in Regi's hand. "What did you find?"

The men came to the desk, waiting for Regi to speak. Glancing up at Morgan, Regi managed to say, "I think I know who took Samuel."

Before Samuel could gain his feet to have the advantage over Trace, the camper door flew open.

Colder outside air swooped in as Trace leaped into the enclosure, grabbed the curtains off the floor, balled them up, and threw them onto the upper bunk and out of the way. He shoved Samuel to the rear of the camper's galley. "This is not my camper! Look what you've done!" He stared at the door then glared at Samuel. Trace's heavy breathing was coated with frost, and it shot from his nostrils like steam. He pulled another syringe from his coat pocket, set it on the small counter, and reached for Samuel.

Still on the floor, Samuel kicked Trace's legs out from under him, knocking Trace's head hard against the cabinets. Samuel tried to worm his way past him to the door, but Trace was dazed for only a second. He charged Samuel like an angry bull, punching him in the gut near his knife wound.

Samuel gulped for air as sharp pain skewered through him. The camper jostled from side to side as they wrestled for control. On top, Trace pinned Samuel to the floor with his knee. Quickly grabbing the syringe from the countertop, he pulled off the cap with his teeth and sunk the needle into Samuel's neck.

Samuel still tried to fight, but his movements grew sluggish and slow. Trace boosted him onto the bench seat as the drug pulsed through Samuel's veins. Moving the portable table and pulling a board into place that allowed the dinette area to become a bed, Trace arranged the cushions and hefted Samuel on top.

Samuel's vision grew fuzzy.

Trace wrapped a blanket around him, eased him down on the cushions, and stuck a pillow beneath his head.

In the distance, Samuel heard a car pull up and stop.

"Great! A cop," Trace spat out.

Samuel could barely lift his head. Trace ripped the tape from Samuel's mouth. Pin pricks of pain needled his face and lips. Trace jammed the tape in his pocket. He checked Samuel one more time. Samuel tried to speak but couldn't.

Trace patted his back and said loud enough for the officer to hear, "Now get some rest." He turned to leave.

"Hi there, officer," Trace said. "Nice day, isn't it?"

"Little cold for my taste. Having trouble?"

With eyes barely open, Samuel saw the top of the officer's hat. *Please, climb in the camper.*

Trace blocked the entrance.

"Nah. My friend's sleeping off a drinking binge is all." Trace hopped down to the ground, eyeing the door as he tried to close it. "Gonna have to fix this."

"Mind if I take a look at your friend?"

Samuel felt the camper jostle as the officer stepped up. Relief filled him. He was saved. Samuel could barely make out a milky image. He tried to talk. "Ahh, uhh." Drool slid down his chin.

The officer patted Samuel. "It's okay, buddy. Sleep it off." He knelt beside Samuel, studying his face. "Looks like he's been beat up."

Samuel tried to focus on the officer. He had to make him listen. But Samuel's mouth wouldn't work.

"Yeah, he got in a scuffle last night," Trace said. "I had to step in and save his sorry hide."

"By the looks of him, the other guy won." The sheriff stood and turned to Trace. Samuel saw their images bleed together. "Where you heading?"

"Washington."

"There's a detour ahead that will take you to Butte."

Butte . . . Montana? No . . . Help me, please! Don't go away!

"Thanks for the warning." Trace followed him out. Their voices muted as the door closed, locking away Samuel's hope.

CHAPTER SEVEN

Disguised as hemlock needle,
Devilfish lures Seal Hunter and Caribou Girl
into Whale's belly.

"Who do you think has taken Samuel?" Morgan reached for the letter and check printout. She willingly gave them to him. Cameron Elliott stood behind the sheriff, his Smoky Bear hat in his hands as he gazed over Morgan's shoulder.

Regi rose from the comfort of the leather chair. If this Shada character had kidnapped Samuel, they were probably on their way to Alaska. *Dang it, Samuel. Why didn't you tell me about this crazy person?*

Morgan finished reading and handed the evidence to Elliott. "I don't know who this Clan is, but, Regi, you're onto something."

"Mom." Jack stepped in front of her. "Tell us what you found."

Morgan answered for her. "It's a letter from somebody in Alaska; they're threatening Samuel."

"Who in Alaska?" Jack asked. "And what kind of threat?"

Lisa stood beside her brother and appeared just as concerned. Wakanda and Claudia watched Regi as though their reaction to this information depended on what she did.

Before Morgan could answer Jack, Elliott said, "I'm familiar with these people. I've read about them in some of the National Park Service e-mails. They're called the Raven Clan. If they are after someone, look out. They mean business."

"What is it they threatened to do?" Jack's cheeks and neck turned red, a sign of frustration.

Regi had to tell him something. "It's not 'they' as much as it is one person threatening to go to the Clan." Regi looked to Morgan. He nodded, meaning she was doing fine. She continued. "And I'm not sure who this person is, but the name is Shada Baranov."

"Why would anyone threaten Samuel?" Lisa asked the question on everyone's minds.

"I'm not sure." Regi had no idea why Shada Baranov wanted to harm Samuel or why Samuel had been sending this person money up until two years ago. She gazed down. Not far away lay drops of blood. *Very likely Samuel's blood.* Regi had to find answers and fast. "Sounds like this Raven Clan can fill in the blank."

"Which makes sense because Samuel's raven statue disappeared." Morgan started for the door. "Elliott, come with me. Maybe you can get on the horn to someone in Alaska while I radio the sheriff in Bounty Falls and fill him in on these new developments. He might be able to check the databanks of the DMV, FBI, or even the census. There's got to be some way of tracking this Shada person down."

The superintendent gave Claudia and Regi a sympathetic smile that said they'd do everything they could; then, with letter and check printout in hand, he followed Morgan to the door. They slipped on their coats and left.

An avalanche of worry fell on Regi. "The first twenty-four hours are crucial to finding kidnapped victims. With that tri-state Amber Alert for the little girl, the police won't be looking for Samuel. And we don't even know what kind of car they'd be in. They might have flown or even taken a train. On top of that, we have no idea what Shada looks like."

"There's no way the kidnapper could get Samuel on a plane or train without this," Claudia added. She held up Samuel's passport, which she'd found in the drawer.

"Criminals don't care about the law. But there are only so many roads that lead to Alaska," Regi said.

Wakanda pulled off her latex gloves and gave Regi a so-are-we-going look.

"Don't give her ideas." Claudia glared at the woman as she returned bank statements to their envelopes. "I'm sure the state troopers can multitask. And Cameron is going to alert the National Park Service in Alaska, so they'll look into this Baranov person."

Regi didn't know how much importance the Alaskan authorities would put on a missing person who may or may not be coming their way, especially if the Clan was involved. The government seemed reluctant to butt heads with Native Alaskans. She glanced at Wakanda.

Her shaman friend tilted her gray head as she met Regi's gaze. She knew exactly what her friend was thinking. Grabbing a notepad, Regi opened the Alaskan bank statement and wrote down the bank's address in Malamute. She tore the note off and shoved it in her jeans pocket. Giving Wakanda a nod, Regi said, "The Jeep's full of gas. Why not?" They grabbed their coats from the hall tree.

Lisa and Jack seemed confused. "Where are you going?" Lisa nervously asked as she watched Regi and Wakanda prepare to leave.

Claudia folded her arms. "You can't take your Jeep all the way to Alaska this time of year. Good grief, you'll freeze to death."

"Mom, you and Wakanda aren't seriously planning to go all the way to Alaska, are you?" Jack passed his mother, blocking her path to the door. Regi looked from him to Lisa to Claudia. Oscar got up from his snooze and came to stand beside Regi, as if to give her support.

Claudia folded her arms, drumming her fingers on her cashmere sweater sleeve.

Still maintaining eye contact with her sister, Regi said, "You're right. It is too cold to go in my Jeep."

Claudia rolled her eyes to the ceiling. "No you don't, sis. Not my Caddy."

"It has a strong heater," Regi tried to reason with her sister. "And cruise control."

With great reluctance, Claudia pulled her keys out of her designer jeans. "It's a good thing I love you and Samuel."

Regi rushed to take them from her, but Claudia pocketed them and grabbed her pink parka. Surprised, Regi asked, "What's the deal?"

"You really don't think I'd let you drive, do you?" Claudia reached for the doorknob.

"Now, wait just a minute," Jack said as he glared at his mother. He gave Lisa a quick look that said, help me talk sense into them.

Lisa chimed in. "You guys can't leave. There's all that food you need to cook for everyone who's coming to the Raindancer for the wedding this afternoon. Remember?"

Claudia wrapped her matching pink scarf around her neck. "You do it, honey. You're a great cook."

Jack scoffed.

Regi nudged her son. "And you can help by telling everyone what's happened and taking care of the Raindancer and Samuel's place until we get back. You took this semester off to earn money. What better way than to work for me?"

"But, Mom," Lisa piped up, "I have school Monday, though I was thinking of dropping French to take Spanish this summer."

"And if I remember right, your other classes were online." Regi didn't want to interfere in her kids' lives, but they were both in positions to help out if they would.

Wakanda huffed and folded her arms like a mighty chief.

Jack ignored her. "Mom, you can't afford to just take off."

Regi looked at her son. Before last fall, Jack had been a self-absorbed kid, but after the ordeal of Romney's murder, he'd changed and was very protective and worried about his mother. Regi smiled. "I can afford it for a couple of weeks, especially if you and Lisa take care of our paying guests."

Times like these made Regi grateful to the Lord for the family and friends He'd placed in her life. However, she knew she still had a mountain to climb in telling Morgan what she planned to do.

Through the haze of a restless sleep, Samuel knew they'd traveled several hours. He'd felt the truck slow, like they'd traveled through a town. He could swear they'd stopped, and he remembered seeing glimpses of someone repairing the camper door. The person had opened and closed it many times. He'd heard Trace speaking in the background.

All of those images disappeared behind horrible dreams that swarmed Samuel with scenes of open, empty graves, of Big Jake's decomposed body reaching out, and of Regi standing at the altar and crying.

A sudden chill and the smell of food cooking brought Samuel wide awake, and he found Trace beside the makeshift bed Samuel lay on. Trace'd pulled the blankets off and hiked up Samuel's shirt so he could examine the knife wound. Samuel's wrists were still bound behind him; his legs remained taped together. Trace peeled off the duct tape and paper towel bandage, making Samuel wince. As Trace swabbed the inflamed skin with betadine, slivers of pain pricked the wound.

Trace glanced at him and noticed he was awake but didn't say anything and kept working.

"How long have I been out?" Samuel asked.

Trace glared with disgust. He didn't answer but rubbed Neosporin on Samuel's wound and placed a large bandage over it. "Hungry?" Trace stood, released the childproof clamp on the cupboard, and threw the garbage into a container within.

Vapors trailed up from a kettle on the small stove. Samuel was starving, yet he didn't want Trace to know. "If you hate me, what's with the bandage and food?"

Trace shook his head. "I do hate you, but . . ." He took bowls from the cupboard and set them on the counter. "I'm not the one to deliver justice."

"Trace . . ."

He stared at Samuel, apparently shocked that he knew his name.

"Look, I may not have recognized you at first at the ranch, but I know who you are." Samuel wanted to reason with him. "I had nothing to do with your grandfather's death. Let me go, and I won't press charges."

"If you had nothing to do with his death, why was Grandfather found on your cabin land?" Trace clenched his jaw as he poured hot stew into the bowls.

"What condition was the body in?"

Trace scowled. "The body . . . You buried *my grandfather* well over ten years ago. What do you think he looked like?" With rage slanting his brows and thinning his lips, Trace grabbed hold of Samuel and, using more force than necessary, helped him sit on the edge of the temporary bed.

"Jake was lost at sea." Samuel remembered that cold, dismal day like it was yesterday. He'd never known sorrow as deep and painful as when he'd searched the seiner, unable to accept that his dear friend had disappeared.

"Liar!" Trace rose, fists clenched so tight his knuckles turned white.

Samuel knew it took all the young man's willpower not to haul off and hit him. But he didn't, so there was a ray of hope. Samuel chanced pressing him more. "Why would I kill him?"

Opening an overhead cupboard and pulling out the raven statute, Trace said, "For this and what was inside it." He slammed the wooden raven on the counter, rattling the bowls.

Samuel stared at the bird. He remembered how Bartholomew Grey, Big Jake's attorney, had given the statue to him after reading the will. Slight of build, with a head too big for his body, the lawyer had stared through thick-lens glasses at Samuel with a mixed look of sympathy and caution. Already uncomfortable after learning he'd inherited Jake's fishing business and boat, Samuel had felt Shada's rage as she'd watched the attorney hand Samuel the raven. Her feelings had permeated the room like rancid perfume. Her copper eyes had glowed like burning embers.

At the time, Samuel'd known that tradition called for the raven to be passed within the family, yet he'd taken it. That was what Big Jake had wanted, even though Shada was his only child and the rightful heir. Tradition had been broken. The Clan held tight to tradition.

Staring at Trace and knowing the poisonous lies his mother had probably filled him with over the years, Samuel couldn't blame the young man for feeling as he did. "Look, I would never kill *anyone*, let alone a man I greatly respected and loved. You have to believe that I had no idea I was even in Jake's will or that he'd give me the raven when he was gone."

Trace rolled his eyes.

"Have you spoken to Bartholomew Grey? He'd tell you."

Trace didn't say anything until he'd dug spoons out of the drawer and placed them in the stew-filled bowls. "You paid off the attorney, so of course he'd say what you wanted him to." Trace filled a spoon, blew on the stew, and brought it to Samuel's mouth.

Samuel refused.

"You have to eat." Trace touched the hot spoon to his lips.

Maybe if Samuel relented, Trace would take his gesture as progress and relax a bit. The rich smell of beef chunks made Samuel's stomach growl. With great reluctance, he took the food, chewed, and swallowed. "I never hurt your grandfather. He was like a father to me."

"Cubs grow up and kill their fathers all the time." Trace ate out of his own bowl. "You made a fortune off my grandfather's death, while my mother . . ." He grew quiet as he stirred Samuel's stew and brought the spoon back up to Samuel's mouth.

"Your mother, what?" Samuel asked as he took another bite.

"Nothing." Trace grimaced and stirred in the bowl again. "You talk too much."

"It's been awhile since I've seen your mother." Samuel knew this was a dangerous subject but one that needed to be discussed to learn what the heck was going on. "How is Shada?"

Trace put down the spoon and leaned back. "She's doing very well now that a witness has stepped forward who saw the murder."

"What?" Flabbergasted, Samuel tried to make sense of what Trace was saying. "Someone claims they saw me murder Big Jake? Who would say such a thing?"

Trace shoved both bowls into the sink and pulled a syringe from the cupboard. "Doesn't matter."

"Sure it does, because whoever it is is lying!" Samuel watched as Trace readied the needle. Where did he get all the syringes? Samuel had to make him listen. "Tell me, please."

Trace reached for Samuel.

He wasn't going to make this easy. Dodging Trace's hands, Samuel fell to the floor, hitting his head. He curled his legs beneath him, trying to rise. "Come on, Trace! You have to believe me."

Trace grabbed Samuel and sunk the needle through his shirt, into his arm.

"Thanks, Bishop Caldwell and Brother Bronson, for coming over on such short notice." They'd given Regi a blessing and were now leaving. She guided the men around the backpacks waiting near the front door. She was anxious to have the bishop and his counselor leave so she could get on the road before Morgan found out what she was up to. She'd decided it would be easier to ask his forgiveness than his permission.

The sheriff and Elliott had been talking on the radio with the Bounty Falls police in Morgan's patrol car outside Samuel's house when Regi'd sent Jack, Lisa, and Claudia back to the Raindancer. Morgan had rolled down his car window before she and Wakanda had climbed into her Jeep and headed home. He'd told her that he'd be in touch. The man must have had his hands full trying to organize some type of rescue for his good friend, or he would have been here before now.

Regi gazed at Brother Bronson as she opened the door. He had one of those youthful faces that would never grow old. She knew he was well into his forties yet didn't look a day over twenty-five. The bishop motioned for Bronson to go to the car, but Bishop Caldwell hung back to speak with Regi.

"I was glad you asked for a blessing before you left. I'm sorry to hear about Samuel." He placed his hand on Regi's shoulder. "This won't give you much comfort, but I feel what has happened is for a reason."

Regi didn't know what to say.

"The Lord works in mysterious ways that are hard for us to comprehend while we're going through certain events and trials."

Regi bit her tongue because she was about to argue, but she remembered the scripture in Samuel's hat rim. The words *tribulations, patience,* and *hope* came to her mind. She wondered if Samuel felt as the bishop did and that's why he'd written the verses. Deep down, beneath her fear and worry, she knew the bishop was right. She nodded. "Thanks for coming."

"Be careful. I'll keep you in my prayers." Bishop Caldwell gave her a hug and left.

Regi nearly sprinted to the living room. Claudia, Wakanda, and Lisa were gone. Jack was looking over the Raindancer's guest register. "Where did everyone go?" Regi asked.

"Lisa's in the kitchen. She's packing some food for you guys." Jack pulled his mother's arm through the crook of his as he went with her to the front door. "And Aunt Claudia and Wakanda are bringing the Caddy around front so you can load your bags."

Regi stopped and gazed into her son's face. His kind eyes looked so much like his late father's. "I really appreciate that you understand why I have to do this."

Jack dug in his pocket and pulled out his cell phone. "If you insist on going, *I insist* you take my cell phone. Even though the reception stinks here in Trailhead, I still want you to have it just in case."

Regi took the gizmo from him. "How do you turn it on?"

He pressed SEND, and a picture of the Raindancer appeared on the small screen. "Now press here." He tapped on a small picture of a phone icon, and a keyboard appeared. "All you have to do is tap in a phone number and hit send."

"Seems easy enough." Regi heard the Caddy drive up and car doors shutting.

Jack dug in his other pocket. "And here's the charger. You need to plug it in at night, or the battery will run down and the phone won't work."

Regi took it from him and stuffed the phone in her pocket and the charger in her backpack. "Thanks, honey. And I don't want you to worry. I'll try to check in with you and Morgan every day."

The door opened. Claudia had on her parka and rushed past them, followed by Wakanda clad in her deerskin coat. Wakanda grabbed her backpack. Regi stood next to hers. Claudia had three suitcases, a travel case, and an Eddie Bauer backpack. She slung her pack on her back, took hold of two suitcases, and left the third and the travel case.

"Let me grab that, Aunt Claudia." Jack picked them up and gave his mom a warning look that his aunt was taking too much.

Claudia didn't notice and announced, "I think we're about ready."

"Wait!" Lisa rushed from the kitchen and crossed the living room to meet them, a cooler in her hands. "I've packed enough to do you for a couple of days."

"Thanks, sweetie." Regi grabbed her mocha-colored parka and tugged it on. Lisa and Jack followed them outside without their coats and hurried to the car to help load the trunk. The twins kissed Claudia and Wakanda good-bye.

Regi gave each of her kids a big hug and kiss. "Sorry you have to tell everyone what's going on."

"It's okay, Mom. I'll make sure they understand." Jack gave her a comforting smile.

"And don't worry about this place." Lisa glanced back at the Raindancer. Regi followed her gaze. Thick snow on the roof, the rustic logs, and the smoke curling out of the chimney made it look like a postcard. "We'll take care of the guests. Just . . ." She sniffed. "Be careful." Her voice turned to a whisper at the end.

Regi knew her kids were torn between worry over their mother and worry over Samuel. New and old emotions were constantly trying to cohabitate inside not only Regi but also her kids. She loved them for their willingness to support her. She knew she'd start crying if she stood there much longer. Claudia and Wakanda were already in the car. Regi opened the passenger door, and Oscar jumped in. She was so used to the dog following her that she hadn't noticed he was by her side. The Irish setter seemed to smile as he settled onto her seat. Regi leaned down to look at Claudia, who sat behind the wheel of the car, to see if she was all right with taking the dog along.

Claudia shrugged. "Well, I did pack his arthritis medicine. But he rides in back."

Regi hustled the dog out and settled him on the backseat next to Wakanda, who welcomed him with cooing and a loving pat. Regi hopped in the front. They were ready to go.

The late afternoon sun made the heavy snow on the ground eerily pretty. For a moment, Regi felt as though nature knew a secret she didn't. Such crazy thoughts!

Regi waved good-bye to the twins. Claudia pulled away from the house then stopped as Sheriff Morgan drove his patrol car in front of them, blocking their exit.

He climbed out and came to the passenger window, motioning with his hand for Regi to roll it down.

"We're in trouble," Claudia muttered.

"Let me do the talking," Regi said as she pressed the button for the window.

"Where do you three think you're going?" he asked. Oscar whined. "Okay, you four?" He glared at Regi.

At first, penned up emotions claimed Regi's vocal cords. How could she explain that if she stayed home waiting to hear something she'd go crazy? Samuel's hat fell over her eyes, giving Regi a chance to think of what to say. She pushed it up. "We're going for a ride."

Morgan looked in the backseat at Wakanda. He leaned over to see Claudia at the wheel, but she wouldn't look at him. "This ride of yours wouldn't take you as far as Alaska, would it?"

Claudia stared forward. No one answered.

"Regi, remember what happened during the Romney case? You nearly got yourself and your sister and friend killed."

"Claudia and Wakanda were safe. And if we hadn't snooped around, you know darn well you might have had to arrest me and I'd be in jail right now." Regi hoped he'd admit that she was right.

"Not so," he said. "I was tracking down a lead when Samuel and I found the mess you'd made of things. If we'd shown up a few minutes later, you would have been dead. I can't let you go. I can't risk something happening to you three. Imagine how Samuel would feel if you were killed while trying to play Wyatt Earp and his gang. Now, come on. Get out of the car." He grabbed the handle, but Regi quickly clicked the button that locked all the doors and, at the same time, pushed the roll-up button for the window.

Morgan banged on the glass. "If I have to, I'll arrest all of you."

"You'll have to catch us first," Regi shouted. She pulled Jack's cell from her pocket and showed him. "I'll keep in touch." Turning to Claudia, she said, "Let's go."

"But?"

"Darn it, Claud, just go!" Regi yelled.

As they drove away, Regi peered through the rear window. Jack and Lisa were talking with Morgan. The sheriff was making big arm gestures as he ranted. But her kids seemed more focused on the car driving away.

Morgan might be as upset as a badger whose hole had been invaded, but Regi had to follow her heart. A sadness filled her. Two days ago she'd believed she would be leaving with Samuel on their honeymoon today. She thought of Bishop Caldwell's parting words when he'd left earlier. *The Lord works in mysterious ways.*

Did mysterious ways involve making the local sheriff, her friend, hopping mad? She didn't think so. But Regi had to do what she felt was right whether Morgan agreed or not. Samuel's life was at stake.

CHAPTER EIGHT

Sent by Raven,
Wise Owl flies into Whale's belly
and builds a fire.

As the miles flipped by, Regi's mind drifted to Samuel. Just a week ago they'd gone to the Cutter Races. Neither of them had a chariot team competing, but both she and Samuel loved the thrill of watching well-trained horses charge down the track.

Overhead heating lamps and barrels of fire strategically placed here and there had warmed the stands. She remembered that as she'd sat next to Samuel, she'd marveled at his rugged good looks. A few wispy gray hairs had played at the sides of his face. Bushy brows had risen above his dark, chocolate-colored eyes. When he'd looked at her, he'd made her heart race.

She loved everything about him, but she liked his hands the most. They were solid, work-worn with callouses on the palms and small scars on the knuckles from years of hard work. His thick, tapered fingers made it difficult for her to thread hers with his. So instead she would take hold of his last two fingers. Whenever they were together, she automatically reached for his hand, wanting to feel his touch and know he was there . . . would be there for the rest of her life.

She remembered during the races how excited he'd become as the horses thundered down the track, mud and snow spraying behind them. Samuel and Regi never gambled at the races; they merely cheered for their favorite teams, drank hot chocolate, and enjoyed the day together. Would there be more days like that?

Claudia'd been driving for hours when the headlights of her Caddy shone on the turnoff for Butte.

"Regi." Claudia looked at her. "I think we better stop, fuel up, and stretch our legs."

Regi glanced at her sister. "In other words, you need the restroom."

"Yes!" Wakanda said from the backseat. "Oscar needs to . . . *rest.*"

Though Regi didn't want to stop, she agreed. If they didn't pace themselves, they'd be in no shape to help Samuel once they reached Malamute.

Claudia pulled into the first truck stop. It also had a café. The booths were packed. Small towns supported their local diners. Before getting out of the car, the women tugged on their coats. Regi walked Oscar while Claudia and Wakanda went inside. When she brought the dog back to the Caddy and wiped snow from his paws, Regi noticed the vanity plate of the vehicle they had parked beside.

Winkie. If Samuel were with her, they'd speculate about the vanity origin: a pet? A person's nickname?

Shutting Oscar in the car, she hurried into the building. Claudia and Wakanda were buying munchies for the road. Regi rushed to the ladies room. When she came out of her stall, she noticed an elderly, blue-haired lady washing her hands. Regi smiled at her, but the woman grimaced, tossed her paper towel into the trash, and left. Regi had the room to herself. She gazed at her reflection.

Her long, mussed-up hair looked straggly beneath Samuel's Stetson. Dark half moons underscored her eyes. She was a mess. No wonder Blue Hair had given her the stink eye. Regi rummaged in her purse and found a pick and hair band. Taking the hat off, she quickly pulled her hair back and combed and braided it. Next, she splashed water over her face. She planned to drive for a while and wanted Claudia to see that she was alert, or her sister would never hand over the keys to her precious car.

Finished, Regi pushed open the restroom door and searched for Claudia and Wakanda. They were waiting near the exit next to the cash register. An elderly fellow was paying, and Blue Hair stood next to him. They were in an earnest conversation with the cashier.

"Please, my wife has been after me since noon about this. Would you please make the call?" The elderly man glared at his wife. The gangly, pimple-faced cashier shrugged his shoulders and picked up the phone.

"I'm just saying," Blue Hair said to her husband. "You can't ignore something like that. I saw what I saw . . . and so did you." She huffed.

Ignoring the couple the best she could, Regi grabbed a Snickers bar and paid for it while the cashier waited on her with the phone stuck to his ear. She skirted around the bickering couple and was about to follow Claudia and Wakanda out the door when Blue Hair said, "He had duct tape over his mouth. And you know it."

Regi stopped and whirled around. "What did you say?"

Blue Hair glared at her. "This is no business of yours."

Regi could barely stop herself from yelling, but she had to remain calm. "I apologize for eavesdropping on your conversation, but did you say there was duct tape on someone's mouth?"

"Well, we're not certain." The husband scowled at his wife like she'd embarrassed him. "I don't see as well as I use to. And it was dark inside that camper."

By this time, Claudia and Wakanda were standing beside Regi like sentinels. Claudia reached her hand out to them. "Hello, I'm Claudia Osborne."

"The late congressman's wife?" Blue Hair seemed quite impressed and shook Claudia's hand.

Claudia nodded. "This is my sister, Regina Bernard." She motioned to Regi. "And our friend, Wakanda." Wakanda moved to stand in back of the couple, keeping them trapped in the conversation. They turned, gave her a quick look, and returned their attention to Claudia, whom they obviously favored.

Regi had had enough of the formalities. Time was wasting. "Did you see a man with duct tape on his mouth?"

Neither of them looked at Regi to reply. Instead, Blue Hair spoke to Claudia. "About noon we were on our way home from visiting my sister in Bounty Falls. She has the gout and lives in a care center there. I still don't think she's getting proper care."

Regi was tempted to tackle the woman and squeeze the information from her, but she clutched the Snickers bar instead.

"What about this man you saw?" Claudia coaxed.

The elderly fellow answered. "Was in the back of a camper. Lookin' out the back door at us, he was. I don't think it was duct tape. Probably sunglasses."

Blue Hair huffed. "We've been arguing about this for hours."

Unable to contain herself, Regi fired off questions. "When did you see him? What kind of camper? What kind of truck? Did you get a license plate number? Why in the world didn't you call the police?"

"Like I said, we saw him around noon. Against my husband's better judgment, I did call the police when we stopped for gas. Told them what we saw." Blue Hair gave Regi a defensive look that said, back off. "They put me on hold for near fifteen minutes, so I hung up. That's plain rude. Like someone else." She glared at Regi. "Anyway, Elmer said he thought the man's sunglasses had slid down his face and it weren't none of our business, so we came on home. But it keeps nagging at me something fierce. In fact, I was so upset I couldn't fix supper, so we came here to eat at the café. Can't get it out of my mind."

"You have to understand," Claudia said, trying to smooth things over, "my sister's fiancé has been abducted. We have every reason to believe the man you saw could have been him."

At that moment, the cashier hung up. "Elmer, the police are coming to talk with you. They want you to stay here."

The gray-headed man nodded to the teen, turned to Regi, and said, "I'm as sorry as I can be about your man. I honestly couldn't see who was in the camper very well. And Edith reads those mystery novels so much she sees crime everywhere she looks." He bit his bottom lip and sighed. As though finally realizing he may have made a big mistake, he said, "It was a camper that looked like one of those sheds you see on TV. The truck was an old Dodge. I didn't get the number on the plates, but they were from Washington."

"Washington?" Regi repeated.

"Thank you, Elmer." Claudia patted the man's arm. "Please tell the police everything you remember."

"I'll make certain of that," Blue Hair added.

Wakanda stepped beside Regi. "Washington is on the way north."

Regi stared at her wise friend. "So you still think we're on the right track?"

Wakanda nodded.

Regi headed for the door. Claudia followed her. "What are you going to do?"

"I'm calling Morgan to see what he thinks about this."

"You'd better let me. He was pretty upset with you." Claudia reached out to Regi for the phone. "Stay with those two and please be nice." She pointed to the elderly couple. "They might remember something else."

Samuel awoke to find the truck wasn't moving. He thought it must be the middle of the night, but there was lamplight filtering through the curtains from somewhere. Cold seeped into his bones even though he wore his parka and was covered with blankets. Once again, he had duct tape on his mouth, and his wrists were still bound behind him. He angled up to gaze through a slit in the curtain. They were parked near a building that had a strong porch light. Where were they? And where was Trace?

Rolling onto his back, he glanced around the camper. From what he could see in the shadows, the dishes had been put away. Everything was clean and orderly. Then something caught Samuel's eye. Something small on the counter. Matches? Trace must have used them to light the stove and forgot to put them away.

Samuel scooted to the edge of the makeshift bed and dropped his bound legs over the side as he rose to a sitting position. Blankets fell to the floor. Cautious of his wound, he managed to stand. Dizziness swirled his vision, the effects of whatever drug Trace kept injecting him with. Blinking several times, Samuel focused on the small object he thought was a matchbook.

He heard muffled voices. Someone was coming, but Samuel was determined to grab the matchbook before the camper door opened. A couple of hops put him next to the counter. Turning so his hands could reach from behind, he found his fingertips barely touched it.

"You can't stay out here. Come in and sleep on the couch. I can heat up some supper for you." A female voice.

"Clara made a great chowder; plus, tonight we had cherry pie." A male voice, but not Trace's.

"Thanks, but I'll be all right out here." That was Trace. What had he told these people? Were they in on his plan? Didn't matter. At any moment, Trace would come in.

Samuel leaned backward, stretching as far as he could. Pain pinched his wounded side, but he ignored it. He didn't know what was in store for him, but whatever Trace planned to do, if Samuel possessed the matches, he would at least have comfort in knowing he had an option that might help him get away.

He heard the keys in the lock. With the tip of his middle finger, Samuel slid the matchbook closer. A little more and he could pick it up. *Come on.*

The doorknob turned. The camper shifted. Trace must have stepped up on the rear bumper to climb in.

Samuel's fingers curled around the matchbook, clutching it in his hand, just as Trace entered.

Seeing Samuel near the counter, Trace spat out, "What are you doing?" Rain sluiced off his slicker as he flipped on the overhead light.

Samuel caught a glimpse behind him. For a second, he saw the back of a man and woman retreating toward a clapboard house. Trace slammed the camper door shut.

Samuel couldn't answer him.

Trace shoved him, knocking Samuel off balance. He hopped to the bed and sat.

Trace tugged off his coat and opened a closet, hanging his rain slicker on a hook. Cupping his hands together, he blew into them and rubbed them together before reaching for the upper cupboard. He searched and searched, moving paper cups and plates around.

Must be looking for the matchbook, Samuel thought.

Trace searched the countertop, shrugged, and grabbed a lighter from the same upper cupboard he'd searched. He removed a vented panel near the door and turned on the gas valve. Samuel could smell propane. Flicking the lighter until it flamed, Trace turned on the heater, and Samuel heard the whoosh of the pilot lighting. With the job accomplished, Trace pocketed the lighter and replaced the panel. He turned up the thermostat, and Samuel immediately felt warmth, though it was little comfort against his worry.

A knock came at the door. "Trace, I brought you some food anyway." The female had returned.

Samuel would have called out to her, but with his mouth taped, he couldn't.

Trace opened the camper door. A woman with a Native American complexion handed him a large grocery bag. As he took it, Trace peeked inside. "I can't take your entire pie."

She smiled up at him. "I made two. I hope you're warm enough out here."

"Just lit the heater. I'll be fine."

"Be careful you don't set the camper on fire. Kashan would not be happy. He went down to the dock to load the boat with supplies." She shivered. "You'd best leave at first light. Neah Bay's weather is fickle this time of year."

Neah Bay? Samuel couldn't recall a town by that name. Still it was slightly familiar, though he didn't know why.

"Tell Kashan thanks. And thank you for the food." Trace seemed awkward standing in the doorway. Samuel knew he was blocking the woman's vision so she couldn't see him.

"If we don't see you in the morning, may Raven guide your ship." She quickly turned on her heel and left.

So they were spending the night in Neah Bay, wherever that was. Samuel watched as Trace took a container of chowder and the pie out of the bag. He collected paper bowls and plates from the cupboard.

Samuel thought about what the woman had said in regard to setting the camper on fire, and a plan formed in his mind. He had to gain the attention of the people in the house. They thought Trace was alone. If Samuel started the camper on fire that would definitely draw their attention. The problem was, what if Trace and Samuel couldn't get out? Or what if Trace got out but left Samuel inside?

The plan had definite flaws, the main one being, how in the world was Samuel going to strike the match with his wrists bound behind him and without drawing Trace's attention? Wait. It was a matchbook. All he had to do was put a match between the flap and the strike pad and pull.

Trace was busy fussing with the food, banging the pots around. All Samuel had to do was wait to strike when Trace made noise, but Samuel would have to position himself so he was near the curtains over the bed.

He scooted back on the cushion closest to the window, tore one match out of the book, placed the match head on the strike strip, and pressed the flap over it, ready to pull. Trace turned on the sink. The water gurgled.

This was Samuel's chance. He jerked the match free and felt the heat of flame. The smell of the lit match was strong, which worried Samuel until he realized Trace was close to the food and there was still a hint of propane from lighting the heater.

Moving his hands near the curtain, Samuel felt heat close to his fingers. It seemed to take hours, but it was only seconds before the curtain caught fire. Samuel scooted away, positioning himself between the flaming curtain and Trace. At any moment, Trace would discover the fire.

At any moment, things were going to get really dicey.

CHAPTER NINE

Through a smoke hole,
Seal Hunter and Caribou Girl escape Whale,
only to be caught by Devilfish.

SAMUEL FELT THE HEAT OF flames behind him as they licked up the curtain. His plan had worked—maybe too well. Smoke was quickly filling the camper. Trace swung around and saw the fire. "What the . . ." He grabbed at part of the curtain that wasn't in flames, trying to pull it down as though he thought he could get it outside before it did real damage. But as he did, the curtain fell to the makeshift bed catching the blankets on fire as well.

Trace shoved open the camper door, took hold of Samuel, and flung him out into the rain mixed with snow.

Samuel could see he was going to land face first, so he turned in midair, falling hard on the concrete driveway on his side—the side with his wound. Hot pain ricocheted through his gut. He labored to breathe through his nose since his mouth was still taped shut. Moaning, he curled into his pain and watched Trace grab a fire extinguisher to fight the blaze. He would have it out soon.

Samuel had only minutes to break free. Ignoring his injury, he pushed himself to a sitting position and scooted across the drive to the opened garage. He peered into the darkness. The porch's light didn't reach inside. Surely something was in there that he could use to cut the tape from his wrists.

He spied a shovel leaning against the wall close to the door. He swung around and feverishly worked his taped wrists against the blade. Unable to see in back of him, he felt his skin burn as the shovel cut through the duct tape and his flesh. Didn't matter. This was his only chance. With one final thrust, he broke free. He quickly yanked the tape from his mouth.

His lips stung. He tried to rip the tape from his legs, but blood from his wrists trickled to his hands, making it difficult for him to grip anything. Frantically, he pulled, but his fingers kept slipping. Time was running out. He had to get inside and tell that woman what Trace was really up to and that he'd been holding Samuel hostage. In a few minutes, this nightmare could be over.

Then he sensed a presence.

Someone stood behind him.

A cold foreboding blew over his skin. Slowly turning about, Samuel found the woman he'd only had a glimpse of before. Relieved, he was about to beg her for help when she raised a double-barreled shotgun and leveled it at his head.

The woman cocked the gun, ready to shoot Samuel should he move or say something that bothered her. Again, his attempt to get away had been thwarted.

"Why do you have to make so much trouble?" Trace joined them and grabbed hold of Samuel's parka, yanking him to his feet.

Though his arms were free, Samuel still had tape around his legs, and he didn't dare move.

The woman kept the gun barrel pointed at Samuel. "I called the fire department when I heard the commotion and saw the flames. Afraid you were trapped. Now that the fire is out, you've got to leave before they get here." She handed him keys. "Take my car. You can spend the rest of the night on the boat and leave at first light."

Trace pocketed the keys and searched the garage for something.

By the loathing in her eyes, Samuel knew she meant business. Her gaze said she knew everything, which meant she knew Shada's view.

Trace returned with a rope. Pulling Samuel's hands behind him, he tied him up and jerked the tape from Samuel's pant legs before pushing him toward a rust-spotted Honda Civic. "Thanks for everything," Trace said. "Sorry about the camper."

She shrugged. "Tell your mom that after she gets what's rightfully hers she owes us a camper."

Once they were in the car, Trace drove away. Fire trucks screamed past them. How many times would Samuel come close to rescue before one took hold? He'd never had such a run of bad luck. It was as though a higher power wanted him to be with Trace. That didn't make any sense at all. But for the first time, Samuel began thinking of his situation in a different light. Part of the scripture he'd tucked in his hatband came to mind.

Knowing that tribulation worketh patience; And patience, experience; and experience, hope.

Patience, experience, and hope. Three words so different in meaning. He'd always thought of himself as a patient man. Samuel'd waited all those years for Regi, and if that wasn't patience, he didn't know what was. And he could see how patience could be connected to experience, since experience came with age and in many cases so did patience. Hope was the oddity. Hope, right now, seemed beyond his grasp.

The car stopped.

Samuel gazed out the smudged windows. Dock lights shone down on moored boats bobbing in their slips, a sight he hadn't seen in a very long time.

"Kashan's not going to be happy about his camper. I'd better talk to him before he sees you." Trace checked Samuel's seat belt and bound hands. "You won't be going anywhere," he said and then left.

Hope teased Samuel again, though now he wondered. Watching Trace walk down to the dock, Samuel had a strong premonition that for some reason Trace needed him.

Impossible.

The kid had beat him up, drugged him, and kidnapped him. Samuel wasn't about to stick around to see what else was in store.

Now was his chance, and he was taking it.

Samuel worked hard against the ropes, but Trace had done an excellent job of tying his hands behind his back. Plus, the seat belt made the task even more difficult. As he worked, he kept his eyes on the docks bathed in light. Before Samuel could do much, Trace and another man, who Samuel assumed was Kashan, emerged from the Bayliner cruiser. Kashan, a strong, sturdy-looking Native American, stood a good foot taller than Trace and had the shoulders of a linebacker. Samuel stopped struggling, catching his breath in despair. He couldn't go up against both of them.

As the two men walked down the dock, Samuel noticed for the first time how Trace's expression reminded him of Big Jake's. He squinted, listened, and pursed his lips in concentration just like his grandfather had. He even tilted his head and walked like his grandfather. Jake had wanted Samuel to watch over his grandson, and Samuel had by sending money until the kid had turned eighteen. Samuel'd been foolish to think his duty ended there. He knew it would have broken Big Jake's heart to see his grandson turn into the thug for the Clan that he was portraying now.

Thinking over the last few days, Samuel could see that Trace could have been downright mean many times, but he hadn't been. Sure, he'd smacked Samuel around at first, but after Trace'd jabbed him with the knife, he had tried the best he could to bandage Samuel's wound. And in the camper, he'd helped Samuel up onto the bed from the floor. He even fed Samuel when he didn't need to. There was some good in Trace.

But that was neither here nor there. Samuel needed to break free. Regi must be out of her mind with worry over him. And he couldn't risk the life he wanted with her because of some strange sentimental notion that he hadn't done a good job watching over Trace. That was ludicrous.

Samuel's attention turned to the boat the other two men had left. A new cruiser. Must belong to some Clan member or one of Shada's lovers. Had Trace made his way down the West Coast by himself? Even if the kid had made it going from one port to the next, he wouldn't be able to do it again and avoid authorities on the way back. So that meant he would have to put out to sea.

It would be extremely dangerous alone—or even with two people—in such a small boat.

Why would Shada place her son in such a horrible situation? Was the woman's hatred for Samuel that strong?

Trace and Kashan neared the car. Samuel thought about Big Jake and how he'd taken care of Samuel when he'd been lost and alone. The pressing weight of responsibility closed in on him. Once again he thought of the voyage ahead of Trace.

This time of year the ocean could turn nasty fast. The Bering Sea west of Alaska was believed to be the most dangerous body of water in the world. Men who had lived their lives on that sea died there every year. Though Trace would not have to cross those angry tempests, his journey was bound to catch some of the treacherous weather blowing in from the Bering Sea. Even with Samuel's help, reaching Malamute Bay this time of year in such a small craft was about as likely as a snowball's chance in the Baha Desert.

All at once, Samuel knew he had to go with this young man. He had to be there not only for Trace but also for Big Jake.

The more Samuel thought about it, the more he realized that if by some miracle they reached Alaska, he wanted to confront Shada, make certain the body was Big Jake's, find out who this eyewitness was, and state his case in a court of law. With the Lord's help, Samuel could get to the bottom of this mess.

He thought of Regi. If she knew what was happening, she would want him to go. She'd want him to make this right. He hated that he couldn't talk with her and tell her what was going on. The heartbreak he'd heard in her voice as Trace had held him captive haunted Samuel. *"He's done it to me again."*

He couldn't blame her for thinking he'd run out on her. But deep down, and after everything they'd been through, didn't she know he loved her and would never purposely hurt her? How he wished he could speak with her for just a second.

Trace unlocked the car door and handed the keys to the other man. As Trace helped Samuel out of the Civic, he talked to Kashan. "Please tell Clara that Mom will send the money for the camper as soon as she gets it." He shoved Samuel ahead of him, toward the path to the dock.

"Once you leave, stay west of the entrance to the Strait of Juan de Fuca," Kashan instructed over the car roof. "That way you can avoid the main shipping lanes and Seattle traffic officers. Don't forget, once you're in Canadian waters, you need to call the CBSA on your cell. If you do that, they might not bother you, especially if you don't anchor or dock. May the Great Spirit light your path." Then Kashan got in the vehicle and drove away.

Samuel'd made up his mind to see this through. As they walked down the swaying dock, Samuel took note of the boat. Drawing nearer, he saw it was much bigger than he'd first thought and now looked to be more than twenty-eight feet long. That was a relief.

Trace ushered Samuel on board and straight to the galley, where he turned on a light. He pulled another syringe from his pocket. Samuel knew fighting him would be futile; still he said, "Are you sure you want to put me under? Getting out of this port is more than a one-man job."

"Can't chance port authorities seeing you and coming aboard. I can handle the boat."

"At least roll up my sleeve before you put the needle in my arm." Samuel tried to delay the inevitable.

Trace reached over and injected the needle through Samuel's pant leg so it hit his outer thigh. "No need."

As Samuel felt the numbness of the drug working in his body, he wondered if he would ever see Regi or set foot on dry land again.

"Where are you this morning?" Morgan's voice echoed from Jack's cell phone.

Regi had brought Oscar outside and had just finished clearing snow off the Cadillac and packing her bag, a couple of Claudia's suitcases, and Wakanda's backpack into the trunk. They'd left Butte, heading north, and had driven right into a blinding snowstorm. When they reached Missoula, Montana, Wakanda had convinced Regi to spend the night there.

While Regi was waiting for Oscar to take care of his business, she decided to try and make amends with Morgan. Claudia had called him last night with the information they got from the elderly couple, but she said Morgan was still pretty steamed. "Missoula. Look, I'm sorry if I've made you worry, but you know darn well if some crazy person kidnapped Hannah you'd do the same thing."

"That's where you're wrong. Unlike you, I'd know that by going up there, I'd just be getting in the way and causing more work for the authorities."

Regi realized that by taking off, she'd shown Morgan that she didn't respect him or the badge he wore, and she didn't mean that at all. "I know you're a good cop. It's the people in Alaska who I've never met that I'm not sure about."

Morgan was quiet for so long Regi was afraid he'd hung up. "Are you still there?"

"Yeah. Guess I can't stop you from being you."

"Thanks." Regi wanted to say, "Finally. It took you long enough," but she didn't want to "poke the bear," so to speak, and get him riled again. Instead, she asked, "Have you heard from anyone?"

"I talked with Sheriff Talbert and gave him the information you got from that elderly couple last night. Said he'd get back to me this morning."

"Hear anything yet?" Regi asked, watching her breath come out in white puffs.

"Yeah . . ." Morgan hesitated a moment. "Said one of the state troopers reported helping a guy with a camper from Washington yesterday. The guy told him his friend was drunk. But the officer was suspicious and took down the plate number. We're running it now." By the tone in Morgan's voice, Regi could tell he was holding something back.

"What aren't you telling me?" she prompted.

"Trooper said the guy's friend was pretty beat up."

Regi's thoughts raced through horrible mental images of Samuel bruised and bloody. She couldn't think like this or she'd go nuts. "So do you think 'the guy' is Shada Baranov? Shada sounds more like a woman's name."

"We'll find out once we track down who the truck belongs to."

"But what if it's not Baranov's truck?" Regi didn't mean to always question—yet again, yes, she did.

"Calm down. We'll find that out too," Morgan reassured her. "I also called the police in Malamute and asked about Baranov and the Raven Clan."

That was good. "What'd they say?" Regi asked.

"I spoke with a Deputy Jones. He wasn't very forthcoming and refused to tell me anything about Baranov. Said he'd talk to his boss and see what they could do."

Disappointed, Regi let out a heavy sigh. Oscar trotted past her, heading for the motel's entrance. He stopped at the door, waiting for her. Regi followed. She peered through the glass and spied Claudia in the lobby paying the bill. She motioned for Regi to come in, but Regi stayed put. She didn't want strangers listening to her private conversation. Taking hold of Oscar's collar, she pulled him aside and said, "Did Elliott learn anything from the park service?"

Claudia opened the door in time to hear the superintendent's name and gave Regi a questioning look. Her backpack hung over her left shoulder; in her left hand was the handle of one of her many suitcases, on her right shoulder the strap of her traveling case, and over her right forearm the strap of her purse. Regi realized it was a good thing she'd already packed her sister's other two suitcases. Regi mouthed that she was talking with Morgan. Claudia stood beside Regi, listening.

"Nope," Morgan said. "He's trying again this morning. I've been waiting to hear from him."

Regi looked at her sister and shrugged a sign that they had no news from Elliott. "Thanks. Please keep me posted."

Claudia leaned near her. "Has Thomas said anything about how yesterday went with Lisa and Jack and what happened when everyone showed up for the wedding?"

"Did you hear that, Morgan?" Regi held the phone so Claudia could listen as well.

"I was hoping you'd ask." Morgan's voice grew soft.

"What happened?" Regi had felt bad leaving Lisa in charge of cooking and entertaining whoever showed up. That Morgan was hoping she'd ask about it was a good sign that things had worked out.

"The entire town of Trailhead found out what happened to Samuel and brought a ton of food over to the Raindancer. Stew brought your favorite chocolate cream pie. By the way, it was delicious."

Regi's heart warmed at her friends' care. "The fridge was already full." Regi couldn't imagine what Lisa would do with all the extra food.

"Your daughter's smart. She called your bishop and asked if there were ward members in need. Jack's taking good care of the Raindancer too. Don't worry. Your kids are doing fine."

"Thanks. I tried to call them earlier but couldn't get through. Please tell them where we are and what's going on." Regi said her good-byes and glanced at Claudia. "Where's Wakanda?"

Claudia gazed around Regi. "I thought she was with you."

Regi spun about, scanning the parking lot and the snowy landscape beyond, searching for her friend. No sign of her deerskin coat anywhere. "She was gone when I got up. She's probably taking a walk. You know how she is. I put her pack in the car already."

Arms loaded, Claudia started toward the vehicle. Regi tried to help by taking the larger suitcase from her.

At that moment, they heard what sounded like a buzz saw coming their way. To the north, Regi spied a snowmobile bouncing over drifts, heading right for them. Two people were on it, one in a parka, wool cap, and snow goggles; the other in a familiar coat.

Regi leaned close to Claudia. "Now what?"

Claudia shrugged. "She's your friend."

"Yours too." Regi knew that despite what her sister said, Claudia thought highly of Wakanda.

Oscar hid behind Regi as the machine pulled in front of them and stopped. The driver killed the engine and took off his snow goggles. He wore what looked like a pirate patch over one eye. The other eye was coal black. Ice caked his bushy brows, mustache, and beard.

Wakanda crawled off the back of the machine. A wide smile split her wind-reddened face. "This here's Tucker. He knows a fast way to Alaska."

For all Regi knew, Wakanda'd bumped into him on the street, and he was selling her a magic carpet ride. "Wakanda, may I speak with you for a minute?" Regi smiled at the Tucker fellow while she guided her friend a few feet away, leaving Claudia and Oscar with the man.

"Who is this guy?" Regi glanced behind to make sure Claudia was all right. She was talking with him, smiling and laughing. She should have known her sister would make friends in a matter of seconds.

Wakanda huffed. "I told you, he's my friend."

"How long have you known him?"

"Long enough." Wakanda sounded irritated. She folded her arms, a sign that Regi was stepping over the line.

"Look, I just got off the phone with Morgan. He has a lead on the truck Elmer and his wife saw from Washington. So, like you thought last night, we need to go there first."

"Last night's storm closed all the freeways. But we can fly to Washington or Alaska." Wakanda smiled as though she had an answer for everything.

"Fly. You're telling me your *friend* has a plane?" Regi noticed a nervous twitch in Wakanda's eye. She'd never seen it before. Wakanda cautiously nodded, giving away the fact that she understood even more than Regi did. Suddenly, the nervous knot in Regi's stomach became twice as heavy.

"Seriously? He's a pilot, and you know him from . . ." Regi wanted Wakanda to fill in the blanks.

Wakanda's happy face turned somber, as if Regi's question had deflated her spirit. She gazed at her snow boots. "I've known him for many years, hard as that is to believe."

Regi didn't mean to offend Wakanda, but she had just been broadsided with the information. In fact, she was plain stunned. "But . . . how . . . when . . . Is this why you had us stay here last night, because you knew this Tucker guy lived here?"

"Snowstorm. Remember?" Wakanda said.

Regi gazed at her friend. "Yeah."

"I'll tell you about my past, but not here. Not now. Later." Wakanda walked toward Tucker.

"Later?" Regi followed.

Wakanda stopped. "At Tucker's. There's much to do." She turned away from Regi and went to her friend, who waited on his Polaris RMK.

Flying would save precious time. But that would also mean leaving Claudia's car behind and maybe even Oscar. Plus, Regi knew Claudia had an aversion to small planes. Anytime she and Morris had traveled to Washington DC when he served in Congress, Claudia had made certain they were on a big plane. She didn't deal well with close spaces. They tended to stress her out, had ever since she was young. Regi leaned near Wakanda and quietly said so no one else could hear, "Sounds like a good idea; just let me be the one to break it to Claudia."

While Wakanda settled in behind Tucker on the snowmobile, Tucker gave Claudia directions to his house. "Once you get on the tar, my place is two far-sees and across the big whoop."

Regi was confused, and by the expression that flitted across Claudia's face, she was puzzled as well. Regi asked, "What tar? What's a far-see? And a big whoop?"

The man chuckled and sniffed as the icicles on his mustache dripped onto his lips. "I forgot you're not from 'round here. *Tar* is the road, though you can't see it now because of the snow. A *far-see* is as far as you can see. And the *big whoop* is right at the end of the second far-see. You'll know what it is when you get to it." He flipped on the Polaris and revved the engine.

"But which road do we take?" Claudia shouted.

Wakanda pointed to the one heading north, away from the hotel and freeway. Tucker gunned it, and the two of them took off across the field.

Regi let out a loud, frustrated scream, making Claudia and Oscar jump. "Sorry, but good grief, now what are we going to do?"

"Come on," Claudia coaxed her toward the Cadillac, her bags in hand. "We can figure this out." She stored her stuff in the backseat while Regi brushed snow from Oscar's paws so he could get in the back with the bags.

Riding in silence much of the way, they traveled as far as they could see, which took them to a bend in the road; the next far-see ended at the foothills that dropped down into a valley. "The valley must be the big whoop? Guess we cross this valley, and we'll be there," Claudia said as she drove.

Regi hoped she was right. She hadn't told her sister about leaving her Caddy behind and making the rest of the journey in a plane. She was still struggling with the idea that Wakanda even knew a pilot. The woman had been homeless and dumpster-diving for food until four months ago. Didn't make sense.

But nothing made sense anymore. An anxiousness grew in the pit of Regi's stomach. Would anything go right? Samuel needed her, and here she was in the middle of nowhere, not knowing what was going on. At that moment, snow began to fall . . . again. They were lost, and now it was snowing.

At the end of the valley, they came to a fork in the road. Claudia stopped the car. "Now what?"

Just then they heard the buzz-saw noise of the snowmobile. Tucker and Wakanda were coming across the field. Tucker drove onto the snow-packed road, heading west, and Claudia followed. Tucker guided them down a road that led to a cabin and a huge hangar nestled in a grove of Ponderosa pines. As they pulled up to the hangar, a young, pretty, blonde woman bundled in a fur jacket and hobbling on a walking cast came out to greet them.

"Do you think that's Tucker's daughter?" Claudia asked as she put the car in park and shut off the engine.

Regi didn't care who it was as long as she could somehow help them on their way. "Did he tell you he had a daughter?" Regi asked.

"No." She put the keys in her Prada purse and zipped it shut. "While you and Wakanda were talking, he told me about the snowmobile races he's won. He was quite proud of the fact that a one-eyed old man beat all those young show-offs."

Regi was surprised to hear her sister call him an old man.

"His words, not mine."

"How old is he?"

"He said he's seventy-five."

"No! Really?"

Claudia nodded. "Hard to believe."

"I'm beginning to believe a lot of things." Regi couldn't wait to see her sister's reaction when she found out that the next leg of their journey would be on a plane this old man piloted.

They crawled out of the car as Tucker and Wakanda dismounted the snow machine. The wind had picked up, and the snow was getting worse. They walked up to the young woman. Tucker took her in his arms and planted a big, slobbery kiss on her lips.

Surprised, Regi glanced at Claudia.

Claudia covered her mouth with her hand to stifle a gasp and turned to Wakanda, who stood with her jaw clenched so tightly that a blood vessel in her forehead bulged.

Was she jealous? Regi could hardly wait to get her friend alone to find out the history between her and this Tucker fellow. They stood there, waiting for the man and girl to finish their passionate greeting. Wakanda cleared her throat, drawing Tucker's attention.

He glanced up. "Sorry." He straightened his stance and said to the young woman in his arms, "Your leg all right?"

The girl blushed and smoothed her long blonde hair over her shoulder while balancing on her cast. "With kisses like that, it will heal lickety-split." She turned to them. "Broke it falling down in the grocery store parking lot. Don't know why Tucker keeps me around; I'm such a clutz."

He hugged her again, and it was obvious to everyone why. As though he couldn't help himself, he nuzzled her ear then spied Wakanda's growly face.

"Captain," he seemed to address Wakanda. "This here's my wife, Kimberly." Tucker slung his arm around Kimberly's shoulders. The twinkle in his eye left no doubt that he loved her.

Wife? Talk about robbing the cradle. She might be all of twenty-six, but that was stretching it. *And why did he call Wakanda captain?* Could be a nickname or some kind of inside joke between friends.

"Pleased to meet ya!" Kimberly held out her hand. She caught sight of Oscar standing next to Regi. "What a beautiful animal."

Regi shook Kimberly's hand and said, "Thanks. His name is Oscar." She turned to Tucker. "Pick them young, don't you?"

Tucker guffawed. "I'm young at heart." He winked.

Despite Regi's first inclination not to like him, she couldn't help but find him very interesting; however, she didn't have time for all this. Claudia shook Kimberly's hand but was very cool toward her, which didn't surprise Regi. She knew her sister was still getting over the fact that her late husband had cheated on her with a younger woman. But it was Wakanda's brusque manner that made Regi look twice.

The older woman's granite face showed no trace of emotion, though Regi sensed an undertow surging within her friend.

Oblivious to the simmering drama around him, Tucker said, "Captain, I know you're anxious to look over Blue Lady, but with this snow falling . . ."

Regi's curiosity piqued. "Why does he keep calling you captain?" she asked Wakanda.

"It's a stupid nickname he gave me years ago. Means nothing." Wakanda glared at Tucker.

He chuckled. "You haven't told them?"

Claudia piped up. "Told us what?"

"Wak and I used to be business partners."

"Business partners?" Regi stared at Wakanda like she'd never seen her before.

"What kind of business?" Claudia asked.

"Bush pilots in Alaska. If it weren't for the Captain, I probably wouldn't be standing here today. Lost an eye, but she saved my life with her fancy flying. I don't go up anymore, but . . ."

"Wait a minute!" Regi felt a full panic attack welling up inside her. Staring directly at Wakanda, she said, "You're the one who is going to fly the plane? *You're* the pilot?"

"Plane? Who said anything about a plane?" Claudia stepped between Wakanda and Regi.

"Captain . . ." Though Tucker was talking to Wakanda, he took his wife's hand and drew it through the crook of his arm as he spoke. "With this snow and wind, you best not fly out today."

"Fly out!" Claudia's shocked look reddened to the shade of a warning flare. She glared at Regi.

Tucker motioned for everyone to follow. "Looks like y'all need to talk. Come on in and rest a spell." He led the way to his spacious-looking cabin.

Regi felt her world had collapsed: Samuel was missing, her sister was having a full meltdown, and now they would have to rely on her homeless friend to pilot them to who-knows-where.

This was about as bad as it could get.

CHAPTER TEN

*Devilfish casts a spell
on his prey,
sending them to separate fates.*

DUMBSTUCK, REGI AND CLAUDIA FOLLOWED behind Wakanda as Tucker and his wife led them into their cabin.

Regi couldn't help but ask, "Wakanda, do you have a license?"

"Course she does. A pilot's license is good for life. However . . ." Tucker looked at Wakanda. "Have you had an FAA physical lately?"

"No! We have an emergency here. I'm not going to stop and get a physical," Wakanda growled.

"Suppose you'll be all right as long as you don't draw attention to yourself." Tucker shrugged it off. "Though there's little or no screening of private aircraft departing from the US, the CBP is clamping down."

Regi had no idea what they were talking about. "What's the CBP?"

Tucker smiled at her naivete. "Customs and Border Protection." He turned his attention back to Wakanda. "To be on the safe side, you'll need to file an electronic notice and manifest on the Internet to the CBP. But it also might be a good idea to avoid landing-rights airports in Canada. If ever there's a case that would be an exception to their rules, yours fits the bill."

Regi had so many questions. Words log-jammed in her brain, and she didn't know where to start. She glanced at her sister.

Claudia looked furious, but her sense of propriety stayed her tongue. She'd never question Wakanda's flying abilities in front of others, though Regi could tell that as soon as her older sister had Regi to herself they were going to have a very long and serious talk.

The strong smells of perked coffee and toast broke through and awakened Regi to the movement around her. She'd quit drinking coffee when she converted to the Church, but she still loved the smell. It almost made her feel normal, like all this baloney about Wakanda being a pilot had never been said.

Tucker stomped snow from his boots and pulled off his knit cap. "Kimberly, darlin'. . ." He tugged off his coat and hung it up before placing his arm around his wife. "Did you make a hootenanny breakfast for us?"

The girl's youthful, loving smile for her husband made Regi think of cheerleaders and pep squads. "After I got your call about Wak, I checked the weather and knew she couldn't fly out today, so I got busy," Kimberly said.

Wakanda grimaced.

"Oh, Wak." Kimberly hobbled to her and took her hand. "You don't mind if I call you Wak like Tucker does, do you?"

Regi had never seen such a split-second slideshow of emotions flicker across her friend's face: disdain, jealousy, anger, and a hint of strained friendliness. In the end, Wakanda seemed to pull herself together and feign a cheerful smile. "Don't mind."

As though on autopilot, Regi, Claudia, and Wakanda took off their coats and hung them up.

Tucker put one arm around Wakanda and one arm around Kimberly. "I'm so glad my best friend and my wife get along." The three of them led the way to the dining area.

Claudia's eyes were as large as whirling propellers. She glared at Regi, and Regi knew that look meant her sister expected her to have the answers to all the questions swimming in her head, especially the ones about Wakanda piloting and this Barbie wife of Tucker's.

Regi shrugged. No answers here. But she planned to find them and soon.

They followed without so much as speaking a word.

The table was set, and in the center was some type of golden-brown egg casserole that rivaled even Claudia's cooking. A plate sat piled high with toast. On another lay crispy bacon. Everything looked good, yet Regi's stomach felt like an anvil weighed her down. The stress of worry about Samuel made her feel nauseated. They sat, and Oscar settled beside Regi's chair. Kimberly tried to pour Regi a cup of coffee.

Regi put her hand over the cup. "No thanks."

Kimberly looked crushed. Regi didn't want to hurt the girl's feelings since she'd been so nice cooking all of this. "Do you have hot chocolate?"

"I can fix some." As though happy again, Kimberly whirled around on her cast and hobbled over to the stove. She filled a teapot with water then turned the burner on high.

Tucker threw the dog a piece of bacon. Oscar chomped twice, and the breakfast meat was gone. His tail thumped against the carpet. Tucker took the plate in front of Wakanda and lifted it up for her. "Tell me 'bout this friend of yours who's been hijacked."

Wakanda started the sorry story, but soon Regi and Claudia were helping fill in the blanks. Tucker nodded with sympathy at the appropriate places. Kimberly gasped off and on with each detail that told of their dire situation while she saw to each of their needs: fixing Regi's cocoa, filling Claudia's coffee mug, and fetching ketchup for Wakanda.

By the time they'd eaten their fill, the tale had been told.

"A sorry bucket of affairs," Tucker said. "Doesn't surprise me none that the Raven Clan would do such a thing. In my glory days of bush piloting, I ran into some scary Clansmen. I always treated them with respect, and they did me as well. Right, Wak?"

Wakanda nodded.

"I'd still be flying if it weren't for this here eye." He pointed to his patch.

Wakanda huffed. "Never stopped Wiley Post. Even with one eye, Post broke speed records and did high-altitude flight."

Tucker seemed to think about what she said then replied, "And look where it got him. Dead at Point Barrow. Killed his best friend too." Tucker turned to Regi. "Okay. I admit it. I lost the fire in my belly to fly after the crash. Plus, when I got married, I promised my wife"—Tucker gave Kimberly a loving smile—"that I'd stop. 'Sides, I made enough money to last us the rest of our lives. Isn't that right, sweet cheeks?"

Kimberly giggled.

He looked at Wakanda. "I repaired Blue Lady in case you decided to take your share of the company out in the plane like I wanted you to. She's a little dusty. Been a couple of years, but she'll fly."

Claudia's face turned stoplight red as she tried to catch her breath, all the while staring at Wakanda like she'd never truly seen her before.

Kimberly handed Claudia a glass of water. She gratefully took it and drank.

"You'll have to excuse my sister," Regi said, looking at Kimberly and Tucker. "But Wakanda has never told us of her past."

"Had my reasons." Wakanda stared at Tucker.

He seemed to note her reluctance and chuckled. Glancing out the window at the blizzard, he said, "Supposed to snow all day. Looks like you'll be here till morning. Let me do the honors of telling you about my best friend's past."

Regi's heart sank as she too glanced at the wild snowstorm. This would set them back another day. However, if they were flying the rest of the way, they could get to Washington, Alaska, or wherever faster than they'd anticipated when they thought they'd be driving. She gazed at Wakanda. She was staring at Tucker.

If looks could kill, Wakanda would have done her old friend in right then and there.

He ignored her. "I met Wakanda twenty years ago . . ."

"Forty," Wakanda corrected.

"Really, that long?" He stared at her, amazed.

Wakanda nodded.

"Okay then, forty years ago, I met Wakanda in a high-stakes poker game in 'Nam."

"'Nam?" Claudia asked. Regi was surprised as well.

"Vietnam. We were stationed there. Not many people know about the women who served in that war. Most think they were only nurses. Women weren't supposed to fly, but when I found out what a good pilot Wakanda was, I had her fly supply planes when we came up short on pilots. She helped fuel choppers too. In that poker game, she was mopping the floor with everyone until I cut myself in and gave her a challenge."

Wakanda scoffed. "You cheated."

"Was caught too." Tucker nodded. "The other fellahs were mighty upset and about to beat the daylights out of me when Wak came to my rescue. She told them if anyone had the right to punch me in the gut, it was her. And doggone if she didn't do it—right there in front of all of them."

"What did you do?" Regi asked Tucker, caught up in the story.

"Well, I didn't hit her, if that's what you're thinking. She can deliver a good punch, but I wasn't about to strike a woman. I do have a little chivalry. Guys in the game seemed satisfied that I'd received due punishment. But that game was the beginning of a wonderful friendship, wasn't it, Wak?"

A smile tugged at the corners of Wakanda's mouth. Regi knew she was reliving the past, yet Regi had a feeling there was much more to this story than what Tucker was telling them. She'd just have to be patient and learn about it later.

Regi watched snow pelt against the living room window in Tucker's cabin, making it nearly impossible to see anything outside. The panicky feeling she carried in her heart for Samuel grew ever stronger. The storm left her with no choice but to stay put.

Regi could hear Claudia in the kitchen with Kimberly. They were making some kind of spicy chili for supper. The smell of chipotle peppers filled the cabin.

Opening Jack's cell phone, Regi punched in Morgan's number. It started to ring and then dropped the signal. She tried again with the same result.

"I'd offer my landline to you, but whenever we have a bad storm like this, it goes out." Tucker handed her a mug of hot chocolate as he came to stand beside her at the window. He held a book in his other hand.

"It's just so darned frustrating." She sipped the cocoa, looking at Tucker over the rim of her mug.

"I remember in 'Nam waiting for Wakanda to fly in with supplies," he spoke in a hushed tone. Turning about, he gazed at Wakanda, who was sitting at the dining table studying the aviation maps he'd laid out. She was madly taking notes as she plotted a course to Washington and another course, should they need it, to Malamute, Alaska. Brushing a gray braid over her shoulder, she repositioned Tucker's reading glasses more securely on her nose. He smiled. "She was always on time, but I still worried for her. She's the closest thing to a sister I've ever had."

"It's strange that she's never mentioned you." Regi took another swallow as she watched Tucker's reaction.

He shrugged. "Doesn't surprise me none. In case you haven't noticed, Wakanda's a private person and guards her feelings and past like a hungry she-wolf."

"Then why don't *you* tell me what the deal is with you two?" Even though it wasn't any of her business, Regi wanted to know.

"The deal?" Tucker cleared his throat and looked over at Wakanda. "The deal is . . . she's one complicated woman, and if you know anything about her—as you say you do—you'd know she wouldn't want us talking behind her back. Tends to make her distrustful and crotchety. Don't think you want your pilot angry." He handed her the book he'd been holding and headed over to the table.

Regi sank down on one of the plush recliners. Oscar sat at her feet and rested his nose on her knee. She patted the dog and eased back to drink the rest of her hot chocolate while looking at the book Tucker thought she needed to read. The title was *Alaska*. She opened the cover and found a section devoted to Malamute.

This was exactly what she needed to make her feel like she was doing something to help Samuel. On one page, a shot of a picturesque village on the shores of the Pacific looked inviting. The place was famous for fishing. People traveled from all over the world to catch salmon there. Another picture showed a man fishing on a riverbank with a bear on the other side. This reminded her of overhearing some Trailhead rangers talking about how a ranger had once found himself across the stream from a grizzly. He thought if he scared the bear, the animal would take off. So the man barked like a dog. However, barking only drew the bear's attention. The grizzly charged across the water after him. Chased him all the way to Smoky Top Ridge lookout. The guy climbed on the roof and stayed there until other rangers came along and scared the bear off.

She wondered if the man in the picture would have had a smile on his face if he'd heard that particular story. Reading the article below, she learned that in some areas of Alaska, bears outnumbered people; and in the winter, rogue bears even broke into cabins for food. Sorry times for the people if they were home. She'd never heard of a bear doing that in Trailhead.

The next page centered on gold mining. She knew Alaska was famous for gold strikes. She'd watched the John Wayne movie *North to Alaska* with Samuel. It was one of his favorites. In its heyday, Malamute had been considered a gold-mining town.

Regi wondered if the land Samuel had inherited from Big Jake had gold on it. Probably not, or it would have been discovered long ago. She was letting her memory of the movie cloud her thinking. Besides, Samuel would have said something if it had. However, he'd never really told her much about his Alaskan past.

She continued to read the history of the Clan and where they'd migrated from, how fur traders negotiated with them, and even how Russia sold Alaska to the US. There was some information about current affairs and how distrustful Alaskan natives had become of US authority because of some misunderstandings about the fishing industry and boundaries. It seemed that the US government and Canada had given the Clan a special waiver when it came to passports between countries because their tribe lived in both.

"Dinner's ready." Claudia carried in a bowl of chili on a tray, along with crackers and a glass of milk. Regi's sister knew what she liked with spicy food. "You've been reading for a while."

Regi's eyes were tired. She glanced out the window. Snow still madly flew to the ground. While she moved the book so Claudia could put the tray on her lap, Regi glanced over at the table. Tucker sat beside Wakanda. They appeared deep in conversation.

Claudia followed her gaze. "I'm feeling a little better about Wakanda taking us up in a plane. I've heard only bits and pieces of what they're saying, but it sounds like she really knows her stuff." Claudia went back to the kitchen.

Regi watched as Tucker moved papers, making a space for Wakanda's chili bowl. The way he looked at her, touched her shoulder, and listened showed the great respect and feelings he had for the woman.

"Sure would like to know more about those two." Claudia had returned and was settling in the other recliner with her own meal tray.

"Me too," Regi added. But her mind was far away as she thought about how tenderly Samuel had watched over her. She missed her man.

Again, the hole in her heart grew deeper.

CHAPTER ELEVEN

Healing water covers land,
putting Seal Hunter in a trance.
Devilfish finds Wise Owl.

THE NEXT MORNING THEY WERE blessed with sunshine. Wakanda would be able to pilot without weather impeding them. Tucker had told them last night that he used the highway as a runway, and it had been freshly plowed. They were good to go.

Regi watched Wakanda check over the old 1970 deHavilland Beaver on wheel skis in the cold and drafty hangar, where Tucker stored his beloved plane. The plane was blue with white stripes down the center of the body and above the tail.

Tucker walked in and dropped several sleeping bags that he insisted they take and a duffle on the pile of Wakanda's and Regi's backpacks. He stared at Claudia's many suitcases. "Someone moving?" he asked. His cheeks were rosy from the cold. The patch he always wore over his right eye now seemed to make his left eye even more sparkly than usual.

"That's my sister's idea of light packing," Regi told him.

Tucker shook his head. "She may need to leave some of it. I've packed emergency equipment for you. Added food for your dog as well."

Oscar stood beside Regi and wagged his tail as though he knew he was being discussed. Regi had included enough dry food for the Irish setter until they reached Alaska, and now, with what Tucker had added, the dog would be set. However, the dog's arthritis medicine would run out soon. Regi had no idea how long they were going to be there. Again she worried. What if she couldn't find Samuel right off? They could be there a week, a month, a year. How long could she afford to leave the Raindancer? Jack and Lisa couldn't watch the place long term. But how could she give up searching for Samuel? Well, she'd cross that rickety bridge when she came to it. For now, she was touched by Tucker's generosity. "Thanks."

Tucker nodded and winked his good eye.

Wakanda peered past the propeller at the engine. "You replaced the piston engine with turboprops?"

Tucker nodded. "Long ago. Adds to its value. If I had an ounce of common sense, I'd sell the thing."

Wakanda's brows teepeed over her eyes.

"Don't worry. I won't sell our plane. It's actually yours." Tucker patted her back. "Common sense left me long ago. Though some guy who flies the Ring of Fire in the peninsula offered me six figures if I'd sell Blue Lady to him."

"Six figures . . ." Wakanda's amazement made Regi wonder if she thought Tucker refusing to sell was impressive or if the plane had been overpriced. But Regi didn't want to dwell on the value of the plane. She wanted to get underway.

Claudia entered the hangar carrying the cooler they'd had in the trunk of the car. "Kimberly added more food to what Lisa packed for us." She set it down by the bags. Though yesterday Claudia had said she was feeling better about their trip, deep furrows crossed her delicate forehead as she stared at the plane up close and personal. Even stressed she looked like she'd stepped out of a fashion magazine with her designer jeans and pink parka. Regi couldn't blame her citified sister for being nervous. She too was worried, but her fear over what was happening to Samuel was stronger than her need for self-preservation.

A cricket noise chirped from Regi's coat pocket. She dug out Jack's cell phone. *Must be his ringtone.* Morgan's number lit the ID bar. Flipping it open, she said, "Hey."

"Regi, that you? Have bad news." Morgan's voice was grave.

Had they found Samuel dead? Regi steeled herself to hear the worst. Breathlessly, she asked, "What?"

"Washington patrol tracked down the truck."

"Well, that's good . . ." Relief filled her.

"The camper had caught fire."

Regi gasped but said nothing.

"They didn't find anyone inside. After the officer threatened to take the couple who owned the truck to jail if they didn't answer his questions, they finally told him that a friend of theirs named Trace Baranov and his traveling companion, which must have been Samuel, were going by boat to Malamute."

"Boat?"

"Yeah."

"But isn't that dangerous this time of year?"

"I would think so."

Regi nearly dropped the cell phone. It wasn't bad enough that this Trace guy had beaten Samuel; now he was taking him out to sea in dangerous waters. She remembered how Samuel had told her about his days fishing and how he hated going during the winter months. But all those years on Big Jake's seiner must have trained Samuel well. Regi couldn't give in to the fear that was charging like a Brahman bull and threatening to overwhelm her. Tightening her hold on the cell phone, she said, "How long will it take them to reach Malamute?"

"If the weather is on their side, maybe several days."

"Several days!" Regi said, alarmed.

"Anything could happen at sea," Morgan added. "Even though I've notified the Alaskan authorities, there are thousands of miles of shore and thousands of small boats. Even with satellite, it will be difficult to pinpoint Trace and Samuel when they arrive. His kidnapper must have chosen to go by boat to avoid driving over the border between Canada and the US."

"Well, what about the Coast Guard? Can't they help?" Regi knew that with all their technology they should be able to do something.

"They'll watch for them, but the ocean is pretty big. Besides, Trace may have already crossed into international waters, and they don't want to butt heads with Canada."

Regi remembered that while searching Samuel's desk they'd come across his passport. But he probably wouldn't need it because if Trace went far enough out in the ocean, no one would stop him.

Out of the corner of Regi's eye, she saw Wakanda climb into the cockpit and put on headphones. Claudia stared at the plane like it was some kind of monster preparing to eat her. Tucker stored most of their gear in the plane, except he set some of Claudia's bigger suitcases aside. She tried to talk with him about them, but Tucker only nodded as he tried to heft Oscar off the ground and put him in the plane as well. The dog squirmed and twisted so much that Tucker dropped him. The Irish setter yelped.

"Are you still there, Reg?" Morgan's voice was worried.

"Yeah. Here's the deal. We're flying to Alaska."

"Flying! How?"

"Uh . . . Wakanda is a pilot."

"No! You're kidding me, right?"

"Nope. She and Tucker—"

"Who's Tucker?" Morgan asked, exasperation threading his words. Of course, he didn't know.

"A friend of Wakanda's. She's full of surprises." Regi tried to sound lighthearted. Oscar cowered behind her as Tucker tried to grab him again. The setter growled. Regi covered the mouthpiece on the phone so Morgan couldn't hear the ruckus.

Morgan continued. "If she flies, she hasn't flown for years, and if you think taking a boat to Alaska is dangerous, it's nothing compared to flying."

"You're making me feel so much better." Regi attempted to move so Tucker could get the dog, but Oscar wormed around her legs, making it impossible. Tucker rolled his good eye, gave up, and went to help Claudia. She was attempting to load the suitcases Tucker had set aside. Tucker took them from her as though he planned to put them in, but he first helped Claudia step into the craft.

Morgan went on, oblivious to the scene unfolding before Regi. "At least wait until I hear back from the Malamute police."

Tucker pulled the wheel props.

Wakanda started the engine. The plane sputtered and roared to life, making further conversation with Morgan impossible. Still, Regi had to say something to him. "I'll call when I get there!" she shouted.

"But—"

She closed the phone, scooped Oscar into her arms, and plopped him into the plane without a problem. Crawling in after him, she found Claudia fit to be tied. She wildly pointed to her suitcases outside on the ground. Regi shrugged, knowing she could do nothing to help.

Wakanda motioned for Regi to come forward. She'd saved her the seat next to the pilot's. Settling in and fastening her seat belt, Regi caught Wakanda's attention and mouthed, "Alaska." Wakanda nodded that she understood. Regi felt she was doing the right thing, even though her dog and sister were racked with apprehension.

Worried for her sister, she glanced back at Claudia. Her white-knuckled fingers were laced together in her lap. Regi gave her a thumbs up. Claudia smiled weakly.

Wakanda pulled out her flight plan to Alaska and studied it for well over ten minutes then put it away and checked the plane's instruments. Then the plane began to move, and Claudia immediately grabbed hold of the armrests of her seat. Her mouth clamped shut, and her eyes filled with *Friday the 13th* terror.

Tapping her headphones, Wakanda motioned to a pair beside Regi's seat and then to a set waiting for Claudia. Regi took off Samuel's Stetson and placed it on her lap so she could put on her headset. She glanced at Claudia. Her sister had put hers on as well. Regi found the press-to-talk button and pressed it. "We'll be fine. Right, Wakanda?"

Wakanda nodded, too busy for verbal communication as she drove the plane out of the hangar.

Oscar settled down on the seat across from Claudia, resting his head on his front paws and keeping his eyes on Regi.

Outside, Kimberly had joined Tucker, and they were standing on the freshly snow-plowed walkway to the hangar. They waved good-bye as the plane passed them. Regi waved back.

With any luck, they would beat Samuel and Trace to Malamute, find this Shada person, and force her to tell them what the heck was going on.

With any luck . . .

No! With the Lord's help.

Taking comfort in holding Samuel's hat, Regi quickly said a prayer as Wakanda taxied onto the snow-covered tarmac and started down the road for takeoff.

Samuel tried repeatedly to rouse himself from slumber. Foggy images and drifting thoughts swirled around him, but he couldn't hold on to them and kept sliding back to sleep. Finally he forced his eyes open and realized he was in an enclosed sleeping berth, still tied up, and wearing his parka. Ice-chilling cold made his limbs stiff. His stomach growled. The bow of the boat bumped hard.

Rough seas.

He couldn't hear the engine running.

How long had he been in here?

Again, the bow of the boat slammed into another wave. Struggling, he sat up. Grogginess threatened to pull him back down onto the mattress, but he'd had enough sleep. Fighting weakness, he scooted to the small door. He kicked at the handle until it opened. Surprised that Trace hadn't locked the hidden berth, Samuel didn't stop to question. Instead, he crawled out.

Another wave hit. This one nearly knocked him back into the berth, but Samuel found his sea legs and managed to remain standing. He stepped up to the helm and into the light of day, though it was cloudy. Frigid wind slapped his face and ruffled his hair, dissipating his grogginess, though he still felt weak.

Trace stood at the ship's wheel, trying to start the engine. With the hood of his parka tied over his head, only his cheeks were wind chapped. He wore flip-mitt gloves. His fingers protruded from the wool and were red from the cold as he tried over and over to start the engine.

The sky billowed with dark, angry clouds heavy with an impending storm. Samuel didn't like the looks of it. "Where are we?" He shouted to be heard over the wind as he scanned the shoreline in the distance.

Trace glanced at Samuel, looking like he wondered whether he should tell him or not, but he finally said, "Just past Prince of Wales Island."

"How long have I been out?" Samuel's head throbbed, his stomach growled, and he had an urgent need for a facility.

"A couple of days."

"What?" No wonder Samuel was hungry.

"Thought it would be easier on both of us to keep you under." Trace remained focused on the job of starting the engine. "Planned to wake you for lunch, and then this storm kicked up and the engine stalled."

Another wave hit. This time water sprayed over the bow. Slushy rain began falling. Waves grew bigger and bigger. "Don't you think we should put in until this passes?" Samuel asked.

"Been trying! The crazy currents and roiling rip keep pulling us out to sea." Trace looked as scared as a rookie drover staring down an angry Hereford bull. At that moment, the boat yawed, turning around from port to starboard. The stern was facing the next building wave. Frantic, Trace tried over and over to start the engine with no success. "You helped my grandfather on his boat. What do you suggest?"

"Untie me!" Samuel turned, exposing his bound hands.

Trace didn't flinch but immediately worked the ropes until Samuel was free.

Water splashed into the aft. With the boat in this position, if they were hit by a large wave, it would flood the engine and roll them. Samuel yelled, "Move!"

Trace stepped away from the helm so Samuel could take charge. Thinking Trace had probably flooded the engine with too much fuel in his attempt to restart it, Samuel didn't try. He knew they needed to get the boat turned about, but with no power, he wasn't sure how he'd do it.

Then he thought of something. "We need drag. Got a heavy sea anchor?" Samuel asked as he fought with the current to right the vessel's direction.

Trace splashed through the water, rummaged in the aft cockpit storage, and finally pulled out a stout canvas bag with a bridle attached.

Samuel motioned to the bow without needing to give Trace further instructions because he knew that's where they needed the anchor tied.

Making his way to the bow, Trace tied the rope onto the clear hollow base and dumped the anchor overboard.

Right away Samuel felt more control on the wheel as the weight of the anchor began to turn the boat in the right direction. The wind was perpendicular to the current, which was causing dangerous irregular waves.

Trace had noticed Samuel's despair. "What?"

"We've got to get the engine started. Conditions are ripe for rogue waves." Samuel flipped the starter, hoping he'd given it enough time. The engine sputtered and stalled. If he kept trying, he could drain the battery. Against his better judgment but knowing they needed it to start, Samuel tried again. This time it coughed a number of times. He stopped for a moment. The battery sounded weak, but he tried again, and it finally roared to life.

"All right!" Trace shouted. "This boat's fast. We'll get out of this."

But Samuel knew better. "A fast boat doesn't mean diddly in this kind of mess." They were trapped in troubled waters.

Another wave came, though this time the bow kept them from taking on water. Samuel didn't know the bottom topography of the ocean here, so he spat out, "Where's your nautical chart?"

"Have a GPS." Trace pointed above the wheel. Next to the compass was a screen giving strange pixilated coordinates. "It's not working!"

"Big Jake and I never used one. Got a paper chart?" Samuel asked as he noticed another rising wave heading their way, this one bigger than the last.

Trace nodded.

"Get it!" It had been years since Samuel had been at sea. Big Jake had brought his seiner this far south only a few times. Along the coastline, water depths constantly changed. With this storm breathing down their necks, their situation could blow up at any moment.

Another wave slammed them.

Even though this one was bigger, they managed to ride over it. Trace disappeared but came back quickly with the chart in hand. Coated with a laminate, it was protected from water.

Samuel eyed the compass and checked the chart. He realized they were in waters over a bottomless channel. Deep water combined with the storm was creating this nasty riptide. Undulating waves would make choosing a safe pathway very tricky . . . if not entirely impossible.

He had to figure out the best angle to steer the boat relative to wave direction. But the waves were growing larger, which could work to their advantage.

Could.

Samuel noticed that, according to the chart, if they went west, they would get out of this mess. Problem was . . . that would take them away from the shoreline and right into an open shipping lane. But they had to do it. "Get our lights up."

"It's not night." Trace looked at him as if he were nuts.

Clinging to the wheel, Samuel said, "No, but when the main storm hits, it might as well be. Bigger ships will have a hard time spotting us without lights. Pull the anchor up while you're on the bow. With the engine running, we don't need it."

Slipping and sliding, Trace put the red light on port and the green light on starboard then fought to pull in the anchor. Finally, he tugged it on board and stowed it away.

Waves were swelling by the second, spraying water everywhere.

"So why are we heading out to sea?" Trace wiped water from his face.

"We've got to tack back and forth to get up on the waves and navigate between crests."

Trace grimaced and looked confused.

"Trust me on this. Now, how many bilge pumps do you have?"

"One. Why?"

"Two would have been better." Samuel didn't want to scare him, but the situation demanded it. "Get the life jackets." They should have put them on long ago.

Trace didn't question but disappeared below.

Samuel knew they might run into another ship. The storm would make Trace's boat nearly impossible to see. Samuel would have to lean on the Lord for guidance. He remembered the picture in the foyer at the church house, the one of Jesus walking on water during a violent storm. Peter tried to follow him, but his lack of faith pulled him under the water.

Samuel prayed that his faith was strong enough to keep them afloat . . . and out of danger.

CHAPTER TWELVE

Raven soars over mountains
and oceans, while Wise Owl
and Devilfish fight.

WAKANDA PILOTED THE PLANE AROUND storms, above the clouds, and through valleys. Regi thought they would make the trip in six or seven hours, but Wakanda explained that they had to refuel every four hundred and fifty miles, so they would have to put down at least three times before they reached Malamute. To be safe, Wakanda wanted to make the journey in two days. Even though the plane had a small heater, they were still cold and learned quickly to bundle up.

At their first stop in Canada to refuel, they were greeted by a customs officer who checked all their papers. Regi was a little worried they'd say something about Wakanda needing a FCC physical, but they didn't. Wakanda seemed to know what to say and when to say it. She filed a flight plan, found out what codes were used in Canada, and learned the weather forecast.

Regi was seeing a completely different side of her friend and could hardly believe that the woman—the same one who made ceremonial potions and avoided most people—talked technical airplane speak and flew a plane like it was second nature.

Wakanda put down for the night in a small town. They stayed in a motel that would have made Norman Bates uncomfortable. Regi received an update from Morgan on the investigation. It seemed the trail died in Neah Bay, Washington. He was getting nowhere with the police in Malamute. Elliott was facing frustration with the park service in Alaska as well. This only fed Regi's anxiety. Wakanda must have sensed her apprehension because as soon as the sun came up, she had them back in the plane and in the air.

On the second day, Regi gazed out of her window at thick forests and stark granite cliffs smothered in snow. If she'd been on vacation, she would have thought the scene beautiful, but now it made her think of death, of white nothingness, and of how empty she felt without Samuel.

In the last few months, he'd become a major part of her life. Truth be told, he always had been, even when they weren't together. All those years that she had been happily married and in love with Earl, she'd still felt something for Samuel. She'd thought it was pure disdain for the way he'd run away from his family . . . and her. But now, she knew it was love hidden beneath her altered life—a deep love that would never go away.

Oh, she had loved Earl. He was reliable and constant. He loved their kids and was an excellent father until the cancer had taken him. Earl had made her feel safe and secure. He'd been Regi's balance, the person who'd listened to her rant and rave and then patiently suggested, "Maybe you should think this over a little more." He'd helped her see reason when she'd felt there was none. Any small grain of patience she'd acquired was due to Earl's guidance. He'd taught her that and so much more. After he'd died, Regi had felt lost and alone, like she did now.

She remembered the first day she'd seen Samuel after Earl had passed. It had been about a month since the funeral, and Samuel was buying feed for his horses when she'd walked into the IFA. For a crazy millisecond, she'd wanted to go to him for solace, but that yearning to find comfort from Samuel had quickly been erased with abhorrence as she'd remembered how he'd refused to sell back the land he'd promised to Earl. She'd nurtured that loathing right up until the trouble over Romney's death, when they'd been able to put their differences aside. And despite the mean things Regi had said and done during that time, Samuel had still said he loved her.

He'd told her that he always would and that even while Earl had been alive, he'd wanted to be with her but had stayed away except when the opportunity to buy Earl's land had come up. Samuel had said he'd leaped at the chance to help Regi. But when it had come time to sell the property back, he couldn't bring himself to do it because that would have broken the tie he'd had with her. Plus, it had made her angry as a mamma grizzly, and at least that was some type of feeling for him. Hate was akin to love. And while she'd been hating him, she'd been thinking about him. That beat apathy by a long shot, or so he'd said.

As Regi thought about it, she guessed Samuel was right, in that love was akin to hate. Their relationship was complex and layered with years of regret and missed opportunities, but now it was topped with love.

More than anything, she wanted to be sealed to Samuel in the temple. She'd never had that opportunity with Earl because when they were married, they weren't members of the Church. The missionaries didn't knock on Regi's door until after Earl had died, and Regi had never gone to the temple. She'd worried about being sealed to Samuel instead of Earl, but she talked to Bishop Caldwell about her fears, and he told her that Father in Heaven would straighten everything out, and the bishop felt she was making the right choice to be sealed to Samuel. But Regi and Samuel would have to wait for a year after Samuel's baptism to go to the temple. That was all right. She'd waited all these years; one more was not a big deal now that she and Samuel had found the gospel.

They'd finally had a chance to start fresh, and then Samuel's Alaskan past had reached out and threatened to steal it away. Regi wasn't about to let that happen. She loved Samuel. He was her first love. And her last. She loved him so much that she wanted to marry him in the temple. She loved him so much that even though she was thirty-nine and already had two children who were in college, she wanted to give him the child he'd always wanted.

Staring out her window, she realized Wakanda was flying awfully close to the cliffs. Too close for Regi's comfort. She pressed the push-to-talk button. "Why don't you fly in the middle space between the mountains?"

"Too much turbulence. Close to the mountain, I know there will be down drafts. Those I can handle, but in the middle, we'd get beat around."

Regi looked at her friend with renewed appreciation. "You really know your stuff."

"Took you a couple of days to figure that out." Wakanda chuckled.

"I noticed. Just didn't want to distract you."

"Not distracting. Talking passes the time."

"So . . . it took you a couple of days to say you wanted to talk?" Regi smiled.

"Waitin' for you is all." Wakanda smiled back.

Surprised and yet grateful for this open door to ask questions, Regi said, "How long ago did you get your license?"

"In my teens. Mom was a WASP."

The first thing that came to mind for Regi was hornets. But that didn't make sense. "What's a wasp?"

"Women Airforce Service Pilots. During World War II, my mother flew supply planes."

That was a surprise. Wakanda had never spoken about her family. Regi just assumed her friend's life had been horrible with parents who didn't want her. Why else would a person adopt the persona of a homeless person? But obviously Regi's assumptions had been wrong. "Wakanda, you've never told me about your family."

"Never saw the need."

"And you never told me about Tucker." Regi could see by the red flush coming over Wakanda's cheeks and neck that these subjects made her uncomfortable.

"Didn't want to." Wakanda straightened. "How you doing back there, Claudia?"

Regi looked at her sister. She was bent over in her seat with her head between her legs. Worried, Regi reached back and nudged her.

Claudia stared up, blurry-eyed. "Are we there yet?"

Regi glanced at Wakanda.

She shook her head. "Might make it late this afternoon."

It seemed Claudia's fear grew worse with each flight. Rarely had Regi seen her big sister so uptight. But then again, Regi hadn't flown in a small plane with her. "You okay?"

Waving Regi off, Claudia leaned against the back of her seat, her complexion a ghostly white. Oscar licked Claudia's cheek, bringing a smile to her face. "I can hang on until then."

"On second thought, it might be tomorrow before we get there," Wakanda said, staring out the front windshield. Wakanda turned a knob and flipped a switch. "Storm's ahead. Don't like the looks of it. If we find a flat place, we might need to put down."

"Put down?" Claudia stared at Regi with terrified eyes.

Regi's gaze shot out the passenger window. No landing strip in sight. They were gliding closer and closer to treetops. Regi wanted to help her friend but couldn't. Instead, she placed her hand on Wakanda's shoulder to reassure her that she trusted her flying abilities. Even so, under her breath she said a silent prayer.

Fighting the cold from the slushy rain and sea spray, Samuel remembered that in troubled seas like this he needed to match the speed of the boat to the speed of the waves. Despite his first instinct to press down on the throttle, he let up on it.

Trace returned. He'd already put on his life jacket. He handed one to Samuel. Taking it from him, Samuel quickly tugged it on, but he didn't dare take his hands away from the wheel long enough to buckle it. Seeing Samuel's problem, Trace did it for him.

When he finished, Trace said, "Why did you slow down?"

"Less speed equals less stress on the hull." Samuel tried to keep the boat at a forty-five degree angle to the wind. Storms caused the wind to blow outward from the heaviest precipitation. He knew once the tempest passed, the winds would ease off and reverse direction. "Check channel 16 on the radio, and see if you can hear something about the storm from the Coast Guard," Samuel said. Trace went below.

Samuel had only taken his eyes away from the sea for a second, but it was long enough for a rogue wave to hit them hard, throwing Samuel back against his seat and nearly onto the floor. He quickly scrambled to his feet. Luckily, the wave hit the bow just right and only made them turn slightly off from the forty-five degree angle.

After a short while, Trace came back. "That was a bad one."

Samuel didn't want to discuss it. He was more interested in what Trace had learned. "Hear anything?"

"They were saying something about boats falling off a wave."

"This storm has it all." Samuel stared at the compass, making sure he was still heading in the right direction. Relieved to find he was, he said, "Did they say where those boats were?"

"Mentioned something about Queen Charlotte Strait."

"Good. That's south of us." Samuel realized that the winds had slacked off, and the waves were now growing farther apart. "Wind's changing direction." Staring up at the sky, he saw a darker gray cloud in the distance. "But we're not out of this yet. With any luck, we might make it to shore before the next round."

The swells between waves were large, but this allowed Samuel to increase his speed between crests. As he made more progress, a feeling overcame him—a powerful feeling that he was missing something.

Something important.

He glanced behind him. Only ocean and storm. And then he saw it. The flash of red and green lights. A ship was heading straight for them.

"Trace, get on the radio and hail that ship!"

"Ship?" He whipped around, staring into the gray stormy world behind them. As soon as he saw it, he cursed under his breath and went into the cabin to call.

Samuel split his attention between where he was guiding the boat and the ship that was fast approaching. The lights were gaining on them.

It had to be a southbound freighter.

Even if Samuel went full throttle, it would be impossible to outrun it. Why was the freighter heading to shore? Or was it? Maybe Samuel's sense of direction was messed up. While fighting the waves, he could have gone off course. He remembered this had happened to Big Jake several times during severe storms.

"They aren't answering!" Trace bounded back up to the helm.

Racking his brain for what else they could do, Samuel said, "Got some high-powered emergency lamps?"

Trace didn't answer but quickly started rummaging in the same compartment he'd pulled the anchor from. He dragged out two lamps, flipped them on, and started frantically waving them.

Samuel prayed the oncoming ship would see.

If not, they were going down.

CHAPTER THIRTEEN

Battle weary,
Devilfish and Wise Owl sing
for peace.

"We can get Popeyed going through that." Wakanda nodded at the threatening clouds ahead. "I'm not taking chances."

Regi had no idea what getting "Popeyed" meant but believed it was pretty bad. The storm heading for them looked angry and ominous. She glanced back at Claudia. Her eyes were closed. Regi doubted that she was asleep at a time like this, but maybe it was best her sister not see what was heading their way.

Staring at the ground below, Regi found they were over a small valley now, with no airport in sight. At that moment, Wakanda pushed down on the stick. The plane descended.

Regi again stared out the window. They were flying toward a small cabin and a few other buildings.

The plane swooped low, flying over the cabin.

"What are you doing?" Regi clung to the armrests of her seat.

"Letting Yepa know we're here."

"Yepa?"

"My friend. Not sure if she's still lives in the cabin. Tucker thought she might and suggested we come this way just in case we ran into bad weather, which happens a lot in these mountains. Haven't seen Yepa in many years, but she'll recognize the plane. We'll wait out the storm, spend the night, and eat." Wakanda pulled up on the stick and flew the plane around for the approach on smooth white snow.

Until a few days ago, Regi had thought she and Claudia were Wakanda's only friends. If they lived through the landing, Regi was determined to have a good heart-to-heart with this woman about her mysterious past.

The freighter was closing fast, its massive bow plowing straight toward them. Samuel issued a quick prayer. "Please, Lord, I'll stand trial—I'll do everything I possibly can to find Big Jake's killer—if you'll please help me know what to do." Staring through the rain over the swells of rolling ocean, he saw the ship still charging them.

Trace pointed the high-powered emergency lamps straight at the vessel. They were closing fast and would collide with them if Samuel didn't do something.

Glancing at the control panel, Samuel decided to turn into the wind, changing their heading. Though it would definitely send them off course, it might take them out of the ship's path in time.

Once he turned the boat, Samuel yelled over the wind and motor, "Give me a lamp, and try to hail them again." He wasn't sure, but they had to try one more time. Trace thrust a light at Samuel and escaped below.

Holding the lamp up with one hand and steering with the other, Samuel maneuvered the boat the best he could. Terror pulsed through him as strong as a coursing river. Flashes of Regi's smiling face as she had sat behind the wheel of her Jeep a few days ago came to mind. Was that the last time he'd ever see her? A moment so brief and fleeting. Not if he had anything to do with it. He gripped hard on the lamp, swinging it with all his might.

Trace leaped up into the helm. "They heard! They're changing their heading!"

Peering through misty rain, Samuel watched with wonder and amazement as the oncoming vessel's red light disappeared. Their starboard was safely abreast. Relief ricocheted through Samuel like a bullet, almost buckling his legs. He handed Trace the lamp and clung to the wheel.

"The guy on the freighter had a thick Slavic accent and sounded pretty shaken up when he finally saw us. Said we weren't showing on his radar. Told me to get a new reflector." Trace sat in the companion seat next to Samuel. "But my radar reflector is a good one and is designed for offshore."

"He had to blame it on something." Samuel wanted Trace to know it wasn't his fault. "Storms like this cause all sorts of trouble. They were probably too busy staying on course to notice us. Don't worry about it." Samuel watched as the mighty freighter passed them then disappeared.

Once Samuel believed they were safe, he changed his heading to guide them to shore. They had to get out of the open ocean. Trace stored the high-powered emergency lamps and returned to sit beside Samuel. The rolling ocean was much easier to handle now that the winds were dying down. Maybe the full force of the storm was over. It would be just the break Samuel was hoping for, but he still kept his eyes on the horizon, sky, and control panel. Even one slip could be disastrous.

"You were praying back there, weren't you?" Trace said.

Samuel nodded. He wasn't aware that Trace had heard him. He'd been too focused on what needed to be done.

"Sure didn't remember you as religious."

Samuel stole a glance at Trace. He wasn't smirking or grinning and seemed sincere. "Years ago, I wasn't."

Trace rubbed his chin.

"What do you remember?" Samuel was curious. Until Trace had jumped him in his home, he hadn't seen him since he was a young boy. By the way he'd treated Samuel, he didn't think Trace remembered much about him.

"I remember when I'd ride on Grandpa's ship you made sure I wore a life jacket. Something you're still doing." He smiled. "And you always gave me a piece of peppermint candy." Trace's mild tone surprised Samuel.

He hadn't remembered doing that, but now that his memory had been jogged, it came back.

"Sure don't remember you praying though." Trace wasn't letting it go.

"Back then, I was angry with God." Samuel hoped the Lord would help him tell Trace what was truly in his heart. To do that, he knew he would have to tell him more than he wanted to, but that was all right. "Don't know what Jake or your mother has told you about me."

"Grandpa didn't tell me much since he died when I was nine. My mother . . . let's just say you're not one of her favorite people."

Samuel wasn't surprised and knew the woman had probably attributed every bad thing that had happened in her and Trace's lives to Samuel. Now he had a chance to tell his side. "I was only seventeen when your grandfather took me under his wing. I was a runaway. Your mother had you a year after I arrived."

"If you ran away, why did you return home after Grandpa died?" A hint of confusion mixed with sorrow returned to Trace's voice.

"I was devastated when Big Jake disappeared. Even searched the sound for weeks. They said he'd fallen overboard, which I found very hard to believe. In the end, your mother convinced me it was so."

Trace looked surprised.

"Yes, your mother. She begged me to give up the search so everyone could move on with their lives." Samuel refrained from telling him how anxious she was to have Jake's will read. "So after all was said and done, I returned home to make peace with my own father."

Silence fell between them. Samuel was willing to let it be, but a prompting came over him to tell Trace more about how he'd become religious and why. "My father didn't want anything to do with me, even up to the day he died. He left me a note that said, 'You win.' Both father figures in my life are gone. That was years ago. I didn't make peace with the Lord until late last fall."

"Last fall?" Trace wiped his brow and looked like he was concentrating on what Samuel was saying.

"My aunt nearly killed the woman I love." Samuel stole a glance at the horizon. It still shamed him that his aunt and brother had been so corrupt and misguided. He looked back at Trace.

His mouth had dropped open as if he were unsure of what he'd heard. "Your aunt?"

"I had a dysfunctional family. I've never known such fear as when I watched Aunt Ida force Regi into the river with a double-barreled shotgun." Flashes of the nightmare came to Samuel's mind as he spoke. "The river was between me and them. My first impulse was to yell at my aunt, but I heard a still, small voice whisper to my soul for me to stay hidden in the willows."

Trace shook his head like he couldn't believe it.

"It's true. Regi, she's my . . ." Samuel didn't want to say *girlfriend*, and saying *fiancée* could be misleading since they weren't engaged at the time the incident had taken place.

"She's the woman you love?" Trace filled in the blank.

"Yes. After she was safe, Regi told me the Holy Ghost was who prompted me. I've learned that He comes to a person in a still, small voice. I followed that prompting though it was the hardest thing I've ever done. When I saw Regi slip under the water, I nearly went out of my mind, but I realized if I stayed where I was, the current would bring her right to me and away from harm." Samuel stopped, overwhelmed with deep gratitude.

"You saved her?" Trace seemed eager to hear more.

"I pulled her from the water. Before I came upon them, as I ran through the aspens toward the river, I prayed. First time since I was a little kid. Prayer opens the door so the Spirit can reach you."

Trace seemed to think that over. "After you prayed today, I could feel the boat turn. You changed our heading. Did that still, small voice direct you?"

Samuel gazed out on the ocean. It had happened so fast that he'd chalked it up to luck. But Trace was right. Once again, Samuel had been directed from above. After reliving what had happened to Regi, and now with them narrowly escaping disaster, he knew God answered prayers. How could he have ever doubted his faith? He stared Trace in the eyes. "Yes, it did. There are times in life—as you're actually experiencing the event—that you know are pivotal. Saving Regi was a pivotal moment for me. It showed me God has a hand in my life." Samuel paused for a moment. He must sound like a crazy old man to Trace. But at some time in Trace's life, he would experience a pivotal moment, and then he'd understand. "What we just went through was a pivotal moment as well. God watches over all His children. Sometimes we get ourselves into bad situations, and sometimes people even die. Why? I don't know, but I do know we're all part of His plan. Our job is to do the best we can to survive by living our best lives. If we pray for His help, He will either guide us to safety or make our suffering bearable. I don't know if that makes any sense to you or not."

"Some." Trace shrugged. "I know before you prayed I'd called and called that freighter, but it was only after your prayer that they heard me." Trace eased back into his seat. "Need to think about this for a while. But after what we've been through, I do know you're not the man my mother said you were."

Relief flooded Samuel. For the first time, he had hope that he might make progress with Trace.

Regi stared at Wakanda. "You're seriously going to land down there?"

Wakanda nodded. "The field looks snow packed. Shouldn't have a problem."

"'Shouldn't,' meaning you don't know for sure?" Claudia grasped the back of Wakanda's seat with her long, thin fingers.

"Done this many times, though it's been awhile," Wakanda said.

Regi gazed out her window at the vast whiteness below and wondered how Wakanda gauged the snow depth from there. But she didn't want to bring it up and worry her sister even more. To take Claudia's mind off of their landing, she asked Wakanda, "This Yepa person won't mind visitors?"

"Likes her solitude, but she'll be happy to see me. Haven't seen her in years." Wakanda looked at Regi. "I could do a touch-and-go first if that would make Claudia feel better."

"Yes, do a touch-and-go—whatever that is," Claudia said as she patted Wakanda's shoulder.

"What's a touch-and-go?" Regi asked curiously.

"I add full power as the skis brush the snow. I'll do this several times, dragging to make a landing strip. Makes for a good runway when we need to takeoff too."

"Sounds like a plan," Regi said, amazed at Wakanda's knowledge.

Wakanda pulled off the power, and as she approached the area she wanted to brush, she added full power, dragging a ways then gliding back up into the air. Clouds of snow kicked up behind them. She did this several times. Regi noticed someone had come out of the snow-covered cabin. *Must be Yepa.*

Wakanda made their final approach, backing off the power and applying full flaps. The skis of the plane glided smoothly over the path she'd made. With the full weight of the plane, more clouds of snow billowed madly behind them and even caught up with them as the plane slowed to a stop near some ropes lying on top of the snow. When the engine died, the windows were completely covered in white, and then as fast as the flurry had come, the air cleared.

They'd landed safely. The droning noise of the engine ceased, and intense silence fell on them until a gust of wind rocked the plane.

Regi checked in back. Claudia's eyes were closed. Regi patted her hand. Claudia opened one eye. "We're alive?" A smile claimed her face. "Don't tell me you weren't scared."

"Wouldn't do that." Regi winked at her.

Oscar whined, wanting out. "Hold on, buddy." Regi glanced at Wakanda, who was already unbuckling her seat belt and taking off her headset. Regi and Claudia did the same, anxious to set foot on the ground.

Wakanda stepped down from the plane and sank to her knees in snow. She held her hood on her head, fighting the wind as she waited for Regi and Claudia.

With the wind blowing a pretty good clip, Regi knew if she wore Samuel's hat it would blow off and probably beat her to Malamute. She decided it was better to store it in the plane. Putting the Stetson up to her face, she breathed in deeply. Samuel's musky scent gave her comfort. She fingered the lining of the hat and the slight bump where the scripture was. It anchored her to the hope of finding her man.

Regi rose and set the cowboy hat on her seat. It would be safe here and would be waiting for her in the morning. She tugged on her gloves.

Claudia crawled out. Oscar leaped to the snowy ground in front of Regi as she climbed down.

Regi stood beside her sister, gazing at the isolated valley. Questions swooped down on her as though riding the wind. What if they couldn't fly out in the morning? What if they were stuck? Would she ever see Samuel again? Regi couldn't let the others, especially Claudia, know the fears that haunted her. But as they made their way toward the cabin a deep foreboding lodged in Regi's heart.

CHAPTER FOURTEEN

While Raven listens to their song,
Caribou Girl meets One Who Was Saved by Land Otters
lost and alone.

THE OCEAN CALMED QUITE A bit as the impending storm skirted by Trace's cruiser. Before nightfall, Samuel caught a glimpse of land. Trace turned on the GPS. The gadget blinked on and charted their position, showing that they were now south of Port Alexander. "The crazy weather must have screwed with the satellite feed or something."

Trace went below for a while. When he returned, he carried two mugs. "Coffee?" He handed one to Samuel.

Samuel didn't want to rebuff Trace's good intention, so he took it but didn't drink. He'd already told Trace so much about the Church he didn't think now was the time to teach him about the Word of Wisdom. They'd been pulled through a wretched storm by the skin of their chattering teeth, and Samuel just wanted to focus on Regi.

If she'd found his note and realized Samuel was in trouble, she'd be terribly worried. He had to get word to her, and to do that, he needed Trace to relax and trust him. A good way to forge trust was to share small talk. "You have a girl back home?"

Trace seemed to think for a moment. "Nothing serious like you. Your Regi must be special."

Samuel nodded. "We'd planned to marry."

"When?" Trace asked.

"The day after you kidnapped me."

Trace didn't say anything.

Samuel knew telling Trace too much about Regi could put her in jeopardy. But after what he and Trace had been through and with this new trust he was trying to develop, Samuel felt he needed to risk it. "She is something, my Regi. We've known each other since we were kids. Probably would have married her right out of high school if I would have stayed in Trailhead."

Relaxed in his seat next to Samuel's, Trace said, "I graduated a couple of years ago. Can't imagine getting married. If you loved her so much, why did you leave Trailhead in the first place?"

Not realizing the conversation would go down the path of him escaping his abusive father, Samuel contemplated what he should say. He certainly couldn't tell him that if he had stayed at home he was afraid his father would have killed him or that he would have killed his father. With Trace thinking Samuel had something to do with Big Jake's death, that wouldn't be a good subject. Clearing his throat, he said, "Long story. But before you kidnapped me, I was finally going to make things right with Regi and start a new life. She's probably very anxious to know where I am." He paused a moment, wondering if he should broach the subject of calling her, and then decided to go for it. "Look, Trace, I plan to willingly go with you and clear my name, but as soon as I can, I'd like to get in touch with Regi and let her know I'm still alive."

Taking a sip of his steaming brew, Trace grew quiet for a moment. "Shouldn't trust you. Mom said you're a liar. But . . . I owe you." He straightened as he made his decision. "We'll stop for fuel in the morning. You can call her then."

A draft of relief breathed over Samuel. He slowed the cruiser as more lights from the shoreline appeared. They rode in silence for a while. There weren't any more clouds. The stars filled the heavens and were a welcomed sight.

Trace set his mug down. He was stowing the gear when he suddenly said, "Look!" He pointed to the water.

Behind the stern was a broad phosphorescent path. Waves breaking around the boat were full of light. Trace looked to Samuel, bewildered.

Samuel remembered a similar incident years ago. "I've seen this before on your grandfather's ship. Big Jake told me when the waters have been disturbed by a storm, tiny marine organisms emit light." Tonight's sighting was quite spectacular, with light-capped waves streaming alongside the cruiser. It looked like an underwater firework display.

Trace turned to Samuel. "It's a sign."

"A sign?" Samuel knew the Raven Clan believed such natural phenomena were messages from the spirit world. After what they'd been through with the storm and nearly being rammed by a freighter, plus their discussion over religion, Samuel could understand why Trace thought it was a sign.

"We're alive because of your prayer. And now you're going back to face the Clan. These lights are a sign that I need to tell you the truth." Trace looked down for a moment, and Samuel could tell he was gathering his thoughts. Gazing up, he said, "Mom told me you're my father."

Samuel was stunned. In a split second his mind went from not believing he'd heard what had just come out of Trace's mouth to knowing that how he reacted to this information was vital to his and Trace's relationship. Samuel wasn't Trace's father. He'd never had a relationship of any kind with Shada. She was just Big Jake's daughter. This was yet another lie she'd concocted. But Samuel needed more information before he disputed the claim. "When did she tell you this?"

"Before she sent me to bring you." Trace sighed. "I wasn't supposed to say anything, but I think you should know. She said she didn't tell you before because she knew you wouldn't believe her, especially when Grandpa was alive. After he died and with all the contention over the will, she thought you wouldn't believe her and that it would look like she was just after the money. But when they found Grandpa's body buried near your cabin, she thought she'd better tell me before it came out during your trial. The fact that you're my father was the other reason she sent me to get you. And . . . why I beat you up. I was mad that you'd left us."

Samuel's mind spun; his sea legs felt rubbery. Just when he thought he was making progress, another obstacle got in the way. How could Shada make up such a story? And what should Samuel say? Denial could be taken several ways. He would sound like he didn't care about Trace or that he didn't want to be his father. And if he said that Shada lied, that would immediately put Trace on the defense.

"Don't tell him," the still, small voice whispered. Samuel was stunned. Not telling Trace would be as bad a lying.

"Don't tell him." Again the whisper. This was a prompting Samuel couldn't ignore. Maybe it was best to have Trace come around to the truth on his own? Still Samuel didn't know what to do except say nothing and keep listening.

Trace added, "No sense in denying it. She showed me the child support checks you sent her until I was eighteen."

Samuel had sent the checks because of Big Jake's will. Plus, Samuel had felt guilty that Big Jake gave him so much and left nothing for Shada.

Samuel should have kept on top of things more. He should have flown up to Alaska once a year to see what was going on. But he hadn't wanted to deal with Shada or the Clan and dig up resentment over the will. So instead of doing something about his deep feelings of guilt and responsibility, Samuel had ignored them, which was never a good thing to do. After all these years, he should have known better. He usually took care of unpleasant business, but in this area . . . the entire situation had been a simmering pot waiting to boil over.

"I did send the checks." So far so good. "And I should have done more. I'm sorry."

"Then it's true?" Trace stared at him.

The feeling to hold back the truth became more powerful than ever. But why not tell him now and get it over with? It would be so easy to say no, it's not true. I'm not your father. Yet the premonition to refrain was just as powerful as the one that prompted Samuel to wait in the willows as he'd watched Regi being forced into the cold waters of the Snake River.

Trace stood before him, eager for an answer. As Samuel stared through the darkness, he realized it was important to Trace for Samuel to be his father. Leaning on the Holy Ghost to feed him words, Samuel opened his mouth and said, "What do you think?"

As though he hadn't expected that answer, Trace leaned back in his seat. "I thought for sure you'd deny it. Mom said you would. When she first told me, I hated you. As I watched you at your home, the hate took root in me."

Samuel rubbed his jaw. "Yeah, tell me about it."

"Sorry." As if ashamed of what he'd done and unable to look at Samuel, Trace rubbed his finger on his coffee mug. "I firmly believed you'd killed my grandfather, and I wanted to make you pay for taking him away, stealing my inheritance, and not being there for my mother and me when we needed you."

Taken back by Trace's willingness to reveal his innermost thoughts, Samuel once again struggled to find words. "Trace, I didn't kill Big Jake. And things were complicated between your mother and me, but please know this . . . If I had known that you wanted me in your life, I would have been there."

"I'm curious. When you found out who I was, why didn't you say something about being my father?"

Trace had a point. If Samuel had really been Trace's father, he would have said something about it right at the beginning. Avoiding the truth until Trace was ready to hear it was going to be a lot like gentling a wild horse. He needed patience and time. "The last few days, we've been at each other like rabid wolves. Let's not look back. You told me that you were sorry; now I'm telling you that I'm sorry about everything in the past. The slate is clean. We're going to find out exactly what happened to Big Jake, and I promise I'm going to make things right by you."

Trace chuckled. "You're not at all like Mom said. That religion you found and this Regi woman really changed you."

Samuel thought about it. Because of Regi, he'd learned to rely on the promptings of the Spirit. She'd led him to the gospel, and now he felt himself grabbing hold with both hands. He was finally realizing that, yes, Regi had changed his life, but it was the Church that had opened his heart. Samuel wanted to do the right thing for the right reason. And though doing so may cost him not only the woman he loved but part of his fortune, he wanted to make things right with Trace . . . and his mother. "I've changed in more ways than I can say."

Yepa stood back as Wakanda, Claudia, and Regi walked toward her. The wind blew swirling white flakes in their faces. They forged on. After running through the snow and stretching his legs, Oscar came to Regi's side like an obedient dog should, which made Regi think that the quiet must scare the setter. The valley was hemmed in with mountains and trees. No roads led to the cabin. There were no telephone wires. This was raw wilderness.

"Wak, is that really you?" Yepa said, hands akimbo, squinting at the woman clad in a deerskin coat much like her own.

"Been so long you can't recognize a friend when you see one?" Wakanda yelled into the wind.

"Well, I'll be moose trampled and grizzly chewed, it is you." Yepa threw her arms around Wakanda, giving her a bear hug. Patting her on the back for good measure, Yepa said, "Thought you were dead."

"What?" Wakanda appeared baffled.

"Let's see, been fifteen or twenty years. So, yeah, I thought you were underground or stuck in a glacier. Tarnation, but it's good seein' you alive!"

Yepa's smile was as genuine as sunrays. She was an interesting character with no false pretense. Wakanda and her friend walked toward the cabin. Regi and Claudia followed.

"Couldn't believe it when I heard your Blue Lady doing a flyby. Never thought I'd see that bird again after the crash." Yepa sniffed loudly.

"Things change," Wakanda said.

Yepa glanced at Regi and Claudia. "Gonna introduce me to your friends?"

Snow began to fall in earnest. Wakanda gave a worried look at the plane but said, "This here is Regi Bernard and her sister, Claudia Osborne." The wind nearly stole her words, so Wakanda raised her voice to a shout again. "Storm looks bad. Need to bed down the plane." She took off.

Yepa nodded to them. "She never was one for formalities. Good to meet you." Gazing up at the black, billowing sky, Yepa started after Wakanda. "You're gonna need help."

Regi stepped forward to follow, but Claudia hung back. When Regi noticed, she turned and stared at her sister. Her face was pale, and she appeared totally drained. Flying with frayed nerves had taken a lot out of her. Though Regi knew her sister was strong when it came to bearing up under difficult circumstances—the death of her husband and the Romney thing proved that—Regi knew Claudia's limit had been reached. "Why don't you go in the cabin? I can help them."

"No. Don't want to give Wakanda anything to hold over me once we're back home. But I think you'd better call Thomas and let him know where we are. He's going to be worried."

"Shoot, you're right." Regi tried to pull her glove off so she could mine the cell phone out of her pocket but was having a hard time of it. Finally, she bit the tip of the middle finger and tugged. The plush, fur-lined glove slipped off. She dug in her coat pocket and pulled out Jack's cell. She could barely make out the face of the phone, but she was able to read *No Service*. "Can't call him from here. I'll try again when we reach civilization."

Claudia gazed about their surroundings. "I've never felt so cut off in my life. Makes me think of Mom and Dad and their Canadian home in the mountains."

Regi hadn't given her parents much thought. She'd sent them an invitation to her wedding, but her mom had replied with a letter. She wished Regi and Samuel every happiness, but they would have to wait to see them until their annual trip to the States in the summer. Scanning the winter setting around her, Regi understood why they couldn't come. For one thing, they were probably snowed in. For another, they hated being around all the hustle and bustle of gatherings.

After Regi found Samuel and after things settled down, she wanted to take him to her folks' place. Glancing at her sister, she said, "Makes me think of them too. Let's go see what we can do to help Wakanda." The sisters made their way back to the plane.

As they drew near, Regi saw that the plane's skis had been blocked. Wakanda was putting a cover over the engine, while Yepa had already covered the wings and was tying down the plane.

"Is that going to hold?" Regi asked.

"Yeah," Yepa said, wiping her lips with the back of her glove. "Each of these ropes is tied around a twenty-four-inch block of wood that I poured water over at the beginning of winter. It's frozen solid. They'll hold even in winds gusting to a hundred knots."

"Anything we can do?" Regi asked.

Wakanda and Yepa finished at the same time. "We got it," Wakanda said as she pointed to the stack of backpacks and sleeping bags she'd pulled out of the plane. "You can help take in our gear."

Regi and Claudia shouldered theirs. Wakanda grabbed hers and another bag filled with Oscar's food.

Yepa picked up the cooler and yelled into the wind, "Got a pot of bear stew warming on the fire. I'm no cook, but you're welcome to try it."

The wind grew stronger. Leaning toward the woman so she could hear, Regi said, "I'm sure it's better than anything I could make."

Claudia heard her and nodded in agreement. Yepa looked from sister to sister, surprised and a little wary, as though she weren't sure if a serious sibling spat was about to take place.

Regi nudged Claudia. "You're my sister. You're supposed to like everything I make."

"Missed that memo," Claudia teased.

Wakanda joined them and laughed as she looked at Yepa. "Regi tends to make burned offerings. But we can also add what Tucker's wife packed in the cooler. Plus, Regi's daughter sent food as well."

The worry on Yepa's face was quickly replaced with a smile. Lugging the cooler, she stepped near Regi. "Have a feeling you and I are kindred spirits." Not waiting for Regi to reply, she trudged away. Regi wondered, did she mean because they were both bad cooks, or was it something else?

Claudia chuckled as she patted Oscar, urging him to follow her. Regi was glad to see her sister's sense of humor return, though her cheeks were still pale and her eyes bloodshot.

The wind blew snow in Regi's face. Pulling her hood tight, she forged ahead.

The wind howled and rattled the logs of Yepa's cabin. Regi sat near the fire, unable to sleep. Oscar was curled up at her feet. After dinner they'd unrolled their sleeping bags near Yepa's bed and the fire since it was the cabin's only source of heat besides the cookstove.

Wakanda dozed off first. After so many years away from flying, the stress had taken its toll on her. She wasn't as young as she used to be. Regi figured Wakanda was in her midseventies.

"Can't sleep?" Wrapped in her blankets, Yepa came to sit with Regi. The woman's wild hair, white as rice, hung to the middle of her back. She pulled her mop behind her ears as she settled down.

Claudia coughed and rolled over.

Yepa grimaced as if she thought her speaking had disturbed her, but Claudia slept on.

"I'm worried." Regi gathered her knees to her chest. She wore thermal underwear, yet she was still cold.

Yepa took one of her blankets and placed it around Regi. "Can't say as I blame you with all that's goin' on. After hearin' your story, makes me glad to be where I am."

"Don't you miss your family?" Regi thought of the twins waiting for news from her at home.

"Don't have none." Yepa added a log to the fire. Flames hungrily curled around the timber.

"Still, don't you miss *people*?"

"Not really."

Surprised by her answer, Regi had a hard time wrapping her mind around the thought of living alone in the middle of nowhere. Though she often sought the solitude of the river or liked riding the range by herself, she enjoyed being with others too. "I don't know whether to feel sorry for you or admire you."

"I'll take the admire part, thank you." Yepa settled down next to Oscar, petting the setter as he raised his head. "It's not that I don't like people. Plenty of pilots stop here. They bring me supplies, check on me. But living here, with the mountains all around, is like living in God's cathedral. He knows my story and why I stay."

"Wish I had your courage. Do you mind my asking what happened to you?" Regi didn't want to pry, but Yepa had brought it up. It only felt natural to ask.

"It's similar to Wakanda's past." She paused, looking at her snoozing friend, who occasionally snorted.

"What do you mean?"

"We were both in 'Nam. Wak never told you?"

Regi shrugged. "I knew she had been in Vietnam but nothing about you."

"I was stationed there as a nurse's aide. Ran into Wak at the evac hospital, where all the women ate with the patients. Being a nurse's aide, it didn't bother me to see missing arms, legs, or eyes. Those guys were my friends, my patients. But when they wanted to touch my hair, it kind of got to me."

"Why did they want to touch your hair?" That seemed odd to Regi.

"There weren't many round-eyed, white-haired women with them. My hair has always been this white. Didn't bother me none until they started crying. There's something so very sad about a man who has the courage to fight in war, even lose a limb, and then cry while he is stroking my hair. A couple of times of that and Wakanda and me would eat as fast as we could and leave. Sometimes she took me to the supply depot where she worked, and we would play poker with the other troops. That's where I met Tucker."

Regi nodded that she knew Tucker. "But why would those experiences make you want to live by yourself in the middle of nowhere?"

"They didn't. It was more the fear of people. See, a white woman's biggest fear in 'Nam was being captured. Those North Vietnamese were offering twenty-five thousand dollars for a white American female. Crud, the government only gave each woman a ten-thousand-dollar life insurance policy. Wak always laughed it off, saying we were worth more to the Vietnamese than our own country. We weren't allowed to carry a weapon . . ." Yepa grew quiet.

"For Pete's sake, why not?"

"Who knows the 'smart' workings of the government? Living with that fear does something to a person, but what really hacked me off and cut my tie to humanity was Operation Babylift. Wak was there too. She never told you about it?"

"No." Wakanda rose from her sleeping bag. Her gruff voice made Claudia stir a little, but she kept sleeping.

Wakanda grumbled as she scooted to join them near the fire. "Why are you dragging up all that baggage? Regi's got enough on her plate without hearing what happened to us in the past. Her man could be dead. She don't need to hear about more cruelty."

Regi had to admit that Wakanda could be right. The thought of Samuel being held against his will by someone who was so sick and twisted that they forcibly took him was a lot to absorb; yet, she did want to know more about Wakanda. And it helped to think of something else. "Wakanda, I'd like to know what happened."

Wakanda's gray braids dangled to her waist as she jerked the sleeping bag up over her shoulders. "Our forces brought out over fifteen thousand children. Tucker piloted the plane we were in. I went along to help with what I could. Yepa was with the nurses assigned to us. We flew into Saigon, and seemed like as soon as the wheels touched the tarmac, people came, holding their babies up to us. Mass chaos. Those children had American fathers, and we knew they'd never survive once the US pulled out. Mothers were crying, screaming, 'Take mine.' We were loading the babies as fast as we could, grabbing kids by their arms and legs. Some civilians hopped on, desperate to get out of the country. The only way they could go was if they became lap holders." Wakanda stopped talking.

"We couldn't take them all," Yepa said. Her eyes were glazed in remembrance. "It was estimated that we left over forty thousand. And we knew darned well what would happen to them, but there wasn't a thing we could do about it." Tears puddled in Yepa's eyes. "That changed Tucker, Wak, and me. All three of us decided we'd had enough of civilization and headed north. When Tucker and Wak started bush piloting in Alaska, I asked them to drop me off. Been here ever since."

"What a horrible ordeal." Regi glanced over at Wakanda. Had that incident been what sent Wakanda over the edge, made her want to become a Native American—something she wasn't—a disguise to escape the ghosts of what had happened? Or was it something else? Something more?

Claudia moaned, drawing Regi's attention. Her sister didn't appear to be awake, but she tossed and turned.

Regi wrapped the blanket over her shoulders and made her way to Claudia. Gazing down on her, she saw that her face was no longer pale but flushed red. Perspiration beaded across her brow. Bending over, Regi felt her sister's forehead.

Claudia was burning with fever.

CHAPTER FIFTEEN

Seal Hunter awakens
and finds Puffin.
He strokes the bird's ruffled feathers.

As REGI GAZED DOWN ON Claudia, she cursed herself for not realizing her sister was ill long before now. She'd been unusually pale, but Regi'd chalked that up to riding in a plane with Wakanda piloting, not sickness. "Yepa, what do you have that could bring down a fever?"

The independent woman, who had lived in the wilds by herself for years and was trained as a nurse's aide, sprang into action, going to a stack of coffee cans near her cooking area. She dug around, looking for something.

"She needs to sweat the fever away," Wakanda said, sitting next to Regi on the floor and gazing down at Claudia. Regi remembered how Wakanda had tried to help her get over a cold last October, making her drink some foul-tasting broth. She'd attempted the sweating ritual as well, but none of those remedies had worked. The broth had left a horrible taste in her mouth, and the added bonus was a putrid smell that had hung on her much of the following day. Claudia would never forgive Regi if she let Wakanda try something like that.

"Let's try what Yepa has in mind first." Regi nudged her friend's arm, hopeful that she wasn't offended. Wakanda was only trying to help, like she always was.

Yepa returned with several cans in her arms and a cup. Written with marker on the resealable plastic lids were the words *catnip*, *sage*, and *mint*. Dried herbs? Not much different from what Wakanda had tried on Regi.

"Don't you have something else? Being a nurse, surely you have antibiotics stored away?"

Yepa looked a little insulted. "Looky here, fevers are brought on by a whole slew of reasons—dehydration, overexertion, insect bites, allergic or toxic reaction. And, of course, there's viral or bacterial infections. Until more symptoms appear, we should use herbs, just to be on the safe side."

Safe side?

Nothing about this trip was on the safe side.

Samuel had been kidnapped and was possibly dead. Wakanda had piloted them to this remote backwoods place. And now Claudia was sick. The safe side? Just what was safe? Cornered and with no other options, Regi said, "Do what you think is best."

Yepa pried open each can and placed equal portions in the cup. She grabbed a pot holder and picked up the wire handle of the blackened-bottom teapot. It was always on the stove, simmering to keep the cold air humid. She poured the steaming water into the cup and stirred. Then she blew on it for a while and dipped the end of her pinkie in it to check the temperature. Satisfied, she motioned to Regi and Wakanda. "It's cooled off enough for her to drink. Sit her up. She's got to swallow as much of this as we can get down her."

Regi slipped her arm beneath Claudia's neck.

"What . . ." Claudia moaned.

"You're sick, sis. You need to drink some of this . . ." Regi didn't know exactly what to call it.

Wakanda finished her sentence, "Healing broth." She got on the other side, helping to keep Claudia from toppling over.

Yepa placed the cup to Claudia's lips and said, "Drink, hon."

Claudia swallowed several times and stopped. As if Regi's words had finally sunk in, she said, "But I'm not sick. Just tired." She blinked, looking like it took all of her concentration to keep her eyes open.

"Did you eat something you shouldn't?" Yepa asked her as she encouraged her to sip again.

More alert now, Claudia stared at the woman. "You're joking, right? My stomach's been doing somersaults all day. I wasn't about to eat and risk vomiting in the plane. The only thing I've had was some of your bear stew."

"I was afraid of that." Yepa shook her head. Gazing at Regi, she added, "Some folks just can't tolerate my cookin'."

The woman wasn't kidding. Regi said, "What did you put in it?"

"Some of the native herbs and plants. I've grown used to them. Have a cast-iron stomach, as I'm pretty certain you and Wakanda do as well. A delicate flower like your sis, here, who has been under so much stress—well, it can take her a while to adapt."

"Unless it becomes worse," Regi said, now more scared than ever. Yepa was no doctor, and Regi wasn't taking her word on the matter. Yet, what could she do? Regi remembered reading that during pioneer times, Eliza R. Snow had begged God to heal her cattle. There had been no men around with priesthood authority to give an actual blessing, so she'd prayed, using only her faith to call down the powers of heaven.

Regi wondered if she could do the same thing. She looked at Wakanda and Yepa, who both stared at her with sympathy. Did Regi dare say a prayer over her sister in front of them? They'd think she'd strayed too far off the reservation.

The truth was, Regi didn't care what they thought. Stroking Claudia's head, she said, "Would you mind if I said a prayer? Ordinarily, I'd ask a priesthood holder to give her a blessing, but we seem to be lacking in that department."

Claudia looked at her sister with glassy eyes. "But I'm not a member of your church. It wouldn't work on me."

"Prayer will work on anyone. All you need is faith."

Claudia stared at Regi. "If you believe it will help me, so do I. Go ahead."

Pushing pillows behind Claudia to support her, Regi motioned for Wakanda and Yepa to come close. Regi took hold of Claudia's hands. "I want you two"— she looked at Wakanda and Yepa—"to be a part of this too. Can you come hold hands with us?" The weight of everyone's hands together filled Regi with comfort. She gave a heartfelt prayer, pleading that if it be the Lord's will, He would heal Claudia. When Regi finished, she looked at her sister.

With teary eyes, Claudia softly said, "Thank you."

Regi smiled and eased Claudia down on her pillow. Once her sister was tucked in, Regi glanced at Yepa and Wakanda.

Both women looked oddly humbled. When they realized Regi saw them staring at her, they both quickly busied themselves. Yepa gathered her herbs and put them away, and Wakanda straightened her sleeping bag.

Regi hoped the Lord would be quick to answer her prayer. But what if He wasn't? What if His will was something else? What if her sister was seriously ill? What then?

Why did Claudia have to become ill on top of them trying to reach Samuel? It didn't seem fair. Fate kept fighting against her the whole way. Maybe she should turn back, give up.

Samuel's chiseled face and crooked smile flashed before her, and she knew he needed her. Regi couldn't let doubt creep into her thoughts. She had to keep the faith, even though right now she felt like she and her sister were smothered with trouble. Images of a battered, cartoon coyote who tried to catch a roadrunner came to mind. Stupid thought.

Her mind quickly reversed to something more serious. She thought of Christ.

Regi thought of Harry Anderson's Second Coming portrayal of Christ. Someone had framed a copy and added words to the side that read, "I didn't say it would be easy; I only said it would be worth it." All these trials would be worth it if by morning Claudia was back to her old self and if they could arrive in Malamute and find Samuel alive and well. Then, and only then, would she feel as though everything they'd been through was worth it.

Staring down on Claudia, Regi smoothed her sister's hair away from her eyes.

Claudia peered up at her. "I'll be fine." She smiled.

"I know you will." Regi leaned over and gave Claudia a kiss on the forehead. "Rest. I'm watching over you."

Claudia's eyelids closed as she fell asleep.

Regi grabbed hold of Claudia's sleeping bag and pulled her closer to the fireplace. She planned to stay up all night until her sister's fever broke, and she wanted her close.

The closer the better.

Yepa finished fussing in the kitchen area and returned to her bed. Wakanda crawled into her sleeping bag. Laying her head on her pillow, Wakanda didn't close her eyes but gazed into the flames of the fire.

Oscar snuggled up to Regi's feet once again, sniffing at Claudia before drifting off.

Regi knew if her sister took a turn for the worse, it would be her fault and her fault alone.

As soon as it was light enough, and as soon as a small port came into view, Samuel steered the cruiser to shore. During the night, he and Trace had taken turns at the helm, catching what shut-eye they could. But at this moment, they were both topside. Nearing the dock, Trace dropped the fenders in place. Once the boat was secured and tied off, they climbed out.

Trace went straight to the fuel pump. As he prepared to fill the cruiser's nearly empty tanks, he said, "I'm sure they have a phone in there. Here's the phone card Mom gave me in case I needed it. Go call your woman."

Walking into the small, shantylike store, Samuel looked about for a pay phone, hoping they had one, but no such luck.

"Need somethin', Mister?" An older fellow was anchored to a stool behind the counter. What hair he had was pulled into a ponytail at the nape of his neck. His jowls hung nearly to his chest. Puffy, red-rimmed eyes clued in Samuel that this guy had led a long, hard life.

"A phone. Do you have one?"

"Where you calling?"

"Don't worry. I have a phone card." Samuel tried to appear friendly and trustworthy.

Reluctantly, the man pulled an old-fashioned, touch-tone phone from behind the counter and set it on top. "By the looks of you, you might want to call for a shave and a doctor." His tired eyes didn't miss much.

Samuel didn't comment but swiped his hand over his face and finger-combed the top of his hair. He could well imagine that he looked like ten miles of road construction. Taking the numbers off the phone card for international calling, Samuel dialed, adding Regi's home number.

The phone rang, but no one answered. Where in the world was she? He thought for certain she would stay close to her phone. But wait . . . if he were in her shoes and she were missing, he wouldn't sit by the phone, waiting for her to call. He would be out doing whatever it took to find her.

A disturbing thought came to him. *What if somehow she figured out that I'm heading for Alaska and is following me? No, she wouldn't do that. She has the Raindancer to take care of and responsibilities. Regi would never leave. Then again, she might.* Disconnecting, he dialed Morgan's office. He'd know where Regi was. The phone rang once, and the sheriff picked up. "Trailhead Sheriff's Department, Sheriff Thomas Morgan speaking."

Samuel wasn't prepared for the emotional rush that overcame him upon hearing his friend's voice. "Morgan!"

"Samuel?"

"Yeah. How's it going?"

"*How's it going?*" Morgan gasped. "Where in the Samhill are you? You disappear for nearly a week, and you're asking me how it's going. Got a tri-state alert out for you. Are you being held against your will?"

"Was, but not now," Samuel managed to get out. "I tried to call Regi."

"What do you mean *was?*" Of course, Morgan wouldn't let that slip. Morgan was a law officer. He'd want to know everything, but Samuel couldn't tell him what had happened with this man at the counter listening to his every word. "Can't go into it now, but things are better. Where's Regi?"

"She's half out of her mind with worry."

"I know."

"So where are you?"

"Not sure. Some little port in Alaska." Samuel looked at the old sea dog behind the counter who eyed him with great interest. Samuel needed to watch what he said or all sorts of trouble would rain down on him and Trace. Though, maybe he should tell this man. But if Samuel did, Trace would never believe him again. Samuel had to keep that connection with the kid. Big Jake would want him to. "This is the first chance I've had to call. Tell Regi I'm all right. We're on our way to Malamute."

"We already pieced that much together. Who took you?"

Samuel knew his friend had been doing everything within his power to find him, just like Regi. "Don't have time to tell you. Please get word to Regi that I'm well."

"'Bout Regi . . ." Morgan's voice trailed off.

"What?"

"You know how she is. Got it in her head to find you. She and Wakanda and Claudia took off for Alaska the day after you went missing."

Though he'd tried to dispel that thought as soon as it had come to his mind, Samuel was afraid of that. "How could you let her go?"

"Since when has anyone been able to tell that woman what to do?" Morgan sounded defensive, but he did have a point. Once Regi got an idea stuck in her head, she'd move heaven and earth and maybe a few other planets to see it through.

"Last I heard from her, she was in Missoula, Montana. Wakanda borrowed a friend's plane . . ."

"Wakanda?" Samuel wondered if he'd heard Morgan right.

"Yes, Wakanda. And she was flying them to Alaska, but . . ."

"What?" Thoughts of the old, homeless woman behind the stick of a plane brought instant worry.

"They should have reached their destination by now, but no one has heard from them."

A chill washed over Samuel's entire body. Having lived in Alaska, he knew full well the dangers of flying in that state. More planes crashed there in a year than in the entire lower forty-eight.

"Sam, are you there?"

"Yeah . . ."

"You have to tell me who you're with."

The man behind the counter learned forward, and Samuel figured he was trying to hear what Morgan was saying on the other end. Samuel turned his back to him. "Please find out all you can about Regi's whereabouts. I'll be in touch."

"Samuel, don't hang up—"

Placing the receiver on the hook was one of the hardest things Samuel had done. Knowing that Regi may have been in a plane crash was too much.

Wakanda, a pilot? Though he'd suspected the woman had led a colorful past, in his wildest dreams, he didn't think she could pilot a plane. Since the day Wakanda had come to Trailhead, everyone'd thought her unstable and a bit crazy.

Everyone except Regi. And later, after the Romney ordeal, Claudia.

Now because of her belief in that screwed-up renegade, Regi might be dead. Though Regi was very frugal when it came to placing her trust in someone, she'd always trusted Wakanda. Just so he wouldn't go mad with frustration, Samuel had to believe that Regi knew what she was doing. Even though facts and statistics pointed to the likelihood that they'd crashed, he had to believe they were alive. He knew plenty of pilots who landed to wait out a storm. And the storm that had nearly sunk the cruiser must be playing havoc inland. Regi was probably all right. *Probably . . .*

"You okay, Mister?" The sea dog behind the counter grabbed the phone and stored it. "Look as though you've seen a ghost."

A ghost . . . Driving his fingers through his hair once again, Samuel left. Walking down the dock toward Trace, who was waiting on the boat, Samuel felt a powerful urgency to reach their destination and fast.

CHAPTER SIXTEEN

While Caribou Girl ponders the fate of
One Who Was Saved by Land Otters,
Night Children sneak by and kick the walrus skull.

REGI CHECKED ON CLAUDIA THROUGHOUT the night. Around two, her fever broke. Many would say that it burned itself out, but Regi knew the prayer she offered had helped. Putting a log on the fire, Regi snuggled down into her bag. Turning on her side to keep an eye on Claudia, Regi placed her hands together beneath her cheeks. Watching her sister sleep reminded Regi of when they were kids and shared a room. If anyone would have told them then that their first husbands would die and the sisters would own a bed and breakfast business together, they would have thought it a crazy notion, let alone the adventures they'd shared beyond that.

Crazy things happened every day. Regi's eyelids closed. The image of Samuel sitting on top of his roan, cowboy hat tilted just so on his head, toothpick between his thick lips, and that lopsided smile of his—that made her insides swirl like the river and helped her drift off.

She was awakened all too soon by Oscar licking her face. "What?" Regi pushed him back and tried to focus. "Is it Claud?" She glanced at her sister, who appeared to be sleeping still. The fire had burned down, and it was darn cold. Glancing at her wristwatch with the illuminated face, she saw it was five in the morning. Wondering about the storm, Regi rose, making certain not to disturb Claudia. Slipping on her cold parka and jamming her feet into her snow boots, Regi made her way across the room and noticed both Wakanda and Yepa were gone.

Regi quickly opened the door and slipped out. The storm had passed. Moonlight cast soft shadows on the airplane. She saw movement. Someone was pulling the coverings off the wings. Another person examined the engine. Yepa and Wakanda were silhouettes against the mountains that rose behind them clear and sharp.

Above the rugged mountain peaks, stars shone with a clear, crisp brilliance Regi had never seen before. As she walked, the air felt dense and frigid.

Must be in the double digits below zero. Her cheeks stung, and her nose hairs prickled.

Making her way through the newly fallen snow toward Wakanda and Yepa, whose flashlights glanced about as they worked, Regi worried that they might not be able to fly out. But if Wakanda didn't think they could, she wouldn't be working to get the plane ready, would she?

The person studying the engine saw Regi and came to meet her. As she neared, Regi realized it was Wakanda. In her hand was a blow torch. She'd turned the flame down. "High pressure system moved in during the night. Could be a problem. Yepa said there's a river close. Very cold, dry air over warm water could make steam fog just after sunrise."

Yepa joined them. "Could fill the entire valley and lock you in."

Regi took a breath. "So we need to get moving."

Wakanda nodded.

"What do you want me to do?" Regi asked, making her way to the plane.

"Been preheating the airplane's engine while Yepa pulled the wing covers and snow off. We'll be ready to leave shortly. Go get ready." Wakanda moved around one of the tie-down ropes, and in that moment, Regi couldn't help but notice the cast of moonlight. Light filled the shafts from the inside out, making the moon seem mystical.

"I've never seen anything like this." Claudia came up from behind. Surprised, Regi turned to find her sister clad in her pink parka, looking pale yet strong. "It's so still, like Mother Nature has cast a spell."

"What are you doing up?" Regi linked her arm with her sister's.

"I'm a little weak, but I'm fine, really. You're not leaving me behind." Claudia sniffed.

"We wouldn't do that."

Claudia gazed at the silent valley. "Seeing raw nature and remembering that touching prayer you said for me makes me think there is a God watching over us." Claudia looked at Regi.

At that moment, they heard the lone howl of a wolf echo through the valley, followed by the answering calls of many others. The wolves were watching their every move. Their howls were warning the humans that they were guests in this timeless world. The animals reminded Regi that danger nipped at her heels, always threatening to overtake her, Claudia, and Wakanda.

"That's a scary sound," Claudia said. "Let's go back to the cabin, pack, and fix something to eat while Wakanda and Yepa see to the plane."

Amazed by her sister's determination not to be pampered, Regi agreed. Once inside the cabin, Claudia set to work in the kitchen while Regi readied their packs. Within a half hour, she'd rolled up their bags and stored their gear in the Blue Lady. Claudia made a passable breakfast of toast and oatmeal. They quickly ate, but as Regi and Claudia grabbed their gear and headed toward the door, Wakanda hung back.

Yepa stood beside her lifelong friend, deep in thought, staring at the raw-lumbered flooring.

"Come with us." Wakanda said.

"I'd love to help Regi find her fellah." Yepa looked up and smiled. "But I'm sure with you along, she's in good hands."

Wakanda took a deep breath, as if pondering what to say next. "Still, I think you should come. I used to think going it alone was the way for me. But they"—tears came to Wakanda's eyes as she looked at Regi and Claudia—"made me realize I needed people. And they needed me."

Regi wanted to set her backpack on the floor and give Wakanda a hug, but she knew such a show of emotion would embarrass her friend, so she just blinked away her own tears and nodded. Claudia elbowed Regi as though to say, we *all* need each other.

"Well, you never know." Yepa heaved a sigh. "Someday you might be lookin' out your window there in Trailhead, Idaho, and I'll be walking toward you." She nudged Wakanda's shoulder with her own. A sorrowful look shot between friends. Regi knew they realized this would probably be the last time they'd see each other.

"Sure you don't want to take some of my bear stew with you?" Yepa said with a twinkle in her eyes.

Wakanda pursed her lips and shook her head.

"I'm sure Claudia would like it," Yepa teased.

"That's very thoughtful." Regi looked at Claudia, wondering if her sister realized the stew may have contributed to her sickness last night. "But I think it's best you keep your secret recipe here."

Yepa laughed and followed them out the door, but she didn't go to the plane with them. Regi didn't know if she just couldn't take emotional good-byes or if she was afraid she might change her mind and get in.

Climbing into the plane, Regi picked up Samuel's Stetson that she'd left on the seat. She took comfort in the sight of it.

Once they were buckled in, Wakanda taxied to the point of takeoff. Oscar whined and placed his front paws on Claudia's lap. Regi gave her sister the thumbs-up sign. Claudia looked pale again, remnants of her sudden illness and getting back in the plane, but she soldiered on. Regi was grateful to have such a wonderful sister and a faithful friend like Wakanda.

Wakanda worked the control panel, flipping switches and piloting the plane. Regi couldn't help but reflect on the story Yepa related about Wakanda and Operation Babylift. What a sad tale.

The plane started down the path, snow flying furiously in the air as the propellers hummed into a frenzy, building momentum. The engine roar was deafening. Soon the plane charged across the snow, racing like a chariot team at the Cutter Races. Regi closed her eyes and said a prayer in her heart as the plane caught flight.

They were once again in the air on their way to Samuel.

Samuel and Trace took turns at the helm as they continued to make their way up the Pacific coastline. Trace sighted a walrus on a small island of rocks close to shore and pointed it out to Samuel. "I remember my grandfather told me that sighting a walrus was good luck to fishermen. Maybe it will be good luck for us."

Samuel had heard the myth as well. "Maybe." He didn't want to squash Trace's hopes, but Samuel wasn't counting on luck to get him out of this. He knew he was beyond luck and was now leaning only on his growing faith in God.

The farther north they traveled, the colder it became. Worry for Regi nearly drove Samuel crazy. He kept a prayer for her safety in his heart. Around midafternoon they glided into Malamute Sound. Their eight-hundred-mile journey was finally over.

Tail flukes of humpback whales appeared periodically in the water. Snowflakes fell, melting into the black, misty sea. A warning horn sounded from a passing trawler where seagulls soared above. The sights, sounds, and smells of the harbor flooded Samuel with memories of the time he'd worked for Big Jake.

Though many years ago, he felt like it was yesterday. If he closed his eyes, he could place himself on Big Jake's seiner and feel the rolling ocean beneath the ship. Big Jake's leathery, tanned face and grizzled beard came to mind. He had a way of looking right through a person with those piercing brown, pebblelike eyes that saw into a man's heart and knew his intentions. He must have inherited the trait from his Russian or Raven Clan heritage. What had happened to his old friend? Who could have killed him? That Jake's body had been buried on land he'd given to Samuel was baffling.

It had to have been someone he trusted because he didn't let just anybody get close. It was probably someone he saw every day. Someone he didn't give a second thought to. That had to be why the Raven Clan believed Samuel was the killer. He could understand their reasoning except for one important factor . . . He hadn't done it.

Whoever killed Big Jake was playing on the Clan's sympathies. And whoever it was had a lot to gain, which pointed the finger of blame on . . . Samuel wracked his brain trying to think of who it could be but couldn't come up with anyone. Yet, he was determined to find out who it was.

They glided past several totem poles peaking through the pines, heavy with snow, that lined the beach. Raven Clan's pole dominated, with a huge raven in flight that staked claim on the land for all who sailed by. The bird's presence said, "This is my land."

It brought to mind a legend Jake'd told Samuel. Raven was angry with his nagging wife so he'd set off to create a world. On the horizon, he came to a camp of men. One man stepped from his tent, and Raven asked him who had created him. The man told him that where the earth and sky met, dust formed. From dust, man was made. Raven told the man he was going to create great lands and seas of the North and asked him to come along.

Samuel remembered Jake had laughed as he'd said Raven's dung had created land. Then Raven had relieved himself to create lakes and streams. Jake thought the myth preposterous. He didn't hold to the Clan's superstitions or beliefs.

As Samuel looked at the rich, natural beauty of the Sound and took a deep breath of cold ocean air, he wondered how anyone, whether they were Alaskan Native or not, could think such a thing, though people could be swayed to believe almost anything, from Raven creating the world to Samuel killing Big Jake. He thought of Shada. She'd distanced herself from her father and had been part of the Clan much of her life. They'd listened to her and must believe her version of who killed her father. Would people who revered Raven as their maker even give Samuel a chance to defend himself?

In the years since Samuel had left, he'd heard that the Clan's ruling government had grown stronger. Still, they had to abide by the law of the land, though in remote villages like Malamute, the state troopers and federal government were hard pressed to keep track of them, and the local law enforcement many times became the last word.

Who was in charge of Malamute law enforcement? Samuel had paid little attention to the police when he lived there before. He couldn't even remember who the sheriff had been.

In the pit of Samuel's stomach, an old churning awakened, reminding him of the animosity he'd felt from the tribal members when they'd heard Big Jake had left all of his money and propriety to Samuel . . . an outsider. Big Jake had gone against the Clan. There had been no potlatch ceremony, no tribute of money left to Clan members.

But Samuel had made sure all the expenses spent in searching for Big Jake's body were paid; in fact, he had Bartholomew Grey, Jake's attorney, double-check that there were no outstanding debts before Samuel left Malamute.

He remembered going before the council. The house master of the Clan was not happy. Chief Taku took special exception to Samuel, claiming that he stole what should have been Shada's, which also would have been in part the Clan's, since she was a member. Big Jake had not been beholden to the Clan for years. Though Samuel had wanted to make things right with them, he'd realized that whatever he offered them would never be enough, so he'd left.

Even now, in memory, Samuel could see the pouting and very angry chief sitting on his high council chair with a tattoo of Raven on his shoulder. Samuel wondered if the bird had been needled there to help the man remember his responsibilities or if the raven was the conscience that whispered in his ear. Taku's calculating eyes looked like caves beneath his stark ledge of a forehead framed by wild brows. He'd hated Samuel. He'd even raised his upper lip and snarled.

"Has it changed?" Trace asked, driving the boat closer to the dock.

The sound of Trace's voice startled Samuel out of his deep thoughts. But he quickly hid his surprise by preparing the fenders. "I hope so."

Trace stared at him, a question on his face.

Realizing Trace had no idea what Samuel had been thinking and that he was asking about the landscape, Samuel said, "You mean the Sound. No. It's the same. Beautiful."

Trace continued to stare at him, but soon a smile tugged at his lips. Since confiding to Samuel that he knew he was his father, Trace's bitter ambivalence had left. Gone was the enraged young man who had kidnapped him, though there was still a wall of resistance.

Nearing the dock, Samuel jumped off the boat onto the perpetually wet wooden planks with the line in his hand. He pulled the cruiser close before he tied the line. As soon as he could, Samuel planned to find a phone and call Morgan again. He'd surely heard something about Regi's whereabouts by now.

Trace cut the engine. Before joining Samuel, he made sure everything was secured and put away. Samuel anxiously waited for him, watching other boats and ships in the Sound. The day was snowy, gray, misty, and dismal, which reflected Samuel's mood. What awaited him? More arguments, more hostility, more . . .

"You ready?" Trace stepped beside him.

"Not really. Think I could make a phone call? I couldn't reach Regi earlier." Samuel didn't dare tell Trace that he'd called Morgan instead.

Trace seemed a little ill at ease, as though he realized letting Samuel call before was probably a huge mistake.

"I'm worried about her." Samuel had to lay it on. "It had to be very disappointing for her to have me disappear the day before our wedding."

Trace nodded. "I can probably find a phone for you."

Samuel zipped his parka to his chin. He wished he'd worn his cowboy hat. That would have made him feel normal.

They walked down the dock. Samuel saw someone clad in a furry parka standing near the steps that led to the parking lot. The hood was tied over the person's head, but he seemed vaguely familiar. As Samuel drew nearer, he saw that beneath the hood was a ledgelike forehead, wild brows, and a stare of hatred. He almost thought it was Chief Taku, but he was unsure because this man looked younger than Samuel imagined the chief would be now.

Trace greeted him by shaking his forearm. The man nodded and said, "My boat served you well. Saw you come up the Sound."

Trace stepped aside. "Chief Skeena, I deliver to you the deceiver of my mother for your justice."

The pain of Trace's words cut Samuel to the heart. For a ridiculous moment, Samuel felt as though his own son had betrayed him.

Skeena stared at Samuel. *Does he expect me to bow?* Resentment, anger, and frustration stopped Samuel from moving. No, he would not bow to the Clan. Big Jake wouldn't want him to. Big Jake would want Samuel to spit in this guy's eye. He wouldn't do it, of course, but he also wouldn't act guilty, and he would not give this Chief What's-His-Name the satisfaction of seeing any type of fear.

Samuel nodded. "I'm not a deceiver. I want justice for Big Jake. If that means talking with you, so be it. I get a phone call, don't I?"

The chief glared at Samuel and turned his back to him. Suddenly, two burly men clad in police jackets came out of nowhere and took hold of Samuel, one on each side.

So the village police answer to the Clan.

As they escorted him past Trace, Samuel glanced at the young man. He appeared upset at the rough handling of Samuel. Shame and regret filled Trace's gaze. Because of Trace's honor to his heritage, Samuel knew he couldn't help handing Samuel over to the Clan. But Samuel could tell doubts were haunting Trace. Wanting Trace to know that he harbored no hard feelings, Samuel winked and forced a smile.

As though unable to witness what would happen next, Trace turned his back.

CHAPTER SEVENTEEN

Wise Owl snatches
Devilfish's radiance from his gills
and flies away.

SAMUEL'S REQUEST TO MAKE A phone call went ignored. The police drove to Raven Hall. Though Samuel had known of it while he lived there years ago, he'd never been inside the impressive building. Raven motif was painted on the front where there were no windows. Above the double doors, a large carving of a raven's head jutted out like a canopy over the entrance. The two officers escorted Samuel inside.

Large nine-foot posts carved with animal and human features supported the massive roof. Tongue-and-groove flooring covered the great hall that was at least fifty feet wide and fifty feet long. The room was filled with people, but as Samuel walked by them, a hush fell over the crowd. At the end sat the justice council in front of a large red wall elaborately painted with black outlined creatures. Even though Big Jake hadn't believed as the Clan did, he'd told Samuel about this place and this wall. He'd called it a nature wall. The central figure represented a raven. He had clawlike feet but human arms that were outstretched. Smaller creatures were symbolic of sea spray.

Five members made up the council. They sat on a platform behind a large banquet table that spanned the length of the wall. As the police walked him before the council, Samuel realized the officers were probably loyal members. He vaguely remembered hearing about a new bill that went before Congress to give tribes and villages in remote regions in Alaska power to see to the legal needs of their villages, though Samuel hoped something as big as murder charges would be handled by the state—that is, if the state even knew about it, which he doubted. This council would determine whether Samuel would be tried for Big Jake's murder.

Three men and two women sat cloaked in black robes. Chief Taku was still in charge and sat in the center. He'd aged. Long white hair hung beneath the domelike chief hat on his head. The man who had greeted Trace at the dock, Skeena, sat beside him. Because he looked so much like the chief, Samuel thought he must be a distant cousin. The other man on the council had the face and body of a walrus: a huge mustache, round bulbous nose, dark purplish eyes, and stout body.

One of the women was elderly. Her wrinkled and wooden face gave away no emotion. Long hair, still jet black except for two shocks of white at her temples, webbed about her shoulders. The other woman, who looked to be in her forties, leaned against her chair, studying Samuel with considerable interest.

Returning her inspection, Samuel thought her quite pretty. Her hair was cropped short. Her cheeks bones were heightened by her native complexion. And even though she seemed pleasant, Samuel sensed she was the wild card of the bunch.

Taku raised his hand, and the teeming crowd paused to give the chief the respect and quiet he deserved. "Who brings this man before us to accuse him of murder?"

Trace came to stand at Samuel's side. "At the bidding of my mother, I do."

Samuel hadn't seen Trace since leaving the docks, but he was glad he was here. He didn't look at the young man, not wanting to draw attention. Had Trace gone home to collect his mother? His loyalty to family ordinarily would have been something Samuel admired. But loyalty was sadly misplaced when it came to a woman like Shada, and there was nothing ordinary about Samuel's current situation.

"Where is the accuser?" the chief asked, panning the faces in the crowd.

They parted, and Shada stepped out, carrying a leather-trimmed talking stick—the shape much like a baseball bat but very sharp at the small end—in one hand and a small wooden box in the other. Short and a little overweight since the last time Samuel had seen her, Shada was still a strikingly beautiful woman in her late thirties. Smooth and sleek hair gathered about her shoulders. Her nose broke high on her Indian face and accented her cheekbones. But it was her eyes that made Samuel take a second look. They were big and round, like Jake's, yet kind of sleepy with the hint of a trickster reflecting in her gaze. Her thick, pretty lips were slathered with frosty pink lipstick.

Shada walked in front of Samuel and off to the side, standing where she could speak directly to the council and keep Samuel in her view. She smiled weakly at Samuel, as though he were a long-lost friend who had wronged her. Then her forehead pinched with worry as those expressive eyes of hers puddled with what Samuel knew were fake tears.

She addressed the council. "I am the accuser." Pointing at Samuel with the talking stick, she added, "He killed my father."

The crowd gasped because anyone holding the talking stick must tell the truth. Samuel knew that the gossip around town had probably already condemned him, but for Shada to make such a boldfaced statement before the justice council while holding the talking stick was a surprise even for them.

Samuel stared at her. Deep in his heart he'd known this was coming, but still, he had a hard time believing Shada was so vindictive. How could she say such a thing? She of all people knew the love Samuel had for her father. *She of all people* knew Samuel had searched and searched the Sound for Jake, long after everyone else had given up.

Walrus-Faced Man on the council leaned forward. "It is easy to make accusations. What proof can you give us?"

Surprised and grateful that the councilman asked, Samuel looked at him more closely. Sloe-eyed, his dark gaze studied Shada and seemed to measure her words.

Taking attention away from herself, Shada glanced condemningly at Samuel. Her lip curled, and her brows flattened. Lifting her chin with strong resolution, she said, "An eyewitness."

The crowd buzzed.

Trace had said there was an eyewitness, but it was still shocking to hear it stated. How had she come up with an eyewitness to a crime Samuel had never committed? A crime that had happened well over ten years ago? What low-life coward would make such a claim? Samuel clenched his hands into fists then released them and clenched then released them again as he steeled himself for what would follow.

"Bring the witness forward." Taku eased back against his chair.

From among the crowd stepped Herman Degelder, the caretaker of Samuel's Alaskan cabin and land. The thin, tall, wiry man stepped forward. The tongue-and-groove floor creaked as he came before the council. He pulled his Thirsty Beaver cap off his head as if to give the council due respect.

His hair was matted to his scalp. Herman hung his head, not taking his gaze from the floor.

"Herman, look up here," the elder woman commanded.

He gazed up.

"Would you give a statement of what you saw in a court of justice?" Taku asked.

Herman nodded.

Taku rolled his eyes. "You need to say yes or no, Herman. A nod means nothing."

"Yes, sir." Herman's gaze dropped to the floor. His face flushed red with a hint of self-deprecation and embarrassment.

Taku scowled. "Are you saying yes to me that you'll answer, or are you saying yes that you'll give a statement?"

"Yes to both, sir," Herman said, wiping at his chin.

"Why didn't you come forward ten years ago?" The chief voiced exactly what Samuel was thinking, which gave him a small measure of comfort. Maybe the chief was a reasonable man. Maybe.

"Back then I was drinking a lot." Herman nervously rubbed his shoulder to his chin. "Couldn't remember one day from the next. Thought I'd dreamed it, especially when they were lookin' for Jake's body in the Sound. But when the backhoe dug him up, it all came back to me."

"Save the rest for the trial." Taku cleared his throat and focused his attention on Samuel. "Samuel Tanner, you will remain in the custody of the Raven Tribal Council until your trial for the murder of Jake Baranov."

Samuel couldn't believe this joke of a judicial system. "Wait a minute! How can you believe the word of someone who admits to being drunk? It could have been anyone." Blank faces stared at him, which only made Samuel feel more desperate. "At least ask him how Jake was killed and then test the remains to see if he's telling the truth."

"How dare you question!" Shada was enraged. "My father has been blocked from making his afterlife passage for over ten years. We gave him the death rites of the Clan, covered him with animal skins and blankets, and sang dirges as flames consumed his body. His ashes are here." She held up the plain wooden box in her other hand. "He will rest for a year, then we will hold the Finishing, and he can rest with those who have gone before him."

Samuel glanced around the room. The crowd's condemning eyes spoke volumes. How could he possibly prove his innocence without an autopsy? He stared at the police officers who flanked him. They would be no help.

The wild-card woman on the council piped up. "Do you have represen-tation, Mr. Tanner?"

Samuel was surprised that she'd asked. He thought of Big Jake's lawyer. "Bartholomew Grey."

"I object!" Shada pounced. "Grey is not a criminal attorney. He deals with trusts, deeds, and *wills*." Samuel knew her main objection was that the man knew too much of her sordid past. Big Jake had confided in Grey as much as he had in Samuel.

Wild Card Woman nodded agreement with Shada. Walrus-Faced Man cleared his throat. "I'll represent him."

A hush fell over the room. Samuel didn't know why. Maybe the council members weren't supposed to become that involved, or maybe . . . Samuel couldn't come up with another reason.

Taku ignored the silence. "Fine. The council will not judge this man. A jury of the village tribe will be selected. Until the trial, Samuel Tanner will be held without bail. We will start the trial Monday."

Monday! Four days away!

How could they possibly find a jury and vet them by that time? Samuel realized they probably already knew who his jury would be, had probably handpicked them shortly after finding Big Jake's body. What kind of kangaroo justice was this? He wanted to say something, tell them they were breaking the law, but what good would it do? Somehow, he had to get word to Morgan of what was going on. He'd know who to call.

Then Samuel thought of Regi.

Bad as things were, he was still more worried about her than his own sorry predicament. That she'd been missing for so long tore at him. Thinking of her helped keep him sane during life's crazy moments. And this was a crazy moment. Regi was his anchor, the person he revolved around and drew breath for.

Taku aimed a stare squarely at his cocouncil member who had volun-teered to represent Samuel. "I hope you know what you're doing, my friend."

Walrus nodded, staring at Samuel like he could measure his worthiness if he looked at him long enough.

The council rose and left the room. The two cops, who had escorted Samuel to the lodge, now flanked him on both sides and led him toward the front of the hall. Before they could exit, Trace caught up to them. He motioned for the guards to stand back. "Give me a minute."

They must have been friends because they stepped aside.

"Samuel, sorry about having to say what I did back there."

"I know." Samuel didn't want Trace beating himself up over what his mother had obviously made him do. "You can do something for me though."

Trace seemed surprised. "Anything."

"Get me a phone."

"Sure." Trace nodded.

"Trace!" Shada made her presence known and stepped beside her son. Samuel gritted his teeth, determined not to show this woman emotion.

"Nothing to say to me, Samuel?" She shrugged. "How unlike you. Come along, Trace. I don't want you talking with the enemy." She walked away and didn't look back, expecting her son to immediately heel.

Trace leaned near so only Samuel could hear. "I'll get that phone to you somehow." He took off after his mother. The two made an odd pair, with Trace towering over Shada. But of the two, Shada had a worse bite. Samuel knew he was about to find out just how deep her fangs could sink.

They'd been in the air for several hours. Regi checked on Claudia periodically, but her sister was sleeping. Each time Regi looked in the back, Oscar gazed at Regi as though to say, all is well.

Regi was glad Claudia was resting and wished she could do the same. But even when she closed her eyes, her worry for Samuel never quieted. That panicky feeling that had taken root in her stomach wouldn't go away until she actually saw him again. Couldn't the plane go faster?

Looking at Wakanda, Regi remembered the conversation they'd had in Yepa's cabin just before they'd found that Claudia was ill. Curious about what had made Wakanda leave Tucker and even Yepa for so many years, she pushed her headset button and said, "Wakanda?"

The woman looked at Regi, acknowledging that she'd heard.

"What happened?"

"Something happened? Did you hear a strange noise?" Concern immediately flinched across Wakanda's leathery face.

"No, relax. I mean, why did you leave Tucker and Yepa?"

Wakanda stared ahead. Regi wondered if she'd offended her friend.

"The past is better left behind." Wakanda glanced at her, brows raised in a hopefulness that Regi would drop the subject.

"I thought we trusted each other," Regi said. "I remember the day I first saw you in Trailhead. You'd painted your body and were sitting in front of the WELCOME TO TRAILHEAD sign. Morgan didn't know what to do with you, so he called me."

Wakanda nodded. "Drank too much. But even though I was seeing double, I saw your spirit's reflection."

"Really?"

"Yeah. A warm, buttery yellow color. I knew I could trust you." Wakanda adjusted the stick and a knob and acted like what she'd said was merely a matter of business and not something she'd kept only to herself.

"I don't know what Claudia and I would have done without you the last few months. You're family, yet I really don't know anything about you." Regi was sincere and hoped Wakanda believed her.

"My mom died when I was seventeen." Wakanda didn't look at Regi.

"That had to be tough on you and your father."

"My father died a few years after. No brothers or sisters. Been on my own most all my life. Didn't need anyone. When the Vietnam thing came up, I went to see what it was all about. Some general knew my mother and father and assigned me to Tucker's squad, though with orders that I couldn't fly. But I did. See, I'd spent hours in the air with my mom. After she died, Dad had me help with his company. We crop dusted for farmers. I could fly better than most men."

"Your parents must have been very special."

"They were." Wakanda bit at her lip.

"Tucker broke the rules and let you fly during the war, so, of course, you fell for him." Regi knew the kink in Wakanda's life that had done a real number on her had to have something to do with that man.

"How did you know?" She smiled and glanced at Regi.

"Guessed."

"Through the horror of Vietnam, Tucker was my saving grace. He made me laugh, made me cry, kept me going when I wanted to quit. Like your Samuel does for you. Yepa tagged along with us, but most of the time, it was Tucker and me"—she chuckled—"and the rest of his men.

"When the war was over, he came up with the bush pilot business idea. We could leave the war behind and everything that reminded us of it. I loved him so much that I would have gone to the South Pole with him if he'd asked."

"Did he ever ask you to marry him?"

"No." The one-syllable word seemed to echo around in the plane, and along with it, a growing tension threatened to end the conversation.

Regi wasn't about to let the moment slide into something bad. With a smile, she asked, "Did you ask him?"

Wakanda laughed. "Thought of it. Wanted to. The man kissed me only once in all those years."

"Okay, now we're getting to the good stuff." Regi coaxed her on. "Was it during the war? Operation Babylift?"

"Was when we crashed in the Chugach Mountains. In the crash, his eye was cut. I put a patch on it the best I could. We were stuck on the site for a week. The fuselage gave us good shelter. Nights were long and cold. We stayed warm by huddling together. His eye caused him a great deal of pain. I tried to help him with what I could, and I guess his one eye saw me as beautiful or something, and he kissed me." Wakanda bit her lips together, as if cherishing the memory.

"And . . ."

Wakanda sighed. "And the next morning the 212 Rescue Squad found us and got us off the mountain. I fooled myself into thinking the kiss meant something more than what it did. But when I visited him in the hospital and saw him flirting with his nurse, I knew the truth. I was once again one of his buddies. Doubt if he even remembers kissing me."

"What a jerk." Regi regretted that she'd treated him nicely.

"No. He was only being himself. When I realized we'd never have a future together and that I'd have to watch him carry on with other women if I stayed, I bolted. Started drinking and roaming about like a homeless dog. Did so for years."

"You were never like a dog." Regi's heart broke for her friend. Such a tragic life—losing both her parents, witnessing the horrible events of a war, and then having the one person whom she thought loved her treat her like that—wasn't fair.

"A person has only so much space for give and take. Once the quota is full, everything melts away." Wakanda's eyes panned the sky as though she wished she were somewhere else.

"I agree there's only so much a person can take on her own. That's why I turned to the Church. Without my firm belief that a loving Heavenly Father watches over us, I couldn't have recovered from Earl's death. Nor could I have gone through all that mess over Romney's murder." Thoughts of those bad times made Regi shiver.

"You had it bad. But I've seen . . ." Wakanda didn't finish.

"You've seen worse, haven't you?" Regi finished for her.

Wakanda nodded. "Does your religion help you understand why innocent babies suffer? Does it tell you why men kill each other? And does it explain why some people have to keep living even when they've gone through hell?"

Wakanda's life scars were deep. Her questions were far beyond Regi's understanding, and anything she said would only sound weak and ignorant compared to what this poor woman felt.

Praying for the right words, Regi said, "In the Book of Mormon, there's a story about some Lamanites."

Wakanda rolled her eyes. "I know. You've told me about them."

"And I gave you the book," Regi reminded her.

"I've read some of it," Wakanda defended.

"Well, you need to read about the Anti-Nephi-Lehies. They were Lamanites who converted to the gospel and swore never to kill again."

That seemed to pique Wakanda's interest.

Regi went on. "Their Lamanite brothers felt betrayed and hated them so much that they decided to kill them.

"Upholding the covenant they made with God, the Anti-Nephi-Lehies went out to meet their Lamanite brothers on the battlefield, but instead of fighting, they prostrated themselves on the ground."

Wakanda's jaw dropped.

"I know. Pretty brave, huh? Over a thousand were slaughtered before the Lamanites put down their weapons."

Wakanda squinted and looked at Regi. "How does that massacre answer my questions?"

"Sometimes God must stand back and allow evil so that the wicked are truly condemned. The innocent and guiltless are rewarded with celestial glory." Regi didn't know if she'd answered Wakanda's questions to her satisfaction or not.

Silence filled the airplane.

"I've never heard it explained that way," Claudia piped up from the backseat. Regi turned around, surprised that her sister had been listening.

Claudia reached over the seat and patted Regi. "I thought that was an amazing story. Makes me understand why you joined that church."

Wakanda gazed at the plane's controls. "We need to stop in Juneau to fuel up. Then it's just a hop over to Malamute."

The tender gospel moment had passed. Hearing about Wakanda's life had made Regi forget her own worries. She hoped that by talking about the past, some of the shadows that followed Wakanda would lessen.

Once again, Regi was thrown back into her worry over Samuel. "Good. I can call Morgan and get an update on what's going on."

Her greatest hope was that he had found Samuel alive.

Her greatest fear was that he hadn't.

CHAPTER EIGHTEEN

Donning a mask,
Seal Hunter struggles to see the Great Beyond,
but instead finds the walrus skull.

AT THE COURTHOUSE, THE COPS locked Samuel in a cell, closed the door between their office and the jail, and left Samuel alone. Glancing around, he found barred windows and a cot in the corner that held a scratchy blanket and a pillow without a pillowcase. He sat on the cot, shoved his hands into his parka pockets, leaned back against the cinderblock wall, and thought over what had happened.

Incredible.

Impossible.

Idiotic.

Vindictive.

Hopeless.

All words that described his situation, Shada, and the Clan. Thinking like this would get him nowhere. He decided to think of something or someone else. Regi.

Beautiful.

Cantankerous.

Spirited.

Playful.

Love.

She was his love, his hope, his everything. If she'd been in a plane crash and killed because she was coming here to help him, he'd never forgive himself. And he'd never forgive Shada. In fact, he'd make sure Shada and the entire Clan would pay somehow.

This entire situation could have been handled differently. There was no need to send Trace after him. No need to lie to the young man and make him think Samuel was dangerous and needed to be hog-tied like an animal so he'd come here. No need to tell Trace that Samuel was his father.

Nope, no need.

If they had told Samuel that Big Jake's body had been found on his land, Samuel would have dropped everything and caught the first plane north. Shada had to know that. And that's why she'd lied about Trace's parentage and sent him. No doubt she'd supplied Trace with the drugs, but where did she get them? Someone else was in on this farce. Someone with a lot to gain and lose. Whoever was in on this with Shada didn't want Samuel coming back on his own terms. Dragging him here made him look guilty. The concocted case against him was ludicrous. He had to convince the Clan that some killer was on the loose and had been all these years. Everyone in the village was in danger.

Who could have killed Big Jake? Samuel had tried to think this through before and had made little progress. But with no distractions now, he might make some headway. What had been going on all those years ago before Jake went missing?

Leon Smarch had been after Jake to sell his seiner to him. But he was one of Jake's best friends. He wouldn't have killed him for his business. Though, if Leon had killed Jake, he'd gotten what he wanted because Samuel sold him everything except the cabin and land. Leon Smarch went on his mental check list.

The only other thing of worth was the land. When Jake disappeared, some gold miners working the Twisted Slue mine up the mountain from Jake's cabin had surveyors redrawing property boundaries. They thought the barbed wire fence Jake had put up was on their side. Jake and Samuel had worked hard between fishing and building that fence to keep the miners at bay. Even though Jake owned more than a hundred acres, he didn't want them making a claim on his property. If he hadn't fenced it off, they could have nested on his land for several years, taken him to court, and seized some of his acreage. Samuel added the owners of the Twisted Slue to the list.

Was there anyone else? Samuel remembered Jake had a lady friend near Anchorage who was always after him to resettle up there. What was her name? . . . Dolly something or other. Dolly Geddes, that was it.

Samuel had seen her only once, maybe twice. A redheaded white woman on the plump side, but Jake always said he liked a woman with love handles to hold. They'd met while on holiday in Nome to celebrate the end of the Iditarod. Shada had absolutely hated the woman and let everyone know it.

Jake didn't care what his daughter thought. After the sordid life Shada'd led, she had little room to begrudge her father some happiness. Yet, she did. Maybe Dolly knew of someone who had it in for Jake. That was a possibility.

The doorknob rattled. Someone was coming.

Not knowing what to expect, Samuel braced himself but was relieved when the walrus-faced councilman walked in dragging a folding chair with him. He shut the door, came near Samuel's cell, and fixed the chair so he could sit down.

Once settled, he reached a hand between the bars and said, "Name's Kenway Stillman. I know you don't remember me, but I remember you."

Samuel got off the cot and shook his hand. "I just saw you; of course I remember you."

"No. I mean from before, when you lived here."

Samuel didn't recall ever seeing him before today. "You're right, I don't remember you. Thanks for volunteering to help me out."

"Not doing it for you." Stillman stared at Samuel. "Doing it for Jake."

"You were a friend of his?" Try as he might, Samuel could not place him.

Stillman shook his head. "The man hated me and everything I stood for."

"So why . . ." Samuel was confused.

"Visited me from the land of the dead, Jake did, and asked me to help you."

Samuel was becoming more confused by the minute. "Don't tell me you're one of those . . ."

"Shaman. When I'm not doctoring animals, I'm communing with the other world. Does that bother you?" Stillman waited patiently for Samuel's answer.

Bits and pieces of Samuel's memory came back. Stillman had come to Jake's boat to talk with him. Jake sent Samuel on an errand, but before leaving, Samuel had noticed how riled Big Jake was at the man. Samuel never saw Stillman around Jake again after that. "I do remember you. You're right; Jake didn't like you."

Samuel also recalled how Jake felt about shamans. He'd thought all the trouble the Clan had could be traced to them. That had to be why Stillman and Jake weren't friends. Jake even said some shamans kept their people living in a past that didn't apply to life now. At the time, Samuel had agreed with him. But after everything he'd been through in the last few months, Samuel knew there was more to the spirit world than most folks thought.

Samuel found his answers in the Church. But others found hope in fortune tellers and shamans. He was not one to judge. Samuel wanted to hear more. "No, it doesn't bother me that you're a shaman. But . . . why would Jake come to you if he didn't like you?"

"He knows I see things hidden from the naked eye." Stillman thought for a moment, acting like he wasn't sure if he should tell Samuel more, but then deciding to risk it, he said, "He also knows you have had a spiritual awakening."

Samuel didn't expect that. "Really?"

"Yes." Stillman assessed Samuel from head to toe. "I'd say it happened late last fall."

"Excuse me?"

Stillman didn't reply at first, merely sat there, waiting, expecting. "You need my help."

In an odd way, Samuel felt relieved. Yet, the man was a bit unsettling. "When Jake came to you, did he tell you who killed him?"

"Doesn't work that way, my friend. Don't know who killed him."

"Well then, why do you think I'm innocent?"

"Jake wouldn't want me to help you if you'd killed him, now would he?" The man had a point.

Samuel wasn't going to look this bit of good fortune in the face and question. Maybe that walrus Trace had spotted from the boat really was a sign of good luck because here sat a man who resembled that beast and he was offering his help. And the cold, hard fact was that Samuel needed him. "I've been thinking about who could have done it."

"Good." Stillman stared at him but didn't ask who.

"Don't you want to know?"

"I suppose."

Samuel didn't expect that response, yet he told Stillman about Leon Smarch and the Twisted Slue mine. He even suggested Stillman get in touch with Dolly. As Samuel talked, he thought the man would ask questions or take notes, but he didn't. He merely listened. Finished, Samuel fell quiet.

Stillman scrubbed his palm over his face and got up, preparing to leave.

"Are you going to check out those people?" Samuel was desperate for some type of normal dialogue with the man who was supposed to help him.

"Sure, after I visit the mountain."

"Visit the mountain?"

"The afterworld is strong there. We're going to need it." Stillman picked up his chair.

Samuel wouldn't argue with that. If going to a mountain made the man feel closer to his great spirit, so be it. Samuel wished he had someone normal to talk to, someone who believed as he did.

"By the way," Stillman set the chair down by the door, "the officers asked me to tell you that Trace arranged it so you could make a phone call. Phone's outside the door. I'll let Officer Jones know you're ready." Stillman left.

Frustrated, Samuel grabbed hold of the bars. He'd spent all this time talking with that man when he could have called about Regi. One of the cops came and unlocked the cell. Samuel followed him to a desk where several officers were playing a game of poker. The phone was there as well.

Dialing Morgan's number, he waited and waited until the familiar voice answered.

Samuel blurted, "Have you heard from Regi?"

Morgan replied. "Nope. Sorry."

His words cut to Samuel's heart.

Juneau had two airports, one for big commercial planes and one for small private planes. Wakanda safely landed at the smaller airport. While she spoke with some men about fuel and while Claudia was walking Oscar around the tarmac, Regi hurried into the small building just off the runway. She could use Jack's cell in there, away from all the noises; plus it was bound to have a nice restroom, maybe a vending machine or two. She'd give anything for a Snickers.

Once inside, she pulled Jack's cell from her pocket. She pushed and pushed the SEND button. But nothing.

"Your battery's dead," a young Native Alaskan teenage boy said as he passed her. "Long as you keep it local, you can use the phone behind the counter."

Regi followed him as he emptied a trash can near a desk at the far end of the room. Aerial maps were pinned on the walls, and a couple of guys sat at another desk discussing how long it would take to fly up to Glacier Bay and whether or not they had enough fuel.

Speaking softly to the boy so only he would hear, Regi said, "Here's the deal. I need to call Trailhead, Idaho. We're late arriving, and I know there are people worried about us there."

"I've been given strict orders that no one is to make long-distance calls on that phone." He started walking away. Regi couldn't let him go.

"I'll pay you fifty dollars." She pulled out her wallet, knowing full well she didn't have fifty dollars inside. Nope, only debit and credit cards. She'd given Wakanda the Raindancer company credit card to pay for the fuel, but she still had her personal cards.

"No, ma'am." He shook his head. "Can't give me enough money that would make me risk losing my job."

Desperate, Regi said, "Look, kid. I've got to use that phone. Can I talk to your boss?"

He nodded toward one of the men at the desk and quickly exited through the door with a full garbage bag tossed over his shoulder like Saint Nick.

Regi made her way to the men, who stopped talking and watched her walk toward them. Had they heard her? No big deal if they had.

"Hi. My name is Regi Bernard. I'm from Trailhead, Idaho." The two stared at her like she'd tromped all over their good-time pie or something. One fellow wore a baseball cap. Beneath his oil-stained coat was another jacket; ragged sleeves peeked from beneath. The fellow behind the desk, said, "Arlen, we'll pick this up a little later. Go see if you can help Buzz." Arlen got up and left, eyeing Regi in a way that gave her the impression he thought she was a good-looking woman.

The man pointed to the empty chair. "Now, what can I do for you, sweetheart?"

Ignoring the jab of annoyance she felt by his condescending comment, she said, "I need to make a call to Trailhead, Idaho."

He shook his head.

"I'll pay you. I don't exactly have the cash on me, but I do have money." A scowl came to his face.

"I have a debit card or a credit card, whichever you prefer." He stared at her and pursed his lips.

"Look." Regi didn't know what else to tell him except everything. "A week ago my fiancé was kidnapped."

The man reared back in his chair.

"We have every reason to believe he has been brought to Alaska by some person. I need to let the sheriff back home know I'm all right, and I need to find out what's been going on. I'm late calling him by a couple of days." There. She'd said more than she probably should have, but it couldn't be retrieved.

Again, the man only stared.

"Are you going to let me call?"

"Nope."

"What!"

"I've heard a lot of sob stories in my time. Yours almost had me. But no." He started thumbing through paperwork on his desk, dismissing Regi.

"Look, mister. I'm not lying. I need to call. I'm not some teenage kid trying to get away with something here. Please . . ."

At that moment, Wakanda stomped in from the cold. "You 'bout ready?" she asked.

The man gave Wakanda a sideways glance then rolled his eyes like she was yet another annoying woman who would take up too much of his precious time.

"I have to call Morgan." Regi sighed. "We're two days late checking in; plus, he might have heard something about Samuel."

"What's wrong with the cell-thingamajig Jack gave you?" Wakanda had never used a cell phone.

"Battery's dead. And I offered to pay the man . . ." Regi pointed to him. His deadpan face didn't even hint at what he was thinking. "But I don't have cash—only credit cards."

Wakanda started rummaging around in her coat pockets then her jeans and pulled out a Ben Franklin. Turning to him, she said, "Would this cover it?"

Regi was amazed. She would never have thought Wakanda carried around hundred dollar bills. But as she thought about it, she remembered that Claudia had started paying Wakanda for helping out at the Raindancer. And the woman didn't pay rent or buy food, so she was bound to have a stash. Regi was just so used to taking care of Wakanda that she didn't think about Wakanda being self-sufficient.

"Well, you can't use the company's phone, but I'll let you use mine." He pulled out his cell and took the money.

"A little steep, don't you think? Don't you owe her some change?" Regi questioned him.

He chuckled as he pocketed the cash. "Not from around these parts, are you?" He didn't wait for an answer to his rhetorical question. "You're in for wallet shock up here, sweetheart."

Unable to digest what he'd said, Regi took the cell from him. She quickly dialed Morgan's number, only to have it ring once and go directly to the answering machine, which meant he was on the line with someone else. Great! Wakanda had sacrificed a hundred-dollar bill only so Regi could leave a message.

Who in the world was he talking to when she needed the sheriff most?

CHAPTER NINETEEN

Stripped of sight,
Seal Hunter must wait for
Raven to spread His magic.

SAMUEL STOOD IN THE HALLWAY with Kenway Stillman behind him and two cops sitting close by. Morgan hadn't heard from Regi. Samuel clutched the phone receiver and took a deep breath, trying to stay his worry. "How long has it been since she last called?"

"Several days." Morgan's otherwise hopeful voice filled with gloom.

"Have you called search and rescue in Alaska?"

"Yes, of course, but they can only do so much." Morgan sounded concerned. "I've been trying to track down this Tucker fellow who owned the plane. Not having much luck. But you know Regi. She beats the odds all the time, and I'm not giving up on her. She'll call. However, I am having doubts about the police department in Malamute."

Maybe Morgan was right. Regi did beat the odds in most everything. Samuel couldn't give up hope. Turning his thoughts to what Morgan said about the Malamute police, Samuel looked at the two officers who feigned playing cards while they listened intently to his side of the conversation. All at once, he wondered if the police were recording his call. Then reality set in. This was the real world, not TV. These guys were probably lucky to get paid, let alone have fancy equipment to tap phone lines, and that was why they were pretending to be involved with their game but were really listening to his every word.

Morgan told Samuel he had a friend in the US Marshals Service in Anchorage. Though they didn't usually get involved with cases like this, he was hopeful his friend could help Samuel.

Then Morgan must have realized Samuel's main worry was not for himself because he said, "We have to believe that Regi and the others are all right. I think that's what your church calls having faith."

Surprised that Morgan brought up religion, Samuel said, "Yes, it is. Thanks. Say a prayer for Regi and me."

"The entire town of Trailhead is praying for both of you."

Samuel was slow to hang up and lose the connection to his friend's familiar voice and the only link to his life back home. Placing the receiver on the hook, Samuel's thoughts returned to Regi. She could be lost somewhere in the mountains of southern Alaska or northern British Columbia. He thought of what Morgan had said about faith. Samuel's faith had been tested many times since this ordeal had started. Faith nurtured hope when there was none.

Samuel felt the weight of worry press hard against his chest. He'd waited all his life for Regi, and now because of her chasing after him, trying to save him, she might very well be . . . dead.

Keep the faith . . .

Samuel glanced at the cop who had fetched him. His name tag read *Officer Jones*. Sympathy creased the officer's brow. An idea came to Samuel, and before he thought it completely through, he said, "Do you know if there are members of The Church of Jesus Christ of Latter-day Saints who live here?"

Jones stared at him with blank eyes.

Samuel needed to talk with someone who wouldn't condemn him or claim to be a shaman. He needed someone who would help him through this and give him comfort.

Stillman had overheard. "You're a Mormon?"

"Not yet, but I plan to become one." Samuel thought of his baptism day and how everything he'd hoped and dreamed had been destroyed.

"Leave this up to me." Stillman patted Samuel's back and left.

Samuel didn't know what he meant—was he going to find some members of the Church, or did he want Samuel to put his faith in Stillman's shamanism?

Jones rose and walked Samuel back to his cell. As he closed the door, he said in hushed tones, "Stillman will find the religious people you asked about. A few members live here." He quickly left and closed the jail door, a look of regret on his face for having talked with Samuel.

Faith and hope worked hand in hand.

Samuel placed his faith in the Lord.

In the air once again, with Wakanda flying over the mountain tops and Claudia in the backseat clinging to her armrests, Regi felt anxiety well up within her. She'd tried to leave a message for Morgan, but the answering machine must have been full because as she's started talking, a dial tone had blared in her ear. She'd have to call Morgan from Malamute.

Right now, she had to control this edgy feeling that was driving her nuts. She'd kept it at bay most of the time by talking with Wakanda about her past or worrying over Claudia, but now a full onset of severe edginess threatened to smother her. Why was she panicking now when they were close to reaching their destination and when she needed to collect her thoughts and act?

Regi concentrated on breathing and staring out the window at snow-capped mountains. She didn't want her friend or sister to realize she was close to a full meltdown. Something nudged her elbow. Glancing back, Regi found Oscar staring at her with soulful eyes. His doggy instinct knew her all too well. She patted his head and massaged his ears. He licked at her hand.

"We're coming up on Malamute's airport." Wakanda nodded toward the front windshield.

Gazing out, Regi saw that the mountains gave way to a seaside town. A landing strip was surrounded by water. A connecting bridge led to the mainland. There was no flight tower, only a windsock to guide Wakanda. She let down the flaps and landing gear. Regi would have been scared to death a week ago, but since flying from Missoula with her friend piloting, she'd learned Wakanda could handle pretty much anything.

They landed with a bump and thud and taxied down the landing strip, pulling off to park the plane near an empty hangar and a small office building. As they scrambled out, Regi grabbed Samuel's Stetson and put it on. She'd hold it in place all day if she had to, but she was wearing it. The wind off the ocean bit at Regi's exposed skin and blew straggling hairs into her face.

Wakanda pointed to a barnlike office building. "Check in there while I take care of the plane." Her deerskin coat seemed to keep her from shivering, though her frosty breath billowed.

Claudia pulled the pink fur-trimmed hood of her parka securely over her head and held Oscar's leash. Regi was glad her sister had thought ahead and was taking care of the dog.

Reaching the building, Regi read a sign on the door. Malamute Airport. She opened the door and looked inside. An African American woman sat behind a desk, next to a space heater. Her frizzy hair was pulled into a ponytail atop her head and was bushed out like a thorny cactus. She wore a sweatshirt with a picture of a salmon on the front.

"Good gads, don't just stand there letting all the cold in." She didn't look up but studied papers on her desk.

"Sorry," Regi said as she, Claudia, and Oscar tumbled inside.

A large Siberian husky sprang from behind the woman's desk and shot over to Oscar. "Didn't say anything about bringing your mutt along." The woman was now staring at them as she tapped a pencil on the desk. Her face puckered as though she had a mouthful of sauerkraut.

The Irish setter dodged behind Claudia. By the terror-filled look on her sister's face, Regi knew she had to intervene. Stepping in front of the husky, she pulled off a glove and offered the animal a sniff of her fisted hand. The canine smelled her and then licked her knuckles.

"I'll be. Roy never takes to strangers." The woman smiled and waved them over. "Since he didn't bite your hand off, you must be all right. Name's Cooper Clawson. What can I do for you?"

"Nice to meet you, Cooper. Hope it's all right if we leave our plane parked out there?"

Cooper nodded. "That's what we're here for. But so we're straight, we're not liable if something happens to your plane."

"Understood. We need a place to stay that will allow a dog." Regi patted Oscar.

"Dogs are as common in these parts as people. Several motels and hotels are on the main drive. You want cheap or classy?"

Claudia piped up. "Clean."

The woman eyed Claudia. "That's the Salmon Run Inn. I can call and have them send a car to pick you up if you'd like."

Regi wondered if a place called Salmon Run would pass Claudia's clean test, but they'd check it out. "That would be great." Hoping to find more answers from the woman, Regi asked, "Can you tell me where I can find Shada Baranov?"

Rearing back, she said, "Didn't see that coming. Nope." Cooper shook her head. "I expect she was at the Clan meeting earlier. Her long-lost boyfriend was being charged in the death of her father, Big Jake."

"But Big Jake died years ago." Regi was all sorts of confused.

"His body was found buried on her boyfriend's land," she said matter-of-factly. Samuel would be upset to learn about Big Jake. Regi hoped she beat him here. Still, something bothered Regi about what the woman had said.

Found on his land. Big Jake had willed his land to Samuel. Realization crystallized in Regi's mind. The "long-lost boyfriend" in this odd situation was Samuel. Regi's stomach nose dived; her skin goosefleshed. This could not be. To validate her thoughts, she asked, "What's her boyfriend's name?"

"Can't remember. Shada sent their son down to the States to fetch him though."

Regi felt like someone had punched her gut. The room swam in a surreal whirlpool. She had to remain calm and focused. If this Cooper woman saw Regi freak out, she'd stop giving information. "You said her boyfriend was charged with the death of her father." Regi's breaths came in short huffs.

She nodded.

Claudia gasped as if she finally connected the dots.

Shaking her head, not wanting to believe this nightmare, Regi muttered, "What have you gotten yourself into, Samuel Tanner?"

"That was his name! How did you know?" The woman blinked then looked at Regi and Claudia with fresh interest.

With shock behind her, Regi's temper simmered with the situation she now faced. "Samuel is a friend of mine." She didn't want to tell Cooper too much, just enough to learn more. "He loved Big Jake like a father. He'd never kill him." Despite her good intentions, Regi's anger suddenly boiled over. "And Samuel is not *her* boyfriend. He's my fiancé."

"Oh, Shada's not going to like that." Cooper tisked.

Livid, Regi spat out, "Shada's thug kidnapped Samuel the day before we were supposed to get married."

Oscar whined, threading his way between Regi and Claudia.

The husky, Roy, crawled under the desk.

Claudia cleared her throat and motioned for Regi to calm down. Regi knew she should, but she couldn't let such a lie go unchallenged.

Cooper seemed to mull over what she'd heard and added, "She didn't send a thug. She sent their son."

"*Their* son?" No! Regi had to hand it to Shada. Her lies could build a good sized igloo. "Samuel does not have a son. I would know if he did."

Cooper glanced beside the desk at her husky as if the dog knew the story and she was conferring with him, wanting his opinion. Looking back to Regi, she said, "Honey, men keep secrets from their secrets. But since my dog licked your hand instead of biting it and because I've opened up a can of outdated tuna by telling you a sled of bad news, I'm going to give you some good advice. Get back on that plane and fly home. I'm a transplant from Louisiana. Been here since Katrina. But I've learned a thing or two about how things work around here. There's nothing you can do for your fiancé. The Clan is having his trial Monday, but he's as good as dead."

CHAPTER TWENTY

Hiding from sorrow,
Caribou Girl must trust
Raven's heart.

"WHAT?" REGI FELT SOMETHING AKIN to Mt. Saint Helens erupt within her. She stared at the woman behind the desk. She had to be mistaken. "You must have misunderstood."

The woman shook her head slowly and deliberately, leaving Regi to understand that she knew exactly what she had said. Regi huffed. "What do they think this is, the wild West? There are laws. They can't arrest someone and have the trial within a week." Regi's mind tumbled with thoughts. Morgan was supposed to talk to the police. Surely they would put a stop to this. "Where's your police station?"

Cooper took a deep breath. "In this town, the police and Clan are one and the same."

"Alaska is part of the United States, is it not?" Claudia jumped in. She nodded.

"The Constitution states that a man cannot be tried without due process." Claudia pulled her hood off and had that I-know-things look about her. "Besides, Samuel was kidnapped and dragged up here against his will. The FBI should be notified."

Proud of her sister's knowledge and background, Regi added, "She knows. Her husband was a congressman."

The woman folded her arms. "Well, for your information, Congress passed an act in 2011 that gave tribes authority over their own villages. Alaska is a big state, and the state troopers can do only so much. I agree they may have stepped over the line in this case, but you're a long way from Washington, honey. The Clan rules here."

Unable to believe what she was hearing, Regi looked at her sister. Claudia's gaze was filled with empathy. "Morris had connections in Washington. I can make some calls."

"Won't do any good," Cooper piped up.

Frustration grabbed Regi by the throat. She'd had enough. "Then you tell me what I can do!"

Picking up her coffee cup, the woman rose. "Go see that man of yours. Make him fess up to his dealings. They *might* let him live if he tells the truth. They've got him in jail."

The thought of finally seeing Samuel after all this time lightened Regi's frustration. Since this crisis had started, she'd been uncertain if she'd ever see Samuel again, and now for the first time in well over a week, the possibility of actually laying eyes on him was a mirage teasing her. But he was here and needed her badly.

"I'll do just that." Regi left, with Claudia and Oscar bringing up the rear. As she walked away, her mind echoed the words *their son*.

Surely Samuel would have told her if he'd known he had a child here. She remembered that day in his house when they'd talked about having children. He had been sincere. He wouldn't have pleaded with her to have a child, except . . . his main argument to have more children had been based on the idea that he wanted a child with her.

Doubt crept into her conviction that Samuel wouldn't keep a secret from her. As she thought about it, Samuel had a whole other life that she really didn't know much about. Was that deliberate on his part or neglectful on hers? She didn't know.

A shadow fell over Regi, but she sidestepped it, refusing to let it catch her when she was this close.

Samuel heard a commotion in the hallway outside the jail. What now? Had Stillman returned? Or had Shada decided to play more tricks?

"I demand to see him!"

Samuel would recognize that voice anywhere.

Regi!

She was alive and standing outside that blasted door!

He leaped to his feet and shot over to the bars of his cell.

"We have our orders." A cop.

"Regi, is that really you?" Samuel yelled.

"Samuel!"

There was a scuffle.

"Look, you mule-headed, stiff-armed piece of work. I've come too far for you to stand in my way!" Regi again. Bless that woman and her chipotle temper.

Samuel had never been so happy to hear Regi spout off. "Sweetheart, they're only doing what they have to."

The sound of muffled voices filtered through the door. He thought he recognized Claudia's and even Wakanda's. And did he hear a dog growl? They'd even brought Oscar? What was going on out there? He tried to think what he could say to ease Regi's mind. "I'm fine. Really. Go find Kenway Stillman. He'll know what to do."

There was a long pause, and Samuel could well imagine Regi staring down the guards and assessing her options. He heard footfalls that steadily grew fainter.

She was going.

But Regi had been here! The thought and the promise of seeing her soon would keep him company through the long, lonely night.

Regi tore out of the building, not caring if the others followed. She was going to find this Stillman fellow, and he'd better have some answers as to why Samuel was locked up. What in the blue blazes was wrong with these people? What kind of evidence did they have against Samuel that led them to believe he'd killed Big Jake? Better be something more than conjecture.

All at once, Regi collided with someone. She'd knocked down a large, moon-faced woman who now lay on the snow-covered ground. She was clad in what looked like a heavy wool blanket made into a coat.

Oscar licked the woman's face as though to apologize for Regi. Wakanda and Claudia helped the poor, heavyset Native Alaskan to her feet, and Regi noticed that tucked into the woman's rubber moonboots were the pant legs of bright yellow sweats that showed signs of heavy wear. Her long black hair was pulled into a ponytail at the nape of her neck. Fluffy feather earrings dangled from her ears. She smiled, embarrassed, then said, "Excuse me." Slightly bowing, she prepared to move away from them.

"No, I'm the one who didn't look where I was going," Regi said. Embarrassed that her temper had blinded her, she added, "I'm sorry."

The woman smiled, bowed slightly, and started away when Regi realized she might be able to help.

"Could you tell me where I could find a man by the name of Kenway Stillman?"

The smiling woman's eyebrows rose. "You just missed him. He's gone to the mountains."

"Shoot!" Regi stuffed her gloved hands into her parka. Stillman was her only hope of getting in to see Samuel. What would she do now?

"Calm down, sis." Claudia almost put her arm around Regi but drew it back.

Regi knew her sister had resisted the urge because she knew better. When Regi was frustrated, no comforting hug would soothe her.

"Is there something I can do?" The woman's brows pinched together with concern.

Wakanda shook her head. "Not unless you can get her in to see Samuel Tanner."

"I'm going to see him now." Her cheeks dimpled as she smiled.

Regi stared at the woman. Could she be Shada Baranov? Regi had no idea what the woman looked like. "What's your name?"

"Morning Joy." She pulled off her mitten and reached to shake Regi's hand.

Regi knew it would be an insult not to take her glove off. She quickly pulled her glove from her hand and accepted the kind offer of friendship. "I'm Regi Bernard." She turned. "This is my sister, Claudia, and my good friend Wakanda." Oscar whined. "And this is Oscar." His tail wagged at the sound of his name. Morning Joy patted him.

After the exchange, Morning Joy tugged her mitten on while she spoke. "Stillman said that Mr. Tanner wanted to speak with someone who was a member of his church. My husband's the branch president, but he's preparing for the Iditarod and is in Anchorage right now. I'm supposed to join him tomorrow. All the other priesthood holders live miles away, so I thought I'd best see what I could do to help."

"Samuel Tanner is my fiancé," Regi said as she pulled her glove on again. "I tried to see him, but the guards wouldn't let me." She hoped this kind woman could pull some magic strings and get her in.

Morning Joy bit her lip and heaved a sigh. "You really should get permission from Chief Taku. But let me see what I can do." She hurried up the path to the lodge and slipped behind the doors.

Wakanda paced. Claudia fidgeted with Oscar's leash, and Regi said a silent prayer as she stared at the police station entrance. A large wooden raven—painted black with wings spread and talons reaching—perched above the double doors. Regi had barely noticed the raven when she'd first entered the building because her mind had been focused on finding Samuel. As she stared at the carving now, she tried to think what the symbolism was there. The raven . . . She'd never really thought much of the bird. Such birds at the ranch were low on the respect pole, right next to magpies.

"Raven is a mythic hero." Wakanda stood beside Regi, gazing up at the carving. "Like the Nez Percé, these people revere stories passed down from their ancestors."

"Do you know the stories?" Regi didn't know what kind of battle lay ahead to get Samuel out of trouble, but to know more about the locals could be helpful.

Wakanda shrugged. "Some. Back in the day, I didn't pay much attention. After Tucker and I had our falling out, I gravitated toward Indian myths and legends. Much like your belief does for you, they gave me great comfort."

Morning Joy poked her head out of the double doors and motioned for them to come inside.

"Regi, I convinced the guards to let you go in with me, but Claudia and Wakanda will have to wait here."

They found a bench and sat down, and Oscar settled by Claudia's legs.

Regi could hardly look at the two men who only moments ago had blocked her from seeing her man.

Morning Joy nodded to the one with the badge that said *Officer Jones* on it. He must have been the one who had agreed to let her in. He rose and opened the door to the jail that held Samuel and motioned for Regi to go in first. Like a horse cutting cattle, Regi charged forward.

CHAPTER TWENTY-ONE

Across the great tundra,
Raven guides Caribou Girl
to find her treasure.

SAMUEL HEARD THE DOOR OPEN. Since they'd refused to let Regi see him, he was in no hurry to find out who was coming in. His gut had twisted with frustration after coming off the high of hearing Regi's voice a while ago and letting the reality sink in that he wasn't able to lay eyes on her.

It tore him up when he couldn't hear her footsteps anymore. Samuel'd imagined their long-awaited greeting. First he would hold her in his arms. Then kiss her all over. Thoughts of nuzzling her swanlike neck, of kissing behind her delicate ears, of breathing in her jasmine scent, nearly drove him crazy—and at the same time, made him feel better.

Whoever was coming through that door could never compare to the woman who had captured his heart. He glanced up.

Regi?

Were his eyes and imagination deceiving him? He blinked then blinked again. Had he gone over the edge of sanity and was seeing her image on whoever walked into the room?

Another woman followed her. He'd never seen her before—some large, Native Alaskan woman with a big smile on her round face. So if he saw her clearly . . . that meant . . . his gaze shot back to Regi.

Yes!

Regi! Wearing his Stetson.

Leaping off the cot, he pounced across his cell like a mountain lion. Reaching through the bars, he pulled her to him, knocking his hat off her head and clutching her as though he were afraid she would disappear. He didn't want to ever let her go.

She said nothing, and despite the bars, she hugged him back. The cold steel between them seemed to melt away. Samuel longed to bury his face in her neck. He took a deep breath. Jasmine. Beautiful jasmine. He leaned back and took hold of her face between his hands, marveling that he was touching her and looking into her dark gem-green eyes puddled with tears. His woman, his love, his life.

Drawing her face between the bars as best he could, he placed his lips on hers and kissed her long and hard, relishing her taste.

He heard movement from behind Regi. At first he was angry that someone would intrude, and then he remembered the woman who had accompanied his love. Reluctantly, he pulled back, but before releasing Regi from his hold, he kissed her forehead and smoothed her long, silky hair with his fingers. Oh, how he'd missed her. But he couldn't afford to be selfish. He had to find out what was going on.

Taking hold of Regi's hand, he stepped back and looked at the woman who had picked up his hat. She beamed a smile. Samuel said, "I don't know who you are, but you must have helped get Regi in here. Thank you."

"It's all right. You two obviously love each other." The woman blushed with embarrassment.

"Who am I indebted to?" Samuel asked.

"This is Morning Joy," Regi said. "Some fellow named Stillman sent her to see you. Her husband is the Church's branch president here. He's not home, so she came."

"I'm glad you did." Samuel could have hugged the woman.

"Preston, my husband, will be gone until about the end of March," Morning Joy said. "But I'll make certain he comes to see you as soon as he gets home. Can I bring you anything? Food?"

The end of March would be too late; the trial would be over. But Samuel didn't want to go into that right now. The woman was in a difficult situation and needed to feel like she could do something. "I'm sure they'll feed me."

"They'll probably give you soup from a can," Morning Joy scoffed.

Samuel smiled at her. "Food would be very thoughtful. Thank you."

"Part of the deal of getting Regi in here was that I'd stay in the room. But don't mind me. I'll stand here by the door and listen to my iPod." Morning Joy handed the hat to Regi, put earbuds in her ears, and turned her back on them to face the wall.

Grateful for the small piece of privacy, Samuel gazed at Regi. "You shouldn't have come." She'd put herself in danger, not only on the flight here, but now she could be a target for whoever had killed Big Jake.

"You would have come for me." She gazed into his eyes, daring him to say he wouldn't.

He couldn't lie. "I know, but that's different."

"How?" She sounded offended.

"I'm a man. I can take care of myself." Even as the words fell from his lips, he regretted them.

Regi chuckled. "And you're doing such a great job." She stared at the bruises on his face. "Looks like you've been knocked around." She lightly touched his cheek.

He took her hand in his. Not wanting to tell her that Trace had beaten him, he said, "I'm fine. And as much as I'm glad to see you, you have to go home."

"The only thing I *have* to do is get you out of here." She pulled a small piece of paper from the inside rim of his hat. "I found this. I know it's something very personal to you, but when I read it . . . well, it gave me faith that we were going to get through this and that I'd see you again."

Samuel never intended for anyone to read the scripture he'd written. After Samuel realized the Lord had guided him in saving Regi, the words in Romans 5:3–5 had nearly leaped out of the New Testament at him.

Regi unfolded the paper and read, "And not only so, but we glory in tribulations also: knowing that tribulation worketh patience; And patience, experience; and experience, hope: And hope maketh not ashamed; because the love of God is shed abroad in our hearts by the Holy Ghost which is given unto us." She looked up. Her eyes shimmered with tears. "Samuel, with the Lord's help, we're going to get through this . . . together."

Nearly overcome with emotion, he couldn't speak.

Regi folded the paper, put it back inside his hat, and tried to hand him the Stetson through the bars.

"You keep it safe for me." Reaching through his cell, he placed the hat on her head. It was too big for her, yet he liked seeing it on her.

She rubbed her forehead and said, "Now, I've pieced together some of what happened. When we arrived, a woman told me that a Shada Baranov claims you killed her father, Big Jake."

Samuel nodded.

She paused a moment, biting her bottom lip, then said, "So . . . how are we going to prove you're innocent?"

How he loved her! "Your heart is in the right place, but seriously, if you get too close, Jake's killer might come after you. You nearly died because of my crazy aunt. I'm not going to put you in jeopardy again."

"I'm not afraid." Regi stared at him with conviction.

He knew her mind was set. "I know you're not. But I am. I can't lose you!"

"You won't, unless you keep being mule-headed about this." A smile teased the corner of her lips.

Samuel heaved a sigh. "Morgan is trying to get in touch with the Marshals in Anchorage. He knows someone in their office who will probably help me, so you don't need to do anything except visit me here in jail."

"Count on that." She smiled.

Samuel felt a ping in his heart.

"Until they get here though, Claudia, Wakanda, and I can do some legwork that would save time."

Samuel thought about what she was saying. Time was not something he had a lot of, and if Regi could help, he would be crazy not to have her check out a few places as long as she was careful. "You promise to just ask a few questions?"

She nodded and gave him an innocent look.

"I guess it wouldn't hurt for you to poke around a little. The trial is Monday."

Regi's brows puckered together.

"I know." He understood her alarm. "Stillman's gone to the mountains but said he would take care of everything. The Clan believes in swift justice."

"Swift? How about ram-it-down-your-throat justice?" Regi huffed. She squeezed his hand. "How do you know this Stillman fellow?"

"He's part of the council and volunteered to represent me."

"Why in the world did he go to the mountains?"

"He's a shaman."

Regi rubbed her temples. "Can't see how that's going to get you out of here. Can you think of anyone who can help us snoop around?"

Samuel shook his head but stopped. "Trace might."

"Who is Trace?"

"Shada's son." As the words left his mouth, Samuel sensed Regi withdraw. A deep worry claimed Samuel. Had Regi heard that Shada claimed Samuel was Trace's father?

No. His mind was conjuring up trouble where there wasn't any. She'd just arrived.

But Regi did have a knack for finding things out. He should tell her right this minute about the lie. But on top of everything else, how much more could Samuel expect Regi to take before she walked away? And it didn't help that Samuel hadn't set Trace straight on his parentage.

He glanced at Morning Joy. She seemed to be listening to her music, but he lowered his voice to be certain she couldn't hear. Staring into Regi's soulful eyes, Samuel knew he had to tell her. "You need to know that Trace believes he's my son. Which is impossible since Shada and I never slept together."

"So why would he think you're his father?" Regi sounded somewhat surprised, and yet she didn't.

"Shada lied. And the fact that I sent her money each month tends to back up her claim, but I was only following Jake's wishes, seeing that the boy was taken care of at least financially until he turned eighteen." Samuel gazed at the ceiling. What was he looking for, a sign from God? Of course not. God wouldn't back up someone who had sidestepped telling the truth. And yet, Samuel felt like he'd been prompted to omit telling Trace that he wasn't his father.

Omission was lying, wasn't it? He was living in the gray area of right and wrong. He gazed at Regi. If she knew his inner turmoil, maybe she could help. Staring her squarely in the eyes, he said, "Regina . . ."

She blinked and stared at him earnestly.

Samuel only used her first name when he was very serious, and she'd picked up on his verbal clue. He continued. "When Trace first told me, I thought it best to hear him out before I told him I wasn't his father. But as I listened, I felt prompted that I wasn't to tell him the truth. How could that kind of prompting come from God? It doesn't make a lick of sense, but I just couldn't do it. I'm still puzzled."

She looped stray hairs behind her ears and took a deep breath. "I know you've been studying the scriptures. Do you remember the story about Abraham and his son, Isaac?"

Samuel nodded. "Sure, but what does that have to do with this? Trace isn't my son, and it's not like I was impressed to sacrifice him."

Regi reached through the bars and took Samuel's hand. "That's not the part of the story we need to focus on. What was truly remarkable was how Abraham was willing to do what God commanded him to do. Can you imagine the questions going through Abraham's mind? He knew the law of God forbade human sacrifice or murder of any kind. Abraham had to wonder if this command to sacrifice Isaac was truly from God because the act of killing is a horrible thing. But Abraham was a man of exceedingly great faith." She gazed into Samuel's eyes. "Believe it or not, Samuel, you have great faith. Bishop Caldwell told me that the Lord works in mysterious ways. We need to put our trust in Him and follow the still, small voice, even though, like Abraham, we don't understand at first."

Samuel didn't know how she'd done it, but Regi had made sense of his moral dilemma. Maybe it was simpler than he'd thought. Still, was he being guided by the Holy Spirit or was he merely avoiding an ugly situation? At that moment, a sure knowledge came to Samuel's mind. He was not one to avoid contention. Samuel knew he'd been guided by a higher power. "Do you mind if I let Trace continue to think I'm his father for a while? The kid has gone through a lot. His mother is a real nutcase. I have no idea who his biological father could be, but I don't want to pull the rug out from under Trace."

Regi placed her palm to Samuel's cheek. "Whatever you think you need to do, I'm behind you."

She took hold of the bars. "However"—her voice rose—"I am concerned about this farce of a trial. People have already convicted you. The woman who told me about Shada said they were going to sentence you to death. And she meant it."

"Excuse me," Morning Joy interrupted. She'd turned away from the wall and had come over to them. "I'm sorry, but I couldn't help but overhear. I can tell you're good people, and I can't stay silent a moment longer. My husband, Preston, has some sway with the justice council. They're not thrilled that he converted to the Church, but his cousin is Chief Taku. Preston might be able to delay the trial. And even though Kenway Stillman is a shaman and a member of the Clan, I know he will do everything he can to see you get a fair deal."

"Thanks," Samuel said.

Regi gave her a friendly hug then turned back to Samuel. "While they're taking care of the trial and the council, Wakanda, Claudia, and I can investigate what really happened to Jake."

"You have to promise me you'll be careful."

"Scout's honor." She held up two fingers.

"You're not a Scout." Samuel chuckled.

"I was a Girl Scout . . . for a week."

"Okay, Miss Girl Scout. I want you to be very careful. Where are you going to stay?"

"We're thinking about the Salmon Run Inn."

"Good. I was afraid you might try to stay at the cabin."

"Oh, that's right. I forgot. You were going to give it to me for a wedding present." Regi's eyes grew large and sparkly.

Samuel couldn't believe she'd found out. He'd only told one person. "Morgan has a big mouth."

"Don't be angry with him. As we were trying to piece together what happened, it came up. I can't wait to see it." Regi seemed to be thinking out loud and changing her mind about where to stay.

"No, Regi. You cannot go there." Samuel had to be strong and not relent on this issue.

She stepped back, surprise showing on her face after his passionate plea. "Why?"

"Herman Degelder is the caretaker and lives in the basement. He's the one claiming that he saw me kill Big Jake."

"He's obviously lying," Regi defended.

Samuel wanted to sweep her up in his arms and kiss her for saying that, but he had to remain serious. "Yes, he is. Which makes one wonder why?"

"He could be the killer." Her eyes got big and round like she'd solved everything.

"Could be." Samuel reached through the bars and took both of her hands in his. "Please promise me you won't hang around the cabin." Samuel prayed Regi understood the gravity of the situation.

Regi squeezed his hands. "Don't worry."

Samuel realized he was coming on a bit strong. "Sorry."

"I understand." Regi gave him her crooked smile that said everything was all right. "Where else *can* I poke around?"

Samuel knew he'd belabored the topic of the cabin, and he needed to give Regi something to do or she'd find her own trouble. "You might check out Leon Smarch, who bought Jake's seiner. And if you have time, look into the Twisted Slue Mining Company."

"That's going to be difficult," Morning Joy said, concern washing her face. "They've shut down for the winter. My husband works for them during the summer, but in the winter, everyone revolves around the Iditarod. Cooper Clawson is flying me up to Anchorage in the morning to be with my husband for the race."

"You're leaving? I thought you were going to talk to your cousin about postponing the trial?" Samuel didn't know how much he could trust Morning Joy.

True, her husband was the branch president, but some people did unscrupulous things to protect their livelihood, even if they were members of a church.

Morning Joy shied away. "He's my husband's cousin. I thought it best I tell Preston your problem in person. He's hard to reach when he's preparing for the race and all. I'll see him tomorrow, and he'll call Chief Taku. Is that all right?"

Samuel cursed himself for flaring up like he did. "I don't want to get him in trouble with his cousin or the mine."

"He'll be careful. If he has a job with someone who could have killed Big Jake, I don't want him working there. He can always fish with his cousin to get the money we need." A reassuring smile returned to Morning Joy's face.

"Thanks. I'd appreciate it." Samuel smiled.

She nodded as though she knew he was under a great deal of stress.

Samuel turned his attention to Regi. "Please talk with Trace if you can. He may think of something."

"Sure. And don't you worry. We're going to get you out of here." Taking off Samuel's cowboy hat, Regi leaned through the bars the best she could and kissed him. Despite the bars blocking him, he pulled her close. "Did I tell you I love you?"

"Not in so many words, but I got the message loud and clear." She kissed him again and reluctantly pulled away.

As he watched Regi leave and the door close behind her, his mind went back to the argument they'd had over her not staying at the cabin, and he realized she hadn't agreed to anything.

CHAPTER TWENTY-TWO

Devilfish seeks
friendships of enemies
he aims to kill.

WHILE DRIVING UP THE LONG, snow-packed road leading to Samuel's cabin, Regi told Claudia and Wakanda some of what she and Samuel had discussed inside the jail. After she finished, they both fell unusually quiet. Even Oscar didn't make a sound. The silence was driving Regi nuts. She had to say something.

"I'm glad Morning Joy lent us her SUV." Regi was not a fan of big, hard-to-drive vehicles, but since her Jeep was thousands of miles away, she was happy for the wheels.

Silence replied.

She pulled over and stopped. "So what's wrong?"

"What could be wrong?" Claudia said, as if pretending to be surprised.

"Don't give me that. Come on. Spill it." Regi glanced in the back. Wakanda would certainly tell her what was up.

"The spirit of the dead will still be where the body was buried." Wakanda didn't disappoint.

"You too?" Regi looked at her sister.

Claudia nodded. "Kind of. I don't want to stay in the same cabin as the caretaker who claims he saw the murder take place. Besides, from what you told us, you promised Samuel we wouldn't."

"I didn't promise. We could go back and stay at Salmon Run—"

"Good." Claudia was quick to jump on the idea.

Regi had to make them understand why she felt they would be all right. "But we'd be safe at the cabin. I brought my gun."

Claudia's eyebrows immediately rose to exclamation points. "You promised me long ago that you'd leave it in the safe—back home."

"How well can a gun protect you if it's locked away? I know how to use it. And I'm not afraid of this Herman fellow. The trial is Monday. We don't have a lot of time, and we need to find out what he knows."

Claudia huffed.

Wakanda cleared her throat. "Not afraid. I'll go."

Regi glanced at Claudia. "I'd hate for us to be separated. I need to focus on who really killed Jake, and I'll need your help, but if you want, I can take you to the inn."

Claudia rolled her eyes. "All right. I'll stay with you two."

Regi glanced into her rearview mirror at Wakanda. "And Jake's spirit won't be there. From what Morning Joy told me before we left, his remains were cremated, and Shada has his ashes. Don't Native Alaskans believe the spirit follows the remains?" Regi couldn't tell what Wakanda was thinking as her expression remained unchanged.

Staring at Regi in the mirror, Wakanda finally said, "The spirit remains where the evil happens."

Great! Just what Claudia needed to hear. Regi looked at her sister, whose forehead furrowed with trepidation. Regi had to say something that would dispel Wakanda's superstitions. "Chances are he wasn't killed at the cabin, so the evil deed didn't happen there."

Wakanda's right eyebrow quirked up. She seemed to know Regi was splitting hairs.

Wanting to focus on another reason to stay at the cabin, Regi said, "The cabin won't cost us anything." She knew she had them with that one. "We might be here a while, and free beats paying any day of the week." This logic should appeal to Claudia, who was the number cruncher for the Raindancer back home.

"Nothing is free," Wakanda said. "His displaced spirit will be there."

Regi avoided her stare. Just when she thought Wakanda had left superstitions behind and become a regular person—flying a plane and sharing her background—she'd reverted back to the superstitious, homeless woman of months ago. Regi wouldn't be surprised if she pulled out a bottle of her ceremonial potion to ward off evil spirits.

"Samuel has money. He'll pay us back." Claudia nervously wrung her hands together.

"Claud . . ." Regi had to state her case in a way her sister could relate to. "Wouldn't you have done everything you could to save Morris before he died?"

"Of course." She squinted cautiously at Regi.

"I have to do everything I can think of to help Samuel. And if that means going against his wishes and staying at the cabin, I'm going to do it. We've been in dangerous situations before. The three of us together can handle anything."

Claudia slumped back into her seat. "All right. But the first sign of trouble, we're going to the Salmon Run Inn."

With that finally settled, Regi drove to the road she'd been told to follow, but she didn't see a cabin.

The snow was as high as their vehicle's windows, but the road had been plowed. As they rounded the bend, a huge three-story cabin came into full view. It was built against a hill, the bottom level was flagstone, and it had a patio area. The rest of the cabin was made of squared logs with red-framed picture windows in every wall overlooking the land.

"Nice," Claudia said as her eyes panned up to the top floor and down again. "Doesn't look haunted to me." She smiled at Regi.

Wakanda grunted from the backseat. "Spirits can't be seen with the naked eye."

"Let's go," Regi said.

As soon as they climbed out of the car, Oscar took off on his own adventure. Bounding over the snow, the Irish setter acted like a young pup. The dog would pay for his burst of energy tonight when his arthritis flared up. Claudia shouldered her pack and started for the ground floor entrance.

"Wait!" Regi called to her.

"What?"

Regi hated to bring it up, but she had to. "That's where the caretaker lives. We need to enter through the main entrance."

Claudia retraced her steps to the car and busied herself helping Wakanda unload other bags.

Hefting her pack over her shoulder, Regi made her way to the cabin. The walk and stairs were cleared of snow, which surprised her. But Herman was paid to upkeep the place, so it only made sense. She followed flat-stone steps up the slight hill to the main level. For a moment, she wondered if she should have knocked on the caretaker's door to let him know they were there, but she felt like she needed to pretend she owned the place so he wouldn't have the advantage.

Reaching the top step, Regi came to a large patio. She realized she didn't have the key. People usually kept one under the welcome mat, but knowing

Samuel, he wouldn't put it there. At the ranch, he kept his emergency house key hidden under a loose brick in the windowsill. The cabin was made of logs, not brick, but she wondered. There was a little octagonal entry window next to the door. She tugged off her right glove and felt around the sill. The jagged ridge of a key grazed her fingertip. Relieved, she pulled it out.

She looked to see where the others were. Claudia and Wakanda were coming up the steps. Oscar sniffed and nosed about the snowy ground past the patio's snow-covered fireplace. The earth dipped where the dog searched.

"That's where I found him."

The male voice startled Regi, and she nearly dropped the key. She glanced over to see a slump-shouldered man standing beside her. He held a can of beer in one hand and an unlit cigarette and lighter in the other. Regi could see that the door to the cabin was open, so that's where he'd come from. The man's haunted eyes reminded her of a gargoyle's.

A shudder glanced through Regi, and it wasn't from the cold. At that moment, Oscar saw the man as well and sounded the alarm with a loud attack bark. He charged across the snow, growling and snarling.

Regi reached for the dog's collar, latching on and holding him back, grateful she'd brought Oscar with her on this long trip. "It's all right, boy," she said then turned to the man. "You're Herman?"

He nodded and stepped away, glaring at the dog as though he were poison.

"I'm Samuel's fiancée, Regi." She watched the man's reaction. He didn't seem surprised.

"Figured you must be *his* people." He set his beer can near his feet, nervously flicked the lighter and lit up, then pocketed the lighter and picked up his beer again.

Regi didn't care for the way he'd said "his." Claudia and Wakanda reached the top step out of breath. They stood beside Regi and the upset dog that had calmed down slightly now that the man was outnumbered.

Regi thought about Herman's first comment. "When you say, that's where you found *him*, do you mean that's where Jake's body was found?"

He appeared rattled, nervously tugging at an eyebrow. "Shada Baranov told me not to talk to anyone about this." Even though Herman had just lit his cigarette, he dropped it into his beer can. It sizzled. The subject obviously upset him enough to waste his smoke.

Irritated, Regi spat out, "I bet she did. Look, Mr. Degelder, Samuel loved Big Jake. Talked of him often. I don't know who you saw kill the man, but it wasn't Samuel."

"Herman," Claudia stepped in. She scowled at Regi before turning her attention back to the man. "Would you show us around the cabin?" Though Regi knew her sister had no desire to stay here and was fearful of this guy, she'd never show it. She knew how to hide behind her diplomacy mask.

He turned and abruptly ran into Wakanda. His fist clenched, and his arm jerked, ready to punch her.

Oscar growled. The fur around his neck rose as the dog bared his teeth.

Herman stared at the Irish setter and then at all of them. Probably realizing he was in a no-win situation, he said, "Sorry. Reflex. You startled me." He opened the door wider so they could go inside.

Regi didn't believe him but walked past him into a beautiful kitchen with pine cabinets and granite countertops. Regi set her pack down. To her right was the living room with a vaulted ceiling, stone fireplace, and landscape window that made the room feel like part of nature. At one side, a sliding glass door led out to a small deck. A plush sea-green couch and cozy chair stood adjacent to the fireplace. The dining room was just off the living room. Above the knotty-pine table hung a chandelier made of moose antlers.

Herman pointed past the kitchen. "The master bedroom is down the hall and to your right. There's a loft upstairs. I'm sure you ladies would like some privacy." He headed to the stairwell and disappeared down the stairs to the basement.

"What a creepy man. Though I sort of feel sorry for him." Claudia glanced around the kitchen then started opening and closing the cabinets, studying the contents. "I don't trust him, and I still don't think we should stay here."

"It will be all right. Besides, we can keep an eye on him if we're here." Regi was sure she was doing the right thing.

"Nice place," Wakanda said, changing the subject as she sat down on the couch.

Regi glanced around again. She had to admit, it didn't look like a cabin that had been neglected for years while Samuel lived in Idaho. But he did plan to give it to her as a wedding present so maybe he'd had it renovated.

"Let's check the rest of the place. I want to know how many doors it has." Regi walked through the kitchen to the hallway and turned right to check the master bedroom. Claudia followed her.

"Spacious." Claudia seemed to admire the king-sized bed and rustic artwork on the walls. Regi peered out a sliding glass door and saw that the deck went the full length of the cabin and included the glass-door exit from the living room. She realized the glass door in the bedroom would make a good place to break in. She double-checked the lock.

"Let's go upstairs." Claudia hurried out.

Regi closed the curtains before leaving, thinking it made the room less inviting from the outside. As she passed the kitchen on her way to the spiral staircase, she remembered that Jack's cell phone needed to be charged. She dug it out of her backpack and plugged it in. That done, she shouldered her pack once again and followed her sister.

Upstairs, they found that the loft had picture windows as well and a balcony overlooking the living room. There was a bathroom at one side and a queen-sized bed pushed up against another wall. Drawn to the railing of the balcony, Regi looked down into the living room and found Wakanda still relaxing on the couch below. "You should come up and take a look."

Wakanda shook her head. "Like where I'm at."

"I don't know about you guys"—Regi looked at Claudia and down at Wakanda—"but I think we should stay in the same room together."

Wakanda nodded, and Claudia agreed.

Regi felt there was safety in numbers. As they made their way down the steps to the main floor, Claudia's eyes were drawn to the stairs where Herman had disappeared. "Do you suppose there's a lock on that door?"

Regi started for the steps.

"Where are you going?" Claudia grabbed her arm.

"To lock it."

"Not now, with him in there. He'll know he made us nervous."

Regi shrugged, pulled her pack around, and dug out her revolver. "I'm not nervous."

"Put that away." Claudia squirmed in her UGG boots.

"Look." Regi pushed the cylinder open. "I always leave one bullet out for safety. There's nothing to fear." She clicked it back in place. "You really should learn how to handle a gun. It would give you more confidence."

"I have plenty of confidence when I need it. I don't want a gun. And I don't want one near me." She sat on the other end of the couch.

Wakanda grabbed her backpack. "Just so you know . . ." She unzipped it and pulled out a Glock G19. "Tucker insisted I take it. A pilot never flies into the back country without a gun of some type."

Regi chuckled. "See, Claud. We're well protected."

Wakanda put it back in her bag and zipped it shut.

"Honestly," Claudia said as she rubbed her forehead. "I don't know what scares me worse—Herman or you two and your guns." She gave a heavy sigh. "But I must admit that I do feel better knowing that you have them."

Wakanda's stomach growled. They hadn't eaten since early morning.

"I'm hungry too," Regi said.

Claudia tapped her chin. "The cabinets are empty, and the fridge is bare, so we need to go back to town."

"While you're buying groceries, Wakanda can track down Leon Smarch. He's the fellow Samuel sold Jake's boat to. And I'll find Trace." Regi felt her pocket for Jack's cell phone and remembered she'd plugged it in. She hoped it had been long enough to get some juice in it. She quickly retrieved the phone. Both Regi and Wakanda shouldered their backpacks.

Claudia stared at the two of them, relief showing on her face that they weren't leaving their packs and what was hidden within. "Well, let's get going."

As Regi pulled away from the cabin, Claudia asked Wakanda what she wanted to eat. Regi saw a basement curtain move. Herman stood at the window, watching them pull away. His steely-eyed stare caught Regi's attention.

A cold shiver streaked over her skin. She now knew what evil looked like.

CHAPTER TWENTY-THREE

A truth revealed,
a secret still hidden,
and Raven watches all.

TRACE SAT ON A CHAIR on the other side of the cell door. Samuel looked at the young man through the bars. When Trace first arrived, he'd told Samuel that he'd stopped to see how he was doing. Samuel told him that Regi had arrived and things were looking up. From there, the conversation had lagged.

"Something bothering you?" Samuel asked, wanting to help and hoping he had the answers.

"Where do I start?" Trace leaned his elbows on his knees and stared down at the floor. "I keep thinking about how awful I treated you. I knocked you unconscious, beat you up, kept you drugged, and then hauled you up here to Alaska."

"You were only doing what your mother and the Clan wanted you to do." Samuel gazed at Trace. He knew by the remorse in his voice that the young man was ashamed about what he'd done. Wanting to lighten the mood, Samuel said, "But when you put it like that, yeah, you were pretty tough on me." Samuel chuckled.

Trace looked up. A slight smile tugged at the corners of his mouth but faded quickly. "I'm sorry." He grew silent again, like he wanted to say something but didn't know how. Rubbing his chin and taking a deep breath, he said, "I keep thinking about that prayer you said when we were in trouble on the boat." Trace leaned back on the folding chair. "You're not a shaman, you don't dress in prayer robes, and yet your prayer was answered."

Samuel nodded. He knew Trace was being prompted by the Spirit to ask questions. Samuel had experienced how the Spirit could guide and direct a person who was in tune and wanted to learn more. "My church believes anyone can pray for help and receive an answer. It may not always be the answer you want, but there's always an answer. I mean, look where I am."

"Thanks to me," Trace added.

Samuel didn't want to turn the conversation back to that. He thought a moment and said, "Trace, have you ever studied the Mormon Church?"

"Never gave it a thought until a few days ago."

Samuel didn't know where to begin. The Church had so many answers to life's questions and was rich with doctrine that helped a person through life. Should he tell him about the miracle of the priesthood and how men were given special keys and powers from God? Should he tell him about the temples and how families could go there and be sealed together for time and all eternity? Or should he tell him about how the gospel came to earth? All at once, he knew what to say. "Trace, there's a scripture in the New Testament. Do you own a Bible?"

Trace shook his head. "You're joking, right?"

This was going to be harder than Samuel thought. "Okay, then." His mind spun, wondering where to start. He thought of the story that struck a chord with him. "In the early 1800s, there was a boy. He was struggling to understand religion. He read in the Bible that anyone who lacked wisdom needed to ask God for help and He'd help them. So early one morning, the boy went to a grove of trees not far from his home so he could pray without being disturbed." This was the part that had always made Samuel wonder, but now, after all he'd been through—not only with Trace but also with Regi—he *knew* this story was indeed true.

Emotion swelled in Samuel, thickening his throat and making his insides quiver. In a low, soft voice, Samuel continued. "While he prayed, a horrible darkness pressed down upon the boy, so strong he thought he would die." Samuel looked straight into Trace's eyes. "But the boy kept praying. A glorious light chased away the darkness and shone all around. Within the light were two Beings."

Caught up in the story, Trace said, "The Great Raven and the Wolf?"

Not certain if Trace were joking, Samuel kept a serious tone. "No. They were personages whose brightness and glory defied description." Samuel paused so Trace could think about what he'd said. He continued. "One of them said, '*This is My Beloved Son. Hear Him!*'"

"So who were they?"

"God the Father and His Son Jesus Christ." Samuel took a deep breath.

"Really." Trace sighed. "I know that a type of god for the Clan is Raven. How could god be a bird? That doesn't make sense. Hasn't since I was old enough to think things through."

"Maybe Raven is a metaphor for God, and as the story was passed down through generations, that was left out. The boy I was telling you about, Joseph Smith, was young like you when he started thinking things through." As Samuel had told the story, he knew it would forever be near and dear to his heart. He hoped it would for Trace as well.

"Only stands to reason that God would be a personage, doesn't it?" Trace asked.

"I think so."

"Where can I learn more about your church?"

"The Book of Mormon is a good place to start. Mine's at home in Idaho, but I'm sure you can get your hands on one somewhere around here." He thought of Morning Joy. "There's a Church leader and his family who live here. He's not home. His wife said he was participating in the Iditarod and is in Anchorage right now, but she's still here. She's not leaving until tomorrow. I'm sure she'd have a copy for you."

"Are you talking about Morning Joy Winder?" Trace perked up.

"She didn't tell me her last name, but she's probably the one. She talked the officers into letting Regi in to see me." Samuel was happy that Trace might know her.

"She and her husband left the Clan because they converted to a different religion. But I didn't think it was the Mormons. It was something like the Church of Jesus." Trace folded his arms, trying to think.

"Yes, that's it. *Mormon* is a nickname for people who are members of The Church of Jesus Christ of Latter-day Saints. It's all the same church." Samuel hoped he hadn't confused Trace too much.

"If my mom found out I was looking into that religion, she'd skin me." Trace's tone sounded concerned, and yet the gleam in his eyes said he was excited at the prospect.

"I don't want to cause family problems. There's enough of that right now." Samuel couldn't afford to give Shada any more ammunition to use against him.

"Mom hasn't been acting normal ever since Herman found Grandfather's body. Herman's been worried about her. Since it happened, he's been over to our place off and on all the time."

Samuel scooted to the edge of his folding chair. Why would Herman be worried about Shada? Why should he care? The puzzle of why the man was now stepping forward, willing to tell a lie that he'd seen Samuel kill Big Jake, was beginning to come together, yet the pieces didn't quite fit. Why would Herman betray Samuel like this? Samuel paid him a good wage for his services and gave him a place to live. All he had to do was take care of the cabin and land.

As Samuel thought about it, he was relieved that he'd warned Regi against staying at the cabin. The puzzlement over Herman kept growing, but Samuel needed more information. "When Herman comes to visit your mother, do you hear what they talk about?"

"No. They usually leave right after he comes. They spend a lot of time at the Thirsty Beaver. Why?"

"Don't you find it odd that after Big Jake was recovered, Herman and your mother started seeing each other?" Samuel asked.

"Yeah. I'll do what I can to find out what's going on with them." Trace stood, folded the chair, and leaned it against the wall.

"Thanks," Samuel said as he watched the young man leave. A nauseating feeling churned in Samuel's gut. He should have told Trace he wasn't his father, but he couldn't. Not now. Not until . . . he didn't know when. He'd have to rely on the Spirit to guide him.

He only hoped he was worthy and in tune enough to receive God's prompting.

CHAPTER TWENTY-FOUR

With nocked arrow in her bow
Caribou Girl hunts
for a sign.

ON THE QUIET RIDE TO town, Regi couldn't shake the image of Herman staring at her through the window. As she pulled into the parking lot of the only grocery store in town, she wondered how wise it was to split up. "Maybe we should stay together."

"I agree," Claudia said. "But we're fighting the clock. We need food, but we need information more. I'll grab a few supplies while you two check on that fellow who owns the boat. I'll be okay. That shouldn't take too long. You can pick me up before you try to find Trace."

"No." Regi couldn't explain it, but she felt they needed to stay together. "It won't take long to grab cheese and crackers."

"We need protein," Wakanda said from the backseat.

"She's right, Reg. We need to keep up our strength." Claudia's cheeks were a little flushed.

Regi realized that fewer than twenty-four hours ago, Claudia had been ill. And she'd already had a lot of drama today. Regi looked at the people coming and going from the market. Shopping for food might ease Claudia's mind and make her feel normal. "You're probably right. But if Herman shows up, don't talk to him." Regi knew she was being paranoid, but she didn't care.

"I won't." Claudia got out of the car. "You two be careful." She shut the door and hurried inside.

With great reluctance, Regi pulled away and drove to the harbor, which wasn't far. Parking the car, Regi looked out on the boats bobbing in the water. The sun was setting even though it was only 4:30 in the afternoon. Most of the fishermen had gone home, except those who lived on their vessels. Regi was hoping Leon stayed on his.

"Any idea where to start?" Wakanda asked as she unbuckled her seat belt.

"Not a clue." Regi got out of the car. Walking down the tin-covered gangplank to the dock, Regi and Wakanda watched as Oscar sniffed here and there ahead of them and then moved on.

The docks rolled with the waves. A pungent, salty-sea smell rode the damp air. An occasional seagull flew overhead. "Samuel once told me that Big Jake's seiner was named the *Isabelle*. I don't know if Mr. Smarch changed the name or not." Regi hoped he'd left it the same.

They walked down row A, passing fishermen who were tending their ships or walking down the dock to go ashore. Some were Native Alaskans, some Caucasians. Regi asked the first person who passed where the *Isabelle* was docked. He glared at her, mumbled, and hurried on his way. The others hurried past before she could say anything. Finding Mr. Smarch and the *Isabelle* was not going to be easy, especially if everyone avoided her as if she had bird flu. "What's the deal?" Regi asked Wakanda.

"Small town, like Trailhead. Word travels fast." Wakanda shrugged.

"Oh, that reminds me. I better call Morgan. Go on ahead and see if any of the boats have the name *Isabelle* painted on them."

Wakanda moved along, leaving Regi alone with Oscar. She pulled Jack's cell from her pocket, grateful she'd recharged it a little. She pressed the RECENT CALL icon and tapped Morgan's number. After eight rings, Regi was about to give up, but Effie answered. "Morgan residence."

"Effie, this is Regi Bernard."

"Regi! Where have you been? Thomas has been sick with worry over you."

Regi felt bad that she hadn't called sooner, but she had tried. "I called this morning but got a busy signal."

"Don't doubt that none. Been as busy as summer roundup around here."

"Can I speak with Morgan?"

"Sorry, hon. After running into so many dead ends trying to find out if you were alive or dead, he packed a suitcase and left."

"What?"

"He's heading to Alaska right this minute."

"But who's watching over Hannah and Trailhead?" Regi felt horrible that Morgan left home to hunt for her.

"Don't you worry none about Hannah. I'm takin' care of her. And Superintendent Elliott is keeping an eye on the town. Let me give you the sheriff's cell number."

After Effie rattled it off and hung up, Regi quickly dialed the sheriff. It went straight to voice mail. And as she tried to think of what to say, the signal dropped. If Regi ran into one more dead end, she was going to—

"No *Isabelle*." Wakanda had returned.

"Well, that's just great!" Regi shoved Jack's phone into her parka pocket and pulled out the keys to the car. As she turned around to head for the vehicle, she noticed that a fellow a few boats down had walked out from his cabin and was scraping ice from the deck. She motioned for Wakanda to follow her.

"Excuse me, sir. Could you direct me to the *Isabelle*?"

He stopped, leaned on his shovel, and said, "Not from around here, are you?" His chin held neglected stubble. His eyes were drawn to Wakanda, taking in her long gray braids and deerskin coat. "'Cept maybe her."

"We're both from Idaho. I need to talk with Leon Smarch, who owns the *Isabelle*." Regi clutched the keys to the SUV in her gloved hand, hoping and praying under her breath that he would guide them in the right direction.

"Why you lookin' for him?" The man sniffed loudly and rubbed his nose on the sleeve of his coat.

"Years ago my fiancé sold him the *Isabelle*." Regi watched the man rear back and blink a few times. She continued. "I hoped I could ask him some questions."

"You're too late." He chipped away at the ice.

"Did he already leave?" Regi panned the parking lot, wondering if Smarch had been one of the men they'd walked past.

"Yeah. 'Bout five years ago." He stopped and glanced at her. "So you're the fiancée of the guy who killed Big Jake?"

Shocked and horrified that this man asked such an absurd question, Regi spat back, "Samuel Tanner didn't kill anyone, let alone the man he thought of as a father."

The man shrugged. "Going to be hard to prove since there's an eyewitness."

"That's a lie." Regi felt the entire town was against them.

Wakanda took hold of Regi's elbow to try to guide her away from confrontation.

The man leaned his shovel on the seiner cabin and leaped to the dock, blocking them. "Sorry to upset you, ma'am. I have a habit of saying what's on my mind without thinking. Come, sit awhile on the *Isabelle*."

Regi glared at him as he guided them onto the boat. "You said the *Isabelle* was gone."

"No, I didn't. I said Leon Smarch was gone." He led them to the cabin and opened the door.

"You misled us into thinking his ship was gone as well," Wakanda said.

"Possibly. But I don't take to strangers asking about my boat."

"Why are you telling us now, then?" Regi pocketed her keys and sat on a bench seat in the dinette area. Wakanda stood beside her. Oscar had followed them in and was sniffing at the cupboards and floor.

"Guess I felt sorry for you. Saw you poking around the docks and knew you were probably looking for me." He pulled off his gloves and sat across from her with the small table between them. "Leon sold me the *Isabelle* 'bout five years ago. After he bought it, he had one thing after another go wrong. So when the ship needed a new engine, he was tapped out. I put a four-hundred-horsepower diesel in her, even refurbished the bridge deck with swivel captain chairs."

Regi glanced around. Years ago, Samuel had been on this very ship. He'd probably eaten many meals at this very table. Regi cleared her throat. "What's your name?"

"Leroy Smarch. Leon is my brother." He smiled like he'd played a joke on them.

Regi wasn't laughing. She'd had enough of this man and his surprises. "Okay, Leroy. Let's get a few things straight."

Wakanda cleared her throat and seemed to step into Claudia's shoes of trying to calm Regi down before she said something she'd regret. It worked.

Regi rethought what she planned to say. "Is there any way we can get in touch with your brother?"

"Moved down to the lower forty-eight."

So Leon was out of the picture. Regi had to deal with Leroy, but her mind was blank as to what to ask next.

Wakanda came to her rescue. "When you refurbished the boat, did you find anything unusual?"

"Not much space on a boat. What you see is pretty much what you get." He glanced around at the close quarters. "When I renovated, I left this pretty much the same as Big Jake had it, though I did replace the floor. The bridge deck was totally redone. I wanted to make it my own. Come take a look." He motioned for them to follow. Oscar was fussing at the door, like he needed to go out.

Before either Regi or Wakanda could do anything, Leroy opened the door, allowing the dog to escape.

Wakanda glared at the man and then glanced at Regi. It was obvious she didn't want to leave Regi alone with this stranger. But Oscar could quickly get lost in this strange town. Regi felt she'd be all right. "Go ahead and get the dog. I won't be long." Besides, if things got out of control, Regi had her gun in her backpack.

Reluctantly, Wakanda trailed after the dog, whistling for him as she left the cabin. That would draw attention to anyone close by. Regi smiled to herself. Her friend was trying her best to do two jobs at the same time.

Regi followed Leroy up the steps to the bridge. He turned on the lights.

He sat in one of the two padded swivel chairs. In front of him was a panel filled with instruments, to the side a laptop computer, and above a radio and mic.

"In all the times I've heard of Big Jake's boat, I never pictured this," she said as her eyes panned the area.

"Wasn't this way when he had it." He motioned to the instrument panel. "Had all this installed. Makes fishing a whole lot easier with this radar showing where fish cluster."

Regi noticed a strip of rawhide with beading tied to the wheel.

Following her eyes, Leroy said, "That's my good luck charm. Don't know what it is exactly. Found it under the dinette stuck between the floor and the wall when we pulled up the linoleum."

The beads were made of bone, red jasper agates, and flint. It looked like it had been part of a bigger piece. "I can see why you kept it; it's pretty." Regi smiled.

"Don't care if it's pretty. Must have been under there even when Big Jake owned the boat, so it's a part of the vessel's history. That's why I kept it." Leroy motioned for Regi to have a seat. "Now that it's just you and me, tell me what you wanted to talk with my brother about."

Regi didn't know if she could trust this Leroy person. After all, he hadn't been exactly upfront with her about who he was and that he owned the *Isabelle*. This man liked to play games. If Leon had been the one who killed Big Jake, his brother might very well have been in on it with him. Leroy saying there was an eyewitness to the crime may have been his way of distracting Regi from getting at the truth. She had to be careful and not tip her hand. "I wondered if he could help me understand what was going on when he bought the boat from Samuel. I mean, did Shada, Big

Jake's daughter, give him a hard time? Or was there anyone else who came snooping around back then?"

"Oh. I was hoping I could help you out. But I was living in Vancouver at that time. Didn't come up here until Leon started having financial troubles." He scrubbed his whiskery face with his calloused hand. "Sorry."

"It's okay. It was a long shot." Regi rose. "Thanks for showing me Jake's boat. I've heard a lot about it." Regi turned to leave when Leroy grabbed her hand. She tried to pull away, but his grasp was firm.

"Be careful." Leroy had a very serious, very concerned look on his face, which struck Regi as odd. This guy really didn't know her at all, yet he seemed earnest. He continued. "There are people in this town who don't like strangers poking around. Especially strangers who are trying to help someone they don't like."

Was that a veiled threat? Or was he really trying to help her? Regi didn't know. What she did know was the ship's bridge was closing in on her, and she had to get out. Wanting to appear calm and not rattled, she replied, "I appreciate the advice." She glanced down at his hand that still held her captive. "Can I go now?"

"Oh, yes." He slowly released her.

Regi quickly made a dash for the exit. She could hear Leroy following close behind. Was he coming after her? Escaping out the door, she found the sun had already set. Only a few meager lights lit the swaying dock. Anxious to put distance between herself and Leroy, she stepped out and immediately slipped and nearly fell on the icy deck, but Leroy caught her.

He steadied her, holding her close. "Ran out of deicer. Been trying to keep the ice off, but it's a constant battle this time of year."

Regi wiggled away. Grabbing the rail, she climbed down from the boat. She wanted to appear nonchalant, so she said, "Be seeing you around."

He waved, and Regi could swear he winked. "Count on it," he said.

So now he was coming on to her? She had to get away from this man. As she walked down the swaying dock, she couldn't see Wakanda or Oscar. Where had they disappeared to?

She thought she heard footsteps behind her. Was Leroy chasing her down? She quickly glanced behind.

No one was there. Fog from the ocean crawled over the dock like tentacles. The world seemed mystical and eerie at the same time.

Her stomach twisted.

Her skin tingled like it did whenever she watched a scary movie. But this wasn't a movie. Trying to calm down, she took comfort that she carried a gun in her backpack and started walking.

Again, she heard footsteps. It had to be her imagination. Not stopping to check, she raced to the tin-covered gangplank and leaped up the steps to the parking area. Wakanda and Oscar should have been there waiting for her, but the lot was empty except for a few trucks and Morning Joy's SUV.

Footsteps pounded up the gangplank, nearly on her heels. She slung her pack around and unzipped it to grab her gun, but a strong hand caught her from behind and swung her around.

Barely able to take a breath, she looked up into the determined eyes of a very tall Native Alaskan.

CHAPTER TWENTY-FIVE

Harpoon ready,
Seal Hunter waits to strike.
Ice freezes the hole.

SAMUEL FINISHED THE MEAL MORNING Joy had brought by the jail. That she'd taken the time to prepare him a meal while packing to join her husband in Anchorage for the beginning of the Iditarod was amazing. Morning Joy must be a genuine, loving person, trying to do what she thought the Lord would want her to do in her husband's absence.

It had been many years since Samuel had tasted salmon baked in skunk cabbage leaves. Rolled within the meat were onions, potatoes, and carrots. And bless her heart, she'd also brought him sugar-coated fried bread covered with raspberry jam. This was the best meal Samuel had eaten in well over a week. Morning Joy had also unexpectedly brought him a copy of the Book of Mormon. Said she'd been prompted to bring it.

Samuel set the empty tray aside on his bed and picked up the book. *If only I'd had this when Trace was here.* At least Samuel had it now. He had told her that Trace wanted to read it and asked Morning Joy if he could give it to him. She was thrilled and told him of course he could.

The doorknob to the jail turned. The guard was probably coming to collect the tray. Samuel grabbed it and went to the bars to meet him as Herman Degelder walked in. Samuel nearly dropped the tray.

"Surprised to see me?" Herman closed the door behind him.

Samuel smelled cigarette smoke and alcohol as his accuser neared. He didn't reply to Herman's question but instead said, "How did you get past the guards?"

Herman cast his eyes to the floor. "Jones was the only one on duty. He got a call about someone shooting a gun and left."

"How do you know?"

"I called it in." A joker smile turned Herman's lips up before he burst into laughter.

"Why?" Samuel didn't know where this was going, but it was obvious that Herman was either very drunk or psychotic.

"Just wanted you to know that I'm quitting as your caretaker." Herman had a defiant air about him, as if he were looking for a fight. Samuel was wary of this man and, at the same time, extremely curious. All these years he thought Herman was just down on his luck, a confirmed bachelor who couldn't catch a break. He'd worked for Samuel for more than ten years. Samuel thought he knew Herman well and that he was trustworthy. "Tell me, Herman, what secret does Shada hold over you that makes you so afraid that you're willing to lie?"

Herman reared back and glared. The mild-mannered redneck who Samuel had felt sorry for all those years was gone. "You think you're so smart. It's not what she knows about *me*. It's what I know about *her*."

Samuel hadn't expected that. "What do you mean?"

"I've said too much." Herman backed away, heading for the door. "Before I move out though, I'll take good care of those lady friends of yours staying at the cabin. Very spirited that one with the cowboy hat. And her snobby sister—she could stand to learn a thing or two."

Regi had gone against his wishes and was staying at the cabin! Pure panic coursed through Samuel's veins. "Herman! If you do anything to harm them, I'll . . ."

"You'll what?" He chuckled. "Not much you can do behind bars." He winked and left.

Samuel threw the empty food tray at the wall. "Get back here!" But Herman was gone, and Samuel knew he wasn't coming back. Rage, fear, guilt, and panic collapsed on him. Frustrated beyond belief, he grabbed the tin tray off the floor and began banging it against the cell door, while yelling at the top of his lungs, "Jones!"

No one came. Dropping the tray to the floor, he grabbed the iron bars and yelled, "Please, God. Help us!"

Through the misty crystals of fog, Regi stared up at the Alaskan. She spat out, "What do you want?" If she pulled the gun out in front of him at this close range, he could easily overpower her and steal the weapon.

"I'm here to help you," he said as he stepped back. "Sorry to grab you like that, but when I saw you leaving my grandfather's boat, I thought I should warn you about Leroy."

This guy didn't look at all like Leroy Smarch. "You're related to Leroy?"

The young man shook his head. "I'm screwin' this up. No. I should have said the *Isabelle used* to belong to my grandfather."

Regi instantly knew who this was. Trace Baranov. The man who had beaten and kidnapped Samuel, the man who had ruined her wedding day, and the man who was claiming that Samuel was his father. A whirlpool of emotions swirled her insides. Staring up at his dark face that she really couldn't see clearly because of fog and poor lighting, she realized he was close to her son's age. She tried to calm down. Even though Samuel had made his peace with Trace, Regi still didn't trust him, especially after the way he'd jumped her just now. "Why did you need to warn me about Leroy?"

"He's not honorable."

Regi tisked. "You're hardly one to talk about honor. I'll have you know that it's only a matter of time before the US Marshals, FBI, and a ton of other authorities beat down your door and charge you with kidnapping." She wanted to get away from him, so she started walking toward the SUV, scanning the lot and hoping for a glimpse of Wakanda and Oscar. They had to be here somewhere.

Unless . . . She stopped and studied Trace. Had he done something to Wakanda and the dog? A nervousness befell her, but she had to hide it.

Trace hadn't moved. "You may not think my bringing Samuel to Alaska was honorable, but it was Clan justice."

She could tell by the tone in his voice that he was sincere; however, that didn't cut it with Regi. She couldn't believe Samuel wanted her to ask Trace for help with investigating. Frustration and anger overcame her fear of being alone with Trace. "Kidnapping is not honorable, no matter what. Plus, you beat him."

Trace hung his head. "You have to understand, I have hated Samuel Tanner for years. He left my mother and me and took all of my grandfather's money, his company, and his home. After they found Grandfather's remains buried at his cabin and Herman told my mother that he'd seen Samuel burying something the night Grandfather disappeared—even though he thought Samuel was working on the water main . . ." Regi heard him suck air between his teeth. "It all came to a head. So when Mom loaded up my bag with syringes and sent me down to get Samuel, all those years, all the deceit, crowded in on me, and I was very angry."

Regi thought about what he'd said regarding Herman. "Wait a minute. I thought Herman claimed he actually saw Samuel kill Big Jake."

"Guess he thinks if he saw him burying my grandfather, that meant Samuel killed him." Trace didn't seem to realize the problem.

"That's a far cry from witnessing someone killing another person." Regi could hardly wait to get ahold of that Stillman fellow and tell him what she'd just learned. "Do you know what mountain Stillman goes to when he does his shaman thing?" She dug in her pocket, anxious to find the SUV key. If she had to, she'd track Stillman down with fog lights. And where in the world did Wakanda and Oscar disappear to?

"No. No one knows. But he should be back tomorrow."

"Shoot." Regi folded her arms, not wanting to accept defeat but knowing that she'd waste time and energy searching for the man at night. "Guess it can wait until then." She scanned the foggy parking lot again. "Did you see an older woman walking a dog when you arrived?"

He shook his head and nervously gazed around. At first Regi thought he was helping her look, but then she realized he seemed more afraid that someone would see him with her, though that was highly unlikely in this fog. Odd. "Trace, are you worried someone will see you talking with me?"

"No . . . yes." He took a deep breath. "It would be best if my mother and the Clan didn't know we were speaking. I took a risk visiting Samuel earlier. But I had to. He's my father."

For a moment, Regi forgot her fear of him when she heard the proud sincerity in his voice. No wonder Samuel didn't have the heart to tell this young man the truth. She wasn't going to meddle with the subject, but she was going to press him for more information. "Who do you think killed your grandfather?"

Trace shrugged. "I was only nine when he disappeared. Don't remember much."

"Leroy Smarch showed me around your grandfather's seiner. Did you ever go fishing with Jake?" Regi thought if she got Trace talking about his grandfather, something might jog his memory.

"I only went on his boat a few times. I didn't see him very often. He and my mother didn't get along." He kicked at a clump of snow that had fallen from the bumper of the SUV. "When he would come to visit, she'd send me out of the room because Mom and Grandpa usually argued." Trace looked away, staring off in the distance.

"What did they argue about?"

"Money." Trace seemed more and more uncomfortable. "My mother hasn't had an easy life. She raised me by herself." A defensive tone rode his words.

"Believe me, Trace, I understand." Regi remembered how hard the last five years had been raising her kids.

Oscar galloped across the parking lot to Regi. The Irish setter sniffed at Trace and growled. "There you are." She patted the dog's head. Relief washed over her. Not only was she glad Oscar was all right, but now she also felt protected. She saw Wakanda's silhouette walking toward them.

Trace became even more nervous. "I want to help you where I can."

Oscar's growls deepened, making Trace step back. He started quickly walking away.

"Find me in the morning, and we'll talk more," Regi called after him.

Wakanda had reached her. "Who was that?"

"One scared kid I don't trust." Regi watched as Trace's shadow disappeared in the fog.

CHAPTER TWENTY-SIX

Wise Owl hides
Devilfish's radiance beneath
his wing while searching for truth.

WHAT HAD HE DONE? AFTER talking with Regi, Trace realized he was between a razor-sharp rock and a very hard place. By doing his mother's and the Clan's bidding and bringing Samuel to Alaska for justice, he'd probably broken a number of laws he'd never thought about. The Clan thought it the honorable thing to do, but he could tell by the way Regi spoke that the rest of the world would not.

However, Samuel seemed to have forgiven Trace. When this was over, he hoped Regi could forgive him too. He pulled his coat collar up around his ears. The fog from the ocean seemed to have lifted in town. Slushy snow clung to his boots, but he plodded toward home. Somewhere between Idaho and Alaska he'd misplaced his knit ski cap, and the chill of the night was biting his cheeks. He'd probably lost it at sea. Thoughts of the storm that nearly sank the boat made him shudder even more. By some kind of fluke, he and Samuel had survived. Though he really didn't think it was a fluke.

No . . . it was an answer to Samuel's prayer. Trace could not deny what he'd seen and what he'd been through. Nor could he deny that he greatly respected Samuel Tanner . . . his father. Over the years, Trace's mother had always said Samuel had stolen Trace's heritage. He'd believed her until he and Samuel were caught in that horrible storm. Now Trace wasn't sure what to believe, except that deep inside he wondered if his mother was wrong.

His mother was a good person. She loved him, and he loved her. She'd always been there for him . . . most of the time. But she meant to always be there. Whenever she would forget to pick him up from school or to come to a hockey game, she always felt bad and told him that she loved him. And whenever she forgot Christmas, she made up for it by buying something even more expensive than what he'd wanted. And every birthday, no matter where she was or what she was doing, at four in the morning, she would wake Trace up and tell him how much she loved him. If she was home, she sang to him and gave him a Pop-Tart with whipped cream and a candle on top. Shada Baranov wasn't the typical PTA, cookies-and-milk kind of mother, but Trace knew she loved him.

He'd arrived at the trailer court where they lived. Theirs was at the end of the lane. Quiet blanketed him as he walked down the road. The kitchen lights were on, which meant Mom had company because she never cooked unless someone was visiting.

Had to be a guy. Trace didn't feel like meeting yet another boyfriend, so he entered through the back and sneaked toward his room. If he was lucky, his mom and her friend would be drunk and wouldn't hear him.

"Does Samuel have a clue what's going on?" a male voice said.

Trace stopped. He didn't recognize the voice right off, but it was familiar. Curious, Trace quietly eased down the hallway. The kitchen was at the far end on the other side of the living room. Drawing near, he chanced a peek.

The man was seated at the table, his back toward Trace.

His mother was pacing. "I think he's still in shock. You shouldn't have risked coming here. What if someone saw you?"

"So what if they did? I could very well be here on Clan business." He reached out and took her hand.

She smiled at him. Trace strained to see who her visitor was. He was older and heavyset. Tempted to step closer, Trace halted when his mother caressed the man's cheek, leaned over, and kissed him on the lips. It grossed Trace out to watch old couples kissing, especially his mother.

When they finished, the man took her hand and kissed it.

"Must have been a real eye-opener when Trace got the drop on ol' Sam and hauled him up here," Shada said. "Trace told me the injections helped a great deal. Thanks for giving them to me. Would've liked to have been a fly on the wall the day Trace nabbed him."

Scenes from the day he'd taken Samuel captive reeled through Trace's mind. He was ashamed and filled with regret for how harshly he'd treated him.

"Samuel may be many things, but he isn't stupid, Shada. He's going to figure this out." The man scooted his chair away from the table and pulled her onto his lap.

She kissed the tip of his nose. "He can't do much in jail. As long as you keep Chief Taku believing a speedy trial is best, the truth will never come out."

"Heard his woman and two others are staying at the cabin," the man said. "They could cause trouble."

Trace's mother caressed the man's forehead. She planted a big slobbery kiss on his lips then leaned back. "Don't worry. Herman will take care of them. And then we can take care of Herman."

"How did you make Herman go along with all this?" Jealousy threaded the man's concerned voice.

"You don't really want to know, do you?" She nuzzled his ear. "Besides, I always save my best for you. Have for years."

The man was old enough to be Trace's grandfather. Sickened by spying, Trace really didn't care anymore who this guy was. He carefully eased back to make his way to his room.

"Our son is quite something going to Idaho and hauling him back here like that." The man's voice, though low, caught Trace midstep.

Son?

Trace felt his gut clench and his vision blur. The walls of the trailer closed in. The man couldn't be talking about him. His mother had said Samuel was his father. She wouldn't have lied about something so important. She may have many faults, but she wouldn't lie to her own son about something like this, would she?

"Trace is very loyal. A trait he didn't inherit from you," his mother said.

They *were* talking about him. Leaning against the wall, Trace felt as though the ground beneath him had given way. He must have heard them wrong. Trace's first instinct was to barrel in there and make them tell him what was going on. What gave them the right to screw around with him? Their son—his mom's and this man's? Why would they say that, especially when they thought they were alone, unless it was true? There was no other explanation for what he'd just heard. Why would they keep such a secret from him? Anger twisted tight in his gut. No more secrets. He was going to make them face him.

About to make his presence known, Trace heard his mother say, "Before we go further, you must tell me why you volunteered to represent Samuel." She stood, allowing the man to stand as well. He came into full view.

Kenway Stillman!

A frisson flashed over Trace's skin. Nausea crawled up his throat as he watched the man who had pretended to be a shaman, the man who had betrayed Samuel, the man who was his father.

Revulsion pulled Trace down the hall and out the back door. He ran fast and hard. Lies buzzed in his head like angry bees, stinging and taunting him. He needed to be alone.

He needed . . .

He needed help.

But he didn't know where to turn or where to go. Samuel. He could go to him, but he was in jail. And besides, how could Trace face him and tell Samuel he wasn't his father? Did Samuel know? If he did, why didn't he tell Trace? Unless he wanted to believe it. Unless Samuel wanted Trace to be his son. Trace's head throbbed.

He ran down the road, out of the trailer park, and onto the highway. He raced up a lane that led to the city park. Leaving the snowplowed street, he tromped through knee-high snow to a grove of secluded pines. He went there often as a child, whenever he couldn't deal with his mother's boyfriends or the fights she had with his grandfather.

Trace went to listen to the pines swish in the wind, feel the breeze pick up his troubles and carry them to Raven. But he was no longer a child who believed in such tales. His mind went to Samuel and his prayer on the boat. When all seemed lost, he'd prayed to his God.

All seemed lost now.

Trace knelt down in the snow and poured out his heart to whatever god would listen.

Regi tossed and turned most of the night. The couch was lumpy. Wakanda snored. And Claudia made funny sleeping sighs. But worse than that, Regi couldn't shut off her mind. First, she worried about Samuel. His face was bruised, and he looked like he'd lost about ten pounds from abuse and worry. She couldn't imagine how he'd lived through the last week.

She planned to visit him first thing in the morning and tell him what Trace had said about Herman. Clearly, he had not seen the actual murder. Even the Clan should know the difference.

Regi turned over, fluffed her pillow, and pulled the goose-down comforter up around her neck. From this position, she could see out the sliding glass door that led to the deck. A strange glow lit the outside. What was going on? Curious, she padded her way to the door for a closer look. Despite her thermal underwear, she shivered as her eyes panned luminescent ribbons arching though the night sky in shades of green and purple light.

The Northern Lights.

Yearning to see them without the barrier of the door, Regi stuck her bare feet into her boots and tugged on her coat. As she pulled the glass door open, Oscar tried to dart out. "No you don't," she whispered. "You'll run off, and an old grizzly will eat you. You're staying inside." She glanced back at the couch and easy chair where Wakanda and Claudia were sleeping. They slept on undisturbed.

Regi slipped past the dog and closed the door. As she walked to the edge of the deck, snow crunched beneath her feet. Herman hadn't shoveled here for a while. She took a deep breath. The cold prickled her nose hairs and stung her cheeks, but she didn't care. The show taking place above her was worth a few moments in the freezing air. Shadows of pine trees were silhouetted by the greenish glow that cast the earth in a surreal, quiet wonder. She felt as though she were on a different planet, far away from the trouble that surrounded her.

She wished Samuel were here with her and hoped he could see the heavenly spectacle.

Samuel didn't hear anyone return until well into the night. As soon as he heard movement in the office, Samuel yelled to draw attention. It took a minute for someone to come to the doorway, and Samuel was disappointed when he noticed it was a deputy he'd never seen before. His name tag read Deputy Taggart. Samuel asked, "Where's Jones?"

"Off duty."

"You've got to call him. Herman prank called him to lure him away, and then Herman broke in to see me." Samuel felt encouraged that Taggart seemed to believe him because he stepped closer to the cell.

"Jones said at the end of his shift that he drove all over town looking for some guy with a gun." Taggart appeared concerned. "He was pretty upset. Said he left the office locked up, but the lock was broken when I arrived."

This bit of information fueled Samuel's fear that Herman would hurt Regi. "You have to call Jones and have him drive out to my cabin. Herman threatened to hurt my fiancée."

"Jones was just coming off a twenty-four hour shift. Told me to not leave the place and put the answering machine on in case another prank call came in." Taggart rubbed the back of his neck, looking pretty tired. "We're shorthanded around here. Jones won't admit it, but he takes his phone off the hook when he goes to bed. There's no way I can get in touch with him unless I go to his place."

"Then go." Samuel was beyond desperate.

"They'd have my badge if I left after Herman broke in here. Can't lock up with the door busted. And if I left the place unlocked to check on a lead a prisoner gave me . . . well, you can see my dilemma. Settle down. When I get off in the morning, I'll swing by your cabin and check on your woman. Herman spouts off when he's drunk. His bark is worse than his bite. I'm sure we'll find him sleeping it off in the morning." Taggart left, shutting the door behind him.

Samuel paced about in his cell like a cornered cougar. Finally, out of pure exhaustion, he sank down on his cot and pulled the scratchy blanket around him. Though he left his clothes on to sleep, he was still cold. What he'd give to take a long, hot shower. He felt grimy and soiled, like a dirty rag. He marveled that his disheveled appearance hadn't phased Regi. She loved him. That she had flown up here to help was nothing short of a miracle. After all Regi had been through, Samuel didn't know if he was worthy of her love. He should have done more—for her and for the others involved. Over the years, he should have done more to help Trace. And he should have done more to help Big Jake.

Big Jake.

How he missed his wise old friend. Samuel's thoughts drifted to the scene of Herman standing outside his cell. After Herman's threats, Samuel couldn't help but think he had something to do with Big Jake's death. Samuel now knew Herman was capable of anything. *Lord, what am I supposed to do?*

Samuel prayed and tossed and turned. And then he noticed a glow coming from his cell window. He knew exactly what it was . . . the Aurora Borealis. He'd seen it many times when he'd lived here before. But tonight he was drawn to it like a river fly to a porch light.

Bathed in light from the window, he watched the green luminescent glow in the sky. Samuel felt that somehow, through the spectacle in the heavens, the Lord was reaching out to him, letting him know all would be well. He and Regi would have a life together. Surely this was a sign. He thought of when Trace had seen the phosphorescent organisms in the ocean after they'd survived the storm and had thought they were a sign as well. Samuel had scoffed under his breath then; but now? Maybe he was reading too much into this extraordinary moment. He didn't know what to think anymore.

Gazing at the bright lights, Samuel thought of long ago when Big Jake had told him about the Aurora Borealis. He had said there were two stories about how the lights came to be: one from the Inuits and one from Saami people in Scandinavia. Though the Inuits were distant relatives of Jake's, he preferred the story from the Saami.

Samuel couldn't remember the entire tale, something about how the Sun fell in love with Moon Daughter. But his heat was too much for her, so she ran away across the icy tundra. Coming to the ocean, she found a hut and slept through the day. At nightfall she was awakened by the arrival of Northern Light warriors and their leader. Moon Daughter hid in the forest while the warriors feasted. Tired, they went to bed—everyone except the warriors' leader. He sensed Moon Daughter's presence. He called to her. She timidly emerged from the shadows. When their eyes met, they fell in love and raced into each other's arms.

Samuel thought of Regi. Their love had finally emerged from the shadows of mistrust, guilt, and sorrow. Things had been back on track for them. They were going to get married and would finally have their happily ever after. And then all this happened. His mind went back to the rest of the story.

The Sun hurtled a burning shaft of light at the warrior leader, but Moon Daughter saved him with her shield until he could escape. However, the Sun seized Moon Daughter and threw her into the arms of Mother Moon. Moon Daughter's shadow still drapes night's silver orb. And so the legend was, when the northern lights shine brightest, the warrior leader and his warriors search for Moon Daughter.

Was Regi like Moon Daughter? And would Samuel always be searching for her, their love forbidden like the legend of the northern lights? Silly thought. Regi and Samuel were human beings of flesh and blood. Samuel loved her. She loved him.

And they would be together.

Somehow.

Someway.

Someday.

Overcome by the chill of subzero weather, Regi decided to go inside. Turning, she was shocked to see Herman Degelder leaning against the cabin next to the door. How did he get there without her hearing him? Unless he had been there when she came out. Had he been silently standing there watching her? Obviously, he wanted to scare her or he would have said something. She decided to ignore him and go back in. But as she neared the door, he stepped in front of her. He stank like a brewery. His head tilted as he studied her.

He cleared his throat and stepped forward. She backed up against the deck railing.

"Enjoying the show?" He glanced up at the sky, but she knew he was aware of her every move. At any moment, he could reach out and grab her.

A claw of terror scraped down Regi's back.

CHAPTER TWENTY-SEVEN

Seal Hunter throws his harpoon,
wounding Devilfish,
yet evil goes undefeated.

KNOWING THAT PANIC WAS HER enemy just as much as Herman, Regi asked, "What are you doing?" Her insides quivered, and her knees threatened to buckle, but she had to hold it together.

"Came out to see the lights, like you." He stepped beside her, reached into his coat pocket, and pulled out a pack of cigarettes and a lighter.

The nerve of the man, scaring her to death and then lighting up next to her like they were friends or something. But wasn't that how a real killer worked? They made their prey think everything was normal before striking. She had to get away, had to get inside.

Then she remembered what Trace had said about Herman and what he claimed he'd seen the night Big Jake had died. Her need for information to free Samuel took over. "I heard from a good source that you merely watched someone bury something on the night Jake went missing. You do know that is completely different from actually seeing someone kill another person, right?"

"Lady . . ." He lit up but kept the lighter flaming for a moment. The glow drew her attention to his pimple-scarred face. Gazing at her in the meager light, he said, "Believe me, I know what murder is." He flipped the lighter shut.

White-hot terror sucked the breath from Regi. She started for the door, but he grabbed her arm. She reflexively twisted his arm back and spun around out of his grasp. He flipped his cigarette into the snow and came at her.

At that moment, Oscar started barking and making a ruckus from behind the glass door of the living room. A light flipped on. Wakanda or Claudia must have heard the dog.

Herman leaped down the snowy deck steps and disappeared around the cabin.

Wakanda opened the sliding glass door. "You all right?" Oscar burst out, charging across the deck, barking and growling.

Regi gasped for breath, relieved to see her friend and the dog. "I am now." She grabbed Oscar's collar and guided him inside. Passing Wakanda, she said, "Call the police."

"An answering machine?" Regi couldn't believe it. "What kind of rinky-dink police department uses an answering machine?" She gazed at Wakanda, who sat beside her on the couch.

Wakanda pulled a blanket around Regi's shoulders. "Doesn't surprise me. Probably won't be anyone there until morning," Wakanda said. "You have to understand that these little towns don't have the manpower. In Trailhead, all Morgan has is Thelma Watts to answer his missed calls."

"But at least she's a person. What do they do here in the case of an emergency?" Claudia sat on the other side of Regi, wide-eyed and staring at the glass door like Herman might charge through at any moment.

"They've learned to deal." Wakanda checked the lock on the door then closed the drapes. Grabbing her backpack off the floor, she took out her Glock. "From what you said, Herman's probably long gone for now. Like most wild animals, he's all bluster."

Regi remembered the threatening tone of his voice. "I don't know, Wak."

"I have my gun, you have yours, and we have Oscar. We're loaded for bear. If he so much as shows his face, he's a dead man. Try to settle down and get some sleep."

"Sleep?" Claudia rubbed her eyes. "Like that's going to happen."

Regi knew Wakanda was right. But she also knew sleep would be impossible. She kept wondering how long Herman had been standing at the door before she stepped out on the deck. Had he been watching them all night? He was a creepy little man. She looked at her sister, who sat beside her, biting her lips together, fear smearing her face. Regi took hold of the blanket Wakanda had placed over her shoulders and reached around her sister, wrapping them both up.

Claudia relaxed a little, leaning on Regi. Regi eased back on the couch and kept her eyes on the door.

Regi was dressed and fixing breakfast when Claudia and Wakanda stirred around eight the next morning. Both looked shocked that Regi had cooked crispy bacon, fried eggs, and golden hash browns. They quickly tugged their clothes on and joined her at the table.

"This looks great. Samuel has been a good influence on you, but shouldn't we just leave?" Claudia glanced nervously at Regi.

Regi had been unable to sleep, so she'd decided to make breakfast in the hopes of waking the others. She wanted to get the heck out of Dodge, but she didn't want to appear panicked out of her mind, even though she was.

Wakanda plopped down on her chair and set her gun on the table, her gray braids in disarray, her puffy eyes barely open. Yawning, she said, "I don't think Herman is in his cave." Wakanda poured maple syrup on her eggs and hash browns as though the absence of pancakes didn't matter to her morning syrup fix. "Didn't hear him."

Regi chuckled. "You've been sleeping."

"I can still hear things." Wakanda grabbed her fork.

Claudia took a bite of bacon then sank down on her chair, giving in to her hunger.

Regi put ketchup on her eggs then said between mouthfuls, "We need to hurry. I want to file a report on Herman and see Samuel right away. Want to let him know I spoke with Trace last night and what we found out from Leroy Smarch on the *Isabelle*."

"Are you going to tell Samuel we're staying at the cabin and what happened last night with Herman?" Claudia chomped her toast and chewed as quickly as she could but still managed to wipe her mouth with her napkin at all the appropriate moments.

Regi did not relish facing Samuel after going directly against his wishes. "Once I explain to him that now the police will be looking more closely into Herman and his motives in all this, well, that might outweigh Samuel being upset with me. Anyway, I hope it does."

"That Smarch guy was odd," Wakanda said.

"Why do you think that?" Regi asked. *Odd* was how most folks described Wakanda, not the other way around.

"Well, why didn't he just lend the money to his brother or go into business with him instead of buying him out? You and Claudia have a partnership at the Raindancer. Might be the younger brother is covering up something for the older brother." Wakanda shoveled the maple-coated eggs into her mouth.

Regi had to admit Wakanda had a point. Plus, she remembered that Trace had said the man wasn't honorable. It could be that Leroy knew more than he was telling. "We'll check into that right after I fess up to Samuel. And I want to track down that Stillman character and tell him what Trace told me about Herman only *seeing* someone burying something. That's a far cry from murder."

"What do you need me to do today?" Claudia asked as she picked up her and Regi's empty plates. Wakanda took her last bite and handed her plate to Claudia, who turned and put the dishes in the sink.

Oscar was whining at the door. Regi had to make a quick stop in the bathroom. "Why don't you and Wakanda take Oscar out? I'll only be a second. We'll talk about what else needs to be done on our way to the police station." She pulled the keys out of her pocket and tossed them to her sister. "And please warm up the car."

Claudia caught the keys and tugged on her parka. Wakanda shouldered her backpack and grabbed her gun off the table. They'd be safe should Herman decide to make an appearance.

"Come on, boy." Claudia opened the door, and Oscar bolted out, followed by the two women.

Regi hurried as fast as she could to finish her business. Even though she knew she was safe, she still didn't like being alone. She scooped her backpack off the floor and left the cabin, locking the door behind her, which reminded her that she needed to talk to Samuel about firing Herman and then get the man's keys from him . . . or change the locks.

Wakanda was getting out of the driver's side of the running SUV when Regi came down the steps. By the look on her face, Regi could tell Wakanda was more comfortable flying a plane than driving a car. Regi was surprised her sister wasn't with her.

"Where's Claudia?"

Wakanda immediately scanned the area. "She was here a minute ago."

"Wak!"

"The dog is with her; she's all right," Wakanda defended, though her graying brows were pinched together with worry. Regi's fear was mushrooming into panic. She marched over to Herman's door and pounded on it just in case he was in there.

Wakanda followed and stood silently beside her, watching. Always watching.

Regi pounded harder. "Herman! Open up!"

Her heart slammed against her ribs. If this nut job hurt her sister, Regi'd tear him apart.

"Regi!" Claudia's voice came from down the road near the bend that headed toward the cabin. She was holding onto Oscar's collar as if afraid to let him go. "Come quick!"

Relief flooded Regi as she and Wakanda hurried down the snow-packed roadway. When they joined Claudia, Regi asked, "What's the matter?"

"Down the road." Claudia was shaking, her face pale. They hurried along.

Coming to the turnoff from the main highway, Regi saw the form of a man lying in the snowbank. "Who is it?" she questioned Claudia as they drew near. Her sister didn't seem able to answer.

Splatters of blood reddened the snow. Worried that the person could be seriously injured, Regi reached out and pulled the man over.

Herman Degelder's cold, lifeless eyes stared up at her.

CHAPTER TWENTY-EIGHT

Blinded by misfortune,
Caribou Girl does not see
the storm swelling overhead.

SAMUEL HARDLY SLEPT. BUT HE was roused from dozing by the sound of scuffling in the outer police office. Something was going on.

"Taggart! Jones!" Samuel yelled. No one came.

The door remained closed, and the noise of many feet faded away. Had they left him alone?

"Hey! Anybody out there?" Samuel yelled again.

The doorknob turned, and in walked a puffy-eyed Officer Jones. He'd obviously been awakened from a deep sleep. "Have a problem in here?" His ledge of bushy brows pinched together.

"What's going on?" Samuel needed to know.

Jones shook his head. "Seems Herman got himself killed last night. Don't know how that happened, do you?" He glared at Samuel through the bars.

Samuel's mouth dropped open. For a second, he forgot to breathe. His mind was hit head-on with fear over what had happened at the cabin. "No idea. Didn't Taggart tell you about last night and how Herman came in here—while you were gone, I might add—and threatened my fiancée?"

Jones studied Samuel for a moment, eyeing him up and down. "Yep. And I find it very strange that the day after your fiancée visited, the star witness in the murder case is run over and killed . . . and she's the person who calls it in. Anything you want to tell me?"

Samuel had to remain calm. Any movement or anything he said could be interpreted wrong. A gut-wrenching feeling tore through him as he realized if Jones was in any way a good investigative cop, he would soon find out that Samuel and Regi had been suspects in Romney's murder case. And though Romney's murder had nothing to do with Samuel's current situation, it definitely looked bad.

Samuel knew if the police could pin Herman's death on Samuel and Regi, they would solve two cases in one blow—Jake's murder from long ago and Herman's. Talk about being dealt a bad hand. Slapping on his poker face, Samuel shrugged. "No."

"Well, from what Taggart told me, you were mighty upset last night, believing that Herman might hurt your girl. Now Herman is dead. Too coincidental for my taste." Jones glared at him through the bars.

What could Samuel say? What could he do? Then he realized the answer. Though he'd been afraid of it, he knew telling the truth, all the truth, was his only course. Jones had tried to reassure Samuel that Stillman would find members of the Church here, so the man had compassion in him . . . somewhere.

"Look . . . Regi and I were going to be married on the day Trace took me. She's a good, honest, hardworking woman. She would never hurt anyone."

Jones skeptically folded his arms looking like he'd heard it all before.

"Yesterday was the first time we'd seen each other in nearly a week. She's been worried sick over me. And I've been worried about her. What do you think we talked about in the ten minutes we were together after being torn apart like that?"

Jones took a deep breath but said nothing.

"If you think we plotted to kill Herman, go ask Morning Joy. She was here the entire time."

"You better believe I will." Jones turned and left.

Samuel stumbled back to his cot. The sun was barely up. What else could go wrong today?

When the last cop car pulled away, Regi felt like she'd been dragged over ten miles of gravel. She turned to find Claudia and Wakanda waiting for her. Their worried faces reflected her own fear, but she had to somehow cheer them up. "Feels like old times, doesn't it?"

Claudia looped her arm through Regi's as they walked back to the cabin. "We'll get through this." Obviously, her sister saw through her act and knew Regi was just as upset as she was.

"Thank heaven we have each other. Did you see the look on their faces?" Regi would never forget the officers' condemning eyes or the skeptical tilt of their heads. She'd seen that look before, in Trailhead when the rangers and state troopers had questioned her about Romney.

Both Claudia and Wakanda were silent.

"They think we killed him," Regi said. The reality of the situation came alive with the spoken word. Regi caught her breath and added, "They think we ran him over."

"But they checked the SUV and couldn't even find a dent." Claudia was always the optimist. "Whoever ran down Herman should have a good dented bumper covered with blood."

Wakanda grunted. "Fresh blood wipes off."

Claudia shot her a work-with-me-here look.

Regi knew her sister had the best intentions, but so did Wakanda. She was a realist, which was what they all needed to be at the moment. They climbed the steps up to the cabin and went inside. Oscar slipped in with them and quickly curled up near a heat vent. Plopping down on a chair, Regi said, "We can't wait for the Malamute cops to put things together. We're going to need some outside help."

They sat at the table, where only hours ago they'd wolfed down their breakfast and had been planning a very different day. Regi pulled out her cell phone and dialed the number Effie had given her for Morgan.

"Who are you calling?" Claudia asked.

"Morgan. I tried to get him yesterday, but Effie said he'd left for Alaska." Claudia huffed. "Thanks for telling us."

"With everything going on last night, I forgot." Regi rubbed her hand over the table as she listened to one ring after another.

"So if he's not home, who are you calling?" Wakanda piped up, concern and curiosity on her somber face.

"Morgan's cell." Regi ended the call. "He's still not picking up. I don't know if he's flying or what. Samuel told me Morgan has a friend with the US Marshals based in Anchorage and that Morgan was calling him about our trouble a day or so ago. Help is on the way. Question is, when will it get here? Could be a couple of hours or a couple of days. We can't wait." She tugged off Samuel's cowboy hat, playing with the rim. Her fingers felt the scripture. The words *tribulation, patience, experience,* and *hope* came to her mind once again. Hope was hard to hang on to. Experience though . . . experience could boil down to doing something you know you should.

"I keep thinking about how Wakanda said last night that we need to deal with our problem. I think we need to be proactive."

"But what else can we do?" Claudia sat on the edge of her seat.

Regi thought for a moment. "We need to fly to Anchorage ourselves."

Claudia looped a lock of hair behind her ear. "You know, Wakanda knows, and I know that Herman's death was no accident and that the police will try to blame us. If we all three leave, it's going to appear mighty suspicious." Claudia had that worried, mother-hen look in her eye. "But maybe we should go because whoever killed Big Jake is afraid we're going to find out who they are. Herman was a warning."

"Even more reason to fly to Anchorage to get help." Regi knew that statement closed the argument.

Silence fell upon them as they realized the seriousness of their situation and the trials they might face.

"It will work," Wakanda said in her Indian-knows-all tone.

Regi prayed she was right.

Regi walked up to the police station, Oscar close to her side. She'd left Wakanda and Claudia in the running car. She just had to see Samuel before flying off to find help. First, she planned to apologize for not doing what he'd asked, and then she was going to tell him what happened last night and that she was off to get the cavalry.

She pushed through the door. A stern-faced officer sat behind the desk. He glanced up and said, "No dogs allowed."

"He's not bothering anyone," Regi defended.

The officer was the same guy who had been on duty when she'd visited yesterday—Jones. By the grimace on his face, he was not pleased to see her. Well, she wasn't thrilled to see him either. Still she asked, "Could I visit Samuel?"

He shook his head. "Not today. And not with a dog."

"Oscar can stay out here with you."

A blank stare.

"Come on. What's the dog going to do?" Regi's patience was threadbare.

Jones sniffed and cleared his throat. "You can't see Tanner because the last time you did a man died the next day. I'm not pointing a finger, merely stating a fact." He resumed looking at the paperwork in front of him.

"That's ridiculous. I had nothing to do with Herman's death." Regi folded her arms, glaring at the man who chose to ignore her even though she stood before his desk. "He was hit by a car. That's it. That has nothing to do with me talking to Samuel."

He glanced up, his face still unamused.

"Your officers checked my SUV and found nothing."

"Time will tell."

With her back against the wall, Regi said, "Samuel doesn't have time. Your shotgun court is Monday. I need to see him now."

"Nope. And you need to work on your flattering bribe routine." Jones picked up the phone, dismissing her.

Regi jerked the receiver out of his hand. "Listen up, bub! A killer is out there. Probably the same man who killed Big Jake. How you can sit here and pass judgment on an innocent man is beyond me. Help is coming for Samuel, and when it gets here, you'll be sorry. I thought—"

"Are you threatening a police officer?" He didn't let her finish. "I know what you're doing. You want me to get mad and throw you in jail with Samuel. Not going to happen. So leave. Leave now, and take your dog with you." He jerked the phone from her hand and pointed to the door with it.

Defeated and feeling like a scolded child, Regi retraced her steps. Stopping at the door, she glanced back. "Officer Jones, I'm saying this in all sincerity—no threat, no ulterior motive—but you're going to regret sending me away." With that, she and Oscar walked out.

Regi could hardly wait to reach Anchorage. She sped to the airport in record time. While Wakanda warmed up the plane, Claudia loaded their gear. Regi's job was to check in with Cooper Clawson.

As Regi walked into Clawson's office, she was surprised to find Morning Joy sitting on her suitcase, tears in her eyes, and no sign of Cooper. "What's wrong?"

Morning Joy swiped her hand over her cheek. "Cooper's plane's broken down. She's in the hangar out back trying to fix it."

"She seems like a capable person. She'll probably have her plane working in no time." Regi patted Morning Joy's back.

"But I'll be too late to help Preston with the dogs. The race starts at ten tomorrow morning. If I don't get there today, it's going to throw him off. As soon as he leaves Anchorage, I'll need to drive his truck to Campbell Airstrip. It's the first checkpoint. I've got to get there. Preston works so hard for this race and his dogs." Morning Joy's bottom lips trembled, her round Alaskan face flushing.

"He'll understand."

"I know. Preston's a good man. But he trains all year for the Iditarod. And if I'm not . . ." Morning Joy put her hand over her mouth like she wanted to take back her words. "I shouldn't be complaining to you. You have a lot more to worry about than I do. I plan to tell Preston all about your troubles as soon as I see him. I know he'll help if he can."

Regi didn't know if the woman had heard about Herman or not, but she didn't want to risk worrying her about something else. "Actually, things are looking better for Samuel." Regi wasn't lying. Herman's death meant someone else was involved in Jake's murder and not Samuel. Problem was, Regi, Claudia, and Wakanda were the only ones to see it. Plus, they were now suspects, but there was no need to bother Morning Joy about all that.

"Oh, that's a relief. I could tell he's a good man. He loves you so much." Morning Joy patted Regi's hand.

"In fact, Wakanda is flying me and Claudia to Anchorage this morning to check on some new leads." A light went on in Regi's mind. "Why don't you ride with us?"

Morning Joy jumped to her feet. "Really?"

Regi didn't think Wakanda would mind.

At that moment, Cooper walked in the back door carrying an engine part in an oily rag, her husky trailing behind. Grease smudged Cooper's cheek. Her oil-stained coveralls looked like they'd never been washed. "Morning Joy, I'm going nowhere until I can get a new carburetor. This one's shot, but I've gotta get this fixed soon. I have to have a flyable plane here in case of emergencies."

"No problem. Regi offered me a ride in their plane." Morning Joy picked up her suitcase.

"You're going to the Iditarod with your man in jail?" Cooper stared at Regi.

"No! We're just going up and back today." Regi didn't want to tell her that she planned on knocking on the Marshals' office door and for good measure the FBI's as well. However, Cooper's accusing words clung to Regi.

"Mind if I hitch a ride? I've got to get my plane fixed." Cooper set the broken carburetor on her desk and wiped her hands on the rag. She grabbed an empty box and placed the engine part in it.

"Why not. Taking your dog?"

"Roy's good here. He keeps watch on the place. Never had a break in." Cooper tugged her coat on then put the box under her arm and headed for the door. Morning Joy followed her, lugging her suitcase. Regi needed to get ahead of them so she could warn Wakanda. But there was no need. Wakanda, followed by Oscar, met them as Cooper closed the door and locked it. She watched as Cooper and Morning Joy made their way across the tarmac to the Blue Lady.

Wakanda turned to Regi. "Where they going?"

Regi quickly explained the situation.

"Five people. That's too much weight in my plane," Wakanda said, staring at Regi.

Again, Cooper's words came to Regi. *You're going with your man in jail?* Regi knew what she had to do. "I'll stay behind. I still need to talk with Samuel. I really don't feel right leaving him anyway."

"But there's a killer on the loose!" Wakanda glared at her.

"Don't you think I know that? If I have to, I'll just hang out at the jail. No one is going to bother me there." Regi had to admit she was scared at the prospects. "Do you want to tell Morning Joy she can't go be with her husband? And Cooper has to have that engine part. Besides, you'll be back before the end of the day."

"Keep Oscar with you at all times." Wakanda reluctantly gave in to the idea.

"I will. I'll be fine," Regi reassured her. "Hurry and leave so you can get back."

By late afternoon, Samuel was nearly out of his mind with worry. He'd expected Regi to visit him. He thought he'd heard her voice a couple of times, but she'd never appeared. Samuel had never been so frustrated in his entire life. In order to take his mind off of Regi, he decided to try to think about who could have run down Herman. Why would someone kill him? Herman was the eyewitness. Whoever did it must have believed that Herman was no longer an asset to the case against Samuel. And if he wasn't an asset, he had turned into a liability. So Herman had to know something that the killer didn't want made public.

Herman had been in over his head. His death was no accident. In a normal court of law, where the eyewitness could no longer testify, the case was dismissed. However, Samuel had a feeling the Clan's justice council didn't work that way. Especially if they believed Regi or Claudia or Wakanda had anything to do with Herman's death.

Samuel had to figure this out and fast.

CHAPTER TWENTY-NINE

*Calamity preys on
all in Raven's world.
The storm billows and blows.*

REGI HAD TRIED EVERYTHING SHE could think of to get Officer Jones to let her in to see Samuel, but he wouldn't budge. Frustrated, she decided she wasn't going to hang out at the police department when she could very well do a little detective work.

She had her gun and Oscar with her. She'd be safe enough. However, she found herself on one wild goose chase after another. At the harbor, she learned that Leroy Smarch had taken a crew out on the *Isabelle* and wasn't expected back until late.

Thanks to an attendant at the gas station, she learned where the Baranovs lived. Trace had said he'd help her today, but she'd been away from the cabin most of the day. And he could have stopped by earlier during all the commotion over finding Herman dead and the cops and paramedics storming the cabin, witnessed the hubbub, and left. Regi tried to remember if Samuel had mentioned that Trace had a job, but nothing came to mind. She knew Trace didn't want to be seen with her, but she didn't think an innocent visit to his house would raise questions. She hoped people would see it as her just wanting to meet the people who had been such a big part of Samuel's life.

Regi drove through the trailer court and pulled up to the Baranov trailer. With Oscar by her side, she walked up to the door, knocked several times, and waited. No one answered.

No one was home. Regi had to admit she had not only come here for Trace, but she'd also wanted to meet Shada. That woman had turned Samuel and Regi's world upside down with her outlandish accusations, and Regi wanted to look her in the eye. But she obviously wasn't home. Regi couldn't very well stand on the porch and wait.

Hungry and wanting a Snickers bar to tide her over until she could think of somewhere else she could go, Regi left. She pulled into the grocery store parking lot. "Don't let anyone in the car," she told Oscar. "And don't go with anyone should they somehow open the door. I'll only be a minute." The Irish setter whined as if he understood. She knew most people would think she was nuts for talking to an animal, but she didn't care. She had to talk to someone . . . something. And, really, who knew how much animals could comprehend?

She planned to keep an eye on the SUV through the store window. On top of everything else, Regi didn't want something to happen to Oscar. She could see the cash registers from here. Surely candy bars were right by the checkout.

After getting out, she locked the doors and headed in. The Snickers were right where she thought they'd be. Thank heaven that was one constant. People wanted their chocolate fixes handy. She waited in line behind a large, walrus-sized man who was buying a loaf of crusty artisan bread, a large bottle of wine, and a round of brie cheese. As the cashier tore his receipt from the till, she said, "Have a good day."

The clerk turned and swiped Regi's candy bar.

"That will be three fifty." The gum-chomping, nail-biting teenage girl held out her hand.

"Three fifty?" Regi was shocked at how expensive it was. She stared at the regular-sized candy bar. "Does something come with it?" Her sarcastic question was lost on the teen, who impatiently waited for Regi to hand over her cash.

Digging in her jacket pocket, she found a five-dollar bill and handed it over. Everything cost so much more up here. Gas, food, peace of mind. The cashier gave her change, and Regi headed out. No more splurging on candy. But she consoled herself with the thought that because she was alone she needed a little extra something. She walked toward the car.

"Are you a friend of Samuel Tanner?"

The voice startled Regi. She turned to find the man who had stood in front of her in line. She'd lost track of him in her amazement over the cost of her candy bar. "I am. And you're?"

"Kenway Stillman. I'm representing Samuel next week." Jostling his grocery bag, he offered Regi his hand to shake.

This was the man whom she had wanted to track down and tell that Herman didn't actually see the murder. But now that Herman was dead, that didn't really matter. Taking the man's hand, she found his grasp sweaty and limp. "I'm Regi Bernard. So you're back from communing with nature?"

"Excuse me?" He seemed confused. His mustache shifted to one side as he thought about what she'd just said.

"Samuel told me you went to the mountains to think before the trial. Said you were a shaman." Regi wanted to hear what he planned to do to help Samuel, so she tried to sound interested, when in actuality, she wanted to quiz him on why he would go out of town when he was supposed to be working on saving Samuel. Shaman or not, she thought his priorities were screwed up.

"I told him that hoping he'd relax a bit."

Regi'd never heard of such a thing. "How would knowing that the person representing him was taking off for the mountains help Samuel relax? Good grief. The man is going to be tried for murder. You should be working on his defense, trying to solve the case, or at the very least notifying authorities about the show-and-pony court that's going on here. I'm not a lawyer, but even I know that trying him Monday negates his right to due process." She suddenly realized she may have said too much. Stillman was part of the community, part of the Raven Clan. In fact, he sat on the council, which should have been a conflict of interest and automatically ruled him out of representing Samuel, but things obviously worked differently here.

"Maybe where you come from, stomping around and shooting off your mouth will get you somewhere." The man glared at her. If looks could kill, Regi would have been mortally wounded. He continued. "But here in Alaska, not so much. Right now, I'm heading over to Chief Taku's place. Going to sip some fine wine, eat bread and cheese, and have a discussion about what to do with Mr. Tanner since the eyewitness has turned up dead. I think I can get the chief to drop the charges if Samuel would be willing to make a token contribution to Jake's daughter and the Clan. Chief Taku is interested in justice and feels that Samuel inheriting all of Jake's assets wasn't fair. Samuel sharing what was rightfully someone else's might satisfy the chief."

"Really?" This was the first good news Regi'd heard in a long, long time. Yet something needled at her subconscious. "You think they'll let him off just like that?"

"I do, or I wouldn't have paid inflated prices for cheap wine. I know what the chief likes." Stillman started walking away.

"Have you told Samuel?" Regi knew he needed to hear some good news.

"Don't want to get his hopes up, but I'll tell him as soon as there's an agreement." Stillman waved good-bye and seemed grateful to be finished with her then got into his car.

Regi hustled to the SUV. Oscar yipped as she climbed in. "Happy to see me?" She rubbed behind his ears. "I'm happy to see you too." Maybe she could drive over to the police station and try her luck at seeing Samuel once again. She thought about what Stillman had said about not getting Samuel's hopes up. And if she was somehow able to get in to see him, she knew she'd tell him. Maybe it was best to wait.

"Shoot." She realized she should have gotten Stillman's phone number so she could check with him later. Sticking the key in the ignition, she decided to go to the cabin, freshen up, let Oscar go for a long run, and then come back to town. Surely by that time, Stillman's meeting with the chief would be over and he would have told Samuel the good news.

And by then Wakanda and Claudia would be back from Anchorage, and hopefully they'd have the Marshals with them so they could investigate Big Jake's murder.

Yes, she would wait until tonight.

Starting the car, she pulled away from the grocery store, hopeful that good news was on the horizon.

Oscar bounded across the snow as Regi unlocked the door to the cabin. He was going to be wet and stinky, but he'd been such a good dog following her around all day. Plus, he was acting like a puppy again. There must be something in the fresh Alaskan air that exhilarated the dog because his arthritis and the pin in his leg had hardly bothered him here.

She'd let him roam a bit while she got him something to eat. Last night when Claudia'd stocked up on groceries, she bought a bag of dog food too. Regi filled one bowl with fresh water then loaded another with dried chunks of bone-shaped food. As she went to the door to call the dog, she heard a noise downstairs.

Downstairs where Herman lived.

Had lived.

What the—? Was someone down there? There'd been no car parked out front when she'd driven up. Wakanda and Claudia weren't there.

She cautiously made her way to the staircase that led to the basement. Herman was dead. She'd seen his stiff body this morning, watched as the paramedics had driven away, answered all the probing questions the cops had thrown at her. No one should be in the cabin except her.

She held still, hoping and praying she'd heard the house settling or the furnace kicking on.

Another thump and bump.

It sounded like furniture tipping over. Someone was down there.

Where was her backpack?

She'd left it on the counter. Stepping ever so slowly and carefully to the bag, she unzipped it and pulled out her Lady Smith. With her right hand firmly holding the handle and her left hand supporting underneath, she pointed the barrel down the staircase.

What was she doing? The best thing to do would be to sneak out, drive to town, and get help.

Yes! A win-win solution.

She quickly put her gun back in her pack, slung it over her shoulder, grabbed her coat, and headed for the door. But she stopped dead in her tracks when she heard a key unlock the basement door and footsteps coming up the stairs.

Nobody had a key except Regi.

And Herman.

But he was dead.

With sudden clarity, Regi knew whoever was coming up had run down Herman and had possibly killed Big Jake.

The door to the jail opened. Samuel leaped to his feet, hopeful it was Regi.

Trace walked in. Worry clouded his face. "We've got to talk."

"What's the matter?" Though he was disappointed it wasn't Regi, Samuel was glad to see the young man. At least he was a friendly face.

"You hear about Herman?" Trace grabbed the folding chair by the door and set it next to the cell. Samuel sat on his.

"Yes. Jones told me. He had some harebrained idea that Regi and I had something to do with it." Samuel was still trying to figure that one out.

Trace stared down at the floor, looking like he was trying to find the words for what he was about to say. He finally looked up. "He's wrong. Herman's death is my fault."

CHAPTER THIRTY

Wise Owl sends
Seal Hunter Devilfish's radiance,
arming him for battle.

"Your fault?" Samuel didn't see that one coming. How could Herman's death be Trace's fault? It didn't make sense, though Samuel knew from past experience that Trace could pack a punch. But Samuel also knew he wasn't capable of actually taking someone's life.

Trace's hand shook as he rubbed his chin and the back of his neck. Wanting him to calm down and tell him what was going on, Samuel tried again. "What happened?"

"I should have gone to the police last night, and he might still be alive, but . . ." Trace huffed. "When I got home, I knew Mom had company so I sneaked in the back and overheard her talking with this . . . man . . ." His voice trailed off.

Samuel didn't know what this had to do with Herman's death, but he knew Trace would eventually tie it together. "Who was it?"

"Kenway Stillman." Trace stared at Samuel, gauging his reaction.

Samuel didn't see anything wrong with Stillman talking with Shada. He was probably asking questions for the trial. But Stillman had said he was going away. "I thought Stillman went to the mountains. But it's not surprising that he spoke with your mother. She is accusing me of murder, and Stillman's representing me, so he's probably snooping around, trying to find out what your mother knows about Jake's death."

"I don't think that was why he was there. He and Mom were . . ." Trace sighed deeply. "They were locking lips and all that."

That was definitely a conflict of interest. While TV dramas showed lawyers of opposing sides being friendly with each other, kissing was taking it a step further, and Shada wasn't a lawyer. Something stunk about this, but was it smelly enough to dismiss the charges? Would the Clan's justice council even listen to Samuel if he were to bring this up, especially since Stillman was part of the council? The only way to make them listen would be if Trace helped. "Would you testify to the Clan about what you saw?"

Trace rubbed his brow. "I don't think it will help. While Mom and Stillman were kissing, they said things."

"To you?"

"No. I stayed hidden. They didn't even know I was there. But as they were talking, Stillman mentioned . . ." Trace clenched his teeth together and shook his head. Looking straight at Samuel, he said, "Stillman said he was my father."

Samuel's jaw dropped.

"And Mom pretty much confirmed it, saying that I inherited certain traits from him."

Samuel's mind whirled with everything he knew about Stillman. He had said he was a shaman, and Samuel had figured that was why Big Jake hadn't cared for the guy, but what if it was something else? What if Big Jake had somehow learned that Stillman was playing around with Shada and got her pregnant? Now that would be a big reason to hate the man, especially if Stillman had refused to marry her. Samuel looked into Trace's eyes. His heart went out to the kid. Reaching through the bars, Samuel patted his shoulder.

Trace stared at him. "But she told me that you were my father. And I believed her. She lied to me, and she lied to you. You sent her that money all those years, and I wasn't even your son." He bit at his lip and stared at the floor, trying to compose himself. When he looked up, his face contorted with embarrassment and confusion. "Did you know?"

"Trace . . ." Samuel remembered how he'd been prompted not to deny being his dad. At the time, he'd thought it odd but had followed what the still, small voice had told him to do. With Trace coming to him after learning the truth, Samuel now knew why. Trace had to learn the truth from his mother so he would accept it. "I didn't know who your father was, but I did know it wasn't me. When you told me, I knew I couldn't deny it because you were in no frame of mind to believe me. And maybe, deep down, I wished you were mine. I've always wanted a son."

Tears came to Trace's eyes. "I beat you up. How could you want to be my father?"

"You were hurting. You were trying to be a good son and a good grandson by bringing who you thought had killed your grandfather to justice. " Samuel had forgiven Trace for everything he'd done to him.

Trace's remorse was tangible and showed in his eyes, in the way he tilted his head, in the sorrow in his voice.

"Finding out that Stillman is your father had to be a big shock," Samuel added. "Did you talk to them and get this out in the open?"

"No way. I took off. I didn't want to face them. They're liars."

Samuel couldn't understand why years ago Stillman hadn't manned up and married Shada. Why didn't he want to be a father to Trace? Why did he hide the truth? The answer had to have something to do with the relationship between Stillman and Big Jake. "Years ago, Stillman used to be friends with Big Jake, didn't he?"

Trace sniffed as he gained more control over his emotions. "Maybe. But I've never seen him with my mother until last night. All these years they've been going behind my back, keeping secrets."

"Which makes me wonder, why would Stillman openly go to Shada last night?" Samuel leaned his elbows on his knees.

"My mom seemed worried about it. Chief Taku is an honorable man who wants justice for the Clan. Justice doesn't hide behind lies. Besides, I think Stillman and Mom were planning to do something to Herman." Trace drove his fingers through his hair. "Mom said Herman was going to take care of Regi . . . and that afterward, she and Stillman were going to take care of Herman."

Samuel leaned back in his chair.

"I should have gone to the police, but I was so upset after learning that Stillman was my father that I could only think about myself. I—" He stared right into Samuel's eyes. "I prayed, like you did out on the ocean. I pleaded with God to help me. But He didn't."

Samuel reached through the bars and grabbed Trace's hand. "Yes, He did. You're here telling me. And together, with the Lord's help, we're going to get through this."

"But Herman's dead."

"And the police think Regi did it." Samuel felt a powerful anxiousness settle upon him. "I have a feeling she's next. Where is your mother now?"

"I don't know. Though with Herman dead, I'm concerned they might be looking for Regi." Despite loving his mother, Trace's mind was clear enough to realize she could possibly be mixed up in Herman's murder, and he seemed willing to help Samuel.

"You've got to get me out of here."

Trace stood. "How?"

"Who was in the office when you came in?"

"Jones."

"He's a fair man, but he'll never let me out. The police put me off last night; they won't check into this immediately." Samuel knew Trace had to somehow get Jones to listen and act. "Tell him what you told me about your mom and Stillman and what you overheard them saying about Herman. Maybe he'll do something for you."

Regi had to get out—now!

A striking woman with sleek black, shoulder-length hair reached the top of the stairs. She smiled, and her large, copper-colored eyes lit up when she saw Regi. It was almost like the woman thought they were long-lost friends. "I knew I heard someone up here."

Totally shocked to see a woman, Regi dropped her pack on the floor and placed her hand over her racing heart, willing it to slow down. "I thought you were . . ." She couldn't tell the woman what she thought.

Oscar barked and scratched at the door, wanting in. Regi reached for the knob, but the woman drew her attention away. She held out her hand for Regi to shake. "I'm a friend of Herman's."

Regi took her hand. "Oh, I'm so sorry about Herman. My sister found him when she took Oscar for his morning walk."

The woman closed her eyes as though willing back tears then opened them. "Yes. His death was quite a shock. He had no family, so it's up to me to see to his services and everything. He gave me a key to his place awhile back when we were dating. Things didn't end well between us." She paused a moment, struggling to fight off tears. Gaining her composure, she shook her head. "Anyway, he needs something nice to be buried in, but I can't find anything that looks decent." She smiled.

Regi noticed her frosty pink lipstick and how it glimmered against her skin. She was a beautiful woman even though she was a little overweight. She could still make a man's head turn. That she'd been in a relationship with Herman was a puzzle.

Regi felt sorry for the woman. "Can I help you find some clothes?"

"Oh, that would be so thoughtful." The woman started down the stairs.

Oscar howled and scratched at the door. "Just a minute." Regi paused. "I need to let him in before he breaks down the door." She didn't know what had gotten into the dog for him to make such a ruckus.

The woman had gone down a few steps but stopped. "I hate to admit this, but I'm very scared of dogs. Especially big dogs that don't know me." She gazed up at Regi. "Do you mind leaving him outside until I get what I need and leave? I promise it will only take a minute."

Regi glanced at Oscar. The dog was barking and carrying on like she'd never seen before. As excited as he was, he could wait outside a while longer. This woman was mourning her ex-boyfriend. She didn't need a dog jumping all over the place. "Sure." Regi grabbed her backpack off the floor and put it and her coat on the counter before she followed the woman to Herman's apartment.

Everything was neat and orderly. A leather couch rested in front of a big screen TV. To the right was a small kitchen nook, to the left a door to what Regi supposed was Herman's bedroom. She shuddered at the thought of going in there.

The woman stopped. "I don't know why I'm doing this. I really couldn't stand Herman."

Regi could relate with that. She glanced around some more. Against the south wall was a bookcase filled with girlie magazines, some paperbacks, and a number of DVDs. The case seemed oddly tilted, which wasn't surprising. Herman himself was oddly tilted.

The woman finger-combed her sleek hair away from her face. "Do you want to know what led to our breakup?"

Regi didn't really. She wanted to find the clothes and get this woman on her way.

She didn't wait for Regi to reply. "He stole the Raven Clan's talking stick. I was the keeper. He swore he didn't take it, but I knew he was lying. I could tell. I can always tell when a man is lying, can't you?"

Regi thought of last fall and the Romney murder investigation. She had sadly misjudged Samuel until toward the end. Regi's problem had been the opposite—she couldn't tell when Samuel was telling her the truth. She hated how close she'd come to losing him because she had been so blind to his true nature and who he really was, but she was not going to tell this woman that, this virtual stranger. She had to get her out of here. "Maybe we should get the clothes?"

"Oh, of course." She walked to the bedroom door but stopped again. "The funny thing is, whoever holds the talking stick is supposed to tell the truth. That he stole it and lied . . . well, it's ironic, don't you think?"

What Regi thought was that the woman talked too much. "Ironic, yeah."

The woman teared up again. "I'm so sorry. I shouldn't be talking like this about the dead."

Great, now what am I supposed to do? Regi felt all sorts of awkward, mainly because she understood how emotions could get all jumbled during a stressful time. "Did you look for the stick?"

"A little in his bedroom, but then I started feeling like a grave robber and decided to just get his clothes and get out. That's when I heard you upstairs. So his bedroom's a little messy. I kinda got carried away until I came to my senses." She opened the door and went in.

Regi stood at the threshold. The room looked like it had been turned upside down. Dresser drawers were dumped on the floor. The bed mattress was half on and half off the frame. Closet doors were open. Clothes were everywhere. The black-haired beauty stood in the middle of the chaos, looking embarrassed. "I'm so ashamed. You must think I'm some kind of a nut." She picked up a black dress shirt from the floor and a pair of black jeans. "What do you think? Would he have wanted to be buried in these?"

Regi shrugged. "Might want some socks and shoes too."

The woman again drove her fingers through her hair as she pilfered through a heap of clothes, finding socks and shoes.

Regi's mind went back to the time she had to buy burial clothes for her late husband. She chose new clothes, wanting Earl to have the very best. She remembered taking the clothes to the mortician and how it tore her heart apart. Regi couldn't help but feel sorry for this woman and wanted to help her. "That truth stick must be mighty important."

She nodded.

Taking pity on her, Regi said, "We might as well search in the living room and kitchen."

The woman smiled. "Really?" She didn't wait for a reply before hurrying past Regi and setting the clothes on the leather couch in the living room. Holding her hands about two feet apart vertically, she said, "The stick is about this big. And has a conelike shape like a baseball bat but with a sharp point on one end. It's pretty old. It has carvings on it, and at the top, it's covered with leather that's decorated with beads and bone."

They both began to search. Regi peered beneath the couch. The woman checked the closet next to the outside door then moved on to the kitchen cupboards. While the woman searched the broom closet, Regi noticed the oddly tilting bookcase again.

Why was it back like that? It didn't seem right.

Placing her head against the wall, Regi strained to see whatever was making it lean. She looked down and saw something on the floor, wedged between the bookcase and the floorboards. Getting down on her hands and knees, she reached behind and touched wood. She tugged and pulled, and finally the thing came loose.

The talking stick? Had to be. It fit the description. Regi noticed the decorated strips of leather with agates, shells, and bones that dangled from around the top.

Regi had seen something like this before.

Recently.

Suddenly, she knew where. On the *Isabelle*! A strap of leather just like this was wrapped around a spoke on the ship's wheel. Leroy Smarch said they'd found it when they replaced the linoleum beneath the dinette. It had been stuck between the wall and flooring. Though the leather on this stick looked faded, it was too similar not to be a match.

Regi turned the stick over until she saw where a piece had been torn off. Leroy had owned the boat for five years, and that piece had been on the floor of the boat for a very long time. Maybe even when Big Jake had owned it.

What was the deal? Why had there been a piece of the covering left on the boat? Why had Herman stolen the truth stick from his ex-girlfriend? She must know the history of the stick and why Herman had taken it. About to call to her, Regi realized the woman had never told her her name.

"You found it." The woman snatched the stick from her.

Regi rose from the floor and brushed off her hands. The woman's back was to her, but that didn't matter. "What did you say your name was?"

"Shada Baranov."

The name echoed off the room's walls and pinged in Regi's ears. Shada Baranov! The woman who had caused so much trouble and pain, the woman who had sent her own son on a vengeful mission, and the woman who had charged Samuel with the murder of Big Jake. Regi felt like a freshly shod horse had kicked her in the stomach.

"And you must be Regi Bernard." Shada whirled around and swung the talking stick like a baseball bat at Regi's head.

CHAPTER THIRTY-ONE

Charging against his foe,
Seal Hunter must find Caribou Girl
or all will be lost.

SAMUEL WATCHED THE DOOR TO the jail close behind Trace. How was Trace going to convince Jones?

Samuel paced as he thought. Shada and Kenway Stillman were partners. Good grief. Big Jake must have suspected something. Earlier, Samuel had wondered if the affair between Shada and Stillman had caused the rift between Jake and Stillman, but what if the two men had become enemies long before? And what if Stillman had started seeing Jake's daughter behind her father's back? That could be why Big Jake left everything to Samuel—because his daughter was playing around with his enemy. The big question was, did Jake know Stillman was Trace's father? Samuel didn't think so. Big Jake had never said anything about it to Samuel, but maybe he'd told his lawyer. One thing was certain: Samuel was calling Bartholomew Grey as soon as possible because there was no way Stillman was going to represent Samuel. And it didn't matter what kind of attorney Grey was; Samuel wanted his help.

Another question came to mind. Why did Shada and Stillman kill Herman?

Whatever the reason, right now, Regi's life, and possibly Claudia's and Wakanda's, were in danger. And Samuel had to do something. He wanted to bend the bars, kick down the door, and yell at the world.

He strained to hear what was going on in the other room. No loud voices. No noise at all. Rubbing his temples, he thought about Regi . . . his bride . . . his life. Why was there always something or someone standing between them and happiness? In a flash, he remembered running away from home when he was a teen and leaving her behind. He remembered trying to write to her but failing, and he remembered how heartbroken he'd been when he'd returned home to find her married with kids.

Another memory streaked before him. When Earl had died, Samuel had wanted to comfort Regi, but mostly he'd wanted to help her. He'd bought most anything she put on the market: livestock, property, even her prized horse. And just when he'd thought she might risk a relationship with him again, Curtis Romney was killed and both of their lives were sent into tailspins.

Somehow, through all their troubles, Samuel and Regi had found each other again. They were finally going to be together, but Shada still stood in their way.

Samuel couldn't allow that to happen. Not again!

The door to the jail opened, and Trace rushed in, keys in hand.

"What did you do?" Samuel asked as he watched Trace unlock his cell door.

"Officer Jones wasn't listening to me, so I had to take matters into my own hands. Let's just say he won't bother us for a while and leave it at that."

Samuel looked pointedly at the boy.

"I locked him in the supply room." Trace smiled for the first time in days.

Samuel followed Trace from the building to a patrol car.

"Where's your car?" Samuel looked over the parking lot, wondering which vehicle was Trace's.

"I don't have one."

"What?" Samuel was surprised. Most enterprising nineteen-year-olds owned their own vehicles. But this was Alaska. And Trace wasn't like most kids.

"I do have keys to one." Trace held up Jones's keychain and tossed it to Samuel. "You're a better driver than I am."

Great. On top of locking up an officer and escaping jail, now they were stealing a patrol car. Samuel opened the driver's side door, while Trace got in on the passenger side.

Samuel shoved the key into the ignition, turned on the car, and peeled out of the parking lot. As he drove, he pleaded, *Please, Lord, keep Regi safe and guide me to know what to do.*

Regi awakened to the strong scent of gasoline. Blinking to focus, she saw Shada, red canister between her hands, splashing gas around the room. Regi looked down. She'd been tied to a chair. "What are you doing?"

"I think it's pretty obvious." Shada continued working.

"Why?" Regi had to keep her talking to stall for time. She fought against the rope that tied her hands in back of the chair. Her fingers fumbled over the knot.

"You know why." Shada set the canister down and patted her pockets, looking for something. "I shouldn't have quit smoking. Always had matches with me. Now, when I need one. . ."

She went to the kitchen and rummaged through cupboards and drawers.

Regi pulled on the ropes, ripping and tearing the skin on her wrists. She only had a few minutes. The knot was firm, but the ropes slackened the more she worked against them. If she could distract Shada, that would give her time. "What is your son, Trace, going to do when he finds out you killed me?"

Shada charged from the kitchen. Stopping abruptly in front of Regi, she leaned over until she was right in her face. "Don't you talk about *my son*! He has nothing to do with this."

"Oh, yes he does." Regi wasn't backing down. "You got him involved when you lied and told him Samuel was his father and sent him to Idaho for him."

Shada raised her hand like she was going to strike Regi.

"But Trace is loyal to you." Regi hoped that would calm her. The rope on her wrists loosened more. Regi tugged the best she could without drawing Shada's attention to the ropes.

Instead of hitting Regi, Shada folded her arms. "You should be thanking me for sending Trace to get Samuel."

"Excuse me?" The gall of the woman was mind-boggling.

"He saved you from marrying a lying freeloader. I plan to get even with Samuel Tanner. He may have stolen my father's love, but he's not going to get away with his money. By the time I'm done with him, Samuel won't have a penny to his name and his home will be a cell no bigger than this room."

Regi noticed the talking stick on the couch next to Herman's burial clothes. "That talking stick doesn't work very well, does it?"

Shada laughed, went over, and picked it up. "Sure it does." She eyed the agates and bones tied to the leather. "My mother was the keeper before me. Trace will be the keeper after I'm gone, though I had to have a new one made when this one came up missing." She chuckled. "No one noticed the change." She fingered the bones. "But this is the one with the real power. I gave it to my father on his boat the night . . . ." Shada shuddered, set the stick back on the couch like she was afraid of it, and headed back to the kitchen.

"The night your father died?" Regi had to keep her talking.

No reply. In a matter of seconds, Shada would find matches since Herman was a smoker. He must have them all over. Regi had to get Shada to tell her more. "You have nothing to lose by telling me what happened. You're going to kill me. At least let me go to my rest knowing why."

Shada came back, a box of matches in her hands. "You have a point. I'd like to think someone would do the same for me. The night my father *disappeared*—died, actually—Stillman and I—" She paused. "You haven't met Stillman, have you?"

"I have." Regi continued to work at the ropes while she spoke. Her plan of keeping Shada diverted was working. "Earlier today, I ran into him at the market. He was on his way to talk with Chief Taku about dropping the charges against Samuel because of Herman's death."

"Is that what he told you?" She cackled. "My man does have a sense of humor."

"*Your man?* He's old enough to be your . . ." Regi was confused.

"My father." Shada cackled again. "Love doesn't look at age."

Shocked, Regi quit fighting the ropes for a moment. She thought of Tucker and Kimberly's relationship. They seemed to be in love. But something was wrong here. Regi's mind spun with questions, though she was unable to form them into a single thought. A calming realization settled upon her. "How long have you and Stillman been involved?"

"Long time. I knew my father didn't care for him because he was a shaman. That's why I sought him out."

"Why would you do that?"

"To prove I could. My father's world revolved around Samuel and fishing. He didn't care about the kid he'd been saddled with since my mother died. Stillman cared. He listened to me. He loved me."

"But not enough to marry you?" Regi asked before thinking, but she really was curious.

"I couldn't very well marry my father's enemy because he would cut me out of his will. He must have known though."

"Is that why Stillman killed your father? He wouldn't accept him as a possible son-in-law?" Regi knew that was a leap, but she might be right.

"You think you're so smart." Stern faced, Shada walked up to Regi and opened the matchbox. "Stillman didn't do it." Sadness reflected in her eyes. Deep sorrow settled on her shoulders. "I took the talking stick with me on the night I told my father who Trace's real father was. Stillman wasn't there. He didn't come until . . . after."

"After what?" Regi managed to pull the rope off one wrist, but there was still another loop. Yet, now she wanted to hold off and keep Shada talking so she could learn what had actually happened.

As though seeing the past reel before her eyes, Shada said, "I was holding the stick when I told him Stillman was my lover. My father said he'd known all along. I was dead to him. He turned his back to walk away, and that's when I told him Stillman was Trace's father. Something snapped in him. He came at me. I tried to defend myself with the stick. He tried to take it from me. We struggled. One thing led to another, and before I knew it, my father lay at my feet, the talking stick in his chest." Tears puddled in her eyes. She looked up at Regi. "Do you know what he said with his last breath?"

Regi shook her head.

"*Samuel.* He called for *Samuel.*"

"So did Herman help you bury Jake?" Regi had to get this information. Shada lit the match. "I think I've said plenty."

Knowing she had to act, Regi yanked the ropes from her hands and dived at Shada. As Shada fell, the match seemed to tumble end over end to the ground like a slow-motion movie scene in Regi's mind and landed on a slick of gasoline.

Flames burst out in one loud swoosh.

Regi pinned Shada down, yelling, "Tell me why Herman said he saw Samuel kill him!"

Shada glared at her, yet in the corner of her eyes she saw fire skitter across the room and up the wall, hungrily licking up the gasoline she'd splashed around. "We've got to get out of here."

"Yes we do, but not until you tell me." Regi was betting that Shada had a strong sense of self-preservation. And pain was not something she tolerated well.

"Herman didn't know until he found the talking stick when he uncovered my father. He knew I was the keeper."

"So?" Regi needed more. Much more.

"He knew I killed my father, but if I could blame Samuel for killing him for his money, that money would revert back to me. Herman wanted a share."

The flames were growing and getting dangerously close to the outside door. "So you had to get rid of Herman eventually, but why run over him before the trial?"

Shada gasped for breath. The smoke grew thick. "Stillman knew what I had to do to keep Herman silent. When he saw Herman walking next to the road, Stillman's anger got the best of him."

Regi had enough. In disgust, she released her hold on Shada and started to get up, but the smoke was too thick. She dropped to her hands and knees. "Stay down, out of the smoke," she warned Shada.

The woman ignored her and leaped up. Regi expected she would sprint for the door, but instead, Shada spun around and kicked Regi hard in the forehead.

Mind-numbing pain shot through her . . . and then she didn't feel anything anymore.

As Samuel sped down the highway toward the cabin, he saw black billowing smoke.

Trace followed his gaze. "What do you think that is?"

"Not sure, but it's not good." Samuel romped on the gas, flooring the pedal. They slid on the snowy road as they rounded the turn to the cabin. Smoke streamed from the windows and leaked out of the roof. Through the windows on the ground floor, orange flames danced amidst black ugly smoke. Though it looked like the fire was contained there, Samuel knew the entire place would be engulfed in a matter of minutes. If anyone was inside, they'd be trapped.

He slammed on the brakes. "Trace, get on the radio and call for help."

"Where are you going?" Trace grabbed the mic.

"I've got to see if Regi's in there."

At that moment, the door to the ground floor opened. Black smoke roiled from the building, followed by undulanting flames. A woman raced out like she'd been emergency ejected.

Regi?

Because of the smoke, he couldn't tell. Flames reached out and caught her back, lighting her clothes and hair on fire.

Samuel's heart stopped.

CHAPTER THIRTY-TWO

On the sharp blade
of a knife,
Raven serves justice to all.

Coughing from the thick smoke awakened Regi. Flat on her back from Shada's blow, Regi's hand hit the talking stick that had rolled to the floor during their fight. Shada had left it behind. Flames roiled above Regi. Still coughing and choking, she grabbed the stick. She had to keep track of the murder weapon that had killed Big Jake. It was key evidence that could free Samuel. Regi glanced at the door leading outside. It was as though a dam had burst, channeling the fire through the exit. How was she going to get out through that? All Regi knew was she had to try because if she stayed here, she'd die for sure.

Crouching over to avoid the billowing flames that crawled on the ceiling, Regi started toward the opening. The building creaked and groaned. About to leap through the flames, Regi stopped when a log crashed to the floor in front of her, blocking the exit. She'd have to find another way.

Spinning around, she saw that the fire hadn't traveled to the other end where the stairs were. The smoke was smothering. Shielding her nose beneath her right arm and tucking the talking stick under her left, she raced to the stairwell. Flames rolled across the ceiling overhead, crackling, hissing, and raining flames and ash.

At the base of the stairs, she turned for a minute, glancing back at the room. Fire framed the walls and laughed at her fear. She had to get out. Leaping two stairs at a time, she slowed as she reached the top.

Smoke dense as black tar filled the cabin, making it impossible to see. Regi knew the kitchen was to her left, and somewhere along the west wall was the door to the deck. She faintly heard Oscar barking outside. Was he still on the deck? Her eyes stung as she tried to see.

Dense black smoke impaired her vision.

Scared out of her mind, she kept the talking stick snug under her left arm and felt the wall. It was hot to the touch. Sinking down on her hands and knees, she crawled over the sweltering floor. Even though she was beneath most of the smoke, the air wasn't much better down there as more smoke leaked through cracks in the failing flooring.

Unable to breathe, she was tempted to stand, but she knew she shouldn't. She had to stay low.

Using the wall as a guide, she came to the outside door. Oscar's barks were on the other side. Reaching up to turn the doorknob, Regi's lungs burned as every breath was filled with soot.

No air!

Her hand slipped on the knob.

Have to get out! Have to . . .

Samuel tackled the woman, rolling her over the snowy ground. He knew as soon as he touched her that she wasn't Regi. Once the flames were out, he carefully rolled the woman over.

Dazed for only a second, Shada stared up, consumed with coughing and sobs. One side of her face was badly burned, much of her hair was gone, and her clothes were seared to her body.

"Where's Regi?" Samuel demanded.

She ignored his question, drawing up in a ball as she tried to catch her breath.

Patience spent, Samuel grabbed her and yelled, "Tell me where she is!"

Shada chokingly laughed, taking pleasure in Samuel's panic. The woman was demented and filled with poisonous hatred.

But Samuel had his answer.

Regi was still in the burning cabin.

Rage shot through him hot and strong like a blacksmith's chisel. It took all his willpower not to hit Shada, but she wasn't worth it. Not when Regi needed him. He'd deal with Shada later. He spun around and raced toward the cabin.

As he neared the building, Trace joined him. "Help is coming!"

"Good." Samuel sidestepped the boy to charge into the burning structure.

Trace grabbed him. "You can't go in there."

"Watch me!" Samuel jerked from his hold.

At that moment, the building trembled. Fresh flames shot out of the door in a new wall of fire.

Samuel stopped dead in his tracks. A terrified feeling overcame him. How could he get in and find her? Panicked out of his mind, he yelled, "Regi! Regi!"

Please, God. Please help me know what to do. He had to get in there. Rushing toward the door, he bent over in hopes of getting beneath the inferno. Another burst of flames shot out of the doorway, blowing him back. The fireball was too much. He was forced to step away.

"Regi!" he yelled at the top of his lungs.

He heard barking. Oscar was on the other side of the cabin, near the patio entrance. The dog had to know something. Leaving Trace behind, Samuel raced around the cabin and up the stone steps to the upper level.

Something pounded from far away. Someone wanted in, but Regi drifted in a sea of black nothingness. Where was everyone? No Claudia, no Wakanda . . . no Samuel. Regi was alone, again. Would she be alone for the rest of her life?

Life?

Samuel was her life. He wanted a baby. Their baby.

He stood in the empty room upstairs in his house, the room he wanted to make into a nursery. He was cuddling something in his arms. As she drew nearer, Regi saw it was a soft baby blanket. Peering over his shoulder, she found the blanket was empty. Samuel's voice cracked as he whispered, "Regi . . ." He buried his face in the empty blanket. She reached out to tell him she was there, but his image disappeared into ash.

"Come back!" she yelled. Regi wanted to hold him, feel his strong arms wrap around her once more. She wanted to tell him she'd have his children. She was sorry that she'd said she was done having babies. She wanted a child with him.

Suddenly, she was on a plane helping Wakanda with Operation Babylift. Frantic mothers handed her crying babies, pleading for Regi to take them. She grabbed two and reached for two more. Her fingertips touched theirs, but she couldn't hold on. Waiflike eyes stared up at her, and suddenly their faces turned into Jack's and Lisa's. Regi's twins.

She was leaving her children. Wakanda shut the airplane doors and stared at her with a judgmental gaze, her brows furrowed with consternation. Ignoring her friend, Regi pounded on the metal door. "We can't leave them!"

The pounding grew louder and louder. Why wouldn't Wakanda open the door? What was wrong with her? Didn't she want to help Regi? Didn't she care?

Regi felt her body lifting. Had the plane taken off?

She floated into light. Cold breathed over her.

"I've got you, sweetheart." That voice. She knew that voice.

Regi blinked. Samuel carried her in his arms. Fresh air stung her lungs and made her cough. The more she breathed the more she coughed. She felt as if her lungs were going to burst. Her head ached like it had been pressed in an iron vise. Bile rose in her throat. No matter what she did, she couldn't hold it. Regi turned away from Samuel and threw up a swell of black phlegm.

He set her on the snowpacked pathway. Her body doubled over with rolling heaves. Holding her hair away from her face, Samuel stroked her back. Tears leaked from her eyes.

"You'll be all right. Are Claudia and Wakanda still in there?" Fear rode Samuel's voice.

Regi shook her head. "No," she eked out. As her stomach settled, Regi wiped strings of spittle from her mouth. "They're safe." She turned and gazed up at the man she thought she'd lost forever.

Samuel smiled. His whiskery face, with tiny lines beside his eyes, softened as he gazed at her. Regi reached to caress his cheek.

Then Oscar jumped between them, licking Regi's face. She hugged the Irish setter.

"He saved your life," Samuel said, stroking the animal's head.

Sirens blared, drawing their attention. Red flashing lights of fire trucks and ambulances headed their way. Regi suddenly remembered what had happened.

"Shada did it!" Her voice croaked. Her throat closed off, making her cough. Regi had to tell him more. "The talking stick! I had it with me." Between coughs, Regi glanced down, hoping that it was still tucked beneath her left arm.

Gone.

"This?" Samuel held it up. "When I scooped you up, you were holding it."

Regi grabbed Samuel's arm. "She killed her father with it." She choked but managed to say, "Stillman killed Herman. We've got to find them." Regi tried to gain her feet but quickly became dizzy and fell into Samuel's waiting arms.

"Regina, it's all right." Samuel held her tight against his chest. "We'll get him later."

The fire trucks and ambulances pulled up. Holding Regi in his arms, Samuel met one of the paramedics as he burst from the vehicle. "She has severe smoke inhalation and has thrown up." The EMT guided him to the rear of the truck. His partner opened the doors and grabbed a couple of cases and hurried over to Trace and Shada. The paramedic with Samuel stepped up into the vehicle, took Regi, and settled her on the gurney. He put an oxygen mask over her face and turned on the tank. Samuel crawled in as well. Oscar tried to jump in, but the paramedic shooed him out. The Irish setter stood by the bumper of the vehicle, anxiously peering in.

"She'll be all right. Just needs rest and some good air. Were there others?"

"Her sister and friend were staying with her, but she told me they're safe," Samuel said. "I don't know if anyone else was trapped inside." Samuel should have gone back in to check, but the cabin had been engulfed with flames. No one could have lived through it. The paramedic seemed to sense Samuel's concern.

"You did all you could and were lucky to get her out."

Samuel heard more vehicles arriving and doors slamming shut.

"That's the one." That was Officer Jones's voice. Since he couldn't see Samuel inside the ambulance, he must be talking about Trace, who was by his mother trying to help the paramedic.

"Hold your horses." A familiar voice. Samuel would recognize that growl anywhere. Sheriff Thomas Morgan.

Making sure Regi was in good hands, Samuel leaped out of the vehicle. There stood his friend, wearing his Trailhead sheriff's parka and, on top of his bald head, his Stetson. Relieved to see his friend, Samuel said, "You have perfect timing, always arriving after I've done all the work."

Morgan reached out and took Samuel in a manly bear hug. "What can I say? I have *all* the luck. Good to see you."

Behind Morgan stood Officer Jones and Officer Taggart flanked by several of the police officers Samuel had seen at the jail. But standing near Morgan was another man he'd never laid eyes on before. His navy blue parka had a US Marshals logo on it, and Samuel assumed he was Morgan's buddy he'd mentioned. Samuel didn't know what he'd done to deserve a good friend like Morgan, but he was awfully glad.

Morgan would wonder where Claudia and Wakanda were. Samuel should have pressed Regi to tell him where they were, but things had happened so fast, and once he knew they were safe, his main concern was seeing to Regi. Now he had to tell Morgan he had no idea where Claudia and Wakanda were. He didn't know where to begin. He knew Morgan and Claudia had been sweethearts in high school, and though they'd both ended up marrying other people, a guy never got over his first love.

"Excuse me." Claudia stepped around the men. Wakanda was with her, a concerned look on her worried brow. They must have arrived with Morgan and the other officers.

Relief at seeing the two women washed over Samuel like spring rain. "Am I glad to see you two!" Samuel reached to give Claudia a hug, but she pushed his arms out of the way. Her eyes were fixed on the burning cabin.

"Where's Regi?" Claudia asked. "Was she in there? Did she get out?"

"Calm down." Samuel couldn't blame her. He knew the sisters were close. Nodding to the ambulance, he said, "She's in there. She has smoke inhalation but should be okay." Upon seeing Regi inside, Claudia gave Samuel a quick hug and stepped into the ambulance to see to her sister.

Wakanda stared at Samuel, looking like she was about to say something but, instead, slugged him and followed Claudia. He guessed it had to be Wakanda's way of acknowledging that she was glad to see him.

Morgan leaned over. "Wakanda flew us here. Darn good pilot too. By the way, I told Cooper Clawson you'd pay to have her engine rebuilt if she'd give up her seat for my friend here."

Samuel had no idea who this Cooper person was, but he'd gladly pay whatever he needed to. Gratitude and awe overwhelmed him as he realized again that he had his friend here as well as another strong arm of the law. The Lord had worked many miracles: helping Samuel escape jail, guiding him to Regi, and even delivering proof of who had actually murdered Big Jake.

Samuel still held the talking stick.

"Where did you get that?" Officer Jones stared at Samuel like he was touching something sacred.

Samuel knew he probably was because members of the Clan revered such tokens. The leather was aged, and some of the beading hung from loose threads. But Samuel wasn't about to answer Jones. He handed it to the marshal and said, "Regi told me this was used to kill Big Jake. Shada confessed the entire story to her."

Samuel gazed at Shada across the way. The paramedics had strapped her to a gurney. Trace held her hand as they rolled her toward a waiting ambulance next to the one Regi was in.

The marshal took the stick. "I'll help Officer Jones and Officer Taggart get to the bottom of it."

"But," Jones pointed to Trace, "he locked me in the supply room and helped this guy"—he pointed to Samuel—"escape." Officer Jones's voice faded as he looked at the marshal, Morgan, and Samuel. "But after what you told me, Sheriff Morgan, I guess I need to reassess the matter." He must have realized the story he'd been told about Samuel might be wrong, that everything he'd been told about Big Jake's murder had been a lie, and that he needed to accept the marshal's help.

Talking to the marshal, Jones said, "Come with me. I'll fill you in on what's been going on with the justice council while we follow the ambulance and keep watch on Ms. Baranov until we can question her and get to the bottom of this." Jones turned and held his hand out to Samuel, wanting the keys to his patrol car.

"Left them inside the vehicle." Samuel remembered what Regi had said about Stillman. "You need to question Kenway Stillman. He's involved in this and knows what happened to Herman."

"I know where he lives. I'll bring him in for questioning," Officer Taggart said as he hurried off to his car.

Before leaving, Jones turned to Morgan. "You will see that Mr. Tanner returns to the office. We're going to need his statement."

"We're right behind you, as soon as he checks on his woman," Morgan said.

Again, Morgan was helping Samuel set things right in his life. Samuel nodded thank you and went to join the love of his life in the back of the ambulance.

EPILOGUE

SAMUEL STOOD NEXT TO BISHOP Caldwell under a canopy of pines, waiting for Regi to walk down the aisle to him. He'd been baptized as soon as he'd returned to Idaho. All his doubts and reservations about the Church had dissipated after seeing how the Lord's hand had saved him so many times during his Alaskan ordeal. Since Samuel had been a Church member for only a few weeks and he couldn't marry Regi in the temple for at least a year, they'd chosen to take civil marriage vows in nature's chapel for the time being.

Above Samuel, the May breeze gently swayed the pine boughs. The fragrant evergreens scented the air. A meadow lark's musical song swelled. All seemed right with Samuel's world. Friends and family sat on split-log pews eagerly waiting for Regi to make her appearance.

Next to Samuel's nephew, Clifford, sat Trace. The guy had lived through an awful spring, finding out his mother had accidentally killed her own father and that Kenway Stillman was his biological dad. Both his mother and Stillman would serve long prison sentences for not only covering up Big Jake's death but for running down Herman and nearly killing Regi. Trace wanted nothing to do with them and had asked Samuel if he could work on his ranch. Bartholomew Grey had helped them with the legal issues of Trace taking Samuel to Alaska. Since Samuel refused to press charges and since Trace was willing to testify against his mother and Stillman, the court forgave any wrongdoing on Trace's part. Samuel was happy to take him in. The kid didn't know much about working on a cattle ranch, but he was eager to learn, and that would make the difference.

Jack and Lisa had really stepped up while their mother was gone. Lisa had managed the Raindancer, and Jack had watched over Samuel's ranch, feeding the horses and checking on the cattle. Regi had done a good job raising those two.

Lisa sat next to Trace. They'd seemed to hit it off. Their eyes sparkled as they whispered to each other. Jack sat on the other side of Lisa, watching for his mother and probably checking out the other young ladies in attendance from the ward. Jack had a scoundrel look about him that women appreciated.

On the other side of the aisle sat Morgan with his wife, Hannah, and their housekeeper, Effie. Morgan smiled and nodded. Samuel owed that man his life and so much more. As the Malamute Police Department had completed the investigation of Big Jake's and Herman's deaths, Morgan had championed Samuel's innocence not only to the authorities but to the Raven Clan as well. With the backup of the Alaskan Marshals, Morgan had convinced the Clan to clear Samuel of all charges. Chief Taku was saddened over the tragedy of Shada killing her father and the years she'd deceived the Clan, but he was most upset over Stillman. He had been the Clan's shaman and was once a trusted member of the council. The chief blessed Samuel and Regi with prosperity and much happiness. As a token of good will, Samuel had signed over Big Jake's land to the Clan. His time in Alaska was over.

Claudia and Wakanda sat on the front pew. Wakanda was dressed in denim and was accented with turquoise jewelry. She sat with her arms folded. Regi had told Samuel about the life Wakanda had led, serving in the military in Vietnam then becoming a bush pilot until Tucker had broken her heart. Samuel hoped that someday he would get to meet Tucker. Samuel'd flown home with Morgan on an airline, while Regi, Claudia, and Wakanda had stopped at Tucker's so Claudia could get her car. But odds were good that Samuel would meet the man, since he and Wakanda were joint owners of the plane parked behind the Raindancer. Wakanda's was an amazing story, and he was grateful she counted him as a friend. Claudia was decked out in a pink chiffon dress, her blonde hair curled about her face and shoulders. Superintendent Cameron Elliot walked in late and squeezed into the seat on the other side of Claudia. Samuel wondered if they'd be the next couple to tie the knot.

Stew, the owner of Twiggs Café, sat in the back and gave Samuel the signal that Regi was on her way. Music should have been playing, but they'd decided nature's music would be enough—the constant sound of a stream rushing by, birds chirping, the wind rustling the pines overhead.

Regi stepped into view. Her eyes locked with Samuel's. A sizzle flamed his insides as he watched the woman he loved walk toward him. He'd never seen her look more beautiful. The hem of her cream-colored lace gown brushed lightly over the grass as she walked alone down the makeshift aisle. Her hair glistened in shafts of sunlight that broke through the trees, spotlighting her as his angel. In her hands was a bouquet of early blooming lilacs.

As she walked toward him, he remembered that as soon as she'd recovered from smoke inhalation, she'd told him she wanted to try to have his baby. She also told him about the strange dream she'd had just before he'd rescued her from the fire. She'd been helping Wakanda with Operation Babylift. Because of that dream, Regi wanted to try to adopt some children from Vietnam as well.

Regi arrived in front of him and reached out. With heartfelt love for the woman he adored, he took her hand in his.

They would finally have their happily ever after.

**Under Raven's watchful eye,
Seal Hunter and Caribou Girl
enter the Great Beyond . . . together.**

ABOUT THE AUTHOR

KATHI ORAM PETERSON LOVES TO write edge-of-your-seat romantic suspense and young adult time travel. The constant thread she sews in both genres is faith in a higher power. She works hard to entertain her readers with clean, uplifting stories. Her path to publication took a detour as she raised three children. During those years, Kathi read all the how-to books on writing that she could find. When her last child graduated high school, she went back to college and earned her BA in English. She was fortunate to do an internship for the University of Utah's *Continuum* magazine, where she learned to edit and write articles in the "real" world. Shortly after graduation, she was hired by a curriculum publisher to write and edit concept and biography books for children. She worked shoulder to shoulder with artists and computer programmers as she watched her children's stories come to life. But the desire to write full-length novels called to her. Leaving the workforce, she devoted herself to writing fiction. You can contact Kathi through her website, www.kathiorampeterson.com, and her blog, www.kathiswritingnook.com.